The Marrilian

Quirni

Book One

By A. & L. Edwards

This Book is Dedicated to Gary,
Loving Husband and Father

The Quirni Series
The Marrilian
Nigh
Claimant Kinsley
Eljay's Promise
Bliss

Table of Contents

The Marrilian

Chapter 1 – The *QSDD Interlude*

The boy stopped fifteen feet away from Erica, halting mid run, shock on his face, spun around and ran to the customs office. He was the second child to do this. The first one hadn't concerned her, young children did odd things, but this one was older.

Nothing about her looked odd or out of place but the boy ran all the way into the building. The bags weren't too big for the kids to carry, or too small to bother. Children carried bigger and smaller bags than hers.

The passengers had all waited under the shade of the ship. No one from Parcles would have anything to do with someone from Tenpole so she stood alone. Now they had children helping with their bags. Only Erica remained. Any child would do, old or young. Instead another one trotted up, took one look at her, turned and ran. Erica sagged with frustration.

Maybe the Parcles prats were telling the kids to stay away from her. She watched the next child come towards her but without a word from any Parcles, they turned and ran. That wasn't it.

Could her long leather coat or wide brimmed leather hat signify something to the residents of this planet? The outfitter on Marril had talked her into the garments. Had he done it as a joke? No one else dressed in such a long coat or wore such a hat. Their coats were shorter and canvas. Their hats were pressed wool or they didn't wear one at all. If it was a joke, she wasn't laughing.

She had bought the coat because she wanted a lot of pockets. As for the hat, the outfitter had claimed it was necessary because of Quirni's harsh climate. That seemed unlikely since the sky was clear and a beautiful blue. The sun shined bright. On the other hand, she had bought the things in Parcles and they didn't have to worry about sun. Their brown skin didn't react like pale Tenpole. Maybe he thought she would fry without the hat. It wasn't the case. The hat would shade her face from a beautiful day and do little else.

No children were close so she allowed her irritation to show

The Marrilian

with a huff and glare at the red shingled building hundreds of yards away. That was the customs office and where she needed to go. Multiple children carried bags towards it, sometimes three to a bag all trying to get paid by one passenger while she still wanted help and even waited for it. They shot glances her way as if worried she would run up and tag them. Blasted kids, what scared them?

Waves of heat rose from the tarmac. At home on Marril this heat was typical and it wouldn't bother Erica but in Quirni's gravity, with a heavy coat, loaded with luggage, that walk wouldn't be easy. Backwater, pisshole Quirni had a third more gravity than Marril. Walking, even standing here under the wing of the ship, took a lot of effort. She grimaced at the idea of carrying a load on her shoulders.

All of that effort would only get her to the lopsided, run down, building, which wouldn't be a decent garage on Marril. The city of Parcles had sky scrapers of white steel and glass. Even old Tenpole had buildings of stone, something of quality. Quirni's customs office was a mess. It should be torn down so the wood could put to decent use. In fact, the entire town looked like it ought to be.

The rooftops of the nearby Padt City rose no higher than three stories. All of it was clay, wood, and brick and she had no idea how the hell they put it together without nails but according to what she had read, they did. Here, they didn't have steel to squander on building houses. Quirni was a metal poor planet and based on what she could see, they were poorer than she had ever imagined.

There was a stable for horses down the road from the base. The animals grazed in a fenced in area there. That was what Quirni used for transport. Not the Quirni Delegate. They had trucks and helicopters.

She twisted and looked back at what had to be the base's motor pool. Half a dozen trucks waited there. They all looked like they could seat six people at least. They appeared to be in reasonably good repair but were ten to twenty years old. She hadn't seen such a model on Marril for at least that long.

A buggy pulled up to the customs office and a round man in a white shirt got out. The driver drove over to the stable afterwards and right into the barn. Nothing else moved except the other passengers and children.

"What a blasted, horse and buggy hellhole," Erica muttered to herself miserably and looked down at her bags. The agents on

Edwards

the ship had lied when they told her the children would carry her possessions. She even had a quid note out for a tip. Screw it, she would carry her own things. She stuffed her money away.

Thank the lords she didn't have much; a computer in a padded case, a few pieces of clothing in a small suitcase that included some ammunition for her gun, and a backpack with antidote smokes for the thayanite. Erica had money and intended to buy anything else she needed but lords only knew what she might be able to purchase in such a backwater pisshole. She could cry.

One of the boys left a group of passengers and trotted towards her. She smiled in relief and tried to look welcoming and friendly but then he too stopped, gawked, gasped "You!" and dashed off.

"What?" Erica tried to yell after the child but instead, coughed. Attempting to yell aggravated the thayanite. It nearly choked her as she coughed harder and harder to clear the phlegm. It had her leaning on her knees and gagging before she was done. The other passengers were coughing too but not as bad. They smoked the antidote cigarettes one after the other. She would smoke when she didn't have to carry her bags because she sure as hell didn't look like she was going to get any help with them.

When she could breathe again she straightened with the resolve to start walking before she had to watch another dingbat child run off in apparent horror. She pulled the computer bag strap onto her shoulder, and placed her backpack strap over it. She held both straps in her right hand and picked up her suitcase with her left.

"Picks for brains," she muttered in an attempt to explain the children but that wasn't it.

Why did they act so shocked when they saw her? Stupidity didn't cover it.

Could Quirni children see she had lived in Tenpole? Did that scare them? Her hair wasn't that light but she did have the starved look, pale skin, and blue eyes. They might know enough to avoid Tenpole. No. That was unlikely. These were Quirni and even if they did know about Tenpole they would also know she couldn't do anything dangerous in this gravity. That wasn't it.

Maybe her gun had scared them? People didn't usually own guns here. She glanced down at her right hip. It was out of sight so that wasn't it. She wore the pistol rather than pack it in a bag and risk it being stolen, same for the money in her belt, and the

The Marrilian

knife at her back but the children couldn't see that. If the gun had been showing she would have sent a message back to Marril to get some ass kicked. At least that would have made sense.

Lords, but carrying her bags was a lot of work in this gravity. She stopped, set down her suitcase, and removed her hat to fan her face. Sweat glued her hair to her forehead. Why didn't the damn ship pull up to the customs terminal?

It sat on old tires and landing gear that could use some paint, the *QSDD Interlude*. She had never seen a ship so used. It still leaked cooling nitrogen from its potbelly.

"Probably burn the damn building down if it got too close," she said. Wood did burn easily. On Marril the customs office would be worth a fortune. On Quirni, a planet covered in trees, it was crap. That had to be why the ship was parked so far away. It came in hot.

The computer bag slipped from her shoulder. She grabbed at it and saved it just before it hit the ground. The near miss made her feel weak. Despite the enormous import duties, she had to bring this one piece of technology. She had to send one message back to Marril. After that it could break. To break it now would be more than she could bear after everything else that had happened.

She had no choice but to come to Quirni. Sirrus was still closed to her because of the exile order. Her options were moving to Quirni or staying on Marril, where thayanite would have soon killed her. Computers were not common on Quirni but she had no choice about that either. The message she needed to send was full of names, dates, and data. That wasn't information she could share over a phone. It would take forever and potentially be overheard. This had to be a private message. After it was sent the computer would no longer be necessary. It would be a curiosity, a toy to play Solitaire, and a repository for some of her most precious data, which she hoped she would never have to use.

Erica placed her hat on her suitcase and pulled the strap to the computer case over her head and around her neck. It caught her dirty blond hair. She pulled it free from the strap, replaced her hat, shrugged her backpack up on her shoulder, and grasped the suitcase.

Then, right on cue, she had another coughing fit. It bent her over. She dropped the backpack and the suitcase. When her throat cleared, she spent a minute with her hands on her knees, bent, and breathing. When she felt her lungs fill fully, she drew a long, rattling breath and then picked up her bags again. Every hundred yards or so she stopped to rest, fan, and then continued.

She finally reached the customs building and dropped her bags in line for the customs agent. Of the dozens of passengers only a couple of groups were left in line. All were rich Marrilian that came to Quirni for short stays. The planet healed thayanite poisoning so it was worth visiting for a few months but the wealthy wouldn't stay. Only poor Marrilians, or exiles like her, became tenants of Quirni.

The men and women around the edge of the room peered out from their cubicles at the new arrivals. One man smoked a cigarette that put off blue steam. A Marrilian. The blue haze was the telltale sign of thayanite antidote. A number of the passengers smoked too. The air in the room hung with haze. Erica could feel the burning phlegm in her throat break up somewhat by that weak dose of antidote so she pulled cigarettes from her coat pocket. She studied the room as she lit one.

The ceiling was in good repair despite all of the strange angles. Apparently, the building had been enlarged a few times. The wood floor had a huge map on it, an intricate design of Quirni's land, seas, and insanely tall mountains. The names of the claims were written in two-inch script. It had taken someone a lot of time to do it. It was pretty and protected by a glossy finish. Maybe they liked art here. That gave her some hope.

A man from one of the cubicles leaned down to a woman sitting in another cubicle and pointed at Erica but as soon as Erica noticed he put his hand down. He turned his back to the room to speak to the lady privately then the lady glanced past his arm. Erica caught her curious gaze but before she could drop her eyes, as any courteous Tenpole should, the woman dropped hers.

That surprised Erica so much she stared. Only Tenpole dropped their eyes. No one gave that respect to Tenpole. No one had ever dropped their eyes for her. That worried her all over again. It was weird, like the children.

'These strange fools don't matter' a thought in the back of her head provided.

Erica blinked when she heard the voice but agreed. They didn't matter if they left her alone. She turned away and took a long pull from the cigarette. Her throat cleared and she breathed easier. The line moved so she slid her bags forward.

A couple of the families exited through the front doors, ready to start their vacation while others talked to the people in the cubicles. None of them had been friendly to Erica despite the time they had spent together on the ship. Once she spoke, they avoided her. No other Tenpole traveled so no one associated with her during the journey. Not many from her part of town would accept coming to Quirni. Better to die on Marril. Erica didn't think so. Here she could live without being chased by the MSDD or forced to bed someone she didn't like or know. It would be nice to finally make decisions about her life.

The customs line shrank. Erica pushed her bags along. The group directly in front of her had ten people in it and they each had at least five bags. It would be a while. She smoked and waited.

Half an hour later she reached the agent, last in line and alone in front of his chest high counter. The man looked young but it was hard to tell age on Quirni. The planet kept its tenants young longer than Marril or Sirrus.

His skin was darker but she couldn't tell if he was tanned or the color of Parcles. Quirni tanned unlike Tenpole, so their skin color was no indication of social status. When Erica had read that she had wondered if the brochure tried to confuse the issue so Parcles didn't act like prats towards everyone they met on Quirni or if it was a warning. Apparently Tenpole could lose their accent and regain some coloring after living here. She hoped so. Her eyes, hair, and skin had been darker once.

The customs agent had long, dark hair with not a bit of grey even though he had a few wrinkles on his forehead. The pamphlets said Quirni men often wore short ponytails and it appeared that could be right because he wore his pulled back. It pleased her to see some of her reading provided accurate information. Pamphlets about Marril or Sirrus tended to include only positive somethings.

The customs agent was a civilian working for the military so he didn't wear a uniform. Instead he wore a white, long sleeved shirt that puffed and twisted around his paunch. He resembled a flopped over pillow on a stool with a head. The man barely moved, but still sweated. The collar of his white shirt was stained yellow from previous sweat stains.

Erica sweated too but she wore the damn leather coat and the gravity pulled hard. Otherwise it did not seem warm to her. She was used to Marril's humid warm days.

"Papers," he requested tiredly, as if worked to exhaustion. He didn't look up but clipped the papers that belonged to the previous group together. Erica held hers out. He dropped documents into a wooden bin and extended his hand. That was when he looked at her.

"Oh!" he exclaimed as his hand touched her papers. He didn't take them. The edge of them lay on his fingers.

Tenpole didn't look authority in the eye unless given reason. That odd exclamation gave her reason. She looked up past the brim of her hat, raising her eyes but only enough to see him. Looking at him directly was out of the question unless she wanted to be harassed and kept waiting longer, or at least that was what would happen on Marril. Lords only knew about Quirni so she stuck with Marrilian manners but that didn't seem to work. The man looked alarmed. He averted his gaze from hers like the woman in the cubicle had.

What in the name of the lords?

"Pardons," she begged for looking at him. She locked her eyes on his chin.

He froze like he saw a bust wall cracking. His mouth twitched. "I uh, see you are-uh, the-uh, last in line?" It was as if he had started to say one thing then changed his mind midway.

Erica smiled to let him know she wouldn't start anything.

He leaned away as if he didn't trust her and that seemed impossible; she had practiced that smile for years! She was from Chaucer. That was obvious. It said so on her passport. It was right there in front of him. He should understand her willingness to please given that, so what was wrong?

His eyes broke from her face and darted around the room then snapped back as if he searched for help. Did he know she wore a gun? Had someone told him? Did everyone on the ship know she had a gun? He couldn't see it. The stupid coat covered it or she would have taken the damn coat off. He hadn't looked at her papers yet so he hadn't read about it.

Chaucer, she needed more Chaucer for this. It always worked. She pulled her gaze up, gave him a more suggestive smile, sloped one of her shoulders and didn't bother to hide her accent at all. "As you will, sir," she replied with a breathy, alluring tone.

The leather coat creaked and half ruined her attempted appeal. Creaking wasn't sexy. She pushed the brim of her hat up to reveal more of her face, her blue eyes and blond hair. He had to understand what she offered. Her accent and coloring would identify her occupation anywhere in Ipet even if he didn't look at her passport or at least it should unless this guy had never heard a Tenpole accent before and never heard of Chaucer. Fat chance.

His reaction to her offer wasn't the reaction she wanted. His eyes grew as if more alarmed. "Uh-" He pressed on a smile. His pupils shrunk to pinpricks. "We'll be through this in a moment," he promised with a high, stressed voice.

He stamped the top documents hard. He didn't pause to read anything, as if doing his best to finish the task fast. His hand shook as it moved papers aside to stamp the next under it. Why? What did he fear from her? Had someone told him she was armed? Guns were rare on Quirni. Carrying one would be a *thing*.

She glanced around the room to see if anyone watched her. No one did but many of her fellow passengers were gone. Those who were still there dealt with their own business. All of them talked to the men and women in the cubicles lined up along the walls. No one seemed to give her a thought not even the man who had pointed at her.

She turned back to the customs agent. He smiled but his lips pressed hard against his teeth, as if he sucked on them to keep his expression in place. He picked up her manifest of belongings. That list described every item she carried. When he read it he would know about her gun and her knife if he didn't already.

Could he make her leave Quirni if her gun worried him that much? Could he stop her from immigrating? She didn't know. The customs office was on a Defense Delegate base. They had all sorts of rules and laws to harass someone like her but if they made her leave she had nowhere to go. That couldn't happen, could it?

That sneering hateful woman on Marril had approved her imports. They were all approved. The gun, the knife, the computer, all of it. The import duties were paid. She would argue the point if she had to, maybe even bribe this man if that was what it took. Damn her ill luck to get this bastard for a customs agent!

The man glanced at Erica when her irritation shifted her stance and made her breathe with a tiny huff. He quickened his pace. He rushed through the check-in process and much to her relief and surprise he didn't look at her manifest. He slipped the list out of her papers, bundled it with a few documents she had to sign, added a stamp over her signature, stamped her passport, clipped the papers together, and dropped everything in the bin.

He had stamped the manifest without a glance. He held her passport out to her. "There you go Miss–ah," he flipped open the passport, glanced down, forced another smile, and then his eyes settled on hers with a pleading fearful quality that amazed Erica. He leaned over the counter. "Ennis," he said her name in a conspiratorial whisper. He glanced around the room then leaned closer so only she could hear him. "I don't want any trouble, Miss Kinsley. I plan on walking out of here and I won't say a thing." He nodded once, as if to cement the agreement between them.

Erica's gut clenched. Kinsley. That was her birth name, Lynn Jillian Kinsley. Apparently he could tell by looking at her that she was one of them. People on Marril could so why not here too? She had the narrow Kinsley face and the full Kinsley mouth along with the wide eyes. At least her eyes weren't the typical Kinsley green.

Hers were blue, a light blue since the thayanite in Tenpole had bleached out so much color. Her hair was bleached lighter by the thayanite as well so she didn't have the dark hair of a powerful family, and her build was light because she had been sick and being an iridim patient made that worse. Her coloring and her size made her look like Tenpole, less like a Kinsley, but she was both.

"My thanks," she responded sweetly, forcing her smile as well, unsure if he warranted any thanks, but she didn't want trouble. She reached over the counter and took her passport from the where he had placed it between them. "My name be Ennis," she added. "Changed it legal."

He leaned back on his stool. "Of course. Have a nice day Miss Ennis." He kept an eye on her until she backed away to put her passport in her pocket and then he stood and collected his papers.

Had this man done a thing to make the Kinsleys angry? Was that what flustered him? He stuffed the papers in a briefcase. If the Kinsleys worried him, he might try to hurt her so she decided to keep him in sight. She coughed and covered her mouth but watched without fail.

The coughing grew harder. Emotions did that. Emotions made thayanite poison more active, a thing about oxygen in the blood reacting with it and the agent had stirred up a wealth of nervousness. She dug in a pocket to find her pack of cigarettes and her matches, then wacked them on the side of her fingers to make a smoke pop out. She took it in her lips. Her eyes left the customs agent only to light it.

Despite the antidote she continued to cough. She covered her mouth with the back of her hand then took another drag from the cigarette. The steam from it caught under the brim of her hat and burned her eyes but she didn't let that stop her from watching. Inhaling deep lessened some of the smoke. She squinted through the rest.

The agent finished stuffing his papers in a briefcase while darting glances at her, as if she were a threat. The briefcase wasn't closed when he scurried away. It was open under his arm, papers fluttering. He noticed and held the flap over the contents until he got to the door. He went through and closed the door after him with the authority he should have displayed at his desk.

The whole scene kept Erica staring. The man's actions made no sense to her, no more than the children or the woman dropping her eyes. What a damn blasted situation. She wasn't even on the planet an hour and already had trouble and she wasn't sure what trouble. The customs agent knew. That seemed clear. He could walk out the door and bring back more trouble. Her eyes narrowed. The best thing to do was disappear. To do that she needed a place to live.

The antidote cleared her throat so she felt ready to tackle the next part of her immigration. According to the pamphlets the representatives of Quirni's claimants would be at the customs office. They could accept her as a tenant someplace, give her a claim to call home, and they were no doubt the people in the cubicles.

Erica studied the map painted on the floor. The bags of a small family sat on the edge of her uncle's claim, Kinsley Claim, far to the north. It bordered what looked like desert according to the color.

All of Erica's life, her family name had hurt her. Quirni could be a new start if she could avoid any association with it, if they didn't interfere. It appeared they far to the north. She would go someplace south.

The base she currently stood on was halfway down the settled part of the continent. She supposed that was far enough south. It was a big continent. Soto Claim was nearby, just north of the base where she had landed. She could walk there within a few days once she got used to the gravity.

A wooden sign stating 'Soto Claim' hung on one of the cubicles and a woman stood in the small space. She busily collected her brochures. As far as Erica could remember, no one had approached her so she didn't have any paperwork beyond that. Erica picked up her bags and started towards her. The woman stuffed her colorful brochures into her bag with as much care as the customs agent. She at least took a moment to tie the bag closed.

Edwards

"Pardons," Erica begged as she set down her belongings.

The lady straightened with a jerk and spun. Her eyes were wide with fright, startled apparently even though Erica couldn't imagine why because she had dropped her bags with enough noise to announce her presence. The women curled her lips in an odd smile, much like the custom agent's forced smile.

Whatever it was that bothered these people Erica couldn't let it stop her from finding a place to live. "Would be fine to live towards the south. Could you-"

The woman's smile fell away. Her eyes stayed wide. "No, please. I've filled the positions we had. My claimant would be furious if…you-you understand?" she added as she pulled down the front of her pink suit coat to straighten it and then ran her hand over her dark hair even though her hair looked fine. Her coat looked fine too but she tugged at it again then forced a wider smile. "May I pass, Miss?"

The woman sounded like she asked. Again, weird. Erica dipped her chin for an answer, a Tenpole 'yes' and then pulled her bags aside. The lady squeezed by with her briefcase clutched to her chest and hurried across the room and out the door. The representative of another southern claim repeated the scene with one difference, the man scowled at her but hurried off nonetheless.

"By the lords," Erica muttered after the last attempt. The door swung shut after two more representatives including the one from Vaughn Claim darted off before she could speak. She didn't bother to move her bags and inquire again. It took too much energy and she was too tired.

Eventually Quirni's clean air would heal her lungs, or so a pamphlet said. For now, the antidote only kept her lungs clear so she wouldn't get full blown pneumonia. Resting, and smoking would help her find strength more than anything. She leaned against the abandoned cubical of Vaughn Claim and inhaled but before she could get a full breath she started coughing.

The pills that the ship's cureman had supplied were supposed to bolster her strength for the gravity. If felt like the one she had taken before leaving the ship had worn off so she searched her coat pockets until she found the bottle and took another one. Without them smoking was like trying to inhale air through a wet sponge. Still, she kept at it.

Sweat trickled down her back. She dragged her hat off and flung it onto her bags. She had left them at the edge of the map, west of Kinsley Claim. She shook her hand through her hair to get it unstuck from her face then sucked hard on the cigarette and held the steam in her lungs.

All the Marrilians had been chain smoking since they arrived except her. Her poisoning had come on so hard and quick she had gone straight to using an antidote chamber. A chain smoking habit would be the only way to care for thayanite pneumonia until her lungs healed. Too often her cigarette would burn out before she thought to light another. They were horrible things, smelly, painful to the eyes if the steam drifted the wrong way. They left a bad taste but without them her lungs would fill.

So she rested against the cubicle and smoked. When she could breathe again she would leave this city and head south. There was no need to approach another representative. Six had denied her. She got the message. They didn't want Tenpole living with them any more than Parcles did.

The cubicle wall was a solid place to lean. One side was tall and the other short so the person sitting inside could see over it. She leaned against the tall side. She could smell the wood.

That was the smell of luxury on Marril. She breathed it in with the antidote and tried to convince herself that any planet with so much wood couldn't be so bad. It wasn't the hellhole Tenpole believed it to be. Lords, she hoped that was true.

"Hello."

Erica looked over her shoulder towards the voice. Kinsley's representative leaned against the tall side of his cubicle and openly stared at her. "Hello," he greeted again when her eyes settled on him.

"Hello," Erica returned, imitating his greeting. Where she came from that word had been shortened to a quick 'Lo'. Erica stared back at the middle-aged man. He had invited her attention so she didn't drop her gaze courteously. She did nothing to invite him closer either.

He smiled in a wry way. "Do you have any particular skills?" he asked and that wasn't a smile at all but a smirk. It was similar to the custom agent's smile right before he whispered her name, somehow conspiratorial, knowing a thing.

"Am not interested in living on Kinsley Claim but many thanks," she answered and then looked away before he could ask to hire her. She didn't need to sell herself anymore. The looks and gestures she had learned were still useful but she didn't have to get paid for them. She would use her body for her own ends now.

"Huh?" he said in surprise. Erica looked back at him. His

grin mixed with a frown. "Tenpole?" He took a few steps towards her and gestured at his throat. His grin faded. "Your accent. It's pretty thick. It is Tenpole isn't it?"

Hadn't he already asked her that? Maybe that wasn't what he meant by *skills*. Maybe he hadn't been referring to her Chaucer skills. "Yes sir, Tenpole." Perhaps he talked only to get closer and get his hands on her. She straightened to defend herself, not taking a defensive posture yet but she was ready. The pill had already given her enough strength to do something. She regarded him over her shoulder. "But truly, sir, no interest in Kinsley Claim. You represent them, so?"

"Yes. I didn't suppose you would be interested but I thought you…" He looked into her eyes intently. He pointed at her. "Your eyes are the wrong color."

Erica's brow knit in irritation. "They be the color they have always been."

"No, I mean, you look like her except for that."

"Really. Who?"

"Matilda Kinsley."

Her stomach turned and her heart sank. That explained why people acted so odd. It was Kinsley crap again. A relative here looked like her. That had to be why they seemed so certain she would be a problem. The girl must be a demon to be treated so. "Suppose she be a cousin or some such," Erica told him as she tried to suppress her dismay. "'Tis of no interest. They caused a spark of trouble back home and well…" She smiled as she leaned against the wall once more as if unconcerned.

This man was a Kinsley Claim representative. It would be best if he didn't call up her uncle and tell him a niece had arrived ready to stir up mischief. That is what most Kinsley's would do. They tended to stomp in and try to take over. "You know how it be when family falls apart. Some things don't fit back together. Changed my name to put an end to such. Wouldn't even be here except for the poison." She lifted the cigarette to make her meaning clear.

His eyes narrowed. "You are a niece to Claimant Kinsley huh?"

Erica took a long draw off the cigarette and held it in her lungs before exhaling. "'Tis a distant uncle who owns a claim here. Great, great grandma went to Sirrus and her brother came here. The families parted, lost touch. Have no interest in them. Came here to get healthy and off Marril. 'Tis all."

"I seriously doubt that is all. It is going to be an issue for

The Marrilian

you."

"Truly none such." Her irritation tinged her tone but she smiled to offset it. She had to convince him she wouldn't start anything. "Have changed my name. No one knows me as Kinsley anymore. 'Tis for sure they will have no part of me. Expect such. Welcome it."

He frowned. "You are going to have problems whatever your name is. Matilda isn't well liked."

"What Kinsley ever was?" she asked then sucked in a long drag of steam, as if smoking was her only concern.

"I mean…" He cut himself off so abruptly she grew curious. She exhaled, stood and faced him. "You mean what?"

"I work for the Kinsleys you know? I probably shouldn't be talking to you." He glanced around. The room had emptied out so they were alone. "But, I mean." He paused. "You are Chaucer, right?" She stiffened. "Don't take me wrong," he added quickly. He extended his hands, palms facing the ceiling, the universal sign of friendship. She could see he held no weapon and no offensive stance started like that. "I would hate if you got hurt. It isn't often we get Chaucer here. They usually go to Sirrus."

Had she heard that right? "Pardons?"

"After the trouble between Matilda and Claimant Kinsley she was kicked out of the family. If Claimant Kinsley learned I was talking to Matilda I'd be in trouble and I don't want to lose this job. It's gravy. I like meeting people. I don't want to lose it."

Erica glanced around. There was no one else there unless they hid in a cubicle and were staying silent. That seemed unlikely. She had seen so many leave.

"You look like her." He continued to stare.

"Pity her," Erica replied with a small attempt at humor because she knew she was attractive if she wanted to be. She was too thin right now but otherwise she had a decent shape and a pretty enough face. She could lure men to do as she wished. She tried to chuckle and ease the man's mind because she wanted to find out why Matilda wasn't liked but instead she began to cough. The man didn't even grin. He took a few steps closer and spoke lower as the coughing subsided.

"You won't find a job. No one in their right mind would hire you. Their claimant would be outraged."

Erica lowered her hand from her mouth. "Well, not to worry." She sounded hoarse. "There be no need for a job." She cleared her throat and stiffened her back to look up at him. "Just want a place to live."

He shrugged. "Same there."

That startled her. How could someone come to a planet and not get a place to live? "You mean no one will accept me as a tenant?"

"Yes, that's what I mean."

Could that even be a thing? How could a person be on a planet and not have a place to live? How did that even work? Claimants owned the land. They rented it to tenants who farmed and ran businesses which the claimant taxed. If she stayed on their land without paying rent or taxes they wouldn't be happy and she would be guilty of a crime. What crime she wasn't sure but there were always crimes to be committed and she found a whole bunch to commit in her days.

Without a tenancy she would have to constantly move, always the visitor. No. There had to be a law against that. "'Tis ridiculous. A person must live someplace. Where does the Kinsley girl live?"

"Actually, no one knows. The QSDD took her."

The QSDD, the blasted Quirni Solar Defense Delegate was involved. Every planet had a Defense Delegate that supposedly kept the peace between claims and the other planets. They had destroyed Erica's life. Sirrus was her home and she would still live there with her family if not for the SSDD. She wouldn't be sick with thayanite poisoning or immigrating to Quirni or need to send a message back to Marril except for the Sirrian Delegate. Then again, hadn't he had said another thing?

She thought a moment, replayed what the man had said about the Delegate. They took Matilda. Her eyes narrowed. "Took her? Why?"

He shrugged again. "They protected her. They caused the riots. They managed to get her out of the city after the trial and since then no one has seen her."

Trial? Riots? By the Quirni Delegate? The military caused riots? By the lords, what had she blundered into? She was almost afraid to ask. "What trial? What did Matilda Kinsley do?" Her stomach began another slow roll as the man took a step back. He didn't want to talk about it. He flushed with fear and worry. "What?" she repeated. "Please."

He looked around again. He considered answering but didn't want to be seen doing it.

She stepped closer. "Please," she begged.

His eyes met hers. There was pity there. His shoulders drooped. He leaned to speak lower and shared what he really didn't want to say. "Matilda wanted to become a claimant and she wasn't willing to wait until she inherited her father's claim. She tried to buy Cobal Claim but the claimants of Cobal refused to sell to her so she decided to make the claim hard for them to keep, turn their tenants against them or something." His face darkened. He paused, swallowed, glanced around, and then continued. His eyes fell to hers and stayed there.

"Up on Cobal Claim they have a filter system for the water that goes into the capital city. It filters out Bacillus *pyrogenzes*. If you drink Quirni water unfiltered, you'll get a fever that kills. It makes you sick. It maddens you. You'll tear yourself apart. After a certain point, nothing can be done. No antibiotic will work." He took a breath and glanced around. They were still alone. "She stole the filter system's replacement parts then hired someone to sabotage the working filter. The water was contaminated before anyone expected. They had no parts to fix the filter. Matilda Kinsley killed over six-thousand people. They were poisoned because of her and they died horrible deaths."

Erica forgot her cigarette.

"Then she walked. She got off free thanks to the QSDD. Everyone knows she is guilty but the QSDD took the judges into a back room and convinced them to find her innocent." He said that with a sneer. "The QSDD protected her. We can only guess why. She owns, or owned, some of the biggest businesses on the planet and they couldn't have them fail, but if anyone ever gets their hands on her, she's dead." He shook his head. "You look like her. I mean, you *really* look a lot like her." He took a breath. "If you want to live I think you should go get the protection of the QSDD too."

Erica's chest felt tight to realize the weird Quirni weren't reacting to her at all but to her cousin. "Why didn't they say something? Was a QSDD ship that brought me here. The crew would have known. Any of them would have known." She spoke with the same low urgent tone he used because that was all she could manage.

He shook his head. "I'm sorry." He picked up his bags and walked away as fast as he could without running.

Erica stared at the door for so long her cigarette burned her. She dropped it. It fell on the map north of Kinsley Claim, in the unclaimed territory that looked like desert. She stamped it out with her boot. She wore good hiking boots. It sounded like she would need them. She would have to stay away from people.

Where was Cobal Claim? She looked for it. It was under her

bags. It butted up against the western edge of Kinsley Claim. Six-thousand dead. She felt like she would be sick. Six-thousand!

She was here because of the Delegate. They wouldn't sell her a ticket to Sirrus and she bet it had something to do with this and not the exile from Sirrus. Her father had been exiled too but he had gone back while she couldn't. This had to be why. The damn Delegate wanted her here. That had to be why the crew didn't say anything to her. She looked like this girl and they wanted her for something. She would be damned if she would fall into their trap.

Lords, but she could be such an idiot sometimes. She should have checked on the Quirni Kinsleys but she had never planned on coming here. She had so little time when she did get a ticket. No doubt that had been their plan. If she had been given any time, she would have checked. Damn the SDD to hell!

She tried to breathe deep, force air into her lungs, but her breath caught and she started coughing again. She sank to the floor with her back to the cubicle. As the fit passed, she drew up her knees and rested her forehead on them. She would keep calm. She would not get upset. She would not be angry. She would not lose hope. She would not cry. Crying would fill her throat and lungs with phlegm. It would weaken her and rob her of breath. She couldn't be weak now.

How could the SDD allow someone to kill over six-thousand people and not be punished?

How could they ever expect her to do anything for them after all they had done to her?

How many times would they mess up her life? If it hadn't been for their meddling she would still be a Kinsley. She would still be on Sirrus.

According to family history, the SDD had killed her great, great uncle Cedric. He had been too successful on Marril and they had killed him. At that time Kinsleys were all from Marril but after his death Cedric's sister, Leta, had moved to Sirrus. Cedric's brother, Cyril, had moved to Quirni.

Erica lifted her head and rested it against the cubicle wall. She lit another smoke, thinking, inhaling deep until the cigarette was gone and then lighting another. Her eyes trailed over the map on the floor. She had to go somewhere. She had to sneak somewhere, not ask permission, not be seen, not settle down at least until the mess with Matilda was over. So where?

There was a lot of land between towns. The further north the more open the land. If she went that way she might go

The Marrilian

anywhere. Maybe all she had to do was camp like all the rich Parcles did when they came to enjoy their Quirni Wilderness Adventures. She could stay away from towns and people and leave the claims altogether by going north.

She rolled out the butt of the cigarette and dropped it in the small pile she made. She lit another.

Her lungs felt better and her throat was clear. She inhaled deep without coughing. With a little maintenance her breathing should stay clear until morning. She knew the feeling of finally getting enough medicine and this was it; clear lungs, deep breath, energy. The gravity still dragged but she had the pills. The cureman on the ship said she should take them as needed. They wouldn't harm her only make her light headed if she took too many. She took another one. She could do this. She could survive this. She had done harder things but where to go?

Her eyes fell to Kinsley Claim. Claimant Kinsley didn't have an argument with her. Could she ask him for help? That would put her back in the Kinsley crap but she could have a claimant at her back. Would he help her if she reminded him of his daughter too much?

It was a risk. Anyone might think she was Matilda and stop her from seeing him. They could jail her and forget about her. Chances were she could wheedle her way out the same way she always had on Marril but was it worth the risk?

If she did manage to see him, how would that help? Erica had heard rumors that Cyril still worked with the Defense Delegate. It was only rumors but she didn't want to be around the SDD. They could nab her and do with her whatever they had planned. Going to her uncle could deliver her to the very thing she wanted to avoid. Should she take the chance?

The Kinsley Claim representative had said her Uncle would fire him for talking to Matilda. He also said the QSDD protected Matilda. Would they protect her if Cyril had kicked her out of the family and they worked with Cyril? That wouldn't make sense. If they worked with Cyril and he no longer recognized Matilda then they wouldn't have anything to do with her. A claimant was a far more important ally than his estranged daughter.

Erica sighed in irritation. She knew more rumors than facts and the rumors didn't make sense. She decided she shouldn't trust anyone. That had worked well in the past. The best plan was to camp and stay away from people altogether until the business with Matilda blew over. That meant going to the least populated area. She would go north, farther north than Kinsley

Claim. North of the claimed territory would be the only safe place.

She slipped a map out of her inside coat pocket and unfolded it. A map of Quirni was on one side and the Southern Padt City on the other. That was where she was, the Southern Padt City. That map had vital information too since she couldn't drag all of her stuff around. There had to be a place to stow it.

Businesses and hotels, banks and restaurants were labeled. The city was set up in blocks around the large court of the Quirni Council Buildings near the center. The Base was at the northeast side of the city. She found a bank on the road that ran straight west to the other side of town starting right from where she sat. It had to be a main road to and from the shipping area. There were no deviations in the road. The Quirni were practical. That made her life easier and that was important right now.

The bank wasn't far away. She stood and put on her hat with her hair hanging down around her face and the hat tipped forward. The wide, flat brim should hide a lot. The pill was working so she gathered her bags without too much effort and then left the customs office with her chin dipped down but aware of every movement around her.

The Marrilian

Chapter 2 – Anxiety

The interior of the bank was cool and that seemed like a small miracle. Another small miracle, the streets weren't busy, as if the people of Quirni built the city and then deserted it. There were no other customers in the bank lobby. Quirni didn't have a large population so maybe this was the norm. Perhaps they liked to overbuild, as if optimistic more people would move to the planet if they built big enough. That suited Erica.

The bank lobby had a grey tiled floor and white walls. It was neat and clean. No paintings, no decorations, nothing but the wooden desks arrayed around the room with a lot of space between them. Each desk had a chair in front of it and one behind it. Most of them were empty, all but one where a woman sat. Erica strode up to her and saw the woman's fear wash over her face.

"Lo," Erica greeted. She smiled her most friendly smile for the terrified teller. "Would make a deposit of Marrilian funds, please." The teller blinked a few times then began to rise from her seat. "Have my ID," Erica added hopefully, trying to stop the woman from leaving. This was the reaction she had expected so she had her passport out. "Erica Ennis," she added and opened the ID so the woman could read it but she was on her feet and backing away.

"One–one…uh…m-moment, please-Miss," she said and backed up until she leaned against a glass wall to the right. She called through the opening. The wall divided the outer desks from three others that all sat in a row at the side of the room. Anyone sitting at a desk behind the wall could watch the entire bank but no one sat there. "Arlo, come here!" She kept an eye on Erica. "Now!"

Beyond the desks a door led to the back of the building. A dark complexion, dark haired man appeared there. He gave the teller a disdainful eye, as if tired of her crap, and then glanced where the teller pointed, at Erica.

His expression fell away as his brow rose with surprise. He walked past the empty desks behind the glass wall with unhurried steps. He was thin and tall and his steps long. Half a dozen took him from the door to the teller where he stopped to speak to her. They disliked each other. His chin stayed up so he looked down his nose at the woman while her arms remained folded tight around her chest and her face set hard.

Erica couldn't hear their conversation. She lay her ID open on the desk. She waited as the teller and the man exchanged an emotional conversation in which the man ended up pressing his hands down with his palms facing the floor, as if he suggested the teller calm down.

Her features darkened during the conversation. The teller shot glances Erica's way the whole time and jabbed a pointed finger at her, as if to tell him she had every right to be upset given who stood in front of her desk. She finished by clenching her fists at her sides, a definite *'I'm not moving. It's your problem'*.

The man scowled and then left her at the opening in the glass wall. He stepped up to the teller's side of the desk to face Erica. He picked up her ID. He wore a smile when he looked up. "Young lady, are you in the wrong place," he told her, apparently amused at her misfortune. He offered his hand. "I'm Arlo Juno. How may I help you?"

Erica's breath caught before she could say anything and she began to cough. She turned away as he watched her struggle then his eyes widened in understanding. This bullshit thayanite cough was supposed to get better since she left Marril and the mines and all the shit in Tenpole. Her cough was worse than ever in spite of smoking all the crap cigarettes!

"You had better get some antidote in you. The Quirni air gets the thayanite stirred up." He spoke like he knew from experience.

Stirred up? Great. Erica nodded and reached in her pocket for the smokes. He produced a match and lit it for her.

"My thanks," she said in a wet, gravelly voice. She tried to clear her throat.

"Janice said you have funds to deposit?"

"Please," Erica told him. "And if there be large security lockers, would place my bags in one." She needed to send a message to Marril with her computer but that would have to wait until she knew exactly what she was up against on Quirni. "Would stow my things here for a while."

He glanced at her bags. "A couple of the largest lockers should be able to hold everything if you are so inclined."

"So," she said without thinking. He might not understand Tenpole agreement. The possibility didn't cross her mind. Getting out of town was the only thing she considered. To do that she needed to finish here. She held her cigarette in her teeth

The Marrilian

in order to free up both of her hands and untie her money belt which was under her shirt and tank top. She pushed back her coat to get to it and revealed her gun. The nickel plating stood out against her dark clothes.

"Oh," Arlo said quietly. "You shouldn't have that in here."

"It is her," the teller squeaked from where she had moved five feet behind Arlo, her eyes so wide the white showed all the way around them. "Nobody has one of those except her. I'm getting the agent." Erica looked up from her efforts with the belt to see the woman had frozen with her eyes locked on her. "Don't try to stop me. He's in the back room and he's armed. He'll hear you." Janice hesitated a moment then suddenly got the nerve and quickly walked to the glass partition faster than Erica had ever seen anyone walk.

"Janice, it's not her!" Arlo snapped over his shoulder. If she heard him it didn't matter because she ran down the hall and fell on the door, going through without a backwards glance.

Erica glared after the woman and returned to the knots on the money belt. They had tightened with her movement and body heat.

"Have no intention of using it," she told Arlo through her teeth.

Her nails slipped on the knots. She tried to inhale to keep the steam out of her eyes. "Blasted," she swore around the cigarette and glanced at the door. What the hell were they doing with an agent here? She assumed the teller meant a Delegate agent.

'You should worry about something other than your health right now' a voice in the back of her head told her.

Erica agreed but she didn't stop working on the knots. The belt should come off easily so she didn't want to stop smoking even though the steam had her eyes stinging. She closed them and concentrated her effort on the knot until she finally got the belt loose. As it dropped away she pulled the cigarette from her mouth and waved the excess steam away. With the other hand she dumped the belt on the desk. "The gun be unloaded," she told Arlo who seemed amused and nothing more.

"Rules you know," he said and picked up the belt. He opened it and started pulling out the Marrilian bank drafts. "How much do you have here?"

"3,983,500 quid."

He didn't seem at all impressed. She thought he would be given Quirni were supposed to be so poor.

"That will make you one of our top hundred depositors." He

began counting. "It entitles you to free services." He stacked the drafts in matching denominations. "What sort of accounts would you like?"

Such matter of fact, unquestioning service was new to Erica. Usually bankers told her what she would do and got angry when she told them. "Where can money be withdrawn?"

He finished stacking the notes and looked up. "Any bank will honor the Bank of Quirni notes on any claim. Where do you plan on going?"

Erica shrugged like Parcles, both shoulders, no tip of her head. She had studied how they acted while on ship. If she spoke like they did and moved like they did she would have a lot fewer problems. At least she hoped to keep others from recognizing her Tenpole and if not that then at least she didn't want them to hear Chaucer Street. Maybe she was succeeding and that was why Arlo was so nice.

"Don't know yet." She used every word she was supposed to use for proper sentence structure and said it very carefully. "Would like to invest two million. The rest can be savings. Can be so until I settle."

"Prudent," he remarked as he sat and began making notations in a ledger. "But I would suggest you put more than two million in investments. It won't take more than a few hundred thousand to buy a nice place." He looked at her for an answer.

"Mayhaps after settling." She sat in the chair opposite him and tried to relax. If the agent saw her sitting and relaxed he wouldn't be alarmed, would he?

"Would you like this changed to Quirni funds–*square*? Since you are depositing bank drafts in quid you can leave your deposit in quid. Only direct bank transfers are automatically exchanged."

"Don't quid be a better investment?"

"Definitely, but I'm supposed to ask," he explained and shrugged with both shoulders just like she had done, no tip of the head to indicate a good or bad thought behind the shrug. "If you don't change it now it will delay withdrawals at other banks. You would have to wait for the exchange rate to be calculated. It could take overnight or you would have to accept the rate for the previous day. Most banks don't have a computer link like we do. They call to get rates in the morning and midday."

"Would be fine. Please, leave it as quid."

"I'd be happy to."

The Marrilian

Janice returned with a QSDD officer, the Agent.

Erica watched him approach with a blank face but her throat got tight. She tried to swallow, tried to relax, but that wasn't possible around the damn SDD. He strode over to the desk and looked down at the drafts then at Erica, his dark brown uniform was stiff, straight and perfect.

The two round pips on his black tie weren't a very high rank, maybe a corporal. He wore a pistol and he had unclipped the leather restraining flap over the butt of the gun so it could be drawn. Worse, he had his hand on it.

"I have been told you are wearing a firearm," he said to Erica sternly.

She didn't move and resisted meeting his eyes. She didn't want to make him nervous so she kept her eyes on his tie and her hands resting on her legs. "Yes sir, 'tis so," she replied as calmly as she could. A cough started to tickle at her throat.

"Remove it and place it on the desk," he demanded.

Erica slowly unbuckled the belt. His shoulders stiffened when she revealed the metal buckle and that gave some small satisfaction to show him she was someone with enough money to buy him trouble…maybe. The belt fell from her hips to the chair behind her. She sat forward and dragged it around herself then placed it on the desk.

The shining nickel plate on the automatic weapon caught everyone's eye. She saw the SDD agent's hand relax. She sat back in her chair.

"Stand up," he ordered as soon as she had settled. She did, once again as slow as she could. She knew his type. She could see it by looking at him, his tension, his distrust. "Remove your coat." Again, she did as she was told and without a word, first grinding out the cigarette with her toe. She swallowed back the tickle that persisted in her throat and dropped the heavy leather coat on the chair. It fell with a solid *thrump* from all the things in the pockets.

She wore a light weight, black shirt over a brown tank top. The tank top was wet with sweat. Her shirt and tank top were tucked in dark brown canvas pants. Her second belt, the one that held up her pants, was a piece of leather tied in a knot as all Quirni wore, or so she had been told.

The agent circled around her. He stopped beside her and kicked her chair so violently that it scudded several yards across the tile floor. He continued to circle her. She felt her knife tugged from its sheath on her belt.

"Did you forget to declare this?" he demanded and held it in front of her face, threatening and pleased with his discovery.

The cough seized Erica at that moment. It burst out. The sudden sound and her movement startled the agent. He grabbed her arm and twisted it behind her. In the next instant the QSDD officer was on the floor and everyone stared at her.

She had untwisted from his grasp and then popped him under the chin with the heel of her hand while at the same time hooking his leg. He had fallen like a rock to his ass. Her knife skidded away on the tile and stopped against the leg of another desk.

"Holy crap," Arlo gulped as the agent jumped to his feet, backed away, and drew his pistol in one fluid motion.

"Put your hands on your head and kneel!" he demanded.

'Shit girl, you just made a world of trouble,' the voice in her head told her.

Erica knew that but the move had been instinctual. He had hurt her and held the knife by her face. Tenpole spent years learning to defend from such attacks. Better trained Tenpole could control the impulse. Any other place or day she might have, but not today. She was too tense.

"That won't happen again," the officer told them all. He looked from face to face. His gun wavered. He breathed fast as he reached in his uniform and pulled out a phone. Arlo, Janice, and Erica watched as he pressed the keypad and held it to his flushed cheek. He didn't say much, only 'seven', waited, and then pressed another button and put the phone back in his pocket.

"What is your name?" He leveled the pistol at Erica's belly.

"Erica Ennis."

"What are you doing on Quirni?"

"Came here because of thayanite poisoning."

The agent made no face to indicate he cared about this. He took a breath. "Are you related to the Kinsleys?"

She finally looked him in the eyes. "Yes."

That brought a flash of fear and Erica felt satisfaction, not that she would ever be able to use the damn name but at least it scared him.

"In what way?"

"Claimant Kinsley be my great, great uncle," she answered. She tried to shift to get her knee off of a crack in the tiles but the pistol came up straighter and aimed at her heart.

"Stay still. Why did you bring that gun here?"

"Here to Quirni or here to the bank?" she asked because she started to get angry. Her bags sat beside her. Anyone could see she had just arrived and hadn't found a place to leave a gun.

"Don't be smart, to Quirni. They aren't common here."

"A life of leisure and hunting. Needed a gun for such," she lied. It actually served two purposes other than hunting, which she loathed, it acted as a status symbol to give her a better life and it hid some things.

The agent looked up at the desk and the stacks of bank notes. "How much money does she have?"

"On this claim you require a warrant for that information," said Arlo. "Unless the depositor allows us to release the amount." He looked at Erica on the floor in front of the desk.

"How much?" the agent demanded.

"As he said, you need a warrant," she hissed. She couldn't help it. Her fear made her say dumb things and in dumb ways. She didn't like fear. She would rather be shot than confess anything while he pointed a gun at her.

'Keep control,' the voice warned.

The agent considered Erica, glanced at the money, and then walked over to her knife and snatched it up. He returned to the desk and took Erica's pistol, belt and all. He holstered his own gun. "After you finish your business with her, call me," he told Arlo and left.

Erica continued to kneel for a few more seconds before lowering her hands. She twisted and looked up at Arlo.

He shrugged. "I'll get the accounts started." He went back through the door behind the glass wall leaving Janice and Erica alone. Janice didn't move. She glared at Erica who slowly got to her feet and retrieved her coat.

After shrugging into it she screeched the chair across the tiled floor back to its original position where she sat and laced her hands over her stomach. Her eyes fixed on the desk, on a plain plastic pen that lay towards the middle of the ink blotter. The teller glared at her. Erica refused to look at the woman or acknowledge her. Only a few moments passed before the teller ruined that plan.

"You're her. I know you are." Her tone dripped with venom.

Erica set her teeth together and kept her eyes on the pen.

"They took you to Marril, taught you to talk like that, changed your eyes and now you're back." Janice swallowed so loud it was as if she had a solid thing in her throat, a ball of fear, or loathing, or a mix of the two. "You are her."

Erica couldn't help it, she looked up. The teller seethed with hatred, pure focused hatred. Her eyes were black with it.

Edwards

The angry woman glanced over her shoulder at the glass wall then leaned over the desk and lowered her voice. She wore a mean grin.

"At least that damned thayanite poisoning got you. It brought you back here and if it doesn't kill you, we will. You killed my sister and her children you filthy, rich, whore and I will hurt you back." Her announcement made her happy and proud to have enough courage to speak. She folded her arms over her chest and sneered down her nose.

Erica held the woman's gaze for several moments then looked back at the pen. Friggin' Matilda Kinsley. Well, at least they had one thing in common, according to this woman they were both whores. Whoring was illegal on Quirni so that meant Matilda broke lots of laws. They had something else in common.

People started to filter back into the bank. Apparently, Erica had arrived during a lunch hour. She pulled her hat down.

"Well," Arlo exclaimed happily when he finally returned. He happened to notice the way Janice stood and glanced at Erica. He didn't say anything but sat down and began to shuffle papers between him and his rich new depositor. He entered numbers and dates into several different accounting books, made receipts, and passed them over.

"This be how you bank here? In ledgers?" she asked.

"No, not entirely. I have to open your accounts on the computer. We do have electricity but only for the one computer. It's solar."

"Some of the investments you suggest be Marrilian and Sirrian," she noticed as she scanned the papers he handed her. "How do you update value?"

"There is a sequence of space station links with those worlds," he answered serenely, as if he repeated the reply often. "They update our information every hour. It isn't as exact to the minute as what you are used to on Marril but it's the best link on Quirni. I'll enter your accounts this afternoon and after that any interest you earn will be calculated by the system. You don't have to worry about human error. It's all automated."

Erica accepted that, not that she had much choice.

He went back to his work. Within an hour they had finished and then stowed the majority of Erica's belongings in two deposit boxes. Arlo gave her the key cards for the boxes then returned her to the chair by Janice's desk. He sent Janice to get the Delegate agent. When the agent returned Arlo told him they were done.

The Marrilian

"Very well," the military man replied politely and placed her gun and knife on the desk. No sign of his earlier animosity showed. "Have a good day," he bid her and returned to the back room. They all stared in surprise.

"What?" Janice exclaimed.

That had been the last thing Erica expected as well. Arlo collected his work from Janice's desk. Janice didn't move.

Erica returned her knife to its sheath on her hip, strapped her gun on, and made a quick exit. All she had with her now was a little money, her backpack, one hundred rounds of ammunition, a change of clothes and necessary personal items.

One thought possessed her–get what she needed to survive in the wilderness and get away from people. She dipped her hat to hide her face and moved as fast as she could to the outfitting store Arlo had described. She was about to become one of the fancy adventurers who came to Quirni for a camping vacation but she would go far, far further than any of them ever had.

Edwards

Chapter 3 – Amon

Erica tried to look casual, like other shoppers from the ship. She wandered in like someone with time to spare. The store was large so she kept distance between herself and any locals. They could be identified by their clothes, thick cloth, drab colors with little style.

The people from Parcles, those from the ship, stood out like a cat amongst dogs with supple fabrics, a lot of bright blue, clean white, and reds in their clothing. Her own clothes almost looked Quirni with the long brown leather coat, brown leather hat, dark pants and shirt. The metal belt buckle at her waist said differently. She kept her hat dipped down as she circled the room to pick out items.

Wooden shelves stood against the walls. Functional Quirni clothes were folded and stacked on tables in the middle of the room. Display racks stood at the ends of the tables. They held the small items in stacked plastic baskets. Not one piece of metal was in sight. Cooking pans were ceramic. Eating utensils were plastic.

She picked out a thermal blanket and a collapsible plastic bowl. The water filters were above them and when she looked up at the water filters, the owner saw her profile. That was enough. He came from behind his counter, snatched an ore that leaned against the wall, and moved towards her like he wanted to squash an rodent infestation.

Erica saw him out of the corner of her eye, a large man coming fast. She faced him and backed away. "Not Matilda Kinsley!" she declared, her palm out to stop him. She gripped what she had already chosen in her other arm. "She be my cousin! Not her!"

He picked up speed as he barreled towards her and raised the ore above his head. He ran and snarled something through his grit teeth that she didn't try to understand. She ran out the door and he chased her into the street screaming. She ducked into an alley, leapt around boxes, made turns down more alleys, and lost him.

When she knew she was safe she stopped and huddled beside a wooden box that served as a garbage bin. It smelled like it and the alley smelled like pee. A wet, narrow gully drained down the middle of it.

"Blast it!" she cursed between her pants for breath. Her heart beat furiously. Sweat dripped down her back and beaded on her face.

"Kinsley!" people yelled in the street.

Erica flinched and gripped her blanket and bowl tighter. The bowl dug into her chest, a bowl she hadn't paid for. That made her a thief here too. Lords, she hadn't meant that but she was glad to have them. She stuffed the items in her backpack and edged away from the noise, hugging close to the walls.

The alley wound behind three story buildings dim and narrow. It reminded her of the alleys back on Marril. Such a place could be good for hiding but only for a short time. It was too easy to get captured in them if a group blocked the exits and slowly worked their way in. For now, she could get out of sight and plan.

She waded through piles of boxes, scattered papers, and the half decayed garbage littering the ground until she found a pile of wood crates that didn't smell like pee, shit, or garbage. She hoped no one expected a Kinsley to hide in such slime. So far, no one yelled or came down the alley behind her. She crouched and lit a badly needed cigarette to clear her lungs and think but kept an eye on the smoke to make sure it didn't curl up and give away her location.

During the trip Erica had done her homework on the planet. She had read all of the brochures about Quirni and learned most of the planet's water was contaminated with deadly bacteria. Just as the people on Cobal Claim had died, so could she if she drank unfiltered water. Quirni born, or those who had lived on the planet long enough, had some immunity, but that only allowed them to bathe in untreated water. Even they would die if they drank it and didn't get the antidote. The recent calamity, of which Erica was now accused, seeing as how she looked like her cousin, was proof enough of that. If she entered the woods without a means to treat the water, she would die.

Starving to death was another problem, and it had become clear she wouldn't be able to buy anything. Going into the wilderness without food would be suicide. The only option left was to steal. "Son-of-a-bitch." The smoke in her lips nearly spit out with her swearing. At this point she wouldn't mind if it fell on the lords forsaken wood building and set the whole place on fire.

Her jaw clenched; the blasted irony of the situation wasn't

lost on her. On Marril she had lived in poverty while having money. She hadn't wanted her father to know she had money so she had banked it and kept it secret. She took money out of the bank, came here and had expected a new start but nobody would let her buy a home or even a dam pot to boil water. They preferred her dead. That blasted cash insisted on staying in the bank. Her jaw and shoulders tensed at the situation.

There had to be someplace she could steal a pan.

A damp area on the cement served to put out her cigarette. Her hands free, she spread her map on one of the boxes. The building at her back was accessible. All of the doors she had passed looked like nothing more than wood planks tied or tacked together by some miracle of wood sticks. Locks were a non entity. Instead of handles, they had a hole. Glancing down at the tiny map of the area, she traced her finger along the alley and counted the divots of buildings to figure out where she was. If she got it wrong it could be the difference between going into a busy pub or the back room of a restaurant. This, hopefully, was a restaurant. Her best guess, this was The Georgetown.

A restaurant might have food and extra pans but if she encountered anyone she would need to fight. The idea made her stomach churn and wish she had her protector, Noel, but he had his drawbacks. Better not to wish for him because if this went poorly, she might get him back for real.

Stuffing everything important in her coat pockets, she discovered she liked this coat. Despite the weight and heat, it was going to save her life if she had to ditch her pack. Nearly everything fit, her bowl, ammunition, passport, smokes, even the map. Now the pack wouldn't be a big loss. Prepared for the worst, she edged up the steps to the door and peeked in the hole.

She feared someone would be staring right back at her, an eye glaring out through the hole. Good lords, but she had to get rid of those fears or she'd never breathe right again.

The hole was only a hole. She could see a light at the far end of the long, dingy hall. Voices and the sound of metal pots and pans rattled in a kitchen but they were down by the light. Holding her breath, Erica slipped inside and found another door off the hall. This one actually had a bolt of wood. She slid the bolt back and passed through then closed the door so it didn't hang open to give alarm. Only a tiny bit of light leaked in from the hall so she struck a match. There, in all its glory, stood a storage room with bread, vegetables, and crackers. Within moments she stuffed her backpack and pockets and began to search for pans.

Edwards

She pawed through the containers, and pulled off lids, but before she could finish her search, the match burned her thumb. She threw it down, stomped it out, and lit another. A search with another match revealed there were no pans. She couldn't risk a third match in this tinderbox.

Erica held her breath as she slid back the bolt of the storage room and placed her eye up to the crack, listening for anyone in the hallway. Once she was sure the coast was as clear, she returned to the alley by the boxes and trash bins to study the map again. The first incursion had gone well. The tickle in her throat relaxed with her emotions. If she could find what she needed she could escape and smoke once out of this horror of a town. So she resolved to try another building.

The map might still show where to find pans or bottles, perhaps a brewery. Before she could spread it, she saw something rush out of the dim light from the corner of her eye so she bolted the other way. She stuffed the map in her pocket as she scrambled over a four foot high tower of crates tossed out behind a liquor store. If she had been more energetic, she might have tried to jump it, but her strength plummeted since the last adrenaline rush. The crates collapsed and scattered under her.

Pain erupted in her side from the small bowl in her pocket. It didn't stop her, nothing stopped her, she couldn't be stopped by this or them. She rolled off the crates and hoped the plastic didn't crack. It could at least capture rain water. Getting to her feet she saw her attacker had doubled. There were two men, not one. Huge Quirni brutes hopped over the crates she had kindly scattered and grabbed at her.

She seized the arm of the closest man and pulled as she stepped aside which rotated him so he lost his balance. He sprawled in the shit. The second man grabbed her pack. She slipped out of it and ran. They wailed for help louder than any Tenpole siren she'd ever heard. Running blurred the jutting backsides of buildings as she dodged around piles of clutter. She had no water and she had lost half her food with the pack. That couldn't concern her right now. Her only hope was the edge of town. If she could get there before the howling madmen caught her, she could hide in the woods. That was the only possible place she might be safe. There was no Tenpole here. There was no one to help her hide, no place to shelter her.

Her breath shortened. Her emotions were too high. The stress would steal her breath as fast as the running and then her strength would give out but how long would it take?

The Marrilian

If she didn't get somewhere safe before she lost her breath, she was going to die at the hands of an angry Quirni mob. She could confront them, use her gun, but if she stood and fought she would not only be a thief but a murderer as well. Her gun had a large bore. No one would survive if she aimed and she wouldn't survive if she didn't aim.

The thought of shedding blood repulsed her. She pushed it away. This was a new start. She couldn't commit that crime again. This time it would be her choice. Running had to be the answer. This wouldn't be the same.

She dodged behind another tooth of the gear-like alleyway and saw trees. She stopped in awe to see the height of them. Her head tilted back, easily a hundred feet high with leaves as big as both her hands spread. Between her and the trees was a road and a line of small buildings, little wooden huts with goods sitting on their porches. No one was outside by the buildings.

Gawkers emerged from the alley doors behind her, called by the commotion of the chase. She glanced back when she heard the doors and that was a mistake. Three of the five people hanging out of the doors recognized her as Matilda. Their eyes flew wide and they ducked back inside. Erica thought that was a perfectly fine reaction, far better than grabbing an ore and chasing her.

She hurried to the end of the alley and peeked out. There was a sidewalk and a wide street. A wagon pulled by two horses passed by but didn't notice her as she darted behind it and towards a road that connected small buildings on the other side. She ran down the road a short distance then cut behind the buildings without anyone raising another alarm. There were bushes and plantings next to a wall so she pushed into them and paused to catch her breath.

No one yelled her name nearby but she knew she had not escaped the hunt. They had simply fallen behind as they searched all the rubbish in the alley. They were far enough behind that this part of town didn't know about her yet. The few people who had seen her run past would join the hunt once they heard about it and they knew where she went.

Reaching the woods wouldn't be an escape but a reprieve; she still had to get water. Confusion and yells erupted behind her but one glance around the corner of the wooden hut assured her she was safe, for the moment. Gawkers had stopped the angry mob to ask questions. More people left their porches and crossed the street to join them.

Edwards

Did that leave the buildings near her empty? Erica left her hiding place in the bushes and peeked around the edge of a wall to see what the buildings were. The one by which she hid had a few pieces of clothing on the porch and the one across from it, the one furthest from her and nearest the woods, had a sign advertising packaged foods. Food meant there might be water. She had seen bottled water in the outfitter's shop. They probably sold it everywhere.

The short road that led to the small shops joined to another road, a green two track lane overhung with trees. It travelled along the edge of the woods. The smart thing to do was use it and get away as far and fast as possible but the food was right there and maybe she could get water.

The mob in the alley gestured and yelled and tried to get organized. Did she have time to run into the store and find water? She would have to cross the short road to get to it.

'Hide,' the voice in her head urged.

Erica frowned. The voice wasn't usually wrong. One more glance between the mob and the store convinced her it was right this time. They could see her if she went there. Her breath had just calmed enough to get running again.

For the sake of speed Erica used the roads but she had to stop soon. She could not outrun healthy Quirni. They would find her, plus, she still had to get water, or some means to make clean water. She would have to go back to steal it but not now.

The woods were thick with undergrowth. That should give her a place to hide and thank the lords for that. Her chest burned. That was warning enough. The running had to stop.

None of the townspeople were in sight so there was time to find a place. They had stopped chasing to make a lot of noise, probably an alarm, not sirens like in Tenpole, but some strange instrument, maybe a drum? She supposed the Quirni didn't have enough metal to make sirens. Whatever they hammered upon, it got attention. She could hear a crowd of people yelling. They would follow soon. There were places to hide in these woods. She just had to pick one.

Erica searched up the main road, half running, crouching, peering under the trees. Finally, a huge mass of bushes looked good. Leaves covered the ground so she wouldn't leave footprints. The bush was a few hundred yards in from the edge of town and half that from the road. It would do.

She passed the spot and threw her hat through the trees so it sailed far ahead and then she doubled back and burrowed into the chosen bush. The branches fought to be separated. Erica struggled into them with a hand in front of her eyes. The bush snagged at her but she wormed her way in. She expected to lay in it, hang like a snake, but instead she found bare ground at the middle covered by a thin layer of moss. She twisted into it and curled up then worked to slow her breathing as well as stop the threatening cough.

Antidote could stop the cough. Since she couldn't smoke she put an unlit cigarette in her mouth and sucked on it. It tasted worse than usual but it seemed to help. Anything to stop from coughing. A cough now would be her death.

Her chin touched her crossed ankles. She massaged her throat. If she absolutely had to cough she would muffle it in her legs, arms, and coat. She sucked on the unlit antidote and concentrated on calm breaths, no sound. Within minutes heavy boots ran by. They receded then came back. People yelled at each other to search bushes with poles, to flay at them. The searching began nearby.

It took all of her concentration and effort to be silent but the need to cough built. She swallowed against it repeatedly but each swallow made the tickle worse. Each breath had to be shallower.

It was the worst thing she could do for her lungs. They needed air and deep breaths. There was antidote in the cigarette but she couldn't smoke so she started chewing it. At least that would get some of the medicine into her even if it didn't go directly to her lungs and get absorbed properly. It was something.

The yelling got louder. They came closer and struck at bushes all around her. She concentrated on holding still. Not one sound. The bushes next to hers rattled. She couldn't make one sound. A stick whacked at her bush, poked into it, but aside from the branches tapping her back and springing away, she was untouched. Another person joined the first to whack at her bush. They plunged sticks into it but they fell short of where Erica crouched. They left together to search the next bush.

Tiny bits of the foam used to make the cigarette broke off. It tasted terrible but Erica had to swallow it. Sweat dripped down her forehead and into her eyes as she worked to do so without gagging. She wanted to wipe the tickling drips away but she dare not move.

She closed her eyes to concentrate on keeping quiet and still. One small movement would move the bush that hid her. The rustle of one branch might draw attention. Oh lords, be still, be still. She concentrated on just that, be still. In her mind she could see the people turn. They would hear the tiny leaf rustle and turn. They would wait for the next movement then beat the bush until it broke and revealed her huddled there. Stay still.

The searchers moved away until she no longer heard them but still she feared them being patient. Anger made people stubborn. The sweat itched as it dripped. It tickled. She hugged her arms tight around her chest and massaged her throat with a finger, the only movement she might make without drawing attention. Their voices and noise grew quieter the longer she waited.

Hours passed as they searched. It became dark. The antidote she chewed helped. It took forever but eventually it calmed the cough and cleared her lungs. Erica remained huddled over her legs, listening, waiting for an ore or stick to crash into the leaves above her again but they gave up as night fell and the damp set in.

The woods grew quiet. Only small animals moved. They no doubt returned to their beds for the night. Was she sitting on a bed? Might she sit where a snake would rest for the cold hours of the night?

She sat up just a few inches to listen. Would she hear if a thing slithered across the ground? She heard nothing but the bugs. She didn't like the idea of a snake joining her but she couldn't move yet. She wasn't sure everyone was gone.

What if someone was as patient as she was? What if someone waited like she did? People had thrashed at the bushes for hours. She wanted to believe it was unlikely. Their stick hadn't hit her. The leaves were big and thick so they hid her. If they had seen her coat it was the color of dirt so they might not recognize it. As long as she stayed still she was safe. If she moved, it was a risk. She would have to move eventually, but now? It was only hours after they'd retreated from the woods.

What if they realized she could hide like this? Someone might sit quietly somewhere and just wait and watch. She would do that if she was out there. If they were enraged like the teller, if they were determined to kill her, they might think of a rational way to lay a trap and wait.

Cold settled. Her knees felt it first. She slowly, quietly, tried to pull her coat closer. A twig snared the leather. The contents of the pockets clinked so she stopped. Dare she try again?

'No. No. No,' her inner thoughts warned.

She carefully replaced the fold of her coat on the ground. For

The Marrilian

the first time in a long time she tried to talk back to the voice in her mind but to no avail. It didn't answer most of the time, just a *conscience*, sort of, but 'no' it had said and she agreed.

She heard something, a small thing, not a person, some sort of little animal. It walked up to the side of her hiding place. It stopped. It stayed still for several minutes then turned around and left. Was this its bed? Had she taken its nest? She hoped not. It might decide to bite her.

'Well, on second thought, maybe we should move into a tree.'

Erica smiled in spite of her situation. She continued to sit still. She would wait until the deepest dark and then she would sneak back and get the rest of what she needed.

'Don't go back you fool.'

Erica shut her eyes tighter and tried to keep calm. *It's the only way. I only got a couple of carrots and crackers in my pockets.*

'Get to the next town. Tellhurst is only a few days walk up the road.'

The next town? I'll have to explore it and I have no water. I know where the stores are here.

'Every house has water and food.'

Go into a house? Break into a house? Erica drew a careful, slow breath. She opened her eyes and tried to see how dark it was through the bushes. She couldn't. Everything was dim and the bush blocked her view of the sky. *Calm down*, she willed herself. Her heart raced at the thought of intruding into homes. People were always the most vicious there.

'You should load the gun you know.'

She hugged her legs. *No.*

'Stupid.'

No. She should not use it on a person. *No.*

'You will die if you don't.'

Have to get water, she thought at the voice, not realizing she was having a conversation.

'I suppose.'

Night fell deep. Erica hadn't heard anything but the wind in the tress and the scurrying of small animals for quite some time but still she waited until the cold made her shiver so hard the bush around her shook.

She lifted her head. The canopy of leaves above brushed her hair. If someone had stayed behind to wait her out she might win against one, two, or maybe three unskilled people. How many wanted Matilda bad enough to stay?

Edwards

The only noise was the insects until an animal chattered nearby, probably a squirrel. It sounded angry. She could hear it scratching at the bark as it ran up and down a tree. It spit out its complaints for half an hour at least then retreated and was gone.

Erica hugged her legs. Ammunition in her pocket rattled, less noise than the squirrel. Nothing reacted. She listened to the insects. Their sounds were a good sign. If there was someone moving about she expected the insects wouldn't make any noise. Or would that be different on Quirni?

Good lords but they hated that stupid cousin of hers.

Friggin' SDD. Why hadn't they told her about Matilda when she was still on board ship? What did they plan? Six thousand people killed.

'It's dark. It's time to go.'

You want me dead. Swear you want me dead.

'It's time to go.'

Erica was accustomed to hearing her *conscience* but not taking its advice. She waited. Let people fall to sleep. She would wait until late night maybe even early morning assuming nothing chased her out of the bush.

Her legs and arms cramped. She worked her toes and made fists to help relieve the tension. She closed her eyes. She tired of making fists. She stopped and rested her cheek on her knee.

A dim red light woke her. It shone through the leaves, casting a bloody hue onto the top of the bush. It was the red moon, Amon. She straightened to look.

The planet she had come from, Marril, had no moons because it was a moon. This was the first moon she had seen since she was eight, well not technically. She had lived on a moon so she saw it every day but in her mind that didn't count.

Moons were pretty in the dark sky. She remembered that from Sirrus. She carefully pushed back a few branches and looked at the red hued sky and puffy red clouds.

'Of course,' her smug inner voice said.

Light! If the red moon was out then the white moon would be out too! Khepri! Khepri is white like a spot of day in the night,' the tourist booklet had said. Crusty blood flaked from the edge of her gaping mouth. She pulled the wad of cigarette mush out and set it on the ground. It had made the inside of her mouth raw. It wasn't meant to be chewed but it had worked. She was still alive but she had to get away.

The question now was how long before Khepri rose? And how long before the third one followed? Big Thoth. 'You can work by it' the saying went. Would the villagers get up to work? Would they be up soon? She didn't remember. It had been a long journey and she had read a lot.

She turned and backed out of the bush on hands and knees. If someone waited for her, she needed to be on her feet before they could strike or call for help. Branches dragged her coat up her back. When clear, she squatted, flipped the coat off her head, then paused to listen and search the trees for movement. The contents of her pockets settled and stilled. Silence. Not a movement. She had certainly been noisy enough to attract attention but nothing.

Only the insects seemed to notice her; they stopped trilling. Dark, silent woods bathed in red light surrounded her. She pushed to her feet, pressing with her palms on her knees to get upright on stiff legs. She worked the stiffness away as she peered through the trees and bushes. She remained ready to fall out of sight. It was absolutely quiet. Too quiet.

She studied the woods in all directions. The insects began to chirp and trill while she stood there, stooped over, peering through the trees, barely willing to take a breath. She straightened and pulled her coat closed with relief. That was warmer.

The ammunition on her pockets clinked when she moved and the bug noise dropped. It was the same as on Marril. Bugs in the brush there reacted the same way. If someone was near they would quiet and listen. That meant it was safe. The bugs had been chirping and trilling for hours. She inhaled. She even cleared her throat the tiniest amount then spat out bits of chewed antidote. She took a deep breath and felt the tickle of a cough but it wasn't bad. She still needed to smoke but not immediately. She couldn't now. She was too close to town and the smell of the antidote steam carried a long way. She carefully cleared her throat until she brought up the knot of phlegm and spit that out as well. Good lords, spitting took effort!

Two more pills would help that. It had been a long time since she had taken any and she had to get supplies before she left. At the very least she needed water and that was back in the town. The moons travelled east to west so she could follow it back. The town was east of her.

Some branches snapped back and slapped at her as she pushed through them. Scratches on her face were the least of her worries. Right now, she needed water and the little store at the edge of town was her target. If nothing else, it should find a pan to purify water. With luck she would get that and bottles.

Every few trees, she stopping to listen then crept on towards the low, dark shape of the store she intended to rob. Red light shone on its clay roofing tiles. It looked eerie, ghostly.

The Sirrian moon was white. When it was full, it reflected off the snow and made walking at night easy. Sirrus. She made a face to think of her home planet and how far she had come from it. She wasn't Sirrian anymore.

Moons, why moons! I'm friggin Marrilian, she thought as she snuck through the dark. *There aren't any damn moons over Marril!* What Marrilian would ever expect so much light at night? Qetesh, the boiling blue and gold planet Marril orbited, didn't even give off so much light.

'*The three Quirni moons create such uneven tides and chaotic waves that the seas are impossible for the wooden Quirni ships to traverse.*' She tried to remember the passage about the phases of the Quirni moons. '*When all three moons rise together the tide can rise twenty-five feet.*' So they didn't usually rise together?

'*Time under only the red moon, Amon, is considered a blessed time to begin a new life.*' Didn't that suggest it wasn't usually up by itself? How long had it been up? She glanced through the trees. It had travelled about a third of the way through the sky but it was passing quickly. She thought she saw a silvery glow through the trees as well and that silvery glow wasn't the glow of electric lights, not on Quirni, it wasn't.

'Quick!' the voice in her head urged.

No! Not quick! My pockets are full and jingling like bells!

She crept forward, stopping, listening, and then inched forward again until she saw the end of the woods. Beyond it was a line of darkness made by planted shrubs, berries she suspected by the sweet odor.

Everything remained quiet. She kept to the lane and shadows until she was even with the store then quickly ducked under the porch awning. She made it to the door without any alarm. The 'lock' was no more than a latch that fell into a wooden slat and it wasn't on the inside but the outside.

She pulled it out of its cradle and paused, waiting in case someone was inside. Still there was no alarm, no voices, no movement. The door hung from leather. No creaks? She pushed. It was quiet. She slipped into the building then closed the door again silently.

'Stupid.'

The room went completely dark. She blinked and tried to see

into the blackness.

'Could you be more stupid? You shouldn't have come back.'

She dug in her pocket until she found matches. She lit one and looked about. Ten feet in front of her stood cartons of Jason's Sparkling Spring Cider and that was the only water she saw. There were not pans. It would have to do. Half a dozen cautious steps, she grabbed the carton of plastic bottles and returned to the door. The match burned out. She listened before pulling the handle then slipped outside.

"There!" someone shouted and a rock smashed into her hip. The packs of cigarettes in her pocket cushioned the blow but it still knocked her sideways. The bottles fell to the dirt as she stumbled off the porch but managed to keep her feet. Of all the things to drop, it was the one thing she came for.

Two men rushed her. They held sticks extended towards the sky. They would have to take several steps to reach her. She rushed at them. She used her speed, slid to the ground, and passed between them.

They swung at her but the sticks swooshed over her head then thwacked on bone. The men yelped in pain. She rolled to her feet and turned to face them. One of the men writhed on the ground and held his face.

The second man swung at her again with a grunt and a curse. She ducked his stick, stepped up and kneed him in the crotch. He dropped the stick on his foot as he grabbed to hold his pain. He crumbled to his knees squeaking. More people ran towards them. That was her chance. She grabbed Jason's Sparkling Spring Cider and ran full out towards the woods. The people stopped to help the men on the ground.

"God damn it! Don't everyone stop! Get her!" a woman yelled. She sounded like Janice.

"The woods!"

"I told you she wasn't gone! By the damn lords! I told you assholes!"

Erica ran with the Cider's plastic holder clutched in her hand. It swung wildly.

The voices faded behind her. She didn't go into the trees but stayed to the road so she might run as fast as she could before her breath failed.

'But someone could be waiting ahead!' warned the voice.

Stay off the road? She stepped off it into the long grass. Walking in the underbrush would be too noisy. She could hide again... No. They wouldn't give up a second time. The grass dragged at her shoes so she stepped back onto the road but continued slower, wary of someone ahead. Her breath came hard and finally caught. It had been too long since she had smoked.

She stifled the noise in her coat sleeve. Calm down. She took deep, slow breaths, trying to ease air down her constricted throat and into her lungs but it didn't help. The best she could do was run half hunched over from the effort of clearing her throat, bottles against her chest, while she dug in her pocket to find her cigarettes. She would have to chew another one but she couldn't find the open pack.

'Quick!'

I can't be quick, she groaned inwardly. *I have to stop and hide again. I have to get more antidote.* Only they wouldn't give up easily this time. They had stayed awake to catch her. They wouldn't go away now. They knew she was close and the brightest moon was rising. It would light the woods like day. She had to go.

She managed another ten feet before her lack of breath weakened her legs. The eroded dirt at the edge of the road gave under foot. She slipped and fell down the grassy slope which wasn't steep or long but she didn't have the strength to climb back up. Instead she lay still, dazed from the sudden fall.

When her wits cleared she rose, sitting up like a drunk on a bender, and looked about for the cider. It had tumbled from her hands to the base of a tree. She crawled through deep grass and fell on it. After laying there long enough to find some energy she righted herself and sat with her back to the tree, the bottles clutched to her chest, listening for her pursuers while her breath wheezed. She couldn't hear them but she bet they could hear her.

'Scare them. Use the gun.'

Erica closed her eyes.

'You have to.'

She put her hand on the holster.

People were close enough now she could hear their cautious steps on the gravel road. She leaned forward to look around the tree. The small silvery white moon had risen. It lit twenty people from behind, their long shadows before them, all spread out, searching for her, listening. They all held sticks or stones. Once they knew she'd shoot at them they wouldn't be hunting her with sticks anymore.

They only weapon she had left was one she never wanted to point at a person. She rested her hand on her gun. It went against everything she had promised herself but it was all she could do.

The crunch of feet on the gravel road came closer. Erica

The Marrilian

stifled her sob and swallowed it down. Her or them. Maybe she could scare them and not fire? She could hope.

Earlier, when she had realized she might need to move quickly she had stuffed her valuables into her pockets. Just about any pocket had ammunition in it. She pulled out a handful of .45 caliber rounds and set the bottles aside so she could draw her pistol.

With her right hand she pressed the button to release the clip. It dropped into her lap. She lay the gun on a flap of her coat and loaded the clip. Five rounds were in her hand.

She inhaled. Could it be a deep breath? Could it give some relief? She coughed. The steps of her pursuers paused. Now they knew where she was. She blinked to clear her tears and loaded the clip, her hands shaking. The clip snapped into the gun with a solid *snick*. She stood, the gun in both hands but still pointed towards the ground, then cocked the automatic weapon, mostly for the effect of the sound so they knew she spoke the truth.

"I be armed," she called out with a rasping voice. She tried to clear her throat but too much phlegm choked her. She spit it out.

She could see the people clearly in the light of Khepri. The road was about three feet above her. She had fallen into a shallow ditch and rolled about five feet. A man at the front pointed towards either side of her. Two men started away.

"You be shot if you come towards me! Stay still!" The men stopped. She cleared her throat and took a quick breath. "You be lit up nice by that pretty white moon. Can't be missed." She clipped her words to sound harsh because she didn't sound strong. Sounding desperate would be fine too, maybe better. They should believe desperate.

The people only carried sticks and rocks. There wasn't a gun or even a bow amongst them. Most of them froze. A few of them glanced over their shoulders at the moon. Two stepped back– only two.

Erica cleared her throat again and shakily climbed the grassy slope to the road. If she could keep them in view she might start walking and keep them at bay. She had the cider in her left hand but set it down before she reached the top. It was too much, too heavy and cumbersome when she could barely get herself up the incline. She would have to get water elsewhere.

When she managed to stand on the side of the road and face the mob she rotated her hand and turned the pistol so it glinted in the silvery light, not that she needed to since the moon lit her well. They could see her clearer than she could see them backlit as they were.

"Do any of you want to die?" She raised the pistol towards the nearest woman. She aimed at her chest. "You?" she demanded of the short, heavy lady as she walked to the middle of the road where no one might come from the woods behind her. They could work their way through and she wouldn't hear them for all of her wheezing.

The woman went two shades paler. Red light shone on her face. Silver light backlit her wildly curly hair and both let Erica see her face pale. She smiled evilly and all of them froze.

"Not that you sots believe me." She took a breath and put on her angriest sneer. "But my name be *Erica* not Matilda." It took everything she had to speak. The sneer was learned in prison. It had backed people off then and she hoped it did now.

"Was stupid of me to come–to this *shit*hole planet without learning about my cousin. My mistake. Yours be–to come closer because–if you touch me–" she paused again to fill her lungs and narrow her eyes a little more, a bit more sinister. "If you attack, nine of you die with me. 'Tis how many bullets in my pistol." She breathed so hard she felt sure it had to be pneumonia.

The gun wavered. "Please, if you would live, walk away. Leave. You had your–" Her voice caught in a wad of phlegm. She cleared her throat. "Chase," she finished and spit. "You caught me. Now–let me go. Not Matilda."

A little ox of a man stepped forward. "I don't care if you riddle me with your stinkin' bullets! You die tonight!" he sneered with a lilting Marrilian accent. He hadn't been born on Quirni but he had lived here long enough to hate Matilda. His accent wasn't Parcles or Tenpole but from some other part of the planet, probably one of the poorer towns that mined the lesser grades of thayanite which would explain why he was on Quirni. He had never saved enough for a ticket to Sirrus.

"Jeff!" the woman beside him yelled and grabbed his arm. She had a hard Quirni accent. He jerked away from her to face Erica.

"And while you are busy shooting me they can attack you." He took several steps. He stopped and squared his shoulders when she aimed at him.

"Stop it!" a voice with authority demanded. A man from the back of the group walked forward. "Don't you hear that poison in her?"

Erica squinted into the silvery outlined face of the man. Arlo? She cleared her throat again and spit out more phlegm. She tried to pull a breath but it felt like a lake in her lungs. She started to feel dizzy. She needed the antidote now.

"Do you hear that?" he asked and pointed at her. He walked to the front of the group and faced Jeff. No one answered. "You will die for nothing or be tried for killing an innocent person if you attack this girl. Worse, you won't be around when Matilda actually does come back."

He pointed at Erica. "I know Matilda and that isn't her. I had to work with that Kinsley brat and in case you don't remember, she is a rude, society bitch and yes, she has a gun but not *that* gun. She doesn't carry an automatic weapon. You people should stop and notice these things, think!"

He looked down the road at the others. "Tell me how could she possibly get thayanite poisoning as bad as this girl has it in so few years? Enough of you are Marrilians. Answer that. Or would you rather be shot?"

A few more people stepped back. Back, but no one left yet.

"And most of all," added Arlo, "I never heard Matilda say the word '*please*' in her life. I doubt she knows the proper use of it."

He walked up to the little suicidal man, putting his body between him and Erica. She lowered the gun.

"Jeff, go home. This isn't Matilda. As much as you want to avenge your mother and father you can't do that on her Marrilian cousin."

Black and red shadows filled the deep furrows in Jeff's face. He glared up at Arlo. "Why do you want to protect her? What have you got to gain by protecting her you money grubber?"

"Jeff," Arlo hissed. "You stink like booze. You haven't got the goddamned brain of a horse on your best day. Don't even consider accusing me of protecting Matilda. You forget what the hell she did to me. I know that bitch and this isn't her."

He shoved Jeff in the chest and back into the woman who had grabbed his arm. She caught him from falling. "Take him home, Bell. All of you get out of here before this girl shoots you for being damned idiots."

Erica lowered the gun further.

"No," a young woman argued. "Arlo, that's her. I know it is." She had been standing behind Bell and Jeff. Her hair blew across her face in the night breeze but Erica recognized the voice of the teller. "I saw her as often as you did. It's her. She dies here tonight!"

"I worked with that Kinsley brat for years! *Years!* You never saw her as much as I did and when you did you saw her across the room from your desk! You never got close enough to see her face! You never had the guts to deal with a Kinsley! Don't tell me I don't know the person who insulted me, badgered me, and sued me!"

His voice quaked. He stopped and when he spoke again, he had regained control. "She ruined me. Do you forget that? There is not one damned reason I would *ever* protect her!" He jabbed his finger at Erica. "This isn't her!"

"You were the money-grubbing asshole that chose to work with her," Jeff reminded him. He righted his balance but he didn't pull away from Bell. "It was your choice and your loss."

A murmur of agreement rose from the people.

"You better believe it was, and that is not her!" Arlo told him and pointed again. "She may be her cousin, and she admits it, some poor innocent that just got off the ship. Listen to her, will you? She's from Tenpole! The Kinsley's abandoned her! She had to live in Tenpole! She is probably the only decent one among them or why else would they get rid of her? And you want to kill her?" He whipped his arm at the whole crowd. "She's worse off than any of you!"

They shifted uncomfortably.

"Prove she isn't Matilda," called someone from the back of the group. "Prove she isn't just acting sick and talking like Tenpole."

Arlo turned towards the voice. It came from the crowd out of the dark but he addressed it. "How the hell am I supposed to do that with a bunch of dimwits like you? Out here in the middle of the night chasing this poor girl? And you think you're good people."

"You're so damn smart, asshole, prove it," demanded a young, dark man standing next to the teller. He took a step forward. "Go ahead."

Arlo drew a long breath and looked over at Erica. "If I had a picture of Matilda you would see it," he told them. "Their eyes aren't even the same color."

"Eye color can be changed," snarled Janice.

"Not from green to blue," Arlo snarled back. "How dumb are you? They can only add color not take it away. Everyone knows that. Hers are the pale blue of Tenpole."

Many in the group grumbled what was probably agreement but they sounded angry too.

"Are her eyes blue?" Jeff asked Janice. "You saw her up close today. Are they?"

Janice sucked in a deep breath then exhaled in a huff. "Yes," she admitted.

"Pale blue?"

Janice didn't reply.

"Tell me," Jeff growled. "I'm not going to be dragged in for murder unless it's Matilda's murder so fucking tell me now, Janice. Are her eyes the pale blue like Tenpole?"

"Yes," Janice snapped and sounded like she hated to say it.

Erica holstered her gun. She felt too weak to hold it up any longer. Plus, if she didn't get the antidote she would die whether they touched her or not. She moved slowly so she wouldn't startle anyone.

She fished in her pocket for her cigarettes. "Am not Matilda. She be a relation." She bumped the pack so she could grab a cigarette with her lips. "Can't prove that if you won't believe it. Just," she drew a breath to keep talking. It wheezed up her throat. She took the cigarette in her lips, struck a match, and lit the end. The light from the match glistened off her sweat briefly.

One breath of the sharp steam and she broke into a coughing fit that sunk her to her knees. She had to put a hand on the road to stay upright. Everyone watched. When she looked up she dripped in sweat and could barely get a breath past wheezing. "Just–tell me–please–wh– *why* if the SDD–be Matilda's savior…if I be her…why aren't they here?"

'Stupid!'

Erica winced.

The woods were silent. The people were silent, unable to answer her question. She took another short draw from the smoke, coughed hard and doubled over further. When the bout passed she sat up again.

She wiped her wet mouth. Blood smeared across her lips and she saw it on her hand. Everyone else saw it. Khepri had risen high enough that the bloody light of Amon would not disguise the smear on her face.

She sunk down until she sat on the road between her heals. There would be no fighting. She needed to get as much of the antidote as possible, as quickly as possible. If they chose to attack she could do nothing.

They watched her for a few more minutes as she smoked and coughed and then, at the back, someone turned, tossed their rock into the woods, and walked away. Jeff heard them go and looked wildly from their departing back to Erica to Janice. "Why aren't they here?" he demanded. "If she's so important to them, where are they?"

Janice couldn't answer. She stared at Erica.

"Wasn't she supposed to have something the SDD wanted? Maybe they got it," The young, dark man said. "So she's been kicked out of where they had her and they deserted her?"

"It isn't her," Bell told the young man sadly. She shook her head. "Go home."

He didn't move.

"They questioned Matilda with Reagent 10. If they wanted something they would have gotten it then," Arlo reminded him. "Before that, the SDD and her father confiscated every business she owned. What they wanted, they took. She had nothing left but frozen bank accounts. Whatever the reason, the QSDD still protects her and this isn't her. Go home."

"Your accent is Tenpole," Jeff accused Erica.

"So," Erica agreed.

Jeff laughed. "Well don't that beat it all to hell? You went to work in the grubbiest, most thayanite ridden hole on Marril, got rich and now you'll die from the poison? It looks like it's gonna kill you." He laughed as he stuck his hands on his hips.

He drew a long breath so his barrel chest rose high. "Hear those lungs?" he asked. "It took eighteen months to breathe like that and I could walk and talk without bleeding when I got here." He paused to sneer at her. "You Kinsleys deserve your thayanite. I hope it kills you. Just do me a favor and die someplace else. Stay away from my town. I can't stand to look at you." With that he walked away and the crowd followed.

Chapter 4 – Cluny

Erica sat alone in the road with her head bowed, exhausted. She drew in the antidote when she could. She coughed and spit out blood. Its coppery slime on her tongue brought up bile. She swallowed it back hard and held her hand over her mouth. She could not be sick. She could not. Slowly she gained control of her stomach. She lowered her hand and concentrated on smoking the antidote.

If Arlo hadn't helped, would she have shot? An image of blood splattered across this lush green planet made her shudder so she shoved it away. He had helped so it didn't matter.

She pulled two packs of smokes from her pocket and set them in the road in front of her knees. She would go through them right now. She would light one after the other so she could breathe right. She would move only when someone came along and hoped that wouldn't be until morning.

But not everyone had left. A pair of man's boots came into view. They were nice boots. They were brown and stitched with a pattern over the toes. They were clean and shiny. She stared at the toes because they stopped on either side of her smokes. Well, if he had stayed to kill her, she couldn't do much about it so she took another drag from her cigarette. The steam filled her lungs. She held it and waited for him to make up his mind. Did she deserve to live? He said nothing and neither did she.

He dropped her leather backpack beside his left leg. She hadn't expected that. Exhaling, she looked up. It was Arlo. Seeing him almost brought a smile to her face. He dropped her hat on top of the pack.

"I took these from their camp when they chased you."

A cough stopped her smile, it bent her over until she choked out more phlegm and blood. She spit it aside. Minutes passed before she straightened again. Arlo still waited.

"Thanks," she told him.

"I didn't expect you to get far today." He replied with a dead tone. "I had to really consider it. You look so much like her I didn't want to help but I figured she has ruined enough lives." He studied her intently. Long moments passed before he continued, enough that Erica drew in several long, clearing doses of antidote. The wheezing in her chest lessened a little. "Anyway, what I'm trying to say is, I heard them talking about you. They said they didn't sell you anything so I bought you some supplies but it will cost you."

He knew she wasn't Matilda but still had to consider whether or not to help. She couldn't imagine how much everyone hated the girl that Arlo was so put off. After what he had done, turning back the mob, helping her in the bank when the teller wouldn't, knowing she wasn't Matilda, in spite of what she could see of his kind nature, he still had to consider helping.

He reached down and grabbed her arm. He pulled her to her feet firmly but gently, as if he expected to support all of her weight and he did.

"Get off the road. People come through here all night." He led her to the grassy slope then retrieved her things and set them beside her. "I bought you a filter for water. Any Quirni water is potentially dangerous so filter it even if you just wash your face, which, by the way, you need to do. Dry the filter completely between each use."

Erica sank back to her knees. Arlo squatted beside her. He rummaged through her backpack and showed her items as he mentioned them.

"I also bought you a few full bottles of water, a map, a blanket, several cartons of the antidote cigarettes, and some staple foods that travel well. Keep them sealed in the bags or the wild dogs will smell you. Your own blanket and soap were still in your pack. I got you a couple bowls, a small pan, matches, and another blanket. You'll have plenty to keep warm now."

He watched her. She didn't say anything but continued to smoke and struggle with coughs. "You have it real bad."

She nodded like the Quirni would nod rather than waste her breath.

"You should be in a clinic, not out here."

"And be around people like them?" Erica asked with a tip of her head down the road.

He twisted to glance towards town. "I think they are convinced. They are all gone." He turned back to her.

"Thank you."

He winced then sighed. "What I would have given to hear Matilda say that." He frowned, as if upset for even thinking such a thing, then stood. "You can write me a withdrawal receipt for the supplies. I think I deserve twice what they are worth. That would be one-hundred-sixty square."

The Marrilian

The bankbook was in her bag. She wrote sixteen-thousand square on the slip and handed it up to him. "You saved my life. Would all be yours if was possible to live without it."

He held the slip up to the moonlight then nodded and stuffed it in his pocket. "If you really want to repay me, you can do it another way."

"Will," she agreed seriously without knowing what he would ask. Where she was from that was called *giving empty*, no thought was given to denying any request. She would fill her empty hands to do whatever he asked. He deserved that, and more.

"When you see your cousin, which I assume you will, you tell her she owes me over 23 million square. She set me up for a fall and she owes me."

No wonder he didn't blink at her 4 million quid when he counted it. It amounted to about 16 million square. He had been far richer. "Will tell her."

He nodded again and watched her as she lit another cigarette off of the last one. She wasn't coughing every time she drew a breath now.

"You took a chance," he told her.

She looked back up at him. "By coming here." She nodded. She knew that now. "Had to. Couldn't get a ticket to Sirrus."

"No, by bringing up the SDD with that group of morons."

The antidote cleared her lungs again and it would be better to move than sit, so she got to her feet. With supplies, she could get away from here. Arlo held her arm as she swayed, dizzy. After steadying, she lifted her head and almost looked him in the eyes but respected him enough she wouldn't meet his eye. "Why?"

"Why did the SDD let you walk out of the bank today?" Arlo asked to answer. "Janice saw you attack an agent. If she weren't such a pea brained idiot she would have realized they *are* helping you. He let you go. I'd like to know why. You should be in jail after hitting him."

Erica shook her head. "Don't know. Would like to know why SDD didn't tell me about Matilda. An SDD ship brought me here. Could have told me about her but didn't."

Arlo grunted and grabbed up her bags. He stuffed her pack of smokes in her pocket and put her hat on her head. "You should get going." He helped her get her bag on her shoulders. "Step off the road when you hear someone coming. They could see your face in the lamplight on their carriages. When you need to sleep, climb a tree, get off the ground. Wild dogs will rip you apart if they find you and are hungry enough, which they often are. I put some rope in your pack so you can tie yourself in place. And, you should know this by now but, stay away from people. The entire planet knows your face."

Erica nodded. "Will. Thank you."

"Sure, you are welcome, but I told you how to thank me."

"So," she agreed. "If we meet, she will be told."

"So," he returned in the Tenpole manner of agreement. He watched her eyes. "You are from Chaucer, aren't you?"

She looked up and in his eyes. If that was what he wanted she would lay down right now.

He shook his head at her reaction. "I'm not asking for anything. I expected nothing more than the check when I followed that group of morons out. I just recognize your mannerisms is all. I lived on Marril and I used to, uh, pass there on occasion. I could afford Chaucer then. I'm a little shocked a Kinsley lived there at all let alone long enough to learn the mannerisms and gain such an accent." He smiled when she didn't respond. "Take care," he said then turned his back and walked away.

She watched until he had put a good long distance between them and then turned and started down the road in the opposite direction.

It wasn't difficult to avoid traffic. She hid behind bushes whenever there was lamplight. Come morning, she left the road altogether and strode into the woods. Quirni's woods were cool with pretty chirping birds and soft breezes. The sun filtered through the leaves. If it rained it was short lived and she stayed dry under the heavy canopy of leaves and the all-weather blanket Arlo had bought her.

The Quirni animals ran from her. They dashed up the trees or slithered away into the underbrush. She ended up laughing at herself for worrying about them. The only dangerous animals were the dogs. They were different. They weren't frightened of her. All of the books warned about them.

According to the guides, they hunted in packs and left indents in the grass where their pack slept. Occasionally there would be a remnant of an animal they had eaten during the night, blood on the leaves or a skull bitten clean of meat. The dogs were gone by the time she arrived each morning. By the end of the first week she walked confidently.

The Marrilian

Her reading on the trip taught her that the dogs were the result of Lord Ahem's attempt to rule all of Quirni, the remains of his crazy dog army. He had brought the animals from Sirrus to fight because he didn't have enough tenants to form an attack force.

The Delegate had actually done its job and killed the dogs and Lord Ahem, but it was inevitable that some of the dogs would survive. They had also thrived. They roamed the woods and were known to attack people when hungry. When Erica heard them barking anywhere nearby she climbed a tree.

According to the books they weighed as much as she did or more, one-hundred pounds. Well, actually, she had no idea how much she weighed on Quirni. It had to be more than one-hundred pounds since that was her weight on Marril. Quirni's gravity was much higher, a third more at least, so she probably weighed a third more. On Sirrus, the dogs would have weighed one-hundred pounds. She felt certain of that. They stood as tall as the wheat that came up to her hip. They were long and would be broad if well fed. Those she saw all appeared hungry.

Arlo had prepared her well to avoid hunger. She found two books that he had forgotten to mention, "The Field Guide to Quirni Edible Plants" and "The Field Guide to Edible Animals." When Erica found these she had blessed him openly and kissed the books then started reading about edible plants.

While strolling through the woods, smoking as necessary, she picked meals. Occasionally she came across a boar-like creature with scaly skin and tusks as thick as her forearm which would take flight whenever it spotted her and even leave behind babies.

She saw various snakes that were supposed to be tasty. They stuck their tongues out as she passed, tasting the air to see what she was. She would have to poke them with a stick to make them move but since they were about eighteen feet long and could kill her with a poisonous bite she didn't care to do that.

The birds were another matter. They were scarlet or yellow and curious, winged nightmares. They liked to land in her camp and try to take things, especially shiny things. Eventually she shot one to warn them off but the birds were dumb as slag because even with the carcass of their dead pal nearby they continued to peck at her belongings. She learned to pack her things out of sight instead of wasting bullets. The birds were part of camping.

The map in the customs office had explained the situation

clearly enough, the entire southern half of the continent was settled. She had to go north to get away from people. There would be a desert to cross, but she had plans to steal a couple of horses from the Kinsleys.

It tickled her sense of justice that she might do that. Her own family would supply her ultimate escape. The desert wasn't wide. She hoped the horses could get across it safely. North would be lonely but she could stay safe there until the anger towards her cousin died.

By staying close to the roads, but off them, she passed Tellhurst without incident, and before long Lud and Market were behind her. Two Quirni weeks, sixteen days, passed without incident.

At Market she veered west. There would be a river, the first one she couldn't swim. According to the "Quirni Adventures" pamphlet, this was Coldwater River, *known for the enjoyable white water river rafting from Veil Falls to the edge of Coldwater Claim.* Erica could not afford to wade across a river with such fast currents, so unless there was a fallen tree or an unmarked bridge, she would have to use the bridge in Cluny.

Her plans to look for a crossing changed when she saw this river. It was in a gorge. Two fifty foot tall walls of wet rock bound a river that was at least as wide as the cliffs were tall. That separated her from her way north. The water looked deep and Coldwater River was aptly named since the air current rising up from the water felt cold. The water had to be colder still.

The source of the noise that she had been hearing for an hour was a ninety-foot waterfall dropping through a mossy canyon.

"Now that's pretty," she said aloud and was a little startled to hear her voice. She closed her mouth and resolved not to talk to herself again. In the past she had talked to her *conscience*, the voice she heard. Every time she did that she validated it, or at least that was how she saw it. The therapist thought she should tell it what to think and ask it how it felt but that was rude. Instead she kept quiet.

Morning sunlight shone on the green walls and sparkled on the tumbling water. To follow the river she would have to scale a ninety foot cliff. The way looked slippery and the rocks looked uneven and crumbly and there could be snakes in the rocks. She could reach for a handhold and end up grabbing a snake. She shook her head. No thanks. She turned towards the road that lay to her west.

The Marrilian

'It's a small cliff. You should do it.'

Erica stopped. She hadn't heard the voice since the Padt City. This was what she got for talking to herself. She didn't reply. She started walking again and it spoke no more that day. The terrain pushed her west.

She reached the road the next morning, the one that headed into Cluny. She had to stop there to get more smokes.

'Steal you mean.'

"Well shit," Erica muttered and drew an irritated breath. She let it out slowly. It had been nice being alone in her head. If she didn't respond, it would go away, right? A vague sense of 'no' pressed into her thoughts.

"Well, could hope for such," Erica sighed. She abandoned her resolve to remain silent. Obviously, it was too late.

Once she had been rid of this sort of nonsense. She guessed the cure needed continuous therapy. The stress of leaving Marril had been too much. "Friggin' Quirni."

Her broken mind would not stop her from surviving. She lived with it. Few people ever even noticed. Since she was going to be alone in the damn woods for the foreseeable future, no one *could* notice. Except when she had to get more antidote, which meant going into Cluny. Could she *steal* the cigarettes without being seen?

She considered her next step. It seemed like a good idea to know how many people lived in the area before she got to Cluny. How many people could attack her? Would there be few enough she could hold them off with her gun?

In reality, it didn't matter. She had to get more smokes and that meant she had to go into Cluny. If it was a big town, she might not be able to hold them off but she would have a better chance of finding the antidote. With any luck at all, even her dismal kind, the town would shut down at night and she could steal the smokes then.

Traffic could give her an idea of the population so when she came to the road she lay on her stomach behind bushes to watch. The grass made her sneeze and smelled like urine. She moved over.

"Blasted pill." She muttered and glared at the spot. "Only needed one friggin' ticket to Sirrus to be sipping lemonade with family instead of lying in pissed filled woods." She put her chin down on the back of her hands. "Blasted SDD," she added since she blamed everything on them.

Five wagons and four horseback riders went by before

sunset. That wasn't many. Farther south wagons passed every half hour or so. She could walk the road and step off when traffic came. It should take two days. She had enough cigarettes for four days. That would give her plenty of time to see where the smokers went to buy more of the antidote.

When she saw the first fields outside of town she climbed a tree to wait for darkness. From that high quite a bit of the town was visible. She doubted anyone would see her even if they glanced up, but remained cautious nonetheless. If the townspeople saw her, they could burn her tree down to get her. She stayed still and she kept the truck of the tree between her and the town, leaning to watch.

The river she needed to cross flowed from a large lake to the northwest. Craggy cliffs and broken land lay farther west. The woods had been cut back around the town for farmland. Fields of wheat, corn, and pasture stretched over rolling hills to the south, north, and to the lake. The hilly woods continued on the other side of the river.

Fields of grain were planted on the hills right up to the edge of the peaceful looking town. Long rows of rock separated the fields. Small groups of houses perched on hills in the distance, probably the farmer's homes. She assumed the rocks denoted property lines. It was a cheap way to mark boundaries and pretty.

The rocks were grey and home to fluffy pink flowers. Erica couldn't stop looking at the town and surrounding land, the pink and grey trimmed golden fields, the waving wheat, the lined up white houses with all of their ivy and gardens. The health and vibrancy charmed her. Wheat grew so tall, so golden and the flowers were so damned colorful.

It was possible this planet was prettier than Sirrus although she didn't really want to accept that. Sirrus was home, or had been, and it held her heart but Sirrus was under snow half the time and it never grew wheat or flowers like that. Anything there would be shorter, paler, and usually frozen before it was harvested completely. Only the native Sirrian plants had short enough growing seasons to do well.

A shake of her head cleared her thoughts of beautiful Quirni. The planet might be pretty, even paradise, but the people ruined it. Sirrus with its long winters was preferable to this hateful world. The snow could be fun. Thayanite heaters allowed all sorts of greenhouses and in some cities a person could walk from one side of town to the other without ever going outside. The

The Marrilian

more she thought about her home planet the more homesick she became and that wasn't something she needed to feel any more than she needed to hate this planet.

Better to consider her position in relationship to the river and the bridge. That was what needed to concern her, the river, the next obstacle to her progress after she got more thayanite antidote. She needed to get to the bridge but it was heavily traveled and in plain sight. The only possible time to cross would be at night.

There would be no sneaking up to it. The woods were gone, crowded out by the town although on the far side, the west side of town, there were only two rows of buildings and they looked like stables and mills that used the river for power. Chances were not many people would be in those buildings at night. A few gardens were planted around the buildings and she could use those for cover until she crossed. Further out in the fields she could use the rock walls to hide. It wasn't much but if no one was looking for a person in the fields it should do.

She continued to sit and watch the town so she might learn their habits. It would be easier to avoid people if she understood that.

The town was the perfect place to live, neat and clean but painted all white. The business district spread over two crossed roads at the center. As the sun set the two and three story buildings stood up in stark relief against a pink sky. It was calm and friendly.

People strolled along the boardwalks and dry dirt streets, stopping to chat. Horses waited by water troughs with their heads sagging in sleep. Apparently, Bacillus *pyrogenzes* didn't bother the animals. A sign near the trough suggested it was unsafe with a big X but the horses sucked the water and no one cared.

No one seemed to care about anything. Nobody seemed to be in a hurry. Nobody seemed to be worried or scared or alone like she was.

Erica frowned and stopped that line of thought. Self-pity didn't help any more than feeling homesick. Yes she was lonely but alive. Life should have been better after leaving Marril but instead she got the same hard line. Accept it. She sighed and watched until the streets grew dark and saw that few people smoked. Of course, she hadn't taken something into account.

'Stupid.'

Erica shook the voice from her head. She agreed with it, but

64

wouldn't admit it. The voice knew Marrilians wouldn't show her where to purchase antidote. They wouldn't walk out of a store holding up their purchases and even if they did they were in bags.

Consequently, she had no idea where a store was that sold the cigarettes. She leaned back on the branch. Stupid was right. She didn't always think of the obvious. Her *conscience* had known what to expect but had declined to mention it. Well, at least she had found a comfortable set of branches that would serve as a place to sleep.

The red moon woke her and that was when she climbed down. It was time to steal some antidote, wherever the hell they kept it.

The road near her tree led to the bridge and through the center of town. She could follow it to the business district. She crept along until she came to the end of the trees. Houses with flower gardens and trailing vines lined the first several blocks. Their yards were fenced, small, and trimmed. She couldn't see beyond the first few houses because of the ornamental shrubs and vines which was good because that was her cover but on closer inspection she would have to hop fences or follow the road to go from garden to garden.

The path she needed to take wound in and out of yards. People were still awake in their homes. She could hear them talking, laughing, partying. Someone could be visiting and go home for the night and she could be seen if they carried any sort of lamp. It didn't look as good down here as it had from the tree.

If seen, people would pour out of those houses to attack her. She returned to the tree to reconsider. Stealing antidote couldn't be avoided but there had to be a better way to get to the business district. If anyone saw her and caught her, it wouldn't be good. The Padt City haunted her. Those people would have killed her. They would have beaten her to death if not for Arlo. There was no Arlo here.

She sat down by the trunk of the tree to hide in the shadows and rested her back against the bark. Going into the town was dangerous but she had to do it. She had studied the area from her tree all day. The options were clear, enter from the road by which she sat or go around and enter at the business district. That meant a long walk in the dark through the fields which could bring her close to dogs. They liked to prowl around farms.

The night seemed chilly even though a warm breeze played across her cheeks. She pulled her coat close and realized how

The Marrilian

dirty she felt. Her skin crawled with itches. A shower would be nice. That made her smile. She wanted a bath. How many times had they scrubbed her so she could accept a client into bed? They had constantly complained about how dirty she stayed. Well, she had reasons for that then. Computer time was more profitable than bedding one of Ilene's clients.

Lords but if it wasn't her father, Ilene, or the SDD, she managed to find some other thing to make her life miserable. Her luck sucked. On any given day, if there was a worse place to be, she would be there.

About the only time she ever got a break was when a handyman at Ilene's warned them to stay inside. Vincent had been a Value's League member in Tenpole once and knew when shit was going to roll. The Value's League didn't let Parcles come into the mining area after dark. During the day they couldn't stop it but at night young Parcles boys thought they could arm themselves and do some hunting. They might get away with it one night but not two and there had been occasions that the Parcles brats were so destructive the Value's League went into Parcles, grabbed the assholes, and dropped them in a pit never to be seen again. If Vincent were here now, he would probably tell her to get inside. Erica sagged against her tree to think of him and how safe she had felt around him. Too bad he was still on Marril. He wouldn't be caught dead on Quirni.

Wishing for him and his amazing fighting techniques wasn't going to get her any antidote. Since the route through the houses was out, that left the fields regardless of dogs. They were barking earlier in the day so she knew they were near but that only meant she had to be careful and avoid animals. They liked to kill sheep, small cows, and chickens. Those would be in pens and barns for the night so she would stay away from those by going out into the fields.

'There were squirrels today. You saw them in the tree,' said a voice that was so loud and startled Erica so much she swung out from behind the tree ready to face an attacker but there was no one there. Her eyes darted around, searching the woods. No one was there. The voice had been so loud it sounded like another person. Her mouth fell open. That had been in her head. Her heart beat like a hammer inside her chest.

Oh hell. Oh blasted hell. She had cracked back apart completely. Her mind was broken again. That voice had been loud. It wasn't a whisper. She closed her eyes to stop tears. Before she was cured the voice had been that loud. She had gone through hell to get rid of it, to stop it. Now it was back. Was the cure gone, completely gone?

If any of it was still intact she would have feelings and memories of her whole past. The voice was a symptom of her problem and her problem was pushing away bad feelings and bad memories to such an extent she separated herself. The cure allowed her remember and be whole. If it was gone…

She leaned against her tree as she tried to remember the worst of her past, to feel the horrors of her passage from Sirrus to Marril and she did remember parts but dispassionately as if it had happened to someone else. Remembering it at all was something but no strong feelings were attached to the memory. The therapy was gone. Tears streamed down her cheeks. It had been so hard, months of therapy, months of remembering things no one should.

She inhaled long, held her breath until she felt calm, then exhaled. *So, you're back and not a blasted thing can be done about it. Don't be an asshole this time.*

'Don't worry.'

"As if," Erica muttered. She blinked at her response. Panic rose in her chest. "Shit." She talked to it. People didn't respond well when she muttered to the voice.

'You have to do it. The squirrels were a good sign.'

She kept her mouth sealed. *There are squirrels because there are farm animals here. The dogs would be after those, not squirrels.*

Why did she answer? She shouldn't but, by the lords, she was lonely. That was why. She was so damn lonely. She hadn't survived Marril and become rich to be alone in the blasted, black, dirty ass woods. She had lived in a city on Marril with lights and water and people. She liked people. She liked their noise and their chaos. The woods were too damn quiet, still, and dark but also comparatively safe. Dogs didn't attack her because of her face. They attacked her because she was meat, and so far, they weren't that hungry.

She returned to the dark under the tree. Her heart thumped in her chest as she tried to convince herself she had to circle the town and enter from the other road. If she came across a thing, she would shoot it.

'Dumb, dumb, dumb. The townspeople would hear that.'

"Damn you, shut up," Erica hissed. She took a big breath and then, with no further thought, crossed the road and forced her way through the woods towards the fields.

Khepri rose over the treetops as Erica crouched at the edge

of the town once again. The path she had taken through the wheat made a nice clear trail right to her. She cast a worried eye at the dark line in the swaying field and could think of no way to hide the damage. Wonderful. Why did the wheat have to be fully grown? She glowered at the absurdity of how a field of food might give away her presence. How many days in her life had she wanted a little food and now a field full of it could end up alerting the town that wanted to kill her.

That damage to the wheat meant she wouldn't be able to come back tomorrow or wait for a better plan. It committed her to acting tonight, right now. She had to get the smokes and be far away by morning.

Her backpack was cumbersome to carry so she stuffed it under the stairs beside her. It would be safe there until she returned and if she didn't return she wouldn't need it. One steadying breath, and she snuck to the closest building in a crouched run with care to step light and not make a noise.

Amon was high enough it shone into the buildings. She pressed her face into the windows. The moon glow lit the interiors. The first building was a restaurant, the second was a bank. She snuck deeper into the town. The farther she went the harder it would be to escape if she were discovered, but she had to go on. Her antidote was gone, smoked earlier to make certain she didn't cough while stealing more.

She passed from building to building, stopping, looking, and going on until she reached the intersection of roads at the center of the business district. From her tree she had seen this spot clearly but what she hadn't seen was the awning over the stores facing west. It cast a shadow on the front of the buildings so no moonlight shone inside.

Now what? Should she go into the stores? If she did that and someone lived in any of them she increased her chances of being heard. The fewer doors she opened the better. She crouched down next to a bench to hide and think.

There were no lights in any windows nearby. All the businesses were closed and if no one lived above them they were empty. That would explain the lack of lights, even gas light. Finally, something good.

'Or someone is watching you from a dark window,' said her inner voice.

What difference did it make if they did? She needed the antidote and beyond that nothing was in her control. The best means to survive this night was to be quick and quiet. If anyone watched, they hadn't raised an alarm yet.

She turned while still in a crouch, straightened, and pressed her face against the window but it was too damn dark. Not a clue to what the building held. Neither Amon nor Khepri were at the right angle to put any light under the awning yet. They would be eventually but not yet.

Khepri did a great job of lighting up the other side of the street. If she went over there she could see into those buildings without a problem but she could also be easily seen and she could see by the signboards above those stores that they were a cobbler, a tailor, and a bookstore. She doubted they sold antidote.

She huddled back down next to the bench. The shadow cast by the moonbeams were at the edge of the boardwalk. It crept towards her. Should she wait for the light to come to the front of this building? If she didn't, once she went in she wouldn't be able to see. She didn't like the idea of using a match like she had in the Padt City. That had been so stupid. No doubt it was how they located her.

'Enough!' warned her *conscience*. 'God! Just sitting and doing nothing! Move!'

Her head jerked in surprise. She wasn't used to hearing the voice anymore. There was a time when she could go about her business while it nagged and she would be able to ignore it. She wouldn't react to it at all. She would have to get that back.

She glanced up and down the roads again. No one was around.

If there were signs above the stores on the other side of the street then there were probably signs above the stores on her side as well. She took a deep breath and walked out into the street. She looked up at the front of the buildings. The signs were there. She ducked back into the shadow and smiled with relief. She was in front of a general store.

Her eyes darted about the deserted town to make sure she hadn't been seen. Hitching posts and water troughs were the only things in the street, no people, no watchmen. She moved to the door and lifted the latch which was a piece of wood sticking through a slot.

That amazed her. None of the Quirni doors had locks. There should be some other kind of alarm so she inched it open and ran her fingers around as much as she could reach. Nothing, no strings. There was no detectable alarm and spending any more time looking for it would be foolish. She pushed the door open wide enough to enter. Everything remained quiet. Nothing fell to make a noise. No alarm. The Quirni were trusting people.

Darkness encompassed her when the door closed. She again lit a match to find her way but this time she stayed by the door, cupped her hand around it, and kept it close to her body to minimize the amount of light that might be seen outside. The antidote cigarettes sat at the front of the store, huge stacks of them at the front counter, right beside tobacco cigarettes. That was all the time she could risk with the light. Now that she knew where they were, she would have to get there in darkness. Erica flicked out the match.

Her eyes took time to adjust. Amon had come around far enough that its pale light seeped through the bottom of the wide glass window. It was enough. She held her hands out to avoid crashing into anything and inched towards the cigarettes. When she touched the stack, she took as many as her deep pockets would hold. The light of Amon brightened the window as she finished stuffing them in.

She turned to leave and saw the red glow on a newspaper. 'Kinsley Girl Returns' read the headline. Erica's ID photograph covered a quarter of the front page. She choked a little. She grabbed the paper and stuffed it between the cartons.

Then she saw a stand of candy and, since she was now a thief on Quirni too, she grabbed a few candy bars. It was some Quirni brand that the wrapper claimed was chocolate and since that was a rare treat for her she didn't resist it. The flat bars slid in next to the cartons of antidote.

She slunk out of the store and back to her pack where she took time to transfer the cartons to it. So many stuffed her pockets they could fall out if she didn't. Her stomach remained tight and her heart raced while she worked to secure everything. Once she knew her supplies were tied in tight she could run to cross the bridge and get lost in the woods on the other side, far enough gone they could never find her.

The streets remained empty until she finished. She shrugged the backpack over her shoulder and dove back into the wheat. It was the only way to circle the town, either that or stay right next to the buildings including the pens of animals. That was where the dogs would be, not that she had heard them but they could be silent too.

She circled around without being seen or heard and came to the mill by the bridge. There she paused to watch and listen but heard or saw no one.

As Thoth rose she crossed the bridge at a fast walk, as if she were a villager out for a midnight stroll. She crossed the wooden structure without a sound from her shoes and then jogged into the dark under the trees. She slipped from sight. The jogging helped throw off some of her anxiety but when her breath started to hitch she slowed and stretched into a long stride. She walked as fast as she could.

As she walked she ate some of the candy she had stolen and shivered in delight at the taste. It had been a long time since she had tasted chocolate. She smiled and actually felt happy. The breeze smelled fresh. Her lungs felt clear. She could move along at a decent clip.

If she were on Marril she would be buried. Maybe Quirni would be alright for a while. It amazed her that the people left their doors unlocked. Of course, they didn't have any metal to make locks but still they could have devised something. She sighed. She could get anything she wanted. She wouldn't starve or go without clothes. In fact, she remembered the paper. She would have news too.

She pulled it from her pocket and spread it so moonlight peaking between leaves fell on the front page. Thoth's light was bright enough she could read while walking.

"These people be mental," she declared out loud. Right under the picture it said 'Erica Ennis' but the caption below it read 'Matilda returned?' "'Tis me, you dolts. What be the mystery?" She stopped in a moonbeam to read. The article held an account of what happened at the Padt City and several eyewitness testimonies but that was weeks ago.

The shadows of leaves covered the top corner. She tipped the paper to move it into the moonlight and examine the date. It was two weeks old. So, news traveled slowly here. The article concluded that Matilda had returned and her accent indicated she had been on Marril. "Great," Erica scoffed. Well, at least it would be good for starting a fire.

She folded the paper and put it in her pack. Time to move. She put the half-eaten candy bar in her pocket and headed northwest. A narrow path ran northwards into the woods so she took it. The town and the river were behind her. She was content for the first time since arriving on the planet.

Was that a growl? Two reactions hit Erica at the same time, panic and climb. She ran, jumped, and grabbed a tree branch then swung herself up before she looked for what she heard. Her coat snagged as she climbed. She pulled up and kicked at what caught her and heard a yelp then the rush of padded feet, the snarl of animals, and the clash of nails against the tree.

That drove Erica up fifteen feet. Her heart hammered as she hugged the tree trunk and looked down to find eight wild dogs jumping and barking up at her. A second later and they would have had her. She carefully squatted down on the branch to get her breath and see them a little better. They were jumping, angry shapes in the shadows. They were huge, bigger than the brochures had warned and she had nearly been their dinner.

How in the hell had they gotten so close? Did they actually hunt at night after all? When did they sleep?

She wiped her sweaty palms off on her pants and lit a smoke. The animals settled under her. Some sat. Some lay down. They all kept looking up.

All these days and nights she had travelled without attracting the dogs and now here they were when she needed to move. It was more of her unbelievably piss poor bad luck. She had probably passed one of their resting places without even realizing it, too caught up in her good fortune to pay attention. Or, perhaps, they had smelled her and were hungry. She didn't usually carry food. That which Arlo had given her was long gone. She usually ate plants when she found them but tonight she carried the candy. She pulled it out of her pocket. She took a bite.

The dogs heard the wrapper. They all jumped to their feet and barked, furious. She dropped the remainder of the bar. The dogs dove for it. They bit and fought to eat every bit of candy and wrapper. It disappeared in a second. "Wouldn't you know it," Erica muttered. Without a thought she had taken the candy and now look where it got her. "Stupid," she said before her *conscience* could.

The dogs circled and sniffed around the base of the tree.

Erica pulled out the second candy bar and dropped it. The animals dove for it again. They snatched it out of the air and fought over it. "'Tis gone you hungry dolts. Leave."

Her voice sent them into frenzy. They jumped to get at her. They were tall, all of her weight and half as much again. Some were tan with black muzzles, others black and white, and one brindle. They had short hair and tall, athletic bodies. Their large heads were squared with long snapping jaws. Fifteen feet was a possible jump for them. Erica retreated a few more branches higher and didn't say anything more.

Amon set and then Khepri dipped to the horizon as well. Thoth followed. Thoth, Erica now knew, would settle over the horizon as the sun rose. The dogs lay under the tree and waited. Erica sat and worried because she wasn't nearly far enough away from Cluny. "Go," she urged the dogs quietly. From where she sat she could still see the tallest buildings in the town. She had to get moving. She had one option but it wasn't good, her gun.

She pulled it out. If she shot, the townspeople would hear but she would still have the rest of the night to get away. If she waited for the dogs to leave, she felt sure the townspeople would find her. They would have to deal with the dogs but they were used to that. They would kill them and then she would have to deal with the townspeople. From where she sat the distant shape of roofs were visible in Thoth's light.

When the town woke people would see her path in the wheat and figure out that she had crossed the bridge. If they realized someone had stolen from the store, they would follow. The barking dogs would give them a good idea where to look. With a grimace she loaded her gun but then rested the weapon on her knee. She gazed down at the vigilant animals.

"Any suggestions would be welcome," she said out loud and wanted the voice to reply. The dogs looked up when she spoke but didn't move. They remained in a pile of bodies under the tree. No suggestions came. Her brow knit in anger then she aimed and fired. She killed the animals with eight shots. Three of them down their throats as they barked up at her.

Afterwards she waited for a while to make sure they were dead. At least a quarter hour passed before she descended the tree where she paused to stand amongst them. If only they had left. She felt sorry for them. They were just wild and hungry.

"Pardons," she said to their carcasses. She liked dogs too much to do this to them. They didn't have dogs on Marril, the thayanite killed them too fast, but she had loved Dopey on Sirrus. The happy, little mongrel had been a joy. She bent and stroked the sleek, tan fur of the closest animal. He was beautiful with a thick muscular chest, strong legs, square head. If they had been loved, they would have been good. Too bad.

She hurried away at a trot. An animal path allowed her to keep jogging until her breath caught. That didn't stop her but only slowed her while she smoked and as soon as she could breathe clearly again she pressed back into a jog. The townspeople would come for her. The gunshots would bring them if the barking dogs hadn't.

By taking the paths through the trees she hoped to obscure the direction she travelled. The first path was well used by something large, probably the wild boar-like animals. She kept on it for an hour before finding a narrower route that forced her to duck under branches and wind around underbrush. That cut her speed but made her harder to track.

The gravity didn't bother her anymore. She had gotten used to that after a week but she had pills left. She dug the plastic bottle from her pocket and popped one in her mouth. The extra energy would put more distance between her and the town. She listened intently for pursuit and did her best to keep her passage quiet so humans or dogs couldn't hear her.

She never saw or heard a thing when the next attack happened. It wasn't dogs but men. An arrow thwacked into her backpack and right through to her shoulder. She gasped in pain and surprise. One moment she wound through a deep woods and the next she was pushed forward, her backpack and right shoulder slammed so hard she lost her balance and stumbled towards a bush.

Something caught her arm, pierced her coat and dug in. It felt like claws. It ripped. It spun her around to face five men all armed with bows. Three had already loosed their arrows. Two more shot as the first arrow spun her around to face them. An arrow grazed her scalp and knocked her back. She fell on the bush and slid into it in shock. The men advanced and nocked more arrows to their bows, aiming them at her, ready.

The world slowed for Erica, as if the men waded through mud. Five of them bore down on her. She dug her heels into the decaying leaves and shoved to gain her feet until the arrow in her shoulder snagged in the bush. She yelped in pain and tried to twist free of it but that made the pain worse. The men stalked up to her with grins.

When she grabbed for the pain in her arm she found the arrow. It wasn't until then that she realized she had been shot. The men approached cautiously, malicious intentions all over their grinning faces. One of them lunged and grabbed her coat sleeve. She yelped again as he dragged her upright by the pierced arm. The bush pulled the arrow in her back free but it remained lodged in her pack, the head of it scraping at the back of her shoulder. The arrow in her arm dragged through the bush and scraped bone.

"It's her! We got her!" The man shoved her towards the others.

No one tried to catch her so she landed on her hands and knees before them, crumpled and trying to still her panic. "I'm-"

she started to say but the man who had grabbed her struck her across the side of her head with his bow which threw her to her side. The arrow in her arm twisted under her but the blow had dazed her so much she hardly noticed.

"Shut up!" he screamed which was the only reason she heard him. The ear he had struck rung. Her other ear was in mud. The chocolate rose in her throat. She shakily drew up her unhurt arm to cover her head. It was a senseless action. It wouldn't help but that was all she could ever do.

"Let's get her back to town before we kill her," the attacker snarled. "Everyone has a right to see her die." He kicked her in the back of the head.

Bright, warm sun woke her. Her head throbbed. She felt nausea and dizzy even lying still on her back. The sun shone down on her and made her squint. A crowd circled her. Some of their faces were obscured by the bright halo of sunlight behind them. They talked about Joe and how far he had to go to get his horse and saddle. When they saw her eyes open some of them spat while others cursed.

"Not Matilda," she told them but the crowd was too loud to hear her and she began to notice her missing belongings. Her backpack, gun, hat, knife, and coat were gone and she could feel the arrowhead was still in her arm. No one here would help her get that out. It surprised her that she was even alive.

A warm glob of spit landed on her neck and another on her chest. Given that and their expressions she wasn't sure how welcome it was to be alive right now. She understood the sneers and disgust they wore. She had seen it enough on her father's face. *If you don't do this, Lynn, I'll beat you harder! I bought that dopey dog for you! Now get on your knees and do what I tell you! I'll kill him if you don't!*

"I'm not Matil-" she started to say again but stopped because she realized she was tied. Her hands were bound in front of her and her feet were together. She lay in the road and she was tied! Oh lords no! She panicked and struggled against the bonds.

The townspeople laughed to see her bite the leather straps. The more she panicked the more they laughed. She didn't listen to them or give any attention to the rain of spit and cursing. They wanted her to die slow and horrible and being tied would allow that. If she could get untied she could fight and, lords, she could hurt them and she would hurt them if only to make them kill her faster, to stop the torture they had planned. As she was, tied and

The Marrilian

harmless, they could do whatever they wanted.

A man stepped on her arm and that pushed her hands away from her mouth. The arrowhead pressed through her bicep. "Stop," she tried to yell but it came out as a begging whimper. Her chance to escape was gone. This was the one who led them. He pressed harder. A scream rose in her but she held it. They loved screams so she stifled it. They wouldn't get the satisfaction of her pain, not anymore. She curled into a ball and didn't even try to wrest herself free of his foot.

He removed it.

The relief was unexpected. It gave Erica hope. She drew her legs up to get them under her and stand. She would face them, answer for whatever crimes they thought she had committed but the man kicked her down. The pain in her head, a concussion at least, made movement difficult. The little tumble from her elbow and knees made her gasp. They laughed.

It took a moment for her head to clear and then she tried to get on her knees again. He kicked her over again and they all laughed harder. That was all the strength she had. The man grabbed the ties on her wrists and jerked her arms straight.

That actually relieved some of the pain from the arrowhead. She twisted to see what he did and saw him take a thick rope from someone in the crowd. He tied it to the leather around her wrists. *What the hell?* He jerked the knots to set them then let out the rope as he walked away towards a horse.

"Oh lords no," she whimpered. He meant to tie to damn rope to the horse. "No! I'm not Matilda!" she screamed.

The man mounted with the rope in hand. The crowd yelled and whooped. He tied the rope to his saddle and then leaned over looking back at her, his lips wet with spittle. "Die slow you lying bitch!" he yelled over the noise of the crowd and then spit towards her.

Erica scrambled to get her feet under her again but the crowd pushed her back down. They did no more than that but as soon as she got an elbow or knee under her and rose a few inches someone darted forward and shoved her then hurried to get away.

Their laughter gained lunatic levels then someone started to chant "Joe! Joe! Joe!" They all joined in. Erica could do nothing so she curled in on herself. This would be the last moment she might be whole. The terror made her throat constrict. She couldn't breathe. Joe jerked the rope.

"Once around!" a woman yelled.

Edwards

Erica lifted her dizzy head in time to see Joe kick.

"Then we'll let the *pyrogenzes* have her!" he called out and took off at a gallop down the gravel street. Erica jerked forward. She felt muscle rip in her shoulders and the arrow pulling through her arm.

The horse galloped and she tumbled. She tried to protect herself but she couldn't keep her legs up against the rushing road. The gravel ground through her pants and shirt in moments. It pulled off her boots. She screamed when she felt it against her bare legs. The horse turned the corner of the two main streets at a gallop right past the store she had robbed. People waited on the boardwalks down which she had so carefully walked the night before. They jumped out of the way. "Faster Joe!" they yelled.

The crowd ran behind while Erica collided with the wooden beams in front of the stores. Her legs shattered and her ribs broke. If she had hit the boards the other way, her back would have broken but that would have been a kindness, perhaps a quick death. Joe stopped his horse at the end of the street, pivoted, and came back at a gallop again. He released the rope so Erica slid head first into the water trough and it was hard enough she felt nothing for several blissful moments. The dragging hadn't lasted long. 'Once around' so someone had said. 'Once around then we'll let the *pyrogenzes* have her,' the Bacillus *pyrogenzes* that contaminated the water.

With Erica broken, cut, and bleeding the man dismounted. She saw him approach but she no longer felt connected to her body. The man grabbed her by the remains of her shirt collar and jerked her up with a powerful arm where he held her for all to see, her eyes open but blank, looking into his but feeling nothing. There was a means to escape torture and she had learned it very young.

She watched the man pull her up and plunge her into the water trough as the crowd cheered and knew she was under water but she didn't feel it. He jerked her back out but she only watched. No sound came from her, no reaction, because she was no longer in that mangled body. Instead she hung from Joe's meaty hand, water rinsing the dirt and blood off of someone's body but not hers. A split let her go. It allowed her to be someone else, not this broken girl.

Joe dunked her again as the crowd yelled. "Make God damn sure! Make sure, Joe!"

Numbness now but she knew how to escape ever further and not witness anything. She had learned that when she was less than five.

"How does that feel you killing whore?" Joe yelled in her face as water drained from her sagging mouth.

Someone grabbed Joe's arm. "Stop it! Stop!"

Sun shined in Erica's eyes so she saw only a flash of brown. It brought her back ever so slightly, curiosity. Someone tried to help?

Joe yelled a stream of curses.

"You are under arrest!" the other man yelled and the crowd hissed and catcalled evilly. Joe dropped her. She fell into the mud at the base of the trough. It was cold. Joe kicked the side of her head as the other person tackled him.

Her ear bled warm against her neck. Warm compared to the water draining from her hair into her eyes and mouth. Voices faded as Joe's shouting increased but Erica hardly noticed. She accepted her last defense for escape after years of being free of it. She no longer watched from far away. She gave up and left.

Edwards

Chapter 5 – The SDD

"She is gaining consciousness," a concerned woman said.

Erica changed from a faraway presence to a close one. The woman sounded kind. "I'm not Matilda." She was unintelligible, her face too swollen and her words too quiet to be clear, but this declaration, which hadn't protected her yet, was the only thing she could think to say.

"Shhh," the woman coaxed. "We're here to help."

Erica opened her eyes as much as she could. She was on her side and still in the mud. Her right arm was under her head but her left was down by her chest so she knew her wrists were no longer tied. Her head felt thick and fuzzy like she might pass out again any moment.

"Lay still," warned a lanky, dark haired man leaning over her. He wore a brown uniform. He touched a medical scanner to activate it then reached behind her and began running it lightly over her spine. He called out injuries to the woman. After scanning he leaned back. "Cox, we need a neck brace and a backboard."

Erica heard someone running away, their footfalls hit heavy on hard road. The runner returned minutes later. They placed a backboard behind her. The thin man leaned over and gently put the neck brace on Erica and then, slowly, three people rolled her onto the board. As careful as they were the pain blurred everything. The man with the scanner sounded far away. "Get the remains of her clothes off. Pull as much as you can out of the cuts."

The young man who had retrieved the backboard was in a brown uniform too. He knelt and pulled the muddy fabric from the deep cuts and abrasions on Erica's arms while the healer scanned her legs. When the remains of her shirt was pulled from her right arm the younger man suddenly sat back.

"She has a tattoo." He pointed at a circlet of rings and thorns around her upper arm.

The lanky dark haired man grunted.

"She looks just like Matilda," the younger man declared.

"We know," the woman said with a tinge of annoyance. Her hand touched Erica's head gently. "Dear, what's your name?

Come on, honey. Try to stay awake. What is your name?"

A shadow fell over them. "She is Erica Ennis," another man answered. He wore brown like the others. Something dropped nearby. "We found her things. It says she is also known as Lynn Jillian Kinsley." He held it so they could see.

The healer and cureman looked. "Good lords," the healer gasped. "Look at that. Without all the bruises and scratches, she looks even more like her."

"I need to get some pain killer in her," the woman said suddenly as if to convince them this meant nothing. She turned away from the passport and dug in her box of supplies.

Dimly, Erica realized the brown was the QSDD uniform. That had been the color the agent wore at the bank. All of these people were part of the Delegate. She closed her eyes. As hard as she had tried to get away from them, now her life depended upon them. A cold swab touched her hand then she felt the jab of a needle.

The healer resumed scanning on Erica's chest. "Betty, you saw she is an iridim patient with your tests?" he asked.

"Of course," the woman replied. She drew a breath. "She's a Kinsley. It's common with them and I already expected we were dealing with that by her build, and it said so on the passport."

The man nodded. "She has a nasty case of thayanite poisoning. The scanner is lighting up like an Marrilian city at night. Plus the Bacillus." His voice ended on a quiet note. Erica heard the question in it and opened her eyes to see why. He looked across at the woman who started an IV.

"She's Marrilian, Lev, so the thayanite is to be expected. I'll manage. You just get her healed. I'll cure the rest."

Erica felt the warmth of pain reliever run up the IV.

"I'll let you know how much healing paste you can use when we get her back to the clinic," the woman added. She knelt over Erica again and touched her hair gently. "It's all right, dear. We're here in plenty of time. Levitus sounds gloomy but he's just a healer. He doesn't know what he's talking about."

Levitus grunted. "*Just* this healer will make her one piece again."

"That's right," Betty agreed as she wiped mud from Erica's eyes with a clean cloth. It left a soothing balm on her skin. "You'll be fine, dear," she cooed as she worked. Her touch felt so gentle and left numb bliss in its wake. Her drugs and her voice lulled her to sleep.

The Marrilian

Short rhythmic beeps followed by a long beep woke Erica. She recognized the sound as hospital equipment. That meant she had to be dying because she wouldn't go to a hospital for anything less. Her heart jumped to realize she had awakened from what should have been death. Why? Weren't they going to let her go? Was it the damn SDD again?

But hadn't she left Marril to escape this? Hadn't she gotten away and sent the message?

The beeping quickened. The heat of the room drenched her in sweat. Tubes and wires draped around her body and it felt like she was tied down. Her eyes snapped open when she realized she couldn't move her leg.

A shape loomed over her, dark and reaching. Erica moved from it but it grabbed her shoulders and held her down. "Don't fight me. Don't-" The thing pushed. "It's alright."

'Erica!' the voice in her head nearly yelled.

She froze.

"You are safe," assured the thing firmly. "You have *pyrogenzes* poisoning. You may be hallucinating from the fever."

Fever? The shadow swelled over her head. She flinched.

A cool compress touched her cheek then her forehead. Another one was tucked next to her neck. The blobby thing seemed to grow then shrink back to the shape of a woman. It kept doing it, growing and shrinking. The thing put more cold compresses around Erica's chest, arms, and legs. The heat in the room subsided and the thing turned into a woman.

Erica's head hurt. Her body felt strange, numb and sore at the same time right into her bones. "Fever?" she asked breathlessly.

The swelling, shrinking woman pressed a mask over her face. It spewed a warm mist that smelled of garbage and shit. That made her grimace and try to turn away with a groan.

"Shhh, you know what this is. It's just the antidote. Take it easy."

She fought to turn her head but the mask followed.

"You need this," the woman said. "It is antidote to thayanite."

Antidote? It did smell like antidote and she did need that. It had been part of the problem hadn't it? Hadn't she gone into town to steal it? Now they gave it to her? The mask pressed her down and she let it. It confused her, made her wonder at this strange planet that withheld antidote then gave it out after all. If it was antidote. It smelled right, like garbage and shit and sour reek. She kept still and breathed.

Edwards

"That's right. Good girl. The fever has already run half its course. Another four days and you'll be cured. Just like I told you, she's good at what she does."

Another four days? Erica asked, or thought she did. She tried to. Everything felt so heavy and hard to move including her mouth.

"It won't be as bad now," the woman assured her.

As Erica breathed her vision cleared. The cold compresses helped. She didn't feel so hot or muddled. She focused on the person and saw it wasn't a woman but a teenage girl who held the mask. Erica rolled her eyes to see the piece of equipment the mask came from, to see if it was the same kind she used on Marril. It was.

The girl followed Erica's gaze. "It's a thayanite antidote chamber. Come on, you recognize it don't you? The box is filled with antidote mist?"

Erica knew that. "Am I–" She began to ask if she was on Quirni or Marril but that had to be obvious. Wasn't this Marril? Four days? Had the SDD been shooting more drugs into her, more stuff to confuse her? Quirni was a bad dream. Arlo had seemed so real and after him she remembered details. Hadn't she gotten on the ship? Had she sent the message? She didn't think so but then that meant she never left Marril.

Why would anyone wake her if she were so close to dying? They let Tenpole die. What did they want to do with her that they kept her alive?

The girl said four days had passed without her being aware. That could be a problem. Had she been conversing? That had happened to Erica a lot once. She would wake someplace she didn't know and meet strangers who said they knew her. They would be happy to greet her and ready to do things with her that she didn't want to do. Such awakenings would usually end with her running out a door.

The girl pulled the mask away and looked at Erica quizzically. "If this is too much for you we can hold off for a bit. You have stopped coughing. We don't have to finish the treatment right now. I am told the mask can cause feelings of claustrophobia."

Her accent wasn't Parcles, Tenpole, or even Marrilian. The teenage girl spoke curt and clear cut rather than the lilting Marrilian vowels. "Don't remember much from the last four days," Erica told her carefully as she tried to mask her own accent.

The Marrilian

The girl's smile faded. "Well, I guess that must be the fever." She flipped a switch on the chamber then set the mask down on the table and got up from her chair. "The cureman and healer want to see you. I'm going to go get them." She left the room.

Erica swallowed back the nausea trying to rise in her throat and chanced lifting her head to look around. Her leg was in a cast but her arms looked whole only they were covered with bruises. She should feel aches with those bruises but she didn't. Her head spun as she turned to look up at the bags hanging next to the bed. She recognized the name on one of them as pain killer. That explained why she felt so heavy and the bruises and breaks didn't ache.

Clearly, she was in a clinic and clearly a bad thing had happened to her. Bruises and broken legs didn't come from nightmares. The hazy memory of an attack couldn't push past the fuzziness of the medicine. Oddly, her mind conjured up images of dogs or arrows but that had to be her imagination. She liked to read and sometimes when she lost time her imagination called up ideas from books to explain what had happened.

Whatever had happened the healer hadn't been able to use enough healer's paste to fix her leg. The paste, she knew from past experience, would react with the iridim in her body. Too much at once and she would have an iridim induced heart attack. Iridim had healed her heart defect when she was an infant but that came with lifelong consequences. She had a small build, fragile bones and she had to avoid many common drugs. Another side effect of iridim was perfect recall but she, unfortunately, didn't have that.

She looked around to try and figure out where she might be. Her room had four beds in it but she was the only patient. White walls reflected light from a window at the far end of the room but drawn blinds obscured her view outside. If she could see out she would know which planet she was on because Quirni was so green and the sky was all blue. Marril's sky was hazy blue with Qetesh usually in some part of it and she would be in a city.

If she were on Marril there would be metal in the room while Quirni shouldn't have any. The blinds had metal parts as did the bed and the door. The healer walked through the door as she stared at the metal hinges. Until she saw those she had nearly convinced herself this was Quirni.

The healer's smile disappeared when he saw her frowning.

"Everything is all right. You're safe." He approached the bed and took hold of her hand which had been gripping the metal rail. "It's all right." His accent had a bit of Marrilian in it or maybe Sirrian but mostly his accent sounded like the girl's. "Your injuries are healing well," he said.

He wore the baggy blue clothes all healers wore in surgery. Nothing except his accent suggested what planet he was from but he looked like the same man who had helped her in the street; thin, tall, dark haired with sharp features, and that man had worn a brown uniform.

The street. She remembered the mud and someone running. Her bags were found. Was it the same healer? She looked up. He bent to catch her eye when she focused on his chin. They stood there, staring at each other. His eyes scanned hers. His smile returned.

"My wife is an excellent cureman so the damage those fools did in Cluny was for nothing. We have antibiotics to fight the disease if it's caught soon enough. You still have a fever but that's for the best. It will protect you later on. You'll have some resistance to the Bacillus after this. You shouldn't get sick unless you drink it."

Bacillus? That meant this was Quirni and he was a Delegate healer.

His eyes stayed on hers. "Your cousin has been informed she has a new relative on the planet. We told her today." He waited for a response but Erica couldn't imagine what to say. Her cousin was of no interest to her, a murderer and capable of causing Erica nothing but pain. "You aren't much for talking are you, Erica?"

"You just don't have the right touch, dear," a woman said as she entered the room, a woman dressed in a brown Delegate uniform. The pin on her tie meant she was a cureman, the emblem was crossed swords with a hissing snake twisting around each sword. The cureman was red haired, round, and soft in the body but stern in the face, slightly shorter than the healer. She circled around to the other side of the bed. "She can be a regular chatterbox if you know the right things to talk about, right dear?"

Good lords, Erica realized she *had* been conversing with them. That meant her problem was really back. That intrusive thought, her *conscience*, had been the first sign.

"She says she doesn't remember much of the last four days," the young woman told them. She had followed the cureman into the room. The girl wasn't in the SDD. She wore a lacy white shirt and blue pants. She looked like the woman but with dark hair like the man. "I figured it was the fever."

The Marrilian

The cureman frowned. She checked a few of the gauges on the equipment around the bed but said nothing.

The healer didn't wait for Erica to comment. "Well, Erica, Betty tells me I can heal your leg soon. Has the itching in your arms gone away?"

Erica nodded, not that she knew that her arms had been itchy but she didn't feel itches anywhere.

He patted her hand, smiled, and leaned close. He almost seemed relieved about something. "I'm a hell of a healer if I do say so myself," he whispered in her right ear. He tapped his ear. "How's the hearing aid working?"

She put her hand up to it. The last thing she had heard out of that ear was funny buzzing.

"That's not bothering you is it? Or are you surprised you are hearing out of it?"

"No, I-" she began. She tried not to frown but she couldn't keep her face under control. "'Tis great," she replied warily. Her stomach lurched to think the SDD had her again and had been doing surgery.

He smiled then glanced at the cureman and gave her a nod. "Of course, I told you I'm excellent but it helped that the generals sprang for the top of the line hearing aid, which was reasonable considering if they had told you about your cousin you wouldn't have walked into danger. I've healed her any number of times. She's a little magnet for trouble too, just like you." His face became serious. "I noticed how often you have been healed, especially your arms."

Despite the fever, Erica felt her face grow hot. Any healer who looked would see where paste had been used to heal bones but they didn't usually look.

The healer pulled up a chair. "How did you break your arms and get skull fractures? I know you are an iridim patient so your bones will be softer than normal but your iridim therapy was exceptionally well handled. You shouldn't have that many breaks."

Erica glanced from the healer to the cureman. No one asked that sort of question. Her father forbid it. He was a Kinsley and what he did in his home was of no concern to anyone, especially a healer. Why didn't this healer know that? Couldn't her father intimidate a healer on Quirni?

Their eyes met. It helped to look at eyes when she wanted to understand what someone was thinking. She could see more that way. The chin or nose just couldn't tell her that much. What she saw in this man was concern. One glance at the Cureman showed her the same. Erica's gaze dropped to the Cureman's brown uniform. Maybe the Quirni Delegate couldn't be intimidated by her father.

Then it hit her, she understood, her father didn't know she was in a clinic yet. It wouldn't take long and he would. Then the questions would stop. They would not want to know the truth and wouldn't appreciate it if she told them. That would mean investigations into Kinsley business and that usually ended badly for anyone but the Kinsley.

"Was a rough childhood," she said simply. Why the hell did her voice have to sound small and frightened? She averted her eyes again.

"Gina, could you leave us and close the door behind you?"

Her heart monitor quickened. The healer glanced at it.

The young woman left. Once the door closed the cureman looked back at Erica with puzzlement. "Erica, you seem different today."

"Different?" Erica repeated with a squeak. She looked up at her with wider eyes than she wished.

The woman opened her mouth but the man interrupted. "There are more important issues for the moment. What I want to know is, who beat you?" His voice became stern, suggesting he had enough of fishing around for an answer.

The monitor beeped faster. Erica's eyes stopped on his again. He really didn't want to know. There was no doubt in her mind about that. Give it time and he would stop asking.

The cureman sighed. "Lev, that doesn't matter. Whoever it was can't hurt her anymore. She's on Quirni now. They are a planet away." She looked back at Erica. "If it helps, we will not try to prosecute whoever hurt you. It isn't usually worth the effort to prosecute old wounds but we can and should let the other SDDs know who has caused you harm. They can keep track of whoever hurt you and make certain they don't do the same to someone else."

"I suppose," the man huffed in displeasure but nodded.

Erica could see he still wanted an answer but he listened to the woman. His features softened. Erica thought he looked concerned. That surprised her. Medical people usually rushed off as soon as they healed the break. They would tell her to be more careful, *you're an iridim patient you know*, and leave.

She found she wanted to answer them. It felt so strange, kind of nice, for someone to act concerned for her when they didn't have an obvious reason to do so. In fact their lives would be better for not knowing. Only it did make sense to tell people what her father was capable of doing. Just to have him watched would be something.

"I..." she began then cleared her throat. "My father hurt me." The healer waited for more. He didn't look away at this point like everyone else. No one wanted to know anything about her father that they ought to report. How much did she really want to tell? How much did he really want to know? The woman suggested it wasn't much. She had already warned him off.

"And?" he pressed. "How did he hurt you? Did he push you around or was there more than that?"

"How?" she repeated in the same small squeak. No one asked that. No one wanted to hear that. *How?* And Good lords, even after all this time and distance, the fear of telling still gripped her. *How?* "He was big and angry."

The healer sat back. He didn't like her answer, which she realized wasn't an answer at all, but then he pressed in a different direction. "Do the injuries go deeper than breaks and bruises?" He tapped the side of his head with two fingers.

The heart monitor gave away her surprise.

He noticed it as much as Erica had. His eyes wavered towards it slightly then settled back on hers, actually held hers. He didn't allow her to look at his nose when she tried to do so. He lifted her chin so she would look at him.

"Do you know why you don't remember the last four days?" asked the cureman.

Erica's eyes widened. Did she tell them something? Usually people would accept her lapses as a sign that she had drank too much or was tired or some such thing, even a fever. "Was the fever?" she suggested.

The cureman shook her head. "It was never that high. I am a good cureman and I made sure of it."

"Do you know why you don't remember the last four days?" the healer repeated.

The heart monitor took another leap in speed. It took some time for Erica to consider what she wanted to reveal. The monitor slowed. It took longer for her to fight the multiple impulses to stay quiet and it took longer still to get up the nerve to speak but they waited unlike anyone else she had ever met.

"Suppose so," Erica answered quietly. "Was cured. Thought it was anyway."

"Cured of what?" the healer asked.

Edwards

Erica winced. "Disso-" Even for trying she couldn't say it. She looked away from them. Before she had come to Quirni she had finally been free of this, the searching for clues about what had happened while she was gone, pretending to know what had happened, pretending she remembered a conversation. Oh, good lords, how could it be back? She closed her eyes.

"I see," he said quietly. "Erica. That is what you call yourself, isn't it?"

She nodded. She had several names.

The healer continued. "I thought so when you didn't correct me."

He had said her name when he came in. She looked back at him. Who were these people? SDD didn't act like this.

"Listen." He leaned forward and took her hand. He squeezed it. His felt warm. She knew hers was cold. It had to be because, despite her fever, his hand felt like fire. "We called up your records from Marril. I know you have Dissociation Disorder. That's the cleaned up, fancy clinical name for what you have. I won't ask you to remember what caused it. We just needed to know if you know or if you deny it. I can see you know. We realize you must be well practiced at making conversation about incidents you don't remember." He smiled as he said this. "We would like it if you didn't do that while you are here."

The heart monitor beeped fast. Erica couldn't stand it anymore. She reached behind herself and pulled the damn patch off. The beeping stopped. She expected the cureman and healer to try and stop her but they didn't. The healer controlled a twitch that would have been a smile.

"So, you seem to know which wires goes to the heart monitor," the cureman remarked coolly. She reached up and turned off the machine then took the wires out of Erica's hand.

"The situation is this," the healer continued as if Erica had done nothing. "We know you have this disorder and we know from your records that Erica is the part of your personality who is usually out, but for the last four days, you haven't been. If you try to cover that up, we won't know what you have missed. For instance, you probably don't know us. Am I right?"

Erica nodded. Her shock didn't let her move any more than that.

"My name is Levitus Amble," the healer added, "and I am a QSDD major, but first, I want you to understand this, I am a healer. This is my wife, Betty Amble. She is also a major in the QSDD but her first concern is also with your health and not any

The Marrilian

SDD plans. It is important for you to remember that." He patted her hand. "Do you think you can?"

Erica stared at Levitus like he was a freak show attraction. He waited patiently until she finally responded. "Yes."

"Good," he replied. "Do you remember why you are here?"

She nodded. "They attacked me."

"Who?"

"Cluny."

He nodded. "Do you remember where we brought you?"

She shook her head.

"You're at the SDD clinic for critical cases in the Southern Padt City."

"All the way back there? No," she whined. She dropped her head back to her pillow, two weeks in the damn woods for nothing.

"All the way back," he affirmed. "It is for the best. You are in good hands here. You should have been checked in when you arrived on planet anyway given the amount of thayanite you have in your lungs. You'll be safe now. We won't let anyone hurt you again even after you leave."

"Leave to where?" she asked as she stared at the ceiling. Where could she go?

"From the clinic," he replied.

"Into the Padt City?" she asked and half laughed. "They would kill me."

"That will change by the time you leave which won't be for a while," he assured her. "I have to heal your leg and you have enough thayanite poisoning you need multiple daily treatments. You will stay here until we get those down to one a day. Then there is your disorder. We have a psychiatrist for you."

Erica pushed up on her elbows and faced him. "No," she said quickly. "No, don't want to talk to a doctor. No."

Levitus sat back in surprise. "Why not?"

Because they would dredge up all the old memories and try to piece her back together and they would cause all sorts of stress, moodiness, anger and lords only knew what else. She could end up dead or in jail. Or how about whatever they did could be blasted by a few hard knocks. "No," she said again.

She pushed herself up to face him squarely. It made her leg pull in the cast and hurt but she would make them understand. "Won't do that again." She looked from Levitus to Betty to see if they were going to force this on her. "Doctors don't help. 'Tis a harm for no good."

Edwards

Neither of them could respond to this. They glanced at each other. Betty nodded. "I understand, dear. We'll discuss it again later but if you don't want that sort of help you don't have to have it. People with your condition often go undiagnosed and lead perfectly normal lives. We won't force you."

They pressed on her shoulders to make her lay back.

"When I leave here I will be attacked again. Was attacked here before Cluny."

Betty disagreed. "You will have agents to watch over you and the population of the city will know you are not to be touched. You will be fine. You will have to stay in town for a while for thayanite therapy so they will know who you are and you will be fine."

'Yeah, right,' Erica's *conscience* remarked darkly.

Erica's eyes widened for hearing the voice so clearly.

She didn't know if she agreed with it or not. These were kind people. She believed what they told her.

Kind agents? Was that possible? Would they help her and release her? It appeared she would have time to find out. She lay back feeling warm. Moving, pressing up to sit, had dislodged all of the ice packs around her and already the fever built. Her face flushed with heat.

Betty touched her cheek. "We'll talk again later," she said kindly. "Get some rest." She placed a cool compress on Erica's forehead and told Levitus to leave then started to tuck the ice packs back in place.

Chapter 6 – Restless Tenpole

Erica had been released from the SDD clinic for a month with orders to return each morning for thayanite treatment. After that she had nothing to do which didn't sit well with her. Agent Jimmy Cox got her an apartment, helped her buy things she had to have, and then trailed after her to warn every potentially threatening person to leave her alone.

When he was there she went to each of the stores. Even with Jimmy along the retailers were rude or downright nasty but they didn't chase her. They wouldn't sell her anything either. Jimmy had to go back to buy what she needed later. That sort of shopping grew old quick so she decided to read archived newspapers at the SDD library. That was when Jimmy quit following. He told her the boundaries in which she would be safe and urged her to stay in them.

Matilda's trial was depressing and newspaper photos showed how much she really did look like her cousin. The description of the disaster sickened her. The trial was a disaster too. The evidence was circumstantial. The defense was poorly prepared, as if her own lawyer thought her guilty and wanted her punished, and then the QSDD intervened and no one believed anything they said. If the account of the trial was accurate there was worse justice on Quirni than on Sirrus. Eventually she stopped reading, but she spent most of her time near the base as per agent Cox's advice.

Since not one restaurant would serve her, she had to eat every meal at the SDD cafeteria. She tried to ignore the agents while she was there, willing to greet Jimmy when she saw him but no one else, and she only ate once a day so she wouldn't have to be on the base any more than necessary. That annoyed Betty who complained when she lost more weight. Erica tried to make Betty happy by eating more at the one sitting but she wouldn't go back for more than one meal.

After her antidote therapy and eating she wandered the town and looked for something to do within the confines of her protected space. People would leave their old newspapers on benches or stuffed in a garbage can so she had those to read on occasion. The papers weren't much and too often she found stories about Matilda, that being herself.

Her computer alone gave her entertainment. With all the computer time she could have made hundreds of thousands of quid if she was still on Marril. She did use the computer to contact Marril once, jumping on the Quirni network briefly to send the one message and after that she didn't get on again. The SDD owned the Network and since she wasn't paying, she was stealing and that was something she shouldn't do here, not while she was under such close supervision. She needed no more problems. The old days were gone. Someday she would visit her businesses and collect the rest of her money but not until she had a legal connection. The four million quid she had in the bank was enough.

Solitaire didn't require a network connection so she used the computer for that but by the time she had won numerous games and beat her best score several times it no longer held her interest. She flipped the laptop closed with a groan then placed it on the floor in the sunlight.

She sat on the floor so she could be in the sun. The only form of electrical energy commonly used on Quirni was solar and her computer didn't hold a charge so she had to keep it in the sun to use it. That wasn't so bad because the heat felt good on her face. She leaned her head against the wall to enjoy the warmth.

Quirni had beautiful weather. When it rained it tended to do so at night. It never got too humid or too dry. The air almost sparkled it was so pure. She loved the trees. They amazed her. Many of them were a hundred feet tall. Betty said some were two hundred feet tall in the south. Marril only had little scrubby bushes, fifteen feet at the most and she didn't remember any trees that tall on Sirrus either.

The warm ray moved off her face and she woke. She had never had this much peace in her life. Betty's promise was good; they kept her safe.

She had played enough solitaire today so she placed her computer in its bag and went to the bank to return it to the safety box. Jimmy had warned her to keep it locked up or it could be stolen from her apartment. The SDD could watch over her but not her stuff.

Arlo sat at one of the side desks when she walked in. He knew why she was there so he got the bank key for her deposit vaults. He led the way. "You look grumpy," he noticed. Arlo, Jimmy, and the Ambles were the only people who spoke to her. His remark surprised her.

The Marrilian

"Am bored," she told him and since she didn't actually feel grumpy and didn't want to look grumpy she tried to smile.

"My friends have kids who say that. I got them jobs cleaning and collecting garbage. It didn't take long and they found different work." Arlo grunted at his thoughts. "One of them got a job at the livery stable mucking out stalls. I couldn't believe he thought that was any better. Stupid kids. It paid less."

Erica wasn't grumpy but she wasn't in the mood for his stories either. If she didn't offer something to the conversation he would tell her about his friend's children all day. He wanted some of his own but hadn't found a woman to have them.

"Would leave. Should go north but the SDD protects me here." She let her thought trail off as he stuck his key in the box and then stepped aside for her to slide her keycard through the sensor.

"I can't blame you. I wouldn't go out on the road looking like you do." He watched her as she stuffed in the computer bag and straightened. "People will still attack you anywhere else on the planet."

"So," she agreed, but she wouldn't need nearly as many smokes after Betty and Levitus finished the therapy for the thayanite. She could take what she needed with her and avoid towns.

"You're considering going anyway aren't you?" Arlo asked. She nodded.

"You're insane." He said it with a smile.

She smiled back and nodded again. She liked Arlo a lot and had long since decided she would do anything for him, or with him, but he never asked. "You be the only one who talks to me outside of the blasted SDD. Did you know that?"

He shrugged and closed the box. "Contrary to what I had to say out on the road that night, I always liked Mati. I had a bit of a crush on her when I was younger. She did end up screwing me but not how I had hoped." He laughed. He led the way back to the front of the bank.

Erica smiled again. His humor lightened her mood. "Need something to do." She looked up at him when he stopped. She had developed enough friendship with him she looked in his eyes. He had remarked on it when she had and congratulated his good character that Tenpole would look him in the eye.

She had tried to explain that wasn't what it was about but he didn't want to hear it. He preferred to tease her and act like he didn't understand so he could continue to tease her. It was part of what made her like him so much. "Might there be garbage to empty around here or might you any other job for me? Would do what you want." She gave him a little smile and big eyes just to let him know she suggested more than a job.

He considered her for a long time then looked away and around the bank. "You know your eyes are totally the wrong color." Before she could respond he looked back at her but not at all how she looked at him.

She added a tilt of her chin. "They be my color," she told him with a softer tone than she usually used. "Mayhaps you can get used to them."

He inhaled, he had noticed what she meant now, and pulled his eyes away. "Maybe you should help exterminate the dogs. You seemed to have a knack for attracting them."

"You blasted prat," she scowled.

"I told you all food had to be sealed so I figure you wanted a few dogs to play tug-of-war or something."

"Should never have told you what happened."

He smiled and looked around the bank. "I could give you a janitorial position without taking any flack. You would be out of sight. We don't have a night janitor right now. The pay is low. As if you care. You could work alone on the night shift scrubbing floors."

Erica grinned both for him giving the offer of a job and ignoring her offer of sex. She liked nighttime work of all sorts. She had accomplished a lot during night shift jobs. "Sounds perfect, Arlo. Should start tonight?"

He stood back at her with a silly smile. "Seriously? Is that really what you are after? You want a job?"

Her eyes were bright. "'Tis something to do so, seriously, yes." And she would have told him she was after more than that but Arlo wasn't the type to be with a woman unless he wanted to commit to a relationship. He would not commit to her in that way. That was clear.

He half laughed. "Can you imagine the comments when people learn Matilda Kinsley is doing janitorial work?"

"I'm not-"

"Yeah well," he said and cut her off with a wave of his hand. "Try to convince fifteen thousand people of that. We only *just* managed to convince about twenty that night, and half of them are kicking themselves for not finishing you off." He shook his head. "I didn't tell you what happened."

Erica stiffened as she stared up at him warily. "What?"

The Marrilian

"They were accused of being bought off."

She sighed. "Good lords. Everyone hates her don't they?"

"Six thousand and twenty-six times over," he said seriously. "And yes, you can start tonight." He showed her what needed to be done and she left.

She returned to the base for dinner that afternoon and ate well for the first time in days. Her appetite had returned with the prospect of something to keep her busy and she would need the extra food to keep Betty happy. She knew from experience that cleaning could be rigorous work if done well. If she showed up with more weight lost, Betty threatened to put her back in the clinic to make certain she ate right. No need for that drama.

That night Erica reported to the bank. The afternoon shift janitor gave her a look that could kill but said nothing until she exited the building. Then the woman began laughing.

"Dummy," Erica muttered and took the bucket with its mop from the cupboard. She understood enough about Quirni water systems now to find the hand pump and fill a ceramic tank. The water needed to be warm so, with a little trouble and an hour of trying, she lit the gas burner under the tank, as Arlo had written, and waited for the thermostat to read the right temperature. A little water, soap, and a clean mop, and she was in business.

The mindless work suited her. Her money and her knife had disappeared in Cluny so she kept her pay in her pocket and used it to try and buy something every few days. Sooner or later a merchant would sell to her. They had to. It was what they did and until she got a book or something else to do her days consisted of a treatment, playing solitaire, eating at the base, then work.

At the end of the second month, the thayanite therapy had made her feel so much better she expected Betty to tell her she was done but Betty didn't think so. Erica asked and Betty shook her head.

"Give it time, dear," she replied.

Erica had learned to respect the cureman so she did give it time when all of her instincts warned her to get away from the SDD, the City, and people.

The beating she had taken in Cluny left a low-level terror huddled in the back of Erica's mind, like another arrow would pierce her when she least expected. The kind treatment she received from Levitus and Betty overcame enough of her anxiety she stayed for now. It remained so until an officer Erica didn't know approached her in the cafeteria.

Edwards

He was a square built man, sort of squat, older, with a lot of ribbons on his chest and a high rank that she thought might be some kind of general given the star on his collar. She sat back warily when he stopped at her table and smiled with a smile she did not like.

It was the type of smile her father would wear when he wanted to be friendly. The smile categorized the man under 'do not trust, abusive prick'. Her plastic fork hovered over her plate. She had just lost her appetite. No one bothered her here and no one talked to her here until now. The cafeteria was no longer a safe place to be.

"Good afternoon, Miss," he greeted. He stood at the other side of the small table and offered his hand. "I'm General White. May I join you?" The cafeteria was empty except for a healer and nurse in a far booth. There was no reason to share the table except to harass her.

She stared up at him and given she didn't want him there and didn't like him she looked him in the eye. She didn't glare because it wasn't safe enough for that. She was on the QSDD base and he was QSDD so she kept her expression blank rather than outwardly hostile.

"Honest, I don't bite," he added with the same creepy smile.

He had hanging jowls and heavy lips that made him look as if he practiced pouting. His hand, which he continued to extend towards her, was thick and so pink on both sides she would have thought he was from Tenpole if she had met him on Marril.

She wanted him to leave, to be left alone, but better she learn what the QSDD had in mind for her than leave and never know until it bit her in the ass. Reluctantly, she stood and took his hand to find it limp and clammy.

"Good afternoon," she replied dully and suppressed the repulsed sneer she nearly made for touching him but couldn't stop from pulling her hand away sooner than she should. She added the polite response she had heard the QSDD make around her when they had welcomed people to their tables. "I would be happy to have your company."

'Damned lie' her *conscience* said.

Go away she thought back at it and smiled as General White sat. It was her flat smile, mouth just taut enough to be taken for a smile.

"You are Erica Ennis are you not?" he asked conversationally but then his tone dropped. "Or I should say Lynn Jillian Kinsley by Quirni law."

The Marrilian

This gave her gut a twinge. "Changed my name legally, sir. 'Tis Erica Ennis." She tried to sound unconcerned and managed well she thought.

"It may be on Marril but, you know, you have to change it here too, you know."

A silent 'oh' formed on her mouth. She wasn't certain where he was going with this so she didn't want to comment. He let her silence hang while he studied her and then continued.

"In order to change it here you have to prove you have no outstanding offences. We don't want people coming here to disappear under an alias, you know? This isn't the drop off planet for thieves and murderers and the like anymore, you know?"

Erica did not like his falsely sweet tone and she liked what he implied even less.

"Of course not," she responded quietly and leaned forward to eat. She rested her arms on either side of her plate. He couldn't threaten her with her past. Her crimes were already paid for with jail time or hidden. She had been careful to not get caught since going to jail.

"If, for now, you prefer to use the name 'Erica' we can see our way to calling you that. For now."

'Damned nice of you, you old bastard,' Erica's *conscience* snapped.

Erica's jaw tightened but she faced her plate so he didn't see it. "A kindness," she told the General and shrugged. "If it suits the law here, however, you should call me by my given name."

'Calling the old, fat asshole's bluff?'

Would you shut up? she thought back at the voice.

"Oh, no, no, no, no." He shook his head as he sat back. He laced his fingers together over his belly. "No, you see, you just need to go through a few formalities. I'm sure a search for records could be quick. Just start the process and you'll be Erica Ennis here too."

So that was it – records. If he didn't have them she wanted it kept that way. "Not much for formalities," she told him and lifted her eyes to his. "*You know*… was a pain to change it on Marril and frankly, doesn't matter to me anymore. Will start using my old name. Thank you for telling me about this."

A frown flashed across his brow before the smile returned. "Oh, now, Miss, uh, well, you see that wasn't exactly what I am here to convey. You need to make the change so it agrees with Marrilian and Sirrian records, in fact, for things like banking and you should have the name you want, you know."

Banking? Something in the back of her mind fluttered with apprehension.

"My old name be fine," she told him which was a flat out lie because the name 'Lynn' did hold issues for her. She shouldn't say it. "You may call me what you like. But," she grunted as she looked down at her plate, "'tis a while since I used it. Will have to get used to answering to it again."

"I see," he said and watched her while she took another bite. "Do you have something to hide?" he asked but hurried into an explanation when she sat back, beginning to bristle. "Because there are always extenuating circumstances and these are taken into account, you know? These records we would need are only private addresses from Marril and release forms for questioning past employers and getting medical information and the like. You know what I mean. It's nothing really. We do all the work. You just have to show up at court for one hour or so."

Medical records? Erica thought Levitus and Betty had those. Apparently, her relationship with them was confidential. She nodded a bit absent mindedly, surprised by that information but happy to hear it.

"Oh good, so you'll be interested in doing that, then good." He began to unfold and lean onto the table as a prelude to rising.

"Uh – no," Erica corrected him. She ate a carrot and smiled.

His eyes darkened. His cheeks flushed in anger. He sat back again. "No? Why?" he demanded and not a trace of the smile remained. "You chose a name and went to all the trouble to change it and just like that," he snapped his pudgy, short fingers, "give it up? That makes no sense."

"*You know*, this wouldn't be a problem except I had to come to Quirni," she told him. "They would respect my choice on Sirrus."

"Well, you are not on Sirrus, Lynn."

Erica tried not to react to the name but she had to fight back the feelings it called, anger, hate. She set her will against the feelings that name called out.

"So, couldn't get tickets," she accused, as if he had something to do with it personally. "Somehow a transport to Quirni was my only option. Strange too since other people got tickets to Sirrus."

"Then perhaps you are not welcome there," he suggested. He still didn't remember to smile. He sneered instead. She had hit a nerve. Maybe he did have something to do with it personally. "You probably do have something to hide? Is that right?"

The Marrilian

'Sure, admit it and let them investigate based on your own confession.'

Hush, Erica thought.

"Well?" the General prodded.

"There be nothing to hide," she told him and did her utmost to look in his eyes without flashing her anger like he had his. "Just, 'tis nothing to gain by changing my name a second time when the first time ends so."

"Actually, you have a lot to gain. Consider how much worse it will be with the name *Lynn Kinsley* here."

'Shit!' her *conscience* yelped as Lynn awoke.

Erica blinked in surprise at the mental yelp of alarm. She straightened in her chair. *Shut the hell up!* She thought at the persistent voice. It reacted to Lynn. Erica forced her breathing to stay calm and even.

The General's eyes narrowed. "Did you know your cousin's middle name is Lynn?" he asked and smiled as if he had hit a bullseye.

Erica did know but she said nothing. She sat back in her chair. She would keep control. She worked on that as he persisted in goading her.

"Interesting don't you think? How will the population react to that? Matilda Lynn Kinsley is now Lynn Kinsley. That's what they'll think."

"'Tis an old family name," Erica hissed. "'Tis how Kinsley's be named."

"You know, I'll bet you a couple of million quid that no one outside of the Kinsley family will know that." He leaned forward with his arms folded on the table and his hands clasped together.

Her eyes narrowed. She didn't like people like him. They were stupid to threaten her and didn't realize it. He would realize it if he continued.

'Listen Stupid, that was a threat. He is going after your account here.'

No kidding. Erica didn't need her *conscience* to tell her that. The problem was what to do about it if anything. Then he smiled again and made up her mind. Her anger diffused as she decided to threaten this asshole in return. Lynn receded and waited. "A couple million? Really," she asked with a sneer.

"Yes," he replied. His head cocked. His brows drew down, confused. He knew there was more going on in the conversation than he heard. He just couldn't put his finger on it.

She leaned forward to eat again. That was the best thing she

Edwards

could do to show her lack of concern, as if she wasn't going to react to him at all. She pierced the first thing her fork touched and stuffed it in her mouth. It was meat, which was perfect to keep her attitude. She didn't like meat as much as she didn't like General White. The two complimented eat other. She chewed hard and swallowed as she watched him watch her.

She knew that look on his face. It surprised him that she did not react the way he expected. He began to think her cold hearted, calculating and emotionless, which wasn't true, she just wasn't feeling the emotion he wanted– fear. That part of her wasn't out. He studied her, expected her to be distressed but she wasn't. She was annoyed and angry. Lynn was angry too. She would attack General White if she got loose. SDD generals had hurt them. Erica worked to suppress her and that made her keep control but doing so was really hard right now because she also wanted to let Lynn out. She wanted this pompous ass to see her courser side.

The SDD on Marril had harassed her this way too. They needled her with inane comments chosen to get an emotional response. Why did they always have to do that? Why did they always try to upset her? Hadn't they learned?

Well, to be fair, they didn't know everything she had done.

She supposed the thing that really annoyed her was how they expected her to react like all the other people they harassed. When would they stop expecting her to be a copy of everyone else and stop trying to control her like everyone else? Why did she have to fit a mold, not talk to herself, be self-controlled, be lawful, and kind and all of that other blasted shit?

'Careful.'

I know, calm down, calm. I am in control. Lords she hated that look on his face as if something was wrong with her, which there was, which really made her mad.

She propped her elbows on the table and pointed her plastic fork at him. She would give Lynn and herself some satisfaction.

"You know," she mimicked him, "if for some reason I be on Quirni, *you know*, for some reason I don't understand and I sit here, doing nothing, useless to everyone, then that be sort of silly don't you think?"

The change of subject didn't faze him. "What sort of reason?"

She shrugged and looked down at her meal, trying to act unconcerned. "It seems a waste of time bringing me here and then letting me go off to go get myself killed. Real waste of time." She looked up. "You know?" She chewed and stared him in the eye.

He leaned back with his arms over his belly, which was barely a belly at all. He was in fine shape but he was a blocky man. "You shouldn't get too clever for yourself, Lynn."

She couldn't swallow so she couldn't answer as fast as she wanted. That part of her simply shouldn't be called out and that was exactly what he was doing, calling her out. It took a mental adjustment to get past the emotions. "Probably," Erica managed to choke.

He grinned as his eyes widened. "That name really bothers you."

Erica speared a carrot and bit off half of it. She swallowed before she glared at him. "Comes with bad memories. 'Tis why it be changed."

He leaned forward. A smile twitched at his mouth. "What sort of memories?"

His dark eyes narrowed and she didn't like the look. He enjoyed harassing her. She could feel that he did. He liked seeing her squirm. He would like to see anyone squirm, an arrogant, abusive bastard. If he was married, she would expect his wife hated him. His children would run as soon as they were able. The military gave him the means to treat people like crap and that was what he liked. She was going to make him suffer.

She held his eyes for several seconds, pausing for affect. He stared back at her with a self-satisfied half sneering smile that made her dislike him so thoroughly she wanted to get rid of him for good and unless he was a complete bastard she knew how. She would remind him of things he had probably done.

She leaned forward, stared straight into his eyes, and spoke in a girlish voice. "When my da would a special thing he called that name, you know. Want to know what be special? Seems to me you would some." His smile fell away incrementally with her words. She guessed he didn't like her tone, or maybe he picked up on where this was going. He had it coming. She leaned forward and hissed, "sex." His response was immediate, sudden color loss. "Started when I was little." She spread her hand to indicate the size of an infant. "That be the size you like?"

He paled and sat back. His grin was gone.

Erica watched and waited, Lynn was quieter, easier to control. She felt a minor relief that he wasn't excited by this. Still, he didn't leave so she continued in the voice of a smaller child. High and tiny. "He called. I hid. He dragged me out and beat me and then did what da shouldn't do but all you men love to do."

Edwards

General White turned a color true to his name. She tipped her head and smiled at him seductively and enjoyed the way his mouth tightened over contents from his stomach which meant he wasn't quite as abusive as she thought. At least the idea of what she said made him feel bad. If it hadn't been for that she would have continued.

She watched him struggle with the mental picture she had drawn then shrugged and returned to her normal tone. "Puts sort of a bad spin on a name, *you know*? Now here you come and say it. 'Tis annoying, *you know?*"

He couldn't respond for several seconds. "That was uncalled for," he finally told her in an attempt at a steely tone but it was too low and soft. He stood stiffly, stepped aside from his chair, and pushed it in hard. He glared at her. "Uncalled for." He walked off.

Erica watched over her shoulder until he had left the cafeteria then said, "Yes, I know," but only wondered if she should be ashamed of herself or happy to be rid of him. She felt happy so she went with that and ate her dinner.

That night she finished her work then sat down at the bank's computer. She wanted to check her accounts. With all the time she had each night she would be able to crack any security the bank had. It would only take time. This was the type of thing she had done on Marril when she wasn't being badgered by Ilene to perform for a customer.

When she touched the old style of the keyboard it's age made her pause in disbelief. The monitor turned on and the cursor blinked in a box labeled 'password'. The best place to start figuring out passwords was at the preinstalled password. Typing anything always gave her ideas so she could start guessing, which was the hard way to do it but guessing was the only option she had since she couldn't go to the nearest store and purchase hardware. She would have to guess at what the computer operator might have set, probably Arlo. That helped because she knew him. Like most people, he would probably use a birthday or anniversary and if not she could search his desk.

She typed in 'password' and hit enter. The screen changed to the banking menu.

Erica froze. Her stomach dropped to see the screen and every alarm bell in her body blared. Her fingers hovered over the keyboard. "Can't be," she mouthed to herself. The default password wasn't supposed to work. It was just a means to get her started. The computer security tech was supposed to change that password. Maybe this was a trap? If she went any further the computer would log off and send an alarm.

Fearing that, she waited and returned to mopping for half an hour in case an alarm had already been sent but the only thing that happened was the screen went dark to save energy.

Erica emptied the bucket, placed her mop in it, and returned it to the janitor's closet. She went to the door that lead to the public side of the bank, the one behind the glass wall, and listened. The bank was quiet. It seemed likely there had been no alarm but that was so damn weird. She moved to the opening in the glass wall and listened again. Nothing, all was silent.

Were the Quirni as trusting with their banking computer as they were in leaving doors open to shops? Could that be it? Her eyes narrowed as she considered, head tipped, thinking, staring at the door leading back to the offices and the computer. Could that be possible? The Quirni were trusting and given that, it was plausible. Not on Marril or Sirrus, but on Quirni, it was plausible.

She returned to the computer and sat. The monitor was dark and the computer had powered down. It was one of the older models too, barely able to fold as small as a pocket. Arlo kept it completely unfolded and he stood it upright on a stand so it made the largest screen, nearly two feet wide. The keyboard was an addition. If he had folded the computer correctly, it would have displayed its own keyboard. Maybe he didn't know that which suggested he was not a savvy user in any respect or he just liked the old style of keyboard. It was strange but this was Quirni.

She took a breath and touched a letter on the board. The screen lit up. It was the same screen all the bankers had on their monitors any time she walked through the bank. The password really had worked. That password was in fact 'password'. How could they be that trusting? How could they leave it unprotected? Didn't that mean her money was unprotected? Lords, it probably did. They *were* Quirni. Then again, no one would know how to use an unprotected computer on Quirni would they? Given the keyboard and the way the computer was set up she suspected even Arlo wasn't used to them and he had lived on Marril once.

Could computer skills be lost? Somehow she doubted it but it wouldn't be the first time she wondered if Quirni's air screwed up people's brains.

Then a new thought occurred, one that explained why he

hadn't installed a password to sign onto the system, he protected each application with a password. That had to be it. That would make her job harder. She would have to guess passwords for each system she wanted to hack and maybe each file or account. Now that was clever.

Her eyes widened in eager delight for the challenge. She had hacked two major banks in the past. Neither had been easy jobs but she only had to break one admin password in either case. Figuring out dozens would be a challenge. She smiled to think of it. Thank goodness she had so much time.

She opened the list of computer files and then tried to open the first application. It opened. Her lips parted in surprise. She stared at the screen. Once the shock passed she closed the file and pulled the mop and bucket back out of the closet and re-mopped the floors. Hacking banks had taught her to be very wary if anything looked too easy.

An hour and a half later nothing had happened. She had mopped the same floors three times now so she could watch the doors. There weren't any security cameras in the bank so if there was an alarm it would go to the base and they would come to the bank but no one was outside. That didn't make her feel better. It only made her wonder if they waited for her to go deep enough into the system to prove her intent and she didn't know how deep would that be because she didn't know the Quirni laws.

It was time for a break so she went to the lounge and leaned her mop against the door within reach if she needed to appear busy and then poured a glass of water from a jug they kept in an ice chest. She sat down on the old leather sofa and stared at the wall and thought. Were the Quirni so trusting they would let her loose by their banking computer when it wasn't protected by a password?

Why had Arlo given her this job? He hadn't asked about her past or asked for references. He hadn't asked about past employment or criminal convictions. He had just given her the job because *she* had asked for it. Her eyes narrowed further. Could that mean the Delegate didn't know or maybe hadn't considered the implications of letting someone like her work in a place like this?

Did the Delegate have any idea of her past? They didn't have her records. Would anything let them know she was capable of hacking a banking computer system if they hadn't seen her records? What would they tell Arlo about his new employee not knowing anything about her?

The Marrilian

Trusting, she mouthed. That had to be the blasted beginning and end of it. The damn Quirni Delegate was as trusting as everyone else on the stinking planet. Nothing else made sense. They would be knocking on the door already if they had an alarm. Why wait for her to go any further into the files? They were simply underinformed and too trusting with their lack of information.

She put the mop away again and returned to the computer. Her stomach turned at the ease of it all but, this time, she didn't pause. File after file was not secure but now she only shook her head in wonder as she jotted down the location of accounts that held the most money. She folded the paper and put the notes in her pocket then turned around in the hard, wooden chair to think her plans through once more.

No security. Amazing. Certainly, there were people other than herself that could access this system.

She still couldn't help feeling this might be a trap but no one had come to stop her. Then again, how could someone on Quirni hack a computer? Those born on Quirni wouldn't know how unless they were Delegate and they wouldn't, amend that, shouldn't hack a computer. Anyone immigrating to the planet had no access even if they had been computer programmers and what if they were? What reason would they have to do what she intended to do? She might be the only person who had access, was capable of hacking, and had reason to do so. General White had been threatening her hadn't he?

Perhaps he hadn't meant to threaten her.

'Get off it you idiot.'

Erica bit her lip.

'They don't like you. You're such an ass.'

"Shut up," Erica snarled. "Just shut up!" She closed her eyes.

She supposed now she had never been cured of the dissociation. Somehow she had gotten strong enough to silence the *conscience* but leaving Marril had been too difficult and she had fallen back to her old defense mechanism, dissociating. That allowed them to come back. Them? Come to think of it she had only heard from Zoe. Erica sighed and fell heavily back in the chair. *There*, she thought, *you have your name back*.

'It was never gone.'

Erica sneered at the voice. It had been nice to be alone but Betty was right, she could live normally but she would have to use the old ways of coping again. At least this time she would know she wasn't insane in the dangerous sense. She just had company, helpers usually, even loud and obnoxious Zoe.

Loud, obnoxious Zoe generally trusted the SDD Erica realized. She didn't trust White.

"'Tis right?" Erica said out loud as she looked back at the computer. She knew it was right. She could feel it was right. It wasn't like Zoe could hide. She wasn't that type of alternate personality anymore. Erica could feel her emotions now, which was basically what her other personalities represented, the stronger aspects of her emotions that she didn't fully control. Her work with the doctor on Marril taught her that much. It brought much of her other parts out in the open so she felt most of what they felt. She couldn't use her emotions like other people; they didn't click into place to react to a situation, but she felt them and if she felt them in time she could use them to try and react correctly and appropriately. But tonight, right now, the important thing was Zoe didn't trust White. Interesting.

Zoe saw the same sorts of things in White that worried Erica. That helped Erica make up her mind. If the bank wasn't going to secure her account, she would.

Now this would be fun because this job would require writing a lot of scripts. It would be simple as far as that went but it would take time and they would have to be perfect. They would have to be tested to hell and back or she could crash the banking system but she had the means to test, her own computer.

Did they do a daily or hourly backup? She hadn't seen any equipment for a backup but she supposed it could be done remotely. It would be recorded in the backup log when they did it so she opened the backup files and found them empty. She checked for alternate software, alternate backup save points, but found none. She looked for all of the possible logs, files, software and hardware that could do a backup, even remotely by the SDD, before falling back in her chair. She felt sick. Holy hell, Quirni's banking system hung by an electrical wire attached to a solar power cell.

"Unbelievable," she muttered. "Bird droppings could do it in." She laughed a short choked laugh at the thought.

If she crashed the banking computers she would never forgive herself. She cleared the evidence of her work then logged off. It wasn't until she noticed the dust on the table that she moved and then she retrieved her dust mop and wiped it away. What she had seen had left her numb. Arlo was kind of a fool but so were the SDD. They should have provided the training and equipment necessary to keep the banks safe. "Blasted Delegate,"

The Marrilian

she muttered.

The next day she worked on her computer by her apartment window. She moved with the sunlight to keep the battery charged. She stopped only to walk over to the base to eat and get her thayanite therapy. When she locked up her computer she watched Arlo to see where he kept the bank key, on a peg above the ice chest.

That night with the doors locked, for the bank did have metal locks and safes, and with her work done, Erica retrieved her computer and began her security operations, as she liked to think of them. She made a backup of the system on her computer then copied the entire banking program. It fit with plenty of room to spare. Her computer was top of the line Marrilian hardware, despite the crappy battery, while the Bank of Quirni had equipment that was easily ten years old. She would use a part of her computer to test her scripts and another to back up the bank records.

Each one of her protective scripts would create problems for anyone trying to take her money. The first one would be activated if a password wasn't used when accessing her accounts for a withdrawal. Her script instructed the teller to ask Erica for a password. It was unusual but the directions would be easy to follow and give the teller a pop-up box to input *fuuSDDaholes*.

If the password was wrong, the script would warn the teller to stop and log the person off. If the password was circumvented then the next script would give another warning that further tampering would result in *Banking Errors*. That meant if they took her money, Erica's money would be returned, undoing their withdrawal. The hacker would then be logged off once more and her new account would be hidden. If her account dipped in value, the sabotage began, although Erica tried to think of it as Compensation.

Quite kindly she informed the thieves at each step how their actions would affect the system. She suspected they would care because she suspected the SDD would be the thieves. Her only fear was the scripts could be triggered by accident and then the bank would need her backup. For Arlo's sake she left him a clue on how to fix such a dilemma. She left him a message. 'You can get in my box any time, Arlo. I'll back you up.' That would lead him to her computer. Hopefully he knew what a backup was.

She liked her work but she had to get around two problems. What if something happened to her and they closed her account?

Edwards

That would trigger the scripts and leave no means to log in and fix the problem. The account would be gone and with it the means to run the scripts. The second problem was scripts themselves were vulnerable to erasure. It was obvious what was in them. If someone with any understanding of computer programs ran across them they would be alarmed so she had to bury them someplace they wouldn't be found accidentally.

Each day she tried something new. It took a few weeks to perfect, to find the right hiding places and give Arlo a simple, one button, ability to fix the errors her scripts would cause in the event her accounts were closed by the bank. She had no idea how much he knew about computers so she had to make it that simple. On the night she was ready to put the scripts on the banking computer she had a second thought. Her '*conscience*' spoke to her.

'You will cause yourself a world of trouble.'

Erica sat still. The 'Enter' key waited. If she didn't do this then the SDD would be able to make her a pauper and not suffer one bit for doing it. General White had mentioned her name was an issue with banking. She had checked and he was right but Arlo had included both of her names when he opened her accounts. White might still argue he could take her money because she hadn't legally changed her name on Quirni, hadn't legally registered her alias. They wanted her name changed to get her records and she expected the blasted SDD would press their case. Her money was the only leverage they had against her. Since she had no means to access her accounts on Marril, she would have no money if they took it.

It could be lawful for the SDD to take her money because of the name discrepancy. They hadn't done it yet but White's threats were just the beginning of pressuring her. It was an attempt to see how cooperative she might be. They waited but they would attack eventually because she wouldn't be cooperative. Now that she had recovered from the attacks in Cluny she expected they would act soon. They had brought her to Quirni for a reason. They would use her money to pressure her into doing as they wished.

'Trust the SDD.'

Trust? You were the one who didn't trust White!

'Trust the SDD.'

Erica seethed at this sudden turnaround. *What's to trust?* Erica wondered at Zoe. *The SDD kills. They killed my family.*

'So do you.'

The Marrilian

"Shut up," Erica hissed through clenched teeth. What the hell was she doing having a conversation? "That was an accident."

'Both times?'

"He didn't die."

'Because you were stopped.'

"You suffer though it next time!" she said loudly. Her voice echoed off the walls. She breathed hard.

'Trust the SDD,' Zoe urged.

Erica pressed Enter. The programs she had written uploaded. She put away her computer then went back to work.

The next day she went to do her thayanite therapy as usual and then she got her computer as usual but returned it early and mentioned something about finally becoming too bored with it. She went to dinner and to work and nothing happened. The next week it was the same and then the next month. White didn't approach her again. Her scripts lay dormant and hidden, as she had planned. At the end of a month she relaxed. Her money would be safe or the Delegate would pay dearly for taking it. Without her scripts she felt sure she would become a victim of some awful end on Quirni. Now she only had to get herself away.

That thought drove her. She paced in the clinic waiting room while she waited for the cureman. "Lo" she greeted Betty as soon as the door opened.

"Aren't you bouncy today," Betty noted with a tired glance.

"I'm feeling good." Erica followed her into the examination room.

Betty pointed to the exam table as she turned on the mister for the therapy then added chemicals into a port. The number of drops had to be counted so Erica took a seat. She noticed Betty looked awful. "What happens?" she asked once she had finished counting the drops.

The cureman looked back at her after adjusting the mister. "What happens? What do you mean?"

"You don't look well," Erica told her.

Betty smiled weakly then returned to her task. "A case kept us up until four in the morning. I am dead on my feet and it's nice of you to notice."

"What kind of case?"

"An accident with a horse," Betty answered as she added water to the antidote chamber. "There is always someone trying to breed a little 'spirit' into them and next thing you know they have a hoof in their head." She held the mask out to Erica who took it. "After you I am going to go home and go to bed." She picked a stethoscope up off the table and listened to her chest while she breathed.

"How much more therapy do I need?" asked Erica after Betty set the stethoscope aside.

"Why, are we in a hurry to go somewhere?" Betty asked tiredly. She leaned against the countertop.

Erica tried not to frown but didn't manage it. "We?"

Betty smiled. "It's a figure of speech, dear." She leaned forward and pushed the mask towards Erica's face. "You could stop now if you want to continue the smoking. Your lungs won't fill with fluid anymore but you will get congestion and lose your breath and start coughing if you exert yourself. If you smoke, which I don't recommend because it becomes a habit, it would take about two years to clear out the rest of the *thayanite*. If you keep coming here, it'll take about three months."

Erica lowered the mask to ask, "What if I didn't smoke at all? I thought Quirni air heals?"

Betty didn't like the sounds of that. She pushed Erica's hand and the mask back in place then crossed her arms over her chest and gazed down at her. "You shouldn't leave the city."

Erica's eyes dropped to the metal button near Betty's waist.

"Stupid, stubborn girl," Betty sighed.

"Don't like it here," Erica said in her defense. "And 'tis fine as long as I stay away from people."

Betty's face tightened as if in pain. "You are going with an SDD escort aren't you? I know they offered."

Erica looked up at the cureman so fast she forgot to move the mask with her face.

"Well, they offered it to someone," Betty added softly. "I heard them." She suddenly looked concerned. "And since you don't seem to be aware of that, you should still consider seeing a psychiatrist."

Erica ignored the tone and the comment. "Do they offer an escort or insist?"

Betty guided Erica's hand and mask back in place again. "I think *insist* would be accurate," she replied quietly.

This was news to Erica. Could Zoe actually be strong enough to take over again? She shuddered to think who else it could be.

"Why do you hate the SDD so much?" Betty asked. "What did we do to you?"

"Who told you I hate SDD?"

The Marrilian

Betty gave her a 'don't be difficult' look.

Erica grimaced. "Pardons."

"Answer the question instead," Betty suggested.

She shook her head. Of all people, a kind agent, a caring cureman, and a mother, she didn't need to hear that.

Betty frowned. "Just exactly how much of your past do you remember?"

Erica blinked and looked at a far wall. A picture of a Quirni mountain range hung there. She remembered her first encounter with the SDD well enough. "A lot of it. I guess…" There was no way to know what had happened in her past if she didn't have the memories anymore. She hadn't been there so as long as no one told her about it she assumed the days had been easy to forget, probably repetitive and dull.

"Don't leave. It won't do you any good. Accept the help we're offering."

"From the damn SDD? Rather not."

"I'm *damn* SDD," snarled Betty.

Erica's eyes widened. She hung her head. "My pardons, meant no offense."

"Perhaps," Betty replied and her frown remained.

Erica set down the mask and stood. She would not leave Betty feeling insulted. She looked up at the woman who faced her with her arms still crossed. "I respect you and your husband. My pardons. Was a stupid thing to say."

That mollified the cureman. Her arms dropped. She smiled the smallest amount. At least the frown was gone. "Nevertheless, you despise the SDD. Why?"

Erica supposed she could explain it a little. Betty didn't have to hear the details about the fucking bastard Razi.

"When the SDD be around me…'tis trouble. 'Tis as if they have it out for my family. They ran me off of Sirrus then they didn't let me return there. My father could but not me. They forced me to come here." She looked back up at the Cureman. "They scare me," she admitted and that was enough of an explanation.

"Or you are paranoid," Betty assessed astutely.

Erica sagged in frustration for trying to explain at all. Everyone always loved to tell her she was paranoid and she probably was but she had every right to be given her crappy luck.

"However," Betty added, and relented as she leaned closer to Erica's left ear. She spoke low. "They did bring you here for a purpose and you are fortunate they did. You would have died if you stayed on Marril any longer. Just be careful." He voice trailed off. She stood back.

Erica's eyes grew wide at this news.

"That's enough of this nonsense," Betty told her and pointed at the mask. "Stay with it for another fifteen minutes. Sit."

Erica started to ask a question but Betty's eyes darkened with irritation and she had never seen Betty like that. It was like she had suddenly turned vicious, and Erica didn't understand how she had upset her. She turned and picked up the mask then slowly sat on the edge of the exam table.

"Good, then enough of that," Betty added. "I know no Delegate would intentionally harm you. It would go against every law that governs the SDD. The SDD and planetary councils set those laws and we don't go against council laws because without council support we don't exist. We wouldn't have funding." The anger in her eyes faded. "This will surprise you but it's not our job to hurt Kinsleys. Your uncle was assassinated by a Marrilian lord, not us."

"Never said it was your business to hurt Kinsley's," Erica replied in defense.

Betty frowned at her.

Erica continued. "I know Marrilian SDD killed him. Was not another lord. He was a lord himself. They don't kill each other. The SDD stormed the mansion, killed him, and forced my great great grandmother and uncle off planet."

"What you know about your family history is filtered through anger and hate. Your relatives caused their own problems. No Marrilian agent ever did a thing to them. Your great great uncle Cedric was dispatched by another lord, or at least someone who became a lord. After that, your grandmother went to Sirrus and your uncle came here and we are happy to have him. He is an excellent claimant."

Cyril Kinsley, Matilda's father, Erica knew about him. He worked with the SDD. Because of Quirni's longevity he was the same person who had fled Marril with Erica's great great grandmother.

"Be careful who you look to for help," Betty warned. "Know your history."

Erica didn't question her further. She dropped her eyes submissively. "Yes Cureman." Betty was far too irritated to ask anything more but what she had said did make Erica wonder who was the fabled other lord the Delegate would blame for her uncle's death. Where had the killer gone after killing him? Why hadn't the SDD punished him? It all seemed so fishy, especially when she had always believed it was the SDD.

None of it made sense, not the family rumors or Betty's version of history. It didn't even make sense that Betty argued about it. It wasn't like her. She was tired, exhausted actually. That explained a lot. When Betty pushed the mask back in place, Erica held it firmly and breathed deep. Neither said another word.

Edwards

Chapter 7 – James and Elsbeth

It was true the SDD wanted to travel with Erica. Agent Cox told her, but Erica didn't want to travel with them. Arlo helped her get away.

He bought her supplies, again, and he brought them to her apartment. Opening the door to see him with all her necessary materials was like the times she'd invited people to her blackmailer's club, expectations high but cautious at the same time. It could be the beginning of something great or a thing that would destroy her.

"I think you're smart to distance yourself from them considering how it turned out for Mati. She has not been heard from since the trial," Arlo told her when he handed over the canvas bag of provisions. "So what about your things at the bank? Are you taking them?" He stepped inside and shut the door.

She shook her head. "Going on foot. Would be too much." She set the bag on the counter. He watched her unload it. "Heading north to get away from the southern settlements altogether."

"And go where? I mean, how far north do you expect to go?"

"Up to Trellis or beyond."

"That far huh? You do realize that's highly mountainous up there and Quirni has at least three deadly types of animals that think humans are a treat?"

Erica gave him a frustrated frown. "Fine, will go to Trellis. There be people there who deadly types of animals can eat instead of me."

Arlo stared at her without blinking.

"Need to go that far at least until this business with Matilda dies down."

"It's already been six years. That won't die down until she's caught and killed or they blame someone else for the Cobal disaster."

"There be time," Erica replied stubbornly. She found a large bottle of vitamins and held them up with an eyebrow raised in question.

"You will need them if you try to survive on Quirni plants

but – uh – you will have to come back for more if you plan to be gone that long."

She smiled at his attempt to see her again then set them amongst the dried fruit and meats, all of which were sealed so dogs wouldn't be attracted. She had learned her lesson after the candy bar and had asked him to pack resealable containers too. "If you say," she agreed.

He dug in the bag and picked out a second bottle he had bought. He rattled it. "Take one every day and get some more if you run out."

She nodded but smiled as if he were nuts. She wouldn't try going into another town again.

He set the bottle back down and watched her for a while. "You aren't really going to Trellis are you?" he asked. "It's illegal to go there."

That caught her by surprise. She paused in her packing and looked up. "Why?"

"Because that is where all of the murderers from Sirrus and Marril are, the criminals who were sent here before Quirni was claimed. They are the original settlers of Quirni. They were sent to Trellis when the claimants came. Only the Delegate is supposed to have contact with them."

Criminals were there? They were her sort. "You mean the Delegate keeps the children of those people and their great grandchildren separate? Thought it was another claim now."

"No, it's not a claim." He shrugged. "I don't know why they are still kept separate. I just know it's illegal to go there."

Erica sighed. That meant if the SDD really wanted her, they would have a reason to take her. She would have to make sure she wasn't caught.

"Guess I'll find out. Can't stay in the south. Has been proven. And the SDD has some sort of plan for me and I'm not interested. Will make myself scarce." She scanned the provisions. Arlo, once again, had done a fine job. "You be a blessing. Thanks." She started to pack her backpack.

He didn't seem as happy as she was. "Just try and stay alive. If the SDD wants you for something then it has to do with Matilda."

"So…" she agreed and it made her stomach queasy. She sighed and paused in her packing. She looked at him. "Arlo, if you should hear anything has happened to me-" He waited for her to go on. She half thought she shouldn't say it. It could get him in trouble. If the SDD did try to steal her money they might

The Marrilian

take her belongings too. Well, she trusted Arlo more than anyone else on the planet. "If *anything* happens, my stuff in lock up be yours." She reached in her pocket and took out the keycards. She held them out. "You keep these. Use them if need be or, mayhaps, if all goes well, you might send me something from my bags. Either way, would my computer be yours and not seized if a thing happens. Take it before any Delegate agent gets it."

Arlo stepped forward. He took the cards from her fingers and looked at them. "I'll hold on to them but hope I never use them except for your sake." He turned them over in his hand then put them in his wallet.

Erica smiled. It was a genuine smile which she didn't use often. She had learned to smile in many different ways to appease others but most of them felt like tacky tape on her lips. Arlo brought out the smile she never tried to change. If she had been free to enjoy her life she would have spent time with him both on her feet and off. "A kindness, thank you."

He shifted his weight uncomfortably and glanced around the room. "Yeah, well, I've gotten used to you. I've been sort of an outcast myself since the deal with Mati." He brought his eyes back to hers. "Everyone knows I left my job to work with her. When I returned I wasn't too popular. I'm sorry to see you go. You're the sort of girl I like, not a prude like most are on this planet."

Erica felt a twang in her heart. She wanted that time off her feet even more. She wanted to make him happy but she couldn't afford to stay. She was feeling better, too much so. Soon the SDD would launch whatever plans they had for her. "Not to worry, we'll see each other again."

How many lives could the Kinsley's ruin? She began to pack her bag forcefully but her anger died quickly when she thought of the programs she had put on Arlo's banking computer. She paused and looked up at him. "Arlo," saying his name made his eyes brighten and he smiled. She liked that. "Arlo, that computer of mine be pretty special. Take good care of it. Use it, but take good care of it."

That perplexed him but he tried to smile. "I will. More important, you take care. I wouldn't be surprised if the SDD wants you to be a double for Matilda. If you were, the planet would stop harassing her and attack you instead. They have protected her for something and you look so much like her you could be used like that."

Erica had thought of that and it upset her.

Arlo grimaced. "It's an awful thought, I know."

"Betty said they would never hurt me."

"I could be wrong but I wouldn't help you leave if I thought they were really protecting you. They have plans. They have left you alone to heal but it won't last."

"She looks enough like me they could give her my identity and get her off planet."

"You do look that much like her," Arlo confirmed. "But what would she do on another planet?"

Erica didn't know. "Blasted Delegate bastards."

Arlo put his arms around her. "I'm sorry. I didn't mean to scare you like that. Getting beaten up for her is a sick thought. I just figured you would have already considered that angle." He rubbed her back.

She rested her head against his shirt. She could hear his heart beating with the hearing aid. Good lords, she remembered how Levitus had commented she had a hearing aid like Matilda and it was even in the same ear. "You may be right," she said scared and quiet. "Seems possible." Still, what would they gain?

Arlo hugged her tighter. "Just get away from them."

She nodded. The more she thought about it, the more she agreed. Whatever they wanted her for, it was not going to be something she was going to enjoy. She did not want to be anywhere near the spotlight.

Arlo walked with her to the edge of town when Amon rose. She kissed him on the cheek and then left. This time she travelled differently. She stayed by the road rather than walk through the woods. She walked during the night until Thoth rose then found a tall, thickly leaved tree with a nice cradle of branches where she could sleep. Dogs, she now believed, did hunt at night and they hunted in the woods. She had just been lucky before.

The nights were cooler after it misted or rained for the evening. Sometimes a light snow fell but she had recovered her warm leather coat and she had a thermal blanket, gloves, a new wide brimmed leather hat with a warm lining and a scarf that she could wrap over her ears. She traveled slowly in order to keep her lungs clear and she hid when the roads became busy. She made certain no one saw her. It took three weeks to reach Cluny this time.

The closer she got to the town, the more her stomach churned, and the heavier her feet seemed to feel. Zoe wouldn't keep quiet when she spotted the same tree she'd used before. She commented on how stupid it was to return to the spot and told

The Marrilian

Erica anyone with any sense would know that.

The tree rose over the village tall as a tower, one she would once again use to watch the people of the horrible little town. The bowl of branches were the same when she climbed up to them. She settled her bag against the trunk, stretched out, and sneered down at the creatures inhabiting Cluny. The people lived on so happy and so oblivious. This time she intended to walk through the center of town with her gun drawn.

She would do it at night and hoped to get through without attracting any attention but if they came after her again they would regret it.

The wait gave her time with her thoughts. Someone had intervened at the water trough. They were damn late but they had stopped the crowd from hurting her more.

Who? She knew it had been an agent of the SDD but she had never learned which agent. It wasn't Cox. She knew his voice. He had found her coat and bag. She had forgotten about the other agent until now. Her brain worked that way, forgetting the bad stuff. Would he still be in Cluny? Could he help her if things went wrong again?

It wouldn't be wise to hope for that.

She settled into the crotch of the branches and ate Quirni's version of a wild potato.

The people who lived in the clean little houses walked in slow easy strides as if nothing had happened, as if they hadn't nearly killed her.

"Just go on and live your perfect, blasted little lives," she muttered as she glowered down at them. "Pissers."

Later in the day a woman tended a garden in her front yard. She drew water from a well down the street and walked back to her yard. The weather was so mild flowers grew even when it got colder. The woman returned several times to water all the gardens in her perfect blasted yard.

"Must be nice to waste an entire day like that," Erica murmured acidly. As much as she wanted to live in one of those nice houses and relax, she couldn't. Instead she had to do the tree sitting thing.

The scent of horses drifted up to her as the breeze shifted. Now that was what she wanted, a horse. She had actually ridden a horse when she was about seven. What freedom. Her heart quickened at the memory.

The money she had deposited at the bank was supposed to rent her property. The horses she'd seen in the pastures and on the streets were as pretty as the dogs. Horses had been a large part of her plan. She had wanted land, horses and to learn how to ride them. She wanted to spend her days with the magnificent beasts, but now, she couldn't even have a house despite all her wealth.

She drew another deep breath to catch the scent again and almost coughed. The leaves hid her well and she was high enough that she felt secure smoking a cigarette. The smoke diffused among the leaves so she just had the butt to worry about. When she finished the smoke she scrubbed out the hot end on the trunk then dropped it. She passed the morning and afternoon smoking more antidote, dozing off, and waiting for dark. She would cross the river before Amon rose.

In the late afternoon she heard someone coming down the road. The clop, clop of their horses' hooves reached her ears before their voices. The branches and leaves she sat in were thick but by leaning she could see the road. Two people rode down it. They wore brown uniforms and brown caps with black brims. SDD agents? Here? They approached slowly. Erica's chest constricted. She gazed down at the pair until she started to feel dizzy and realized she was holding her breath. She straightened to hide as they came near. They stopped below her and she could hear them talking.

"How can she disappear? She's right here," the man protested.

"I don't know. She's close. Did you hear yourself?" the woman asked.

"Yeah," he replied. His head swiveled as he looked around.

Erica heard it too. She had a hard time accepting it but she heard it, the voice of the man with about a two second delay repeated through some sort of device. Somehow, they could hear themselves because she was near. They could hear themselves through her. Her heart thumped hard at the implications of that.

The horses scuffed their hooves as the man and woman turned them to peer into the woods. "I can't-" the man started but the woman interrupted him with a gesture. Several quiet moments passed then the horses walked towards town.

Erica leaned ever so carefully to watch them around the other side of the tree. They were framed by gently swaying leaves. She stretched her neck to see them through the small hole when the breeze blew. The agents stopped about forty feet away. The woman held a small computer flipped open. She turned her horse. Erica leaned back as the woman pointed at the tree where she hid. They had her pinpointed. They had a positioning device on her and Erica had thought she had been so slick to escape. She shook her head in dismay and dropped it against the branch. *Say it Zoe, I am an idiot.* Zoe didn't offer any criticism.

They would find her unless they were complete morons. Their horses started back.

Erica didn't want them to know she had seen the computer or heard them. That could be valuable to her later. She lay on the branch and eased herself into a sleeping position. Perhaps they would believe she had been sleeping and never heard a thing. Perhaps this was the stupidest thing she had done yet but she could think of nothing else.

Blasted SDD! Had they heard everything she said? When did they put the device on her?

Relax, she thought. She would think about that later.

She had talked out loud to Zoe. Good lords, what had she said?

Quiet. Put all thoughts away. She closed her eyes and willed each muscle in her body to relax. Stop the thoughts. Stop the worries. There was nothing she could do about this right now. Sleep.

Soon she relaxed so much her foot slid down the trunk and landed on her bag. It scraped the bark and made a small sound. The agents heard it.

"Up there," the woman said quietly. "No wonder we couldn't find her, we never looked up."

"Where?" the man asked.

They were silent for several moments then feint whispers drifted up followed by the crunch of feet in brittle twigs and leaves. Erica chose that moment to react. She feigned waking, as if startled by the sound. She sat up too fast and slipped off her branch. She grabbed the tree as her bag and hat fell to the ground. The agents jumped back in alarm. Nice. She saw her bag tumble onto man. She clung to the limb thirty feet above them, but her eyes had trailed it down. She couldn't have planned whacking an agent better if she had tried.

She swung herself back up and gazed down at the agents, who she half expected would be aiming guns. Instead they looked up dumbly, or at least the man did. He stood by the tree with one hand holding his head and his other hand on a low branch. He looked like he was ready to climb.

Erica lay belly down on her branch and stared at them in what she thought should be surprise and disgust. The man gazed up at her then bent and picked up his cap. He didn't put it back on but held it. He wore a smile as he gazed up. The woman kept her head lowered so her face was hidden by her cap.

"Lynn?" he called.

Erica's eyes narrowed. Her lip curled.

"You have been sleeping?" he asked loudly. "Hello. We were looking for you."

The woman looked up to hear her answer. She took off her cap and still had to crane her neck severely to see Erica from the base of the tree, which was the only place free enough of leaves to see.

Erica scowled at them.

"Uh-" the woman started to say then seemed to be struggling with herself and looked back at the man. She put her cap back on. Erica thought she heard her laughing.

"We are supposed to make sure you are safe," the man added and glanced at the woman.

She took her cap off again and craned her neck around to look up. She smiled broadly. "You need to cross the river here in Cluny so we came to see you made it all right," she said. She sounded too happy. Erica suspected she *had* been laughing but at what?

"Yeah," the man agreed and grinned up at Erica like it was normal for SDD to help people cross rivers.

"You follow," Erica finally accused and did her best to sound mad but why was the agent laughing? "You followed from the City. How the hell have you done that? Haven't seen a soul."

"You have to use the bridge don't you?" asked the woman. "We knew you would be here sooner or later. And well," she saw something on the ground and picked it up. She practically leapt for it like it would save her "We saw your cigarette butts. You have left a few of them around. You haven't been hard to keep up with being on foot so it left us time to look." She tossed the butt back at the base of the tree, glanced at the man, and then looked up once again with a smile.

Clever woman, Erica thought. If she hadn't seen the tracking computer she might have believed that.

'You would,' Zoe commented dully.

Ah go to hell, Erica thought at the voice and deflated on the tree limb.

'That would be too much fun for you,' the voice commented. Erica sneered at it.

"Are you coming down?" the man called up and sounded

The Marrilian

hopeful.

"'Tis light out," Erica told him. "There be a whole town ahead. Would be stupid."

He looked over his shoulder at Cluny. "They won't hurt you with us along." He rested his hand against the tree trunk so he could lean and see her without bending his neck so far. He was handsome in a cute way, hardly the rough SDD look she expected except for his shoulders being wide and round. His dark blond hair fell in his eyes. He pushed it out of his way, running his fingers through it and back. "They already got in trouble once for attacking you. They know you're not Mati now."

Mati? Not Matilda? He must know her. She didn't reply. He smiled up with such a boyish grin she frowned. She liked that sort of face on a man. Her heart leapt. She clamped her teeth together hard. Staying upset with him was going to be a difficult challenge.

"Come on down," he coaxed in a tone that made her want to go, or at least some part of her.

"No thank you," Erica replied resolutely. Cluny was way too close.

"We won't let anything happen to you," the woman insisted. "We're SDD. They won't attack you while you're with us. You can bet on it."

"Will bet on it when it gets dark. You can go now," Erica told them. Fat chance she thought. "Will be down later."

"We'll wait," the man replied. He and the woman spoke for a while in hushed tones before she looked back up at Erica.

"Lynn, if we get you a horse, will you ride with us?" she asked. "We are going to follow you anyways. You will be safer with us and if you are on a horse you can outrun any problems. How about it?"

Erica lay along the branch with her ankles crossed and her toes hooked to either side of it. She let her arm fall and swing. Her chin rested on her other hand. Her hat had fallen next to her bag below so now her hair hung in a tangled mess. She typically had it tucked up in the hat.

"Will I ever to get away from you people?" she called down. "What the hell do you want?" If they were Marrilian she could imagine half a dozen answers but they weren't Marrilian. As far as she knew, the QSDD and MSDD didn't prosecute each other's criminals.

They both shrugged and smiled up dumbly. No answer. Erica was too smart to ever believe any SDD was dumb, especially any with rank. These two appeared to have that. She couldn't see how much since she was too far away but the insignia on their ties and shoulders looked fancy. She wouldn't be getting away from them especially with a GPS device tracking her and a horse would be wonderful. She could ride until she found the device and destroyed it.

"Very well," she agreed although reluctantly. "Get the horse and will come down but can't ride one bit." And she would just have to hope they didn't tie her up and drag her off someplace.

The woman nudged the man in the ribs. "Something gentle. Go."

The man mounted his animal and trotted into town. At the crossroads he stopped to ask a question then hurried off to the west side of town.

The woman collected the horse she had been riding and another animal that wore a bulky assortment of packs. She led them off the path and let both of them graze below the tree. The animals were out of site of the road unless someone looked amongst the shadows as they passed.

"By the way, my name is Elsbeth," the SDD woman called up. "My partner is James."

"Pleasure," Erica said but didn't sound like she meant it. "And by the way, prefer to be called Erica."

"I thought you were going by your legal name."

Erica snorted. "General White told you that."

"Yes," Elsbeth replied. She stretched her neck to one side then the other. "Why don't you come down? It's not pleasant talking to you like this. Plus, the townspeople are going to wonder why I'm talking to a tree."

Erica had already thought of that. If someone passed and did happen to see the agent talking to the tree it would look odd especially since the other agent had just gone into town to buy an extra horse. Erica sighed at the imposition but she climbed down.

"That's better," said Elsbeth when Erica stood beside her. "I've been looking forward to meeting you. I know your cousin." She put out her hand to shake but Erica ignored it.

"How nice," Erica replied and glanced towards the road to see how much she could see of it. It was too much. A good twenty feet was visible through various parts of the undergrowth. She stepped into the woods out of sight.

Elsbeth followed her partway. She was at least six inches taller than Erica. She looked strong and tough. Her dark red hair hung well down her back in a braid. She had freckles across her nose, light skin. Her high cheekbones and a narrow chin made her look impish. Her eyes were light brown with a nearly crystalline quality. They were bright and clear. This woman was no idiot and no one Erica would take lightly. She glanced at the insignia on her tie. She was a major. She was definitely no idiot.

Elsbeth regarded Erica as if she tried to decide what to make of her. She lowered her hand. "She's a nice person. She didn't do any of the things of which they accuse her."

"Really," Erica replied in a flat tone that let Elsbeth know she didn't believe her and she wasn't interested. There was a wide tree she could hide behind if needed so she leaned her shoulder against it to be close and crossed her arms over her chest.

"Really," Elsbeth repeated as her smile started to fade.

Erica watched the horses. "Well, good criminals never plead guilty, do they?"

"I suppose," Elsbeth agreed almost reluctantly and fell quiet.

The horses munched along the grass towards Erica who hoped to say no more. Elsbeth crossed her arms over her chest and turned away so she could watch the road. With the conversation brought to an end, she and Erica waited for James in silence.

He returned with a dark palomino. When Erica saw the horse her heart jumped. He was beautiful. In fact they both were, the man and the horse. When the man's eyes caught Erica's her heart not only jumped but felt like it skipped to a stop. His serene smile disarmed her. He had gentle eyes and a sweet, boyish face that weakened her knees. It was so strange but she felt as if she knew his character, as if she knew him heart and soul. She knew what to expect from him. He would be kind, compassionate, have a temper but be slow to react. He was a man who could complete her life. Looking at him felt like a blessing.

People in Tenpole described what it meant to find the right partner. It was everything she felt. They claimed the feelings would well up in the heart at first sight. She closed her mouth, stiffened her back, and dropped her eyes to the grass. He was SDD!

He rode his horse into the tall grass and led the palomino by its reins. He spoke. "This is Turnbull."

Her heart skipped again. It hurt. Her breath caught. He seemed proud of his acquisition but his pride was so understated and pleasant, not the boasting of so many men.

"He is one of Turnings," he added to Elsbeth as if that should mean something.

Edwards

Elsbeth nodded her approval as Erica recovered. She couldn't be attracted to SDD! She would not look at him. She centered her attention on the horse which James had led up to her. She reached out a trembling hand and touched its muzzle. It felt like velvet. Thick whiskers poked out from the velvet. Turnbull stretched his neck and snuffed at her face, exhaling large amounts of air. He tickled her nose with his whiskers. Erica backed away. He tossed his head and then began to graze at her feet. James draped the reins over the palomino's saddle.

"Turning's horses are known for being gentle," he said. He dismounted and came around his horse so he could pat Turnbull's neck.

Erica kept her eyes down. James' presence felt like a protective blanket. She suppressed a shudder. She had only felt this safe once before but that man was gone, Vincent, left behind on Marril. This wasn't the same anyway. This was deeper. This wasn't just safe but complete, warm, comforting. She suspected the feelings meant this agent was her *life*, the one meant for her. If so she couldn't, shouldn't, deny her feelings. That would lead to a nothing but pain.

She had learned about *life* from the ladies at her house, how to recognize it, what to do about it. It made her weak to think any SDD could be that for her. She raised her eyes to the insignia on his tie, a captain. A captain. He would be committed to his career.

"Let's get your bag stowed," he suggested and retrieved Erica's gear. He held out her hat to her. She took it without looking at him and put it on. He secured her bag behind her saddle. He didn't even look in it. He strapped it down then returned and started explaining the basics of riding. Erica tried to listen but she couldn't focus on anything and she couldn't look at him. She let her eyes fall to his chest.

"Do you understand?" he asked her gently and bent to see under the brim of her hat. His eyes were bright blue and happy. She gaped at him. "Can you do it?" he prodded.

"So," she replied, nearly choked to see him like that. He was perfect. "Uh, yes."

He reached for her. "Come here. I'll help you up."

He touched her arm, pulled her towards him and the horse. She had to move with him or pull away from his touch. She didn't want to pull away. He got behind her and put his hands on her waist to position her beside the animal.

"You are trembling. It's all right," he assured her. He leaned over her shoulder to see her face. "Turnbull will be good."

Before she knew what he intended, he lifted her up and over the back of the horse. She tried to thank him for his help, to respond somehow, but she only squeaked as her legs eased over the saddle. James settled her lightly. It was as if she didn't weigh anything for him. Could these people be that strong or had she lost that much weight? He gathered the reins and placed them in her hands. His fingers were course in places. His hands were large and tan. Hers were thin, pale and disappeared under half of his but his touch was light and gentle.

"Pull his head up," he instructed.

She tugged on the reins but Turnbull pulled back. She ended up splayed on his neck with the reins falling free. They fell to the ground.

James held her arm to stop her fall. He helped her sit back up. "It's all right." Turnbull continued to graze. "You have to keep your toes up, your heels down, and settle into the seat," James explained again. "Try leaning back a little to put some weight in your pull." He handed her the reins once more.

She tried to pull Turnbull's head up. He completely ignored her.

"Turnbull," James scolded gently.

The horse shook his head, as if a fly bothered him but there weren't any flies around. Then he continued to eat.

"Seems he won't have me."

Elsbeth chuckled. "You don't have a seat." She went around the horse and adjusted the stirrup higher. James adjusted the other one. "He knows you haven't got a clue." She took the reins and got on her own horse. "I'll lead you for now all right?"

Erica had no idea if it was all right or not. She sat on the animal and that was that and it was still light and Elsbeth mounted her horse. James mounted his horse. They started towards the town. They almost left the woods. Now? In broad daylight? Erica jumped off.

"No," she told them breathlessly. She retreated back into the woods. The agents stopped and looked back at her. Turnbull stopped and looked as well. She backed away from them. "Will not go during light." Her voice sounded high and stressed and she didn't bother to hide her accent.

Elsbeth and James glanced at each other. They both turned their horses and got off them. "We understand," Elsbeth agreed kindly. "We'll wait for dark." They led the horses back into the woods and found a comfortable place to sit and wait. James used

Edwards

the time to go back into Cluny and buy provisions. When he returned they ate cold sandwiches.

Soon after the sun set they mounted again. "Can you do it this time?" Elsbeth asked. "We are simply going to ride through the town and cross the bridge. Cluny will be well behind us before Thoth rises."

Erica shuddered at the thought of going through the town. She had planned to do just this, to go through once it got dark and to walk down the center of the streets but when it came right to it, she doubted she could have done it. Returning to Cluny terrified her.

"You can ride between us," suggested James. "The only way someone will see you is if they walk up to us with a lantern and we won't let them do that."

"We are armed," Elsbeth added. "No one can hurt you."

They waited for her reply. Erica already sat on the horse and she planned to ride with them so what had she expected to happen but this? Horses didn't sneak through the woods and grass. They walked down roads. That was what the roads were for. She supposed she hadn't considered that far ahead. That was so like her. She felt disgusted at herself. That disgust translated into determination to make the best of her stupidity. She wouldn't back out. She'd keep her word.

"So," she agreed. "Can do it. Let's go."

Elsbeth pulled Turnbull up beside her own horse and they headed out with James and the packhorse on one side and Elsbeth on the other.

They saw no one in the streets. They passed houses with feint lights glowing inside and occasional laughter or loud conversation. They walked the horses down the same stretch of road that Erica had been dragged a few months earlier.

Turnbull pranced and started at Erica's trembling but Elsbeth held him.

"Relax," James urged. Erica wasn't sure if he spoke to her or the horse.

"Here's the bridge," Elsbeth announced as the clomp of the horses hooves sounded upon it.

As they crossed, Erica twisted and looked back at the town. No one was there. No one had come out of the houses. Could she have walked down the street that night? If she had, would she have simply stolen what she needed then walked over the bridge and been gone? There would have been no lines in the wheat to warn of an intruder. The barking dogs would have meant

The Marrilian

nothing. She wouldn't have need to shoot them. They would have been barking like they always did.

She faced forward. If's and could-have-beens were all shit. She put them out of her head. She was past Cluny. That was what mattered.

As the night progressed the agents started to talk. Erica didn't join their conversations even though Elsbeth and James tried to include her but she told them she had to concentrate on riding.

She didn't want to be rude. They had just bought her a horse, gotten her through Cluny, and they both seemed like nice people. Her excuse, however, caused James to explain once again how she should sit and hold the reins and that brought him too close.

She had never been attracted to a man before and it blasted everything to pure hell that she liked one now. Her *life*? Could he be?

He held the reins out to her and went through the basics while she nodded repeatedly. None of the instruction helped, probably because she was so distracted, so when James was done Erica returned to sliding around on the saddle and not being able to keep Turnbull's head up. Elsbeth took the reins back and returned to leading the animal so Erica could hold on.

Eventually the agents fell quiet. Elsbeth changed the rig on Turnbull so she could lead him with a rope rather than the reins. Erica was supposed to keep the reins in her hands, as if riding, and get used to holding them instead of the saddle. The agents broke apart and Elsbeth led Turnbull from ahead while James trailed behind, bracketing Erica between them.

In the morning, at Erica's insistence, they stopped. The agents gave each other a look that Erica didn't understand. It seemed to her they knew each other so well they could speak volumes with such looks.

They set up camp by a little stream. Erica collected wild carrots and potatoes while James produced meat from the packhorse bags and cooked it in actual metal pans. The vegetables delighted the agents. Erica enjoyed them cooked with their spices. She had been eating them raw since she carried one small pan and that she used to boil water.

"Would you like to bathe?" asked Elsbeth once they had eaten. "We have all day since you don't want to ride until after dark. We can warm water for you."

Edwards

Erica hadn't washed in so long she knew she stank and her clothes felt like she had mud crusted in every seam. "So very much," she agreed with a hopeful smile. "Mayhaps rinse my clothes too."

"Definitely," Elsbeth agreed and smiled back. She filled all of their pans and set them around the fire. "It won't take long to heat," she told her. She added a few drops of chemical purifier to each pan. "When it's warm I'll pour it over you. Get your clothes off. James will refill the pots as long as you want."

Erica started to remove her coat right there.

Elsbeth cocked an eyebrow. "I have a towel for you," she suggested.

"For drying?" Erica asked. She worked at her belt and looked up at Elsbeth. "So?"

Elsbeth considered how to respond, glanced at James whose eyes were wide as he watched.

"Yeah, for drying," Elsbeth muttered. "James, go get it for her."

He heard his name and jerked his head around. "Huh?"

"Go get a towel for her."

"A towel?"

"Yes, a towel."

He got up with an annoyed bend in his mouth.

Erica tossed her coat on the log next to James' spot and dropped her pants in a heap around her ankles. She kicked them aside and started on her shirt buttons. They actually had so much mud on some of them, she had to crack it to get the buttons through the holes.

James tossed the towel in Elsbeth's face and returned to his seat on the log.

"Erica, come over here," Elsbeth suggested. "We don't need to give James a show."

"A show?"

Elsbeth blinked at her.

Erica pulled her shirt off and dropped it on her pants.

"Or for lords sake," Elsbeth complained and took Erica's arm. "You shouldn't undress right in front of a man." She led them to a grassy area where the water would drain away from camp and held up the towel.

Erica didn't know how she could avoid undressing in front of him when he was in the camp.

"Continue," Elsbeth told her. "James, check the water temperature," she called back to him.

The Marrilian

Erica removed her tank top and undergarments. She tossed those aside and stood naked behind the towel then waited to see how Elsbeth would poor the water over her and hold the towel at the same time. James clanked around the pans while Elsbeth stood with the towel raised and her face drawing into a frown.

"I guess you will have to do without privacy while I pour the water over you," she finally realized.

"So," Erica agreed. "Privacy be nothing. 'Tis fine."

Elsbeth didn't seem so sure about that. She glanced back at James.

"Doesn't bother me a bit," Erica told her. She didn't like to show her scars but most of those were on her back so if James had to see her, she would simply not turn her back to him. Easy enough.

With a long, hard sigh, Elsbeth lowered the towel. James pulled one of the pans from the fire. "This is good," he said and offered it as Elsbeth came over.

Dirt sluiced off Erica's face and shoulders. James walked over pans and Elsbeth soaked her hair. Erica soaped it, let Elsbeth rinse, and then asked if she might wash it again.

"Certainly," Elsbeth agreed.

Erica scrubbed it clean and enjoyed the warm water. Then she used a cloth to scrub at her body. Elsbeth rinsed her off as James kept the pans coming, using hotter water to warm the cold. Erica scrubbed every spot twice. Once she was clean she dried with the towel and then turned her face to the warm Quirni sun.

"Let me get out the tangles," Elsbeth suggested.

Erica opened her eyes to see what she meant and found the agent with a comb and brush. "You would brush my hair?"

"It's a mess, Erica. I don't think you could get through it as fast as I could. Do you mind me doing it for you?"

Sort of, she did, but Elsbeth was no General White. She wasn't anything like Razi either. Erica had never met such nice people, agents or otherwise, except for Arlo. What would it hurt to accept her help?

"Go ahead, please," Erica said and turned her back to her.

Elsbeth worked for a long time to straighten all of tangles. She talked most of the time too, telling stories about her younger sister and how she used to brush her hair, and how she knew it felt good to have clean hair. Erica learned she kept her hair in a braid because of a Delegate uniform rule.

When she finished James gave Erica some clean clothes,

pants that were dark brown canvas, and a dark green button down shirt along with undergarments. "'Tis my size," Erica commented as she held the pants up to herself and looked at the agents. Neither of them could get one leg in the pants she held.

Elsbeth shrugged. "We knew we'd be traveling with you sooner or later and you couldn't have carried much so we bought you a few things."

Erica stared. She couldn't imagine what to say. No one had ever bought her anything unless they wanted her to pleasure them. She waited for them to ask. They didn't. "Thank you?" she told them. "'Would you something in return?" Her gaze stopped on James, questioning, expectant.

"You're welcome," James replied. "We don't need anything except for you to get dressed."

Erica stared at him, puzzled. Elsbeth and James exchanged one of their long looks. They said nothing more so she dressed.

Elsbeth retrieved another piece of clothing before she put the outer shirt on over a lightweight tank top. "You need this too. Wear it under your shirt so it can't be seen."

It was a vest of dark brown fabric. It had a wide hook and loop tape closure in the front and it looked like it was quilted.

"Why?" Erica asked. She took it from her to look at it closer. The padding in it was actually little hardened plates of fabric.

"I know we bragged you wouldn't be attacked as long as you are with us but we can't protect you against everything," Elsbeth explained. She pulled the vest open and held it for her. "This is arrow proof, bullet proof, and knife proof. We want you to wear it."

"For protection?" Erica asked.

"Of course to protect you," James said and smiled at her apprehension.

Erica tried to return his smile but she was too stunned.

Elsbeth jiggled the vest. "Come on."

After Erica slipped into it, Elsbeth settled it on her shoulders then turned her around and ran her hand down the front. It molded around her breasts as if they had measured the thing for her.

Elsbeth returned to the fire. One of the pots now had food in it. She stirred it. Other pots had water, soap and Erica's dirty things.

Erica settled down to watch. Elsbeth and James made lunch, served it, and then pulled her old clothes out of the pot and rinsed them in another. Erica had expected them to burn the

The Marrilian

things they were so dirty. When they were done they tied a line between some trees at the edge of the camp and hung them there to dry. Once all the chores were done Erica and Elsbeth sat on a log that James had rolled to the fireside and flattened into three rough seats with a small axe.

It didn't take long before Elsbeth was up again. The colorful, flapping birds that had invaded their camp since they stopped suddenly bothered her. She cursed at them and chased them away. Some of them hopped up into trees to look down while others flapped around her head or on the ground, staying just out of reach.

James took Elsbeth's vacated seat, much to Erica's dismay. He tossed the wood chips from the log he had shaped into the fire. "Are you comfortable in the vest?" He didn't look at her, thankfully, because he brushed bits of wood chips from his uniform.

Erica couldn't speak. She watched him and grunted a sort of 'sure' sound then pulled her eyes away. She held her hands up to the fire. She wasn't cold but she trembled.

Elsbeth kicked at one of the yellow birds that landed by her foot. It was relentless. It jumped away from the kick and flapped up and onto Elsbeth's shoulder. She shooed it away but it hopped to her arm and nipped at her hand. It had no fear. "Damn these things!" Elsbeth growled. She shook her arm violently. The bird hovered above her while she swung at it, missing repeatedly.

James ignored her. "Is the vest rubbing on you anywhere?" he asked.

Lords, another question? She had to answer. She couldn't just grunt at him all day. "No," she said and glanced at him. Oh why did she look at him? Every time she did her mind went numb. But she *liked* to look at him. He had the sweetest face she had ever seen. She wanted to stare at him.

"Erica, we won't get half as far traveling by night as we would by day," he said. "We have to go so much slower in the dark. You are protected with the vest. What do you think about traveling by day?"

He had said her name.

"Would you be willing?" he prodded.

Willing? What? She looked at him again and wondered what the hell he was saying.

"Can we travel by day now that you have the vest?" he asked. His eyes were wide and hopeful.

134

Edwards

She stared into them and wanted to do whatever he wanted not even sure what that was but it was something about riding. She pulled her gaze away from his. It was madness to do what SDD wanted! Wasn't it?

"Travelling in the dark makes it harder for us to see too. It's easier to protect you if we travel by day. Are you all right with that?"

Oh, he wanted to travel when it was light. Would two agents be enough to stop another Cluny? Where they going somewhere that it mattered when they got there? Her stomach constricted in apprehension.

A thick leaf popped in the fire and a glob of sap shot into the air. She twisted away from it.

James cursed in surprise and jerked back from the hot glob too. "Damn me, I put a churl leaf in," he complained sheepishly as he watched the sap cool on the ground behind them.

"Seems so," Erica replied as she watched the glob sink out of site. She had no idea what the hell a churl leaf was but felt grateful it had changed the subject. When she raised her head, her eyes caught his. They both stared while she blissfully forgot his question.

"Stupid, friggin' birds!" Elsbeth bellowed. Erica and James both looked across the camp to see why Elsbeth was so upset. She shook her fist at the canopy of trees where a dozen birds hopped along the branches. "Damn thing got my bracelet!" she told them. She pulled back the sleeve of her uniform to show her wrist while walking back to the fire. "Do you see that? A metal bracelet for a damn bird! It grabbed it right off my wrist!" The hurt in her voice was palpable.

Erica scanned the branches. Sure enough a yellow bird held a twinkling object. Other birds gathered around it and tried to peck the bracelet away.

"Mayhaps it will drop it," Erica suggested although she was not at all convinced. She had seen the birds in action enough. She could shoot it but she didn't expect the agents would care for her brandishing her gun. Then again, they had let her keep it. Erica frowned as she wondered why they had done that. The bird continued to hop. It flew to another branch farther away.

"No," Elsbeth groaned sadly. "Come on. Come back." She watched it go. The bird took another short flight to keep its prize safe. Elsbeth sat down and fell quiet. She looked like she could cry.

Erica actually felt sorry for the woman. The bird was still

close enough to have a good shot. She put her hand on her gun. "Mayhaps I could shoot it?" She leaned forward to see Elsbeth around James. "But I might hit your bracelet."

James snorted. "Feel free," he said offhandedly like he didn't expect her to.

Elsbeth shook her head. "Don't waste the bullet. It's too far away and flying all over the place. It's just that bracelet was a gift, and I hate to lose it."

Erica looked for the bird again. "Not too far."

Elsbeth perked up and looked for the bird. It was easy to find since every other bird tried to get close. "You think you can?"

Erica nodded. Elsbeth looked hopeful.

The bird hopped on a low branch no more than thirty feet away. Erica drew her gun, released the clip, and set the pistol aside on the log between her and James. She pulled two bullets from one of her pockets. James watched her closely as she picked up her pistol, her eyes on the bird so she wouldn't lose it, and slid the clip into place. She cocked the weapon. She aimed and fired. Elsbeth jumped off the log.

"She hit it!" James yelled.

Elsbeth gaped in disbelief then sprinted to the dead animal before any other birds could take the prize. She strode back with a smile on her face. "You can shoot!" she told Erica. "You can really shoot!" She dangled the bracelet before them then wrapped her hand around it protectively.

Erica understood from their reaction that they hadn't seen any of her records yet. They would have known she had won tournaments on Marril for target shooting if they had. It had been a thing her father has insisted upon and it was the one thing she had continued to do with him. She had met a lot of powerful people at the gun clubs and learned a whole lot about them.

Elsbeth stood over Erica and inspected the damage on the bracelet as James retrieved the carcass of the bird. "Would anyone care for roasted foul?" he asked with a grin. "I haven't had one of these in ages."

Erica grimaced. "You eat those?" He held the bird by its legs. It hung well past the length of his arm. The bullet had pierced its chest, gone through the bird and been lost. Lead was by far the cheapest metal to import so Erica didn't mind. It was the casing that had true value. She collected that then unloaded her gun.

"They are a delicacy, very rich and meaty." He held the bird up to look at the hole Erica's bullet had made then added with a silly grin, "usually."

The thought of eating the animal made Erica somewhat ill.

James didn't notice her lack of enthusiasm. He plucked the bird, gut it and began cooking it right then. He and Elsbeth both ate and seemed to enjoy it but Erica shook her head when they offered her a share. They shrugged and split her share for seconds. Pots were scrubbed again and dishes were stowed and James kept on packing.

Erica watched him pick up more and more of the camp. He put away her clothes. He cleaned his axe. He didn't look like he intended to stay for dark. Elsbeth kept an eye on Erica for a while then seemed to make up her mind and got up to help him. She collapsed the tent.

Damn it, Erica thought, they intended to travel by day. Her stomach rolled with fear. Would the vest protect her? The arrow the Cluny man had shot had penetrated her backpack and still stuck in her. It had gone through cartons of cigarettes, clothes, and the backpack itself. She felt a cough beginning from her agitation. She lit up some antidote.

Soon the packing stopped and James came over to her. "Well?" he asked. "Shall we go?" As if to answer the question he put her hat on her head.

Erica looked up at him from under the brim. He gave her a broader version of the perpetual little smile that was always on his face. Of all the people for her to meet now he had to be the first man who could move her to do what *he* wanted. "Where to with such a hurry?" she asked dryly.

He smiled even wider but with a tip of his head and shrug of his shoulders. He almost did the Tenpole sign for 'who cares'. "North," he answered.

It was his smile that persuaded her to not argue. *Cute friggin' SDD agent,* she thought. Lords he had her heart completely. He had to be her *life*. She lowered her eyes and took a long draw off her cigarette. "Where North?"

"You'll see when we get there. You'll like it. I'll promise you that much."

Erica's mouth hardened. "Great," she muttered. She got up and tried not to complain but it wasn't easy. She would be going with them one way or another until she found the GPS device and destroyed it.

They left camp by early afternoon and followed the road northwest.

The Marrilian

As the town of Lakeview drew near, they passed too many people for Erica's comfort. The presence of the agents did make the people look the other way but not enough. People noticed her. One group of children on foot gawked at Erica and whispered to each other as she passed. The agents became nervous.

They pulled their horses up to either side of her when a group of five men on horseback appeared on the road in the distance.

"You should keep your hair down," Elsbeth said as she reached over and lifted Erica's hat to let her hair fall. "It's quite a bit lighter than Mati's especially now that it's clean." She added a short laugh.

James reached over and pushed the front of her hat down. He nodded ahead at the men.

"The less they see the better. There is no need to press our luck." He reached in Erica's coat pocket and pulled out her cigarettes. He bumped the pack and offered her one. "Why don't you smoke? Marrilians smoke. Native Quirni rarely do and your cousin is native. Plus, it's easy to see this isn't tobacco. It's blue steam not white smoke."

Erica nodded and lit the antidote. From that point on she dipped her chin, chain smoked any time she was around people, and allowed her hair to hide her face. They drew far fewer looks and no one stared.

They settled into a routine. They woke as the sun rose and ate a warm breakfast before breaking camp. James cooked and he would pack a lunch each morning that they ate while they rode, usually some sort of sandwich made from the cheeses and meats they carried on the packhorse. At the campfire each night Elsbeth and James talked and Erica listened. Sometimes she laughed. They were funny. They told her stories about other jobs and friends and especially other agents. Even when Erica brooded about her situation, they could make her laugh, especially James. He could be silly while Erica suspected he was nothing of the sort. She felt that part of him was misplaced. He had a good sense of humor but the silliness was an act for her, an attempt to charm her, as if he needed to.

Soon the town of Terns was behind them. While they rode, the agents taught her how to control her horse. Elsbeth was the better teacher so she showed Erica the amount of force to use on the reins and how to relax into the saddle so she moved with the horse rather than sitting upon him stiffly.

Edwards

When Erica finally understood and actually started to ride Turnbull rather than just sit on him, Elsbeth no longer had to lead. They didn't have to wait for Erica to resituate herself every time they turned a corner so they traveled faster. James appreciated the good time they were making. Erica accepted that they were going the direction she wanted and even though she dwelled on the tracking device she was beginning to enjoy riding with the agents. She admitted they were good company.

Still, she did look for the tracking device every chance she got and hadn't found it after a week, a long eight-day Quirni week. It annoyed her that she hadn't found it. She didn't have that much stuff with her and she doubted it was so small that she couldn't see it. It had to have an energy source that could last. Elsbeth and James had tracked her for two weeks. Even on Marril that meant the device had to be at least as big as her thumbnail. Either that or it had to be next to a heat source.

Then one afternoon, while passing through a town she saw a clinic and it came to her. She knew with certainty where it was, no, *what* it was.

"*Betty!*" She gasped under her breath. She had started to doze off in her saddle but bolted awake. Her sudden movement startled Turnbull. He jumped ahead and Erica had to grab the saddle to stay on him.

James caught Turnbull's reins. "What?" he asked and glanced around the woods on either side.

"Oh, uh, pardons, fell to sleep," Erica apologized.

He didn't seem satisfied with the explanation. He held her gaze, searching her eyes.

Elsbeth came to life ahead of them. She turned around in the saddle. "Is everything okay?"

"Fine," Erica reassured her and smiled sheepishly. "Fell to sleep and then jerked awake. Surprised Turnbull. My pardons."

Elsbeth watched her for a few moments then turned back around and fell silent again. James released Turnbull and the horses plodded on.

The GPS device, Erica realized, was in her. It was the hearing aid. That was how they could hear her. That was why she couldn't find it in her belongings. That explained why Betty had been so short with her when she figured out she was leaving. That had been so unlike the cureman but Erica figured she had wanted to put a stop the conversation and any questions Erica might have had. The wrong question would have made Betty seem to accept, even support, Erica's plans.

The Marrilian

She had leaned close to speak in her left ear and told her the SDD did have plans for her. She had also said it was lucky for her they did because she would have died on Marril.

Did that mean the Sirrians wouldn't let her go to Sirrus? She wasn't allowed a ticket to her home planet?

She scowled at the thought and dismissed it. It wasn't a question she could answer. The important part of Betty's message was how she spoke in Erica's left ear. It was her right ear that had been damaged so it was possible that Betty could speak low near her left ear and not be heard by the right which was exactly what Betty had done. There was another clue. Levitus had mentioned how the hearing aid was 'top of the line'. Would an average hearing aid have a tracking device? She doubted it.

Another clue was how Elsbeth and James had been so sure they had located her that day by Cluny. How could they have been if a device was stashed in her things? Anything she carried could have been left behind but an internal device could not. Nothing else made sense. She felt certain she was right. So, how could she get rid of it?

Now this took up most of Erica's thoughts, how to get rid of it. It would have to be surgically removed but there was no one she could trust. What healer would be willing to mess with SDD equipment? Would one who was willing still be a good enough surgeon and a good enough person she should trust him to remove the device?

'Good luck,' Zoe told her.

Erica frowned. *No kidding.* As the days passed, Erica grew sullen. How could she find a healer if she couldn't go near people? If she did find such a healer she would need a lot of money to pay for the work but getting to a bank would be difficult. She couldn't even relieve herself without Elsbeth keeping her within sight. She could never take a large withdrawal from a bank let alone see a healer, not with James and Elsbeth around and she couldn't get away from them as long as the hearing aid tracked her.

She grew a darker frown for the next week as she pondered what to do. The best she could come up with was to injure herself in order to see a healer. Once there she could ask him to remove the tracking device. But why would he if she didn't have any money? So, the first thing she had to do was to get to a bank. How would she do that?

Erica's mood seemed to infect James and Elsbeth. They

talked and joked less as the days passed. Finally, they stopped talking altogether. It was just after they had passed another town. Occasionally they exchanged a look or a few quiet words but they didn't chat like they usually did. They didn't try to draw her into conversation either which was just as well. Erica didn't want to talk. She would snap at them if they tried. What gave them the right to do this to her?

James scanned the woods repeatedly, his eyes flicking about, his head jerking at every little sound. She supposed that was what happened when he kept quiet, he got agitated. Elsbeth sat ramrod straight in her saddle.

She felt a little guilty for that. These two certainly hadn't tagged her with the hearing aid. James' darting eyes finally got the better of her. "Are we stop –"

He put his finger over his lips with a stern glare. His expression startled her. She hadn't seen it before but this was the man she expected he truly was, in control, hard, and ready for anything.

That side of him attracted her as much as the silliness and his sweet boyish face. Stinkin' cute SDD bastard. That internal complaint was her only means to lessen the effect he had on her. It didn't work very well. James could be *stinkin* or a *bastard* or any other number of things and still he would get her complete attention. It was annoying but in such a nice way.

She took a moment to memorize his stern face. He flashed a quick smile, apparently aware of her gaze so she pulled her eyes away and glanced around. The woods closed in on either side. Deep underbrush rose right up next to the road. She began to feel the concern they exhibited. They had passed Potterville only a few miles ago. Was there danger from there?

James took Turnbull's reins from Erica and trotted him up beside Elsbeth's horse. Elsbeth, Erica now saw, also scanned the woods. She shot James one of those looks they passed between them, more in it than Erica could decipher, and nodded towards a spot in front of them,

"By the rock," she told him.

James nodded slightly in return.

Elsbeth took Turnbull's reins from Erica and then placed Erica's hands on her saddle. She held Erica's hands there and fixed her with a rigid stare like James had. "Hold on tight!" she hissed.

Erica tightened her grip. She had no idea what they had in mind but it worried her. Both of them were acting like they expected a thing. James rode up close to her left and pushed her forward.

"Sit like that so you don't fall back when we start to gallop."

Gallop? The fear in her eyes made him smile reassuringly but that didn't help much. Her fingers turned white waiting for the *galloping* to start.

They reached the rock and the agents kicked their horses. The packhorse clanked loudly as it galloped after them.

A man stepped into the road. The three of them bore down on him as he raised his bow. There was nothing they could do but try to get past him. He nocked an arrow and shot. Elsbeth and James urged the horses to go faster. The arrow fell between Erica and James. The man nocked another arrow. This time they were much closer to him.

Elsbeth shoved Erica's face into Turnbull's neck, the front of the saddle digging into her stomach, so Erica never saw where the arrow went. The horses flew by the archer who had to dive to the side.

They galloped down the road. Elsbeth released Erica as their horses drifted apart. Erica sat up but as soon as she did something hit her hard. It slammed her forward so her face hit Turnbull's neck and made her slip. James pushed her shoulder and shoved her back into the saddle. Erica tried to breathe. Whatever had hit her felt like it had cracked her spine. Could it have been an arrow? It felt like a tree had fallen on her. She clung to Turnbull's neck out of pain and fear. He snorted and ran. The agents didn't slow until they galloped from the deepest part of the woods.

By that time Erica coughed relentlessly. Her back hurt so much she couldn't sit. Turnbull began to trot and the choppy gait made her slip again. Her foot came out of the stirrup and then the saddle slipped. Elsbeth's strong hand seized her coat sleeve and dragged her back. She held Erica as they slowed to a walk then broke off the road into a grassy opening where they stopped.

Elsbeth dismounted and circled to Turnbull's side. She dragged Erica down, pulled off her coat and threw it down. She started to unbutton her shirt.

"What are you doing?" Erica complained. She backed away then had to stop and cough.

Elsbeth jerked her upright, pulled her shirt open, and ripped open the closures on the vest. "I want to make sure that arrow didn't hurt you," she replied curtly. She spun Erica around and lifted the vest then rubbed her hand under it, over Erica's back. Satisfied, she spun Erica back around and closed the vest with a quick run of her hand down the front. "Get dressed," Elsbeth commanded and walked to the road where she looked up and down it with James who still sat on his horse.

Erica glared at Elsbeth's back while she buttoned her shirt. She picked up her coat and noticed another hole in the back.

"Great, dirty, damn, stupid, blasted, fucking expensive coat," she snarled then coughed but not so bad she couldn't shrug into the coat. She dug her smokes from a pocket and had one in hand, ready to light it, when Elsbeth returned, grabbed her and flung her onto Turnbull. The cigarette was smashed against the saddle. Erica glared at it and then threw it at Elsbeth's feet. "Not a doll!" she yelled.

"Live with it," Elsbeth replied as she took Turnbull's reins and mounted her horse.

Erica scowled at Elsbeth's back wishing ill on the woman then realized maybe not. She had been checking to see if she was hurt. That confused the issue. Who had ever done that but Betty and Levitus? None of the healers her father paid ever had. He paid them to not notice things while fixing the damage he had done. Or did Elsbeth care because it was her duty?

"Hold on," Elsbeth barked at her.

Erica gripped the saddle, just now realizing from Elsbeth's stressed tone that they weren't that far from the attacker. They needed to move.

Coughs tickled Erica's throat, probably because she was annoyed. These agents were plenty strong enough to toss her around but damn it, she didn't like it! She pulled out another smoke and managed to light it as the horses picked their way out of the grass. They took off at a trot once they got to the road. Erica tried repeatedly so smoke the cigarette but it broke on her nose. She gave up and tossed it to the road. She coughed and held on.

They got away from the woods by evening which was when they returned Turnbull's reins to Erica. The threat had apparently passed but they didn't stop until the sun began to set. They entered the rolling foothills when Elsbeth reined her horse off the road. Trees still dotted the landscape but they weren't thick or tall. They set up camp in a valley by a pond where they couldn't be seen from any direction and trees surrounded them.

Erica couldn't have been more grateful that they stopped. Her mood had calmed to a sedate unease with quiet concentration to endure the pain in her back. It hurt to breathe or sit up. She felt certain a few of her ribs were broken.

"That guy had a hell of an arm," she commented as the others dismounted. She sat forward with her forearms resting on the saddle. She tried to raise her leg to get down but found it took too much effort. She lay forward on Turnbull's neck with a groan and decided to stay there.

"Come here, Doll," James quipped and before she could open her eyes he had pulled her from Turnbull's back and set her on her feet.

"Not a Doll!" Erica told his back with as much volume as her breath could allow. It wasn't much but he heard. He chuckled and walked away. He had been waiting to call her that since she lost her temper at Elsbeth. Now they pitched a tent and glanced her way and laughed.

Erica wanted to walk over and deck them both. Unless they knew her method of fighting she felt sure she could do it but when she tried to move she winced and groaned. If her back wasn't broken, it felt like it ought to be. She watched Elsbeth and James laugh at her and could do nothing about it. She wanted revenge. "You don't toss me around. Not a Doll," she muttered to herself and then remembered the hearing aid. She dug her toe into the dirt and regretted it. It hurt all the way to her neck. She would get back at them eventually on the day she disappeared.

Edwards

Chapter 8 – Friends?

The next morning Elsbeth and James let Erica sleep. The sun woke her mid day. It shined in her eyes through the open flap of the little tent. The coolness of the morning was gone. The breeze almost felt warm. Erica looked out to see James and Elsbeth talking quietly by the fire. They sat on another log. He seemed to like using the little axe cutting seats in logs whenever he could. It made sense why she dreamed of Tenpole. In her dream the sound of his chopping had turned into rocks falling in the mines. She had been willing the rocks to miss the miners by calling 'Bless you!' to the men at the bottom.

"Good morning Doll," Elsbeth called. She got up and squatted by the tent flap. "How are you feeling?"

Erica scowled at the 'Doll.' "Fine," she sneered but then tried to move. Her back was so stiff and sore she couldn't roll over. She clamped her teeth hard to stop her moan, closed her eyes, and breathed shallow. She just had to move a little to get through this. She just had to start it, so she tried again and gasped then relaxed back on her stomach.

"Figured," Elsbeth said with a grin and slipped her hands under Erica's waist. "Come on," she coaxed gently and lifted her. Erica pulled her knees under her with Elsbeth's help. "The vest stops the arrow from penetrating but you still have to take the force of the blow."

"Arrow?" Erica grunted as she got her legs under her. "The guy fired a rocket." Elsbeth slowly helped her crawl out of the tent then sit back on her heals. The sun was almost above them. "We get a late start today?"

"We're staying here until tomorrow," Elsbeth informed her.

"'Tis good news," Erica sighed. She tried to breathe deep but winced. She tried to twist and gasped. Elsbeth rested a steadying hand on her arm while she waited for that shot of pain to pass. Erica looked up at her. "Riding could hurt."

"Most likely," Elsbeth agreed and glanced at James with a smirk. "Can you stand?"

Erica struggled to her feet with Elsbeth's help. "Try to relax," Elsbeth instructed and began to gently massage her back. It felt good but Erica still winced. She ended up standing as stiff and straight as she could. That seemed the best position. "Relax," Elsbeth repeated.

"So," replied Erica with a snap in her tone that spoke volumes.

Elsbeth sighed. "Try harder."

Erica closed her eyes and willed her back to loosen. It didn't help. Every time she let go of the stiff posture a shot of pain ran up and down.

Elsbeth snorted and continued to rub. "We are on Jennings Claim. The claimants here aren't much for supporting the SDD. We don't make the local laws, we only enforce them so if the claimants don't help us we can't deter tenants from attacking. We have decided it is best to stay away from towns and get off this claim as soon as possible. What happened yesterday was only a taste of what could happen by a larger town."

Erica gasped as Elsbeth touched a particularly sore spot.

"Sorry," Elsbeth offered and massaged the area a little more, then stopped.

"So," Erica returned with a dropping tone at the end of the word to accept her apology. She hobbled over to the fire where she turned around and used the heat to help loosen her muscles.

"Now you see things my way?" she asked and arched her back. She took a slow deep breath and forced herself to ignore the pain "Never wanted to ride during the day."

Elsbeth tried to hold her eyes but Erica avoided them. "Yeah, well, I'm sorry."

Erica hadn't expected one apology from an agent let alone an agent insisting on making them. It turned things around the wrong way. "None such," she found herself saying. "If I had stayed down he wouldn't have hit me." She realized she meant it. She grunted at her own stupidity. "Was hit with an arrow before but was not like that. Was a blasted rocket. Would have gone through without the vest. The man had two arms in one. The vest be amazing."

James sighed and shook his head.

"I agree but I intend to avoid needing it again," Elsbeth grumbled. "We are going due west to Knoll Claim and then Lund Claim. We'll be traveling across country from now on, through the foothills then north once when we're below Mois Claim."

She tried to remember the map, remember where Mois Claim was in relationship to Trellis. Her breath caught as she realized even if she did get to Trellis, or farther, the SDD would still be able to find her with the hearing aid. Her whole plan was just a bust wall now. She wanted to sigh, but didn't want to irritate her back, so instead, she turned around and examined the fire to see what they cooked.

A pan had warmed bread and several strips of bacon. She bent to take the bread and groaned as her back knotted up again. She dropped the bread and grabbed at her back.

James got up and helped her to the log. "Take a load off, Doll."

Erica tried to glare at him for calling her 'Doll' but his eyes sparkled. He was so cute she couldn't be mad at him and he practically carried her to the log and that was what she needed. "You big hulking Quirni," she muttered as he gently placed her.

"Big?" Elsbeth laughed. "James is a runt."

Erica flashed a skeptical frown through her pain.

"Most Quirni men are well over six feet tall," James explained. "I'm six foot even. That's the average height of a Quirni born woman."

"'Tis still six inches taller than me," Erica told him. "And strong as any miner with the heaviest pick. You would be in the deep pits for sure."

He wondered at that as if attempting to decide if it was a compliment. "Thank you?"

Elsbeth laughed. Erica smiled.

James sat next to Erica and gently massaged her as Elsbeth had done but he touched exactly the right spots in just the right way.

"My," Erica sighed. "Do that and call me Doll if you want." She sagged in relief. He continued.

"It seems I lost a job," Elsbeth commented and gave Erica her bread.

Erica nodded, ate, and mewed at James' continued attention.

The next day they headed out first thing in the morning. They left the roads and saw spectacular sights. Erica decided Quirni was the most underrated planet of the system. The photographs never showed how massive and tall the mountains were or how clear the lakes were. The glaciers sparkled in the pure air. The grasses were deep green, cut with red, pink, and yellow flowers and the sky was such a deep blue, Erica finally had to admit Quirni was the prettiest. The saturation of colors mesmerized her.

Elsbeth and James allowed her to pause and look as much as she wanted. She began to forget the reason they accompanied her. It wasn't as if she never thought of it or how to get away from them but she thought of it less and less often. There wasn't much she could do about getting rid of the GPS device without a healer, so she gave up pondering the idea and enjoyed the ride.

Never before had she been with people she liked for so long. She had always been with her father, alone, or fellow employees waiting on work, people she couldn't trust. She hadn't realized how much she could enjoy another person's company and just that, just their company. James and Elsbeth talked to her about anything and wanted nothing. They laughed with her and not *at* her. She could laugh with them and not wonder when they would stop laughing to start business. It was the prettiest relationship Erica had ever known.

James and Elsbeth didn't control every movement she made. They kept an eye on her and if she was headed towards any danger they told her. Erica knew they were ordered to guard her but she felt like they might be friends except she wasn't sure. She wasn't sure what a real friendship was. It had to be something like this.

"Mois Claim is better," Elsbeth told her as they looked down a gorge to a river. In the distance they could see falls.

"'Tis where we go?" Erica asked as the damp breeze came up the cliff before her and blew back her hair, which was clean since they had helped her with another bath that morning. They all took turns with baths. She had seen more of James and was completely taken. She had offered herself to him but after a gulp, he had declined.

The offer hadn't changed his attitude towards her either, which she found wonderful. He kept sexually distant while remaining friendly and caring, nothing more. She didn't know if he declined because she was under his care, because Elsbeth was there, or if he wasn't interested. She had told him Elsbeth could join them and saw how it shocked him. She laughed at that, how proper he was. Maybe he thought she'd been joking. He laughed as if he knew she only teased him and everything returned to normal.

It was James who decided on the grassy hill for a camp. Erica couldn't imagine why since it was so early in the day but when she took a short walk she saw the gorge. She sank down and sat in the ankle deep grass to appreciate it.

Elsbeth settled next to her. "Why do you mistrust the SDD?" she asked out of nowhere.

When Erica thought about it she realized the question

probably wasn't Elsbeth's but one she had been told to ask.
Elsbeth had a phone and talked on it every few days. Sometimes
they stopped early when she found good reception. She had
talked on it the day before and now this odd question. Erica
considered answering it until she remembered Betty had asked
the same question. Who was so curious?

She pulled her eyes from the gorge to Elsbeth who watched
her and waited.

Erica liked this woman, her company, her gentle manners.
The long solitude of the ride had given Erica some peace, more
peace than she had ever had.

Zoe hardly spoke anymore but Erica realized she felt
feelings on occasion that didn't suit the moment, just like the old
times. Zoe was close and there were days that time passed so fast
Erica suspected Zoe, or someone, had been out and living the
time instead of her. Her alternate sides were expressing
themselves but James and Elsbeth didn't mention anything odd
so she doubted they had noticed. Most people never did. They
just got angry she said one thing one day and another thing the
next. The easiest way to avoid any problems was to never say
anything. It was a rule she lived by to cope with her condition.
She decided to break that rule right now.

"The SDD made bad times," she answered simply but not
completely, not if Elsbeth pressed which she did.

"Like what?"

Erica shrugged as she considered whether there was any
reason the QSDD shouldn't know.

The SDD command would learn whatever Erica shared.
Elsbeth would report it or they would hear over the transmitter
in the hearing aid. For a signal to travel far enough for someone
to pick it up out here, it would have to be an extremely powerful
transmitter. Not impossible, but Erica didn't think she was worth
that sort of surveillance. No, Elsbeth would report it. She called
in every few days. That had to be why. Erica drew a breath. Why
not answer the question? They would know sooner or later. It
would be in their records, which, apparently, they still didn't
have

"My da and I were kicked off Sirrus." She squinted at her
answer then sighed. "No...'tis the end of the story." She started
again. "You know how Sirrians be intolerant of ..." So this was
hard to say even when she wanted to say it. She ran her fingers
up a long blade of grass. "Well..."

"Intolerance on Sirrus?" Elsbeth asked quietly. "There is only

one thing that might get you exiled from anywhere, homicide."
She waited for a reply but Erica didn't offer one. "You don't mean
that do you?"

"Yes." Erica yanked the long grass from the ground and
twisted it. She kept her eyes on it. She didn't want to see Elsbeth's
expression.

"That usually ends up in corporal punishment," Elsbeth
noted.

"Was too young," Erica told her and threw the twisted grass
towards the cliff. It fell short, blown back by the breeze. "Too
young for execution, but not to face charges given the nature of
the crime."

Elsbeth took so long to reply, Erica looked up. She gaped at
Erica with a mixture of sadness and wonder. "You? Not your
father?"

Erica returned her gaze to the waterfalls. "The SSDD insisted
we leave Sirrus. Between the fact we be Kinsley's and our family
be from Marril and the fact the Sirrian government be, as the
SDD said, *confused about the laws*, they moved us to Marril, away
from my birth family."

"They didn't have the right to do that."

Erica shrugged. "They did when my da agreed to it so he
didn't have to face trial. He was in trouble too. Was me who
pulled the trigger but he told me to. SSDD couldn't prove that so
they bargained. Lessened the charges to manslaughter with exile.
If da didn't bargain he would have a trial with Reagent 10
questioning. He be a lawyer. Not a great one but knew enough
about Reagent 10. Such questioning would prove he told me to
shoot. Would be murder then and execution for him. Would let
me go with manslaughter or less if my wits be daft." She shook
her head. "He took the bargain. Had to move. The rest of the
family stayed on Sirrus. Guess the SSDD wanted them safe."

"That doesn't make any sense. The SDD doesn't get involved
in choices like that. You're either guilty or not. And a claimant's
family gets punished by the planetary council not the SDD."

Erica took a long breath and exhaled slowly. She had to
explain it all. "Da taught me to shoot when I was about seven.
My twin sissies came out to learn later. Was a huge hobby of da's.
He wanted us all perfect so we could win some friggin'
tournaments he loved. We gave him reason to go to them but not
shoot. He met people there. 'Tis a big thing on Sirrus and Marril.
Didn't like it but got good enough to win. My sissies didn't try to
improve though. They only played. That made da mad."

The Marrilian

Erica paused to remember the day. She stared at the gorge but didn't see it. It was one of those memories that seemed unreal, like she had dissociated from it then found it again after a long time.

She could see the teal Sirrian sky and tall yellow-green grass. "Tory and Chase were younger than me. Twins. They had fun together. Was all fun to them. They climbed a rock and tried to push each other off. They both stood on the rock and pushed and shoved each other. Got angry I couldn't play too. Da yelled to get their attention. Didn't work. He told me to shoot at them. *'Go ahead'*, he told me, *'you'll miss them anyway. You couldn't hit a house if you stood on the porch.'*"

"Could too," Elsbeth whispered. It was so soft it felt like Zoe.

Erica nodded. "Took his word and aimed at them rather than away. They stood next to each other. One shot…" she added in a choked voice and could describe no more. Her tears fell for the memory. She stopped and tried to wipe that awful image from her mind, the two of them tumbling off the rock, the red splashing the grass.

Elsbeth waited.

Erica wiped her cheeks. It took a while before she continued. Elsbeth waited.

"The crime didn't fit Sirrian laws. Was too young. Da hadn't pulled the trigger. They were going to let us go, called it accidental so the SSDD took over. Said the Sirrian Council played favorites with a claimant's family, a powerful claimant on Quirni and another on Marril. They said it was their duty to enforce the Sirrian laws when the Council refused to do it. Da got a choice and he chose a reduced plea of manslaughter with twenty years exile."

"I see. Since the Sirrian Council didn't follow the letter of their own law, that would be right. The SSDD would do that."

"So," Erica replied. "Was the start of it. Things got worse from there. He always hurt me but Marril made him worse. If the SDD had left us alone would be with my family. Might have had help."

"Help from what?"

Elsbeth dug in a place Erica couldn't go. Not only were the memories she had too painful but there were some she didn't have. Her alternate selves had them. They could keep them too.

"Is that where you got the scars?" Elsbeth asked. She did so gently, apparently aware of how Erica felt about them. "I noticed your scars when I helped you bathe. Did your father whip you?

Did he cut you?"

Erica shook her head and dropped her eyes. She brushed the back of her hand across the grass at her crossed ankles. She had scars all over her. Most were from him. She didn't want to think about that. She didn't want to bring those up too.

"Did he cut you?"

Erica shook her head. She didn't want to answer that. These were among her worst memories. Some of them were shut down so hard she couldn't remember them and wouldn't try. It felt like her chest was trying to constrict itself to death, like the thayanite was back digging into her lungs.

"We are Quirni SDD, not Sirrian SDD or Marrilian SDD," Elsbeth said softly. "We wouldn't have left you in his hands here. People are more important to us here. We don't have enough tenants on this planet. We react to cruelty."

"All Delegate follow the same laws. He knows how to avoid you."

"We might have the same sort of laws but not the same leaders," Elsbeth responded quickly. "Laws are interpreted." She didn't even have to think about that.

Erica dipped her chin to let Elsbeth know she agreed and that she might be right, they might have stopped Samuel's abuse on Quirni, but then remembered these people didn't know Tenpole sign language. "So," she added.

"Why do you still carry a gun?" asked James. Erica jumped when he spoke. She twisted around. The sun was over his head. She shaded her eyes to look up at him. "I would think after something like that you would never touch a gun."

Erica turned back to Elsbeth who had a questioning expression as well, then she returned to staring at the far away falls. "Wasn't given that choice. We moved to Marril when eight years old. Da told me would help him make new connections so we went to tournaments. Was so until a few years ago."

"Eight," James repeated. "A Sirrian eight?"

Erica nodded. She looked back at him again when he drew a hard breath which he released slowly, as if to calm a temper. His eyes rose to stare at the far mountains. She turned back around and gave them both time to ask questions but they didn't.

"You be right, James," Erica said after a while. "Don't carry the pistol to shoot people. 'Tis not for defense. Never took off the safety in the Padt City." Elsbeth listened to her intently, as if to see if she really meant that. "Brought it here because it be a status symbol, heavy with metal and all that. Thought it might help me settle somewhere better, being Tenpole, lower class. Thought it might help. Thought you ought to know. Noticed you let me continue to carry it but won't help." Erica looked at Elsbeth to see if she could appreciate this. Elsbeth looked sad but also worried. Erica sighed and stopped talking before she said too much.

James stood behind them for a while then returned to his fire.

"I thought you had shown a great deal of restraint when the archer faced us in the road," noted Elsbeth.

"No," Erica replied. The image of her sisters dying in the Sirrian grass kept rising and threatening to make her cry. Remembering how they bled to death in that meadow, how no one could do anything, broke her heart even after twenty years. She didn't want to see that happen to anyone again.

"Erica, that gives you reason to dislike the SDD but I think it gives you more reason to dislike your father. You said he was worse after you left Sirrus. What did he do to you?"

"Won't talk about that," Erica replied brusquely and got up. Her back still ached a little, but with James' massages it felt better than she would have expected.

She strolled away from Elsbeth and over to the fire where she found James with an odd glint in his eye. He held something behind his back.

"You shot the bird that took Elsbeth's bracelet so I know you shoot animals, and I would love a boar," he said and then showed her the long gun he had been hiding. "We have all day here. We have to cross the river outside of Mesen late tonight. We won't pack up until after dark so in the meantime," he smiled, "I saw some boar." He held the rifle out to her with one hand.

There was no doubt in Erica's mind as to how much James loved to eat meat. He complained if they didn't have any. They had salted fish, beef, and pork with them that he usually apologized for since it wasn't fresh. Erica preferred the dried, bloodless stuff he pulled from the packs. The flush of hope and expectation on his face was testament to how much he preferred it dripping red.

Erica hid the grimace trying to creep onto her face and slowly took the gun from him. It was a rifle and a good sized one. She had no doubt it could kill one of the animals and if she hit it in the heart she could do so quickly. The problem was, she had no idea where the heart was in a native Quirni boar. He handed her a box of cartridges. "Where did you see them?" she asked without the least trace of excitement. It would be horrible if she had to keep shooting it to kill it.

He looked nearly maniacal he was so thrilled. He pointed east to a grove of twenty-foot tall pines. "I saw them when I was collecting wood for the fire. There were six of them."

"Did they see you?"

He shook he head and shrugged. "I don't know."

"Could be gone if they did."

"But maybe not," he returned, too excited at the prospect of fresh meat. "I can't shoot worth a damn so I waited for you. You'll do it won't you? I haven't had one in ages. They taste incredible."

Erica found herself willing, which surprised her. Then again, this was James and she would do just about anything for him. She sighted down the rifle. "How does it shoot?" she asked in a flat tone.

"With the trigger," he replied with a crease between his eyes. "I thought you were a tournament winner? Don't you know how to shoot a rifle?"

Erica almost laughed but then what if he wasn't joking? She eyed him as she tried to decide. "Does it shoot high or low or left or right?"

He took off his uniform coat, folded it, lay it on his saddle, and then placed his cap on the coat. He rolled up his sleeves as he shook his head. "I have no idea. It's a gun. It shoots. You'll do it won't you?"

Erica stared at him both to see him undress and to hear how unfamiliar he was with a rifle and then blinked and dropped her eyes. She was being rude.

"So," she agreed. "Do you happen to know where the heart be in the creatures?" she asked as he grabbed a tarp and led her away from the camp. He answered with the precision of a surgeon. Apparently he had cut bore up on more than one occasion.

The animals were still in the same place and that afternoon they ate wild boar with wild onions and carrots that she found as she preceded him back to camp. He had carried the kill over his shoulder wrapped in a tarp so it wouldn't dirty his shirt. She marveled that the weight of the big animal didn't faze him. He even kept an eye on her, even warned her before she walked into a snake hole. He removed the rest of his clothes and then dressed the animal near the gorge tossing the entrails over the edge so they wouldn't attract dogs.

The Marrilian

Erica watched every moment of him working.

Elsbeth sat right alongside her. "I have to admit it, I like it when he gets his hands on big game."

James' back and shoulders glistened in the sun from the sweat he had built.

"Blasted horrible and gorgeous," Erica said.

Elsbeth laughed lightly.

"Why does he take off his clothes?"

"To keep them clean."

"Ah," Erica replied. It made sense. "Does he do so every time?"

"If he is dressing a boar he does."

"Then would like to get him more. He be so happy." She pointed at him. "Sight of that makes me happy."

Elsbeth laughed harder. "Yeah," she agreed. "Don't tell him."

"Don't want to make him self-conscious?"

"Something like that."

"So," Erica agreed.

James finished and rinsed the blood off his body then put his pants back on but he left his shirt off. He washed his shirts so he didn't have one to wear.

As evening arrived, they ate. Elsbeth and James took full plates of meat and didn't say a word until they finished and took another plateful that included some vegetables. Erica managed to eat one bite of the beast and that had been crisped to near burnt. It tasted too much like any other meat she had ever had, bloody. She let them have it and ate the wild onions and carrots.

It took James a while to move again after his feast and then he pulled the rest of the meat off the carcass and seasoned it. He said he would dry it into jerky by the time they broke camp or they wouldn't break camp. He gave Elsbeth a meaningful stare that she returned with a shrug.

When they crossed the gorge with dog proof packs full of dried boar meat they were on Lund Claim. The pass to Mois claim lay only a few days ahead.

Erica noticed the agent's conversation begin to change. It began to sound nostalgic about their barracks as if they were thinking of home. The long ride would end soon. Mois Claim was their goal. She would be delivered into the hands of whoever waited for her and then Elsbeth and James would return south and it was bound to happen for she had not found a means to get rid of the hearing aid. As their hearts lightened, hers grew heavy.

The pass into Mois Claim turned out to be the prettiest part of the trip just as Elsbeth had promised. They slowly wound their way down the side of a gorge and ended up by a river. The insects buzzed around them, rising from the water at night in masses, but they didn't bite. Erica fell to sleep with the river gurgling nearby. It was clean water too, Bacillus *pyrogenzes* free water, Elsbeth informed them. It was glacial water and too cold for the bacteria so they bathed in it freely even if they did freeze. Mois Claim could be paradise.

They saw more wild boar so James tied the rifle to Erica's saddle.

"Mayhaps you be hungry again?" she asked and pulled her leg out of his way.

"Mayhaps starving," he replied. "All of our real meat is gone. Even jerky is better than the old, salted crap we have. So when we see a boar you get another one, ok?" He glanced up at her, flashing a smile that made her sigh and look away. "Or even a couple of those birds?" He pointed at the colorful flying thieves.

Erica watched them hop about in the trees. "They be easy. You can have those any time you want."

"Then they are coming to dinner tonight." He paused and took her hand between his and gazed into her eyes intently. "With another boar, if you can, Doll."

His bright eyes and hopeful grin were infectious. She smiled. "Alright," she agreed and loaded her pistol so she would be ready. James had already loaded the rifle.

That night she shot two birds. Early on the forth morning she saw a boar and shot it. James was ecstatic. He dried most of the meat but saved some raw chunks and planned a stew.

That same day they rode into Nigh. Erica was mostly nervous but partly excited. Matilda might be in the town. She was likely somewhere on Mois Claim. Claimant Mois had been her defense lawyer so this seemed a likely place.

They passed white washed houses and fences on the way into the business district. It reminded Erica of Cluny. Would these people welcome her because the Claimants told them to, or would they be like Cluny? Elsbeth and James pulled their horses up to a boardwalk.

"We're just getting supplies," Elsbeth informed her to stop her from dismounting.

"We still travel?" Erica asked in surprise. "Expected we arrived."

The Marrilian

"It's about six days from here at the pace we have been going," James informed her and dismounted. He was still excited about the boar meat. "I'm making stew tonight," he added and hurried into the store.

According to a map they'd shown her when she asked, six days meant they were probably going to Pey, the capital seat of Mois Claim. Somehow Erica had expected they were taking her to see Matilda but in the capital seat of a claim? It didn't seem likely. The idea that a claimant could keep a killer of her magnitude in their capital seemed ludicrous. Unless, she wasn't guilty.

Erica frowned. How sad it would be to have received the beating she had in Cluny if Matilda was actually innocent. What if the reason for the beating itself was as misguided as the barbarians that had beaten her? What a depressing thought. Erica shook her head and glanced around the town from beneath her wide brimmed hat.

People strolled along the boardwalk in front of her but after they noticed Elsbeth, they didn't look. They averted their eyes and hurried along when Elsbeth glared at them and this was with Elsbeth's uniform looking less than perfect. Elsbeth and James had several uniforms with them but they were not ironed or clean after the long trip. An imperfect SDD uniform was a rarity. If Erica had been walking along that boardwalk she would have been hard put to avert her eyes and she was Tenpole.

James returned with several bags and stowed them on the packhorse. "I got it all," he announced with a grin. His eyes flashed from the packs to Erica and Elsbeth as he talked and stuffed the bags in place. "Carrots, turnips, onions and potatoes, all the spices and sour dough bread." He continued with his choice of spices as he mounted, "Mace, thyme, allspice, pepper, salt and basil. Sugar and salt for the rub." They left the town as he described how he would tenderize the meat and spice it before cooking. "We will end our meal with wild strawberries soaked in sugar, cinnamon, and brandy."

Erica grimaced until he mentioned the strawberries. "'Tis strange I still have two legs," she told James. "You and your meat, would be a cannibal if Elsbeth were not watching."

Elsbeth laughed.

"A man must eat right, Doll, or he'll fade away," he replied with conviction.

They rode side by side, all three of them. Mois Claim was the safest claim they would travel and they relaxed.

Edwards

"Brandy and sugar?" Erica asked incredulously. "'Tis eating right?"

"Yes, it 'tis," he assured her and she didn't even mind him mimicking her with the way he smiled. "Brandy cleans the teeth, lubes the arteries, and it gives the liver a nice workout, a pure necessity of a healthy man." He sounded serious but she couldn't decide if he was. One thing was certain, he was happy. "We're stopping early," he added. "I want the stew to have a nice long time to simmer."

Erica thought this explained James all too well; eat well and be happy. A simple meal and he couldn't be happier even if he did do all the cooking. She guessed he loved to cook as much as he loved to eat. He was enjoyable, easy company. She would miss him far more than she ought to when he went back to his other duties. Everything about him was perfect.

Elsbeth, on the other hand, needed to know things, why this, why that, why did you do that? She would eat the plants Erica found and be satisfied as long as she knew what they were; how do you know you can eat it?

Erica had shared her edible plants book with her long ago. They had crunched on wild potatoes while James looked on. 'At least cook them' he had said with dismay but never an argument. Elsbeth was always up for an argument. Erica would miss her too. Arguments could be fun. They once argued about whether James would be happier with a boar or the same pounds in birds. They almost made a bet on it, but in the end, they both agreed, it had to be the boar.

The road continued to wind along the river. They went slow. "We will stop at the first meadow we see after the sun passes noon," James informed them. Neither Erica nor Elsbeth had the courage to disagree in the face of such high spirits.

James finally fell silent. They rode in the fresh air and sunshine. The river ran quickly to the left of them. The woods twittered with birds to the right. Erica relaxed in her saddle and simply tried to enjoy the scenery. If she could be made happy as easily as James she would be happy now but the damn SDD and their plans plagued her. Well, if James and Elsbeth were any indication, the *Quirni* SDD weren't so bad. But why take her to Mois Claim? Would she meet her cousin here?

"I'm surprised Matilda be on a claim so close to Kinsley Claim," Erica said. It was one of those comments she made hoping to catch Elsbeth or James unaware so they would spill a tidbit of information. It hadn't worked yet. They were both more than up to the task of guessing the motive of her questions but it had become fun to try.

"She made friends with Claimant Mois a number of years ago," Elsbeth replied.

"Really?" Erica hardly contained her excitement. Her voice nearly cracked. She didn't trust herself to say more. Elsbeth had all but admitted Matilda was on Mois Claim.

"Matilda helped Claimant Mois. She knew her father had some plans that would cause Claimant Mois financial hardship. She decided to try and help. At that point in time she would have done anything to hurt her father. He had hurt her and she wanted to do the same back, only financially."

"She used Claimant Mois to get back at Claimant Kinsley?" Erica asked. She realized Elsbeth's words sounded rehearsed.

"Mois knew it," Elsbeth replied. "It was to his advantage. We later learned what Cyril Kinsley intended. It was scandalous. It would have badly hurt Mois Claim if she hadn't stepped in when she did."

"He did something as bad as killing 6,026 people?" Erica asked.

"She didn't do that," Elsbeth said flatly with a harsh glace at Erica. "The two of us traveled with her then." She nodded at James to indicate she meant the two of them. "I was her bodyguard and her physical therapist. I know she didn't kill them but at a critical moment we were away and the prosecutor said she had acted at that time so I couldn't prove it."

"Convenient," Erica replied dryly.

Elsbeth gave her another sidelong glance coupled with a frown. "She's a good person, a little self-absorbed, somewhat immature but young. She was a risk taker. Not unlike you, Doll."

Erica glared at her for the 'Doll'. It was one thing for James to say it but another to hear it from Elsbeth. "I have a thing or two to teach you about that," she muttered but smiled.

"Excuse me?" Elsbeth asked not that she hadn't heard. Her smile gave that fact away.

Erica beamed back. "Mayhaps someday we'll see who can fling you about."

Elsbeth laughed. "A pipsqueak like you couldn't fling me anywhere!"

"Aw, someday," Erica threatened coolly then had to wait for Elsbeth to stop laughing. "So how was Matilda hurt?" She was not really interested anymore but why not hear the whole story?

"She was in an explosion," Elsbeth answered as she glanced

up the road.

Erica's skeptical expression made Elsbeth laugh again.

"God, you look like her when you do that," she said then explained. "Cyril Kinsley is an advanced chemist, trained at a Marrilian university. He worked for the QSDD. He had a lab that we built for him. Some compounds he made were dangerous. He taught Matilda some chemistry so she could help him. Later he used the lab to threaten Mati or, so Mati believes. He told her she had to make a particular chemical with supplies from the QSDD. She knew enough to realize the job was dangerous. He insisted it wasn't, but she thought it would blow up, that one of the chemicals was impure. He told her it wouldn't blow up if she did it right. Instead of doing it small, she did it like nothing would happen, full scale, and blew up the lab with her in it."

"Good God," Erica declared and stared at Elsbeth. "She must be young. Children be so stupid."

Elsbeth shook her head. "It's not that, she's 29 now and that is Quirni years, but it wasn't such a stupid thing to do really."

"'Tis a head full of slag," Erica scoffed.

Elsbeth shrugged. "It had its logic. By destroying the lab she knew no one could use it against her again. The lab could kill her in ways she *wouldn't* expect. This way she thought she protected herself. The lab was designed for safety. She had a room she could go into when a dangerous experiment was underway. She was in the room because she knew the experiment was going to fail."

"But she was hurt," Erica reminded Elsbeth.

"Yeah, well, she was and her brother was killed, Johnny. The whole thing flared through the SDD command for a long time. Claimant Kinsley sued us over it. The engineers were blamed for their design then the builders were blamed for their construction and then the suppliers because of their sub quality supplies. The explosion destroyed the roof of the lab and it caved into the safety room. Mati was partly crushed. Her brother..." Elsbeth shook her head at the memory.

Erica rode in silence long enough for the memory to pass. "Her plan was stupid," she reasserted. "And deadly."

Elsbeth shook her head. "Like I said, Erica, you and Mati have traits in common. It must be the Kinsley blood or why else would you be trying to go north alone when we are here for you? Why would you attempt to go north of the claims? It is deadly there."

"Never told you I wanted to go north of the claims," Erica

The Marrilian

said slowly.

Elsbeth shrugged but she wasn't really listening. She looked up the road searching the woods. "Did you see that?" she asked James who rode on the other side of Erica.

He nodded.

"Get ready to ride fast," Elsbeth told them. Erica could now control her horse but any surprises could still make her lose her seat.

"What did you see?" she asked quietly.

"People in the woods," James answered. He spoke with his no-nonsense tone.

The road led into trees as it bent away from the bank of the river. They quickened their pace but nothing happened.

They began to relax again when suddenly the woods erupted in a chorus of yells. Men jumped from the trees screaming and throwing rocks. The horses jumped and took off at a run. Erica barely managed to stay on Turnbull as he bolted ahead, staying in line with the other horses.

James saw the rope strung across the road. So did Elsbeth. They knew how to make their horses jump but Erica didn't see it and neither did Turnbull. As the packhorse, James, and Elsbeth's horses cleared the rope Turnbull tripped and fell. He collapsed to his knees.

Erica rolled past his shoulder. She curled and tucked in her head to stop from breaking her neck. Instinct from years of falling in sparring matches made her seek an upright position as fast as her speed would allow. She had fallen from a gallop and spun out the energy in somersaults. She came up in a squat, pushing up with a hand, bruised and winded.

Her eyes rose to a man emerging from the woods on horseback. He held an arrow in his bow. He aimed at her chest. Before she could react, he shot. His arrow slammed into her and threw her back. The arrow bounced off.

"God damned vest!" The man yelled in anger. "We're ready for you anyway, bitch!"

The blow left Erica witless. She lay on the road with her arms splayed out to her sides. She hadn't moved when a second arrow pierced her left bicep. She grabbed it. The man's horse pranced near her feet. The hooves bumped her legs. She curled them up but he edged the horse towards her hips. She rolled from the horse's legs, but it didn't want to step on her. It pranced all around her.

Erica sobbed in fear and tugged at the arrow again. It

wouldn't come loose.

The rider urged the horse forward but it still wouldn't step on her. He made it rear up but its feet came back down away from her.

Erica yanked at the shaft. It didn't come free and it hurt like hell.

The horseman backed his animal away.

Erica stopped pulling and faced him. He wore a brown coat, sunglasses, a hat low on his brow, and a bandana under the hat that covered his hair. She could see the collar of his uniform. It was brown with a black tie and a white shirt. Her stomach rolled. She swallowed back sickness. She recognized the color of brown he wore. She knew the knot in his tie. He was an agent.

Erica looked past her attacker to see a second horseman shooting arrows at Elsbeth and James. They turned their horses and Elsbeth drew her gun. She fired at the second archer and missed. The archer shot her in the chest. She toppled backwards off her horse and lay still.

Erica yanked at the arrow harder. These men were going to kill all of them!

James ran his horse at the archer. He grabbed at the man so he could haul him from his saddle. Their horses pranced and bumped. The second archer couldn't get his bow up and James couldn't get his hands on him. The horses danced and spun. The men hit and grabbed until the second archer reined his horse around and galloped back towards Erica with James chasing.

Erica panicked to see the second archer pull an arrow, turn, and shoot at James. The arrow missed. James drew his gun and shot. She grit her teeth together and yanked at the shaft pinning her arm to the road. It didn't budge.

The first archer laughed. He sneered in malice and reached behind his back.

She let go of the arrow and fell back in dismay. He was going to shoot her again and she could do nothing about it. He could put it through her throat.

'Not likely' said a deep male voice. 'He's playing with you. He is an animal watching his prey suffer.'

"Noel!" Erica's eyes grew. She smiled. *Help me Noel!*

The archer paused, unsure why she smiled. He pulled the arrow from his quiver and brought it over his shoulder. He nocked it in the bow.

'Perhaps. This can be handled.'

Then handle it! Lords I've missed you. Where were you in Cluny?

The Marrilian

'You didn't need me. You were helped.'

Yes, Erica thought. She fell into his calmness, put away her shock and pain. *You knew I would be helped. You always know.*

The horseman's sneer disappeared. He frowned. He nocked the arrow and shot it through her right leg.

She grunted but nothing else. She hardly felt it. Noel was there.

'I will help today. You need it today.'

Please, she begged and the pain eased. She breathed.

'Let's change a thing or two here.'

Yes, Erica agreed.

'They are fools. Don't they know we have a gun?'

Don't kill.

'You challenge that all survive? Are you so sure I can find a way to achieve that?'

Erica couldn't answer.

The other part of her chuckled. Noel dropped her hand to her side and popped the restraining leather from the butt of her gun. He drew the weapon, moved it to the hand of her pinned arm and cocked it in a fluid, fast motion.

'Arrows against bullets aren't fair but I am unable to stand. I can give him a chance. It is his choice now.'

Erica viewed Noel's actions from a dream. Her hand brought up the gun and aimed at the archer, safety off. The horseman drew another arrow from his quiver. As he did, he revealed the cuff of his uniform and Erica saw an SDD cufflink. It was just like the ones James wore. This man was a captain. Erica noticed this, then she relaxed. She did not want to interfere with Noel. She completely trusted this part of herself.

The horseman held his bow out to his side as he started to nock the arrow. That was when Noel shot. The bow splintered. Wood splinters stuck in the captain's face and hand, otherwise he was unharmed.

'I am so good,' remarked Noel. He grinned as the archer gaped at the debris in his hand. He dropped the arrow then wiped the splinters from his cheek as his horse spun and pranced back. He couldn't keep his horse under control with the bow string tangling up his arms.

The second archer yelled as he galloped towards them.

Noel rose his head from the road and watched James and the second archer come closer. He waited, waited, waited, for the second archer to hold his bow away from his body. The archer reached for an arrow. The bow arm extended.

Edwards

'How much do you want to bet he is too nervous to hit me?' asked Noel. 'He is galloping towards a very large caliber gun. That would make me nervous. And it is a gun that was just proven to be expertly aimed.'

Erica watched in horror as Noel allowed the second archer to finish nocking his arrow and shoot. It missed. A horse made a pained sound.

'I win that bet,' Noel announced. When the second archer drew another arrow Noel shot his bow into fragments.

The first rider untangled from his bowstring and threw it down. "Die you God damned whore!" he swore and drove his horse towards Erica. James yelled and shot. She couldn't move to stop from being trampled. She pressed herself flat or Noel did. The horse jumped over her.

The second horseman dropped his bow as he galloped between Erica and Turnbull who had gotten to his feet and stood quivering. James yelled and galloped after the attackers, the hoof beats of his horse pounded into Erica's back. They passed. The staccato beats of the three horses faded. Erica relaxed spread eagle on the road. Her hand and gun fell out to her side.

'What a lovely blue,' Noel remarked of the sky. He left and the pain returned.

Calls of men came from the river. It was the men on foot. They had a boat and used the swift current to flee. Elsbeth ran past holding her chest. She stumbled into a run and shot towards them. They were too far away to capture so she gave up and came back to Erica.

"You're alive," Erica gasped at her.

"Yeah," she replied with pain choking her voice. She used a knife to cut Erica's coat sleeve. "God, you've been moving. Stay still now. It's bleeding fast." She cut a strip of cloth from Erica's shirt sleeve and fed the strip under Erica's arm.

Erica closed her eyes and set her jaw. Sweat broke out on her face.

The road vibrated with the hoof beats of a horse. Elsbeth didn't seem alarmed so it had to be James returning.

He flung himself to the ground beside the two of them and clutched Elsbeth's arm with a questioning look. "You're hurt." He touched the side of her face where blood ran freely. "He shot you."

Elsbeth wiped at it, looked at the blood on her hand, and frowned. "My head hit the road." She patted her chest and even winced at her own small touch. "I'm wearing my vest. I'm sore but whole." She pointed at Erica. "Finish that tourniquet then get her free." She stood back and watched the road.

James knelt and tied the strip of cloth tight. He winced when Erica grimaced at the pain he caused. "The bleeding has stopped," he informed Elsbeth.

"Be quick," she told him. "I'll get the healer's paste for her."

He examined the arrow in Erica's arm. He leaned over and put his cheek practically on the road to look rather than move her, which she thought was sweet of him but damn, it hurt so much already she didn't see the point. He gave her an apologetic look then pulled at the shaft and head of the arrow together. Erica grunted at the sudden jerk as he freed it from the hard packed dirt. He did the same for the one pinning her leg before she had a chance to recover from the first. He bent the feather end of the shafts until they broke then slowly pulled the lengths through.

She woke on the road. Leaves and sky filled her view.

"Good boy," James said quietly beside her. "Good boy. Yeah I know, I know. It's all right. Do you think you can go?" the soft clop of hooves, one hesitant, sounded beside her.

"The pack horse was hit by a bullet," said Elsbeth. "It was one of us," she added in disgust.

"Why do they even arm us with these things?" James muttered.

Erica turned her head and saw James leading Turnbull. The horse had shiny salve on his bloodied, raw knees.

"Get what you can out of the packs. At the very least try to get the rest of the bandages, the red clay antidote, food, the–"

"I know. Rest," James told Elsbeth. He dropped Turnbull's reins and hurried away.

Elsbeth moaned as she sat down next to Erica who she noticed was awake. "They may come back. We have to get out of here. You have to ride."

Anything if arrows would be avoided. Erica tucked her hurt arm close and tried to sit but only got half raised before she had to pause and deal with the pain of her leg. It didn't go away or lessen so when Elsbeth offered her arm Erica took it and pulled herself up. Her coat was gone and her shirtsleeve was cut and one leg of her pants was cut. Someone had wrapped bandages around her wounds. Elsbeth stood to help her stand.

"Can you get up?"

"In a bit," Erica answered and tried to find the strength to do that and deal with the pain. Her injuries hurt as much as some of the beatings her father had given her. Her shoulders and back felt bruised from the fall. Her hands were scraped. At least her coat had saved her back and shoulders from being dragged on the road. The thought of that made her wince.

James returned. He set down some supplies and put his hand through Erica's gun belt. He pulled her up gently as Elsbeth steadied her then Elsbeth continued to hold her as James picked up Erica's pistol and put it back in its holster.

"I think Turnbull will be fine for now," he said as he fastened the restraining strap over the pistol. "We put some healing paste on his knees. We put some on you too, not much, you're an iridim patient, but enough to stop the bleeding and lessen the pain." He straightened and almost looked like he meant to say more but thought better of it. "We have painkiller too. It's for an iridim patient. I suggest you take it." He held out a bottle of pills. "Two of them," he instructed and placed the bottle in her hand then hurried back to the dead packhorse.

Turnbull stood behind Erica so she leaned against him. She managed to stand by herself that way as James strapped bags on the horses and Elsbeth helped him go through the packs that the packhorse wasn't laying on. Erica tried to free her canteen from the back of her saddle but her pain kept making her pause.

James brought a bundle over to Turnbull. "You can ride with me if you need to," he told her. "It won't be comfortable but I can hold you if you don't think you can stay on." He nodded towards her leg. He handed her the canteen.

"Will manage," Erica assured him. She swallowed the pills with water. He tied another bundle behind her saddle then took the canteen, closed it, and put it back in the holder.

"All right, Doll, then up you go." He picked her up by the waist and held her high enough she could get her foot in the stirrup. When she had managed that he helped her get her leg over the saddle then situated the remains of her pants under it.

James and Elsbeth both glanced nervously up and down the road when they mounted. "Are you sure you want to ride Turnbull?" he asked one last time before leaving.

Erica's heart hammered in her chest. She leaned over Turnbull's neck. "Did-" she began to ask but then stopped. It felt like the iridim in her system was reacting with the healer's paste but why worry them about that? If it was the healer's paste she could be having an iridim induced heart attack. If that was the case, they could do nothing.

The Marrilian

"Did – what?" Elsbeth asked breathlessly.

"Don't you have a phone?" Erica asked. She fought the pain in her back and shoulders to raise her head. "Can't you call for help? Those helicopters be for medical flights, right? Think we could use one."

Elsbeth looked pained then reached into her uniform and pulled out a smashed pile of electronics. "Did," she answered simply. She tipped her head towards James. "Captains don't carry phones."

"We're on our own until we are late calling in," James explained. "Two days from now," he added. "After that, they have to get worried enough to look for us." He glanced down the road towards town. "Let's get going. Pey is our destination and we need to get there as soon as possible."

"Can we go back to town?" asked Erica.

They were both silent.

"What?" Erica looked from one to the other of them.

"Do you want to risk meeting up with that group again? They probably want us to return to town," explained James. "We were lucky to see them the first time and have a warning. There were a lot of them."

Erica understood. "Of course," she agreed quietly. Then she remembered the attackers were SDD. It didn't make sense. James and Elsbeth were attacked too. That meant they weren't in on whatever the SDD planned. Could agents work against agents? Did that happen?

Elsbeth and James turned their horses but Turnbull remained still. Erica couldn't sit straight let alone manage the reins. She couldn't use the horse. James gently took Turnbull's reins from her fingers. "Just stay on," he begged and led him away.

Edwards

The Marrilian

Chapter 9 – After Nigh

No one spoke as they rode. Erica held her arm against her chest. The pills helped with that injury and the pain in her back and shoulders but the drying blood on her ripped pants was too much. It rasped against the saddle. The painkillers peaked and ebbed before a few hours had passed and by early afternoon Erica couldn't stand it any longer so she called a halt.

"Need new pants and my coat," she told them. "'Tis cold."

James dismounted and helped her. He taped up the sleeve of her coat to mend it while Elsbeth remained on her horse, still and silent, and held her chest. Soon they were moving again.

When they stopped to rest, they had nothing for shelter. The packhorse had been lying on the tent and James hadn't been able to free it so they only slept briefly on the blankets he had tied to their saddles. They rode again when Khepri rose. Erica understood they needed to get to Pey but James pushed too hard. When she asked to stop and sleep he told her to sleep on the horse and once again offered to hold her if necessary. She told him it wasn't. James led both Elsbeth and Erica's horses through the night.

By the second day Elsbeth sat straighter and Erica felt stronger. They improved their time. The small provisions James had saved were mostly the dried meat of the boar, brandy, bread, and cheeses. They ate as they rode.

When James offered food for lunch on the fourth day Erica shook her head. "Can't. Sick," she answered and he quickened the pace even more. That night Erica fell too ill to ride.

She sat by the fire sweating and shivering. Her heart still hurt after four days and she didn't understand that because she had quit taking the pain pills. Elsbeth felt better now so Erica thought she should too. They had both fallen off their moving horses but Erica could no longer sit. Elsbeth helped her lay back on a blanket.

"What are you feeling?" she asked with far too much concern.

"Must look bad," Erica answered. "You sound worried." The firelight danced on one side of Elsbeth's face and made her hard to focus upon. "Feel like hell," she added with a quavering voice.

Edwards

"Caught the worse flu ever." Through the haze of the chills then fever, the constant throbs in her chest, arm, and leg she could hardly stand it. Her chest hurt especially. It felt like someone drilled into her. She closed her eyes to try and ignore the aches and get through this.

"We didn't tell you but those arrows were packed with red clay."

Erica had no idea what that meant. She opened her eyes again.

"It's what is making you sick," Elsbeth explained. "I don't know if you can take the antidote," she added with a tight voice. "It never came up in my briefing. James doesn't remember General Desante mentioning it either."

A log in the fire cracked. The sap popped and hissed as Erica considered this. "What be red clay?" she asked even though her heart felt like it was crushing itself and it was hard to speak at all.

"It's a type of poisonous clay. It's pliable and sticky and it was in the arrowheads. We guess they figured if they couldn't kill you outright they would be able to poison you. But we have the antidote. It's always in first aid kits only we don't want to give it to you. We don't know if an iridim patient can take it."

The attackers certainly had time to prepare. Erica remembered the brown collar and cuff of the uniform. She closed her eyes to rest.

"Get up." Elsbeth slipped her hand behind Erica's head. "If you get much worse we'll have to give it to you and we shouldn't. We need to get you to Pey where a cureman can take care of you. We're close. Get up. You have rested as long as we can allow."

Erica groaned and clutched her fists to her chest. "My heart. 'Tis bad since the attack. Must be why, that poison."

Elsbeth slowly lowered her back to the blanket. "Since the attack? Why didn't you tell us?"

Erica tried to fight the growing pressure. Her arm ached from more than the arrow wound. "Give me the antidote," she told them through closed teeth.

"No," James argued. "It could kill you." He stood over them. He glanced between Erica and Elsbeth repeatedly.

"It may," Erica told him and hardly got the words out. "Clay will. 'Tis a heart attack. Must be." She had heard about them. It was building fast now and it would kill. "Hurts like a house on me."

She heard pills shaking in a bottle.

The Marrilian

"No!" James hissed. He squatted beside them. "Just a little farther. It could kill her." He sat and pulled Erica onto his lap. He hugged her close to his chest.

She curled around the pain and leaned against him, shivering and dripping with sweat.

"We have to," Elsbeth begged. "I'm sorry, James, we have to."

"I'll take her on my horse. I can gallop the rest of the way."

Erica shuddered. His warmth felt so good. She clutched at his uniform.

"You can't. Look at her. We have to. It would take half the night to get there even at a gallop. I don't think we have that much time. I've seen someone have a heart attack. It looks like this. It hurts like hell." She put the pill in his hand. "You have to."

He wrapped his fist around it. He hugged Erica close. He held her and warmed her as long as Elsbeth allowed but then the pain took Erica's breath.

"James," Elsbeth warned. "Do it before she can't swallow the damn thing!"

He made up his mind. He pressed the pill against Erica's lips then forced it into her mouth then helped her drink. "Sleep. I'll keep you safe," he promised and kissed her hair. After she swallowed he held her tighter.

The pill threatened to come up and she feared it was too late. She tried to breathe. She tried to survive this night. If she could hold on another minute then another one and one more after that then the pill might work. It took time, a lot of time, hours, but the pain subsided and she nodded off in his arms. He laid her next to the fire when she finally slept.

Elsbeth and James were by her side as soon as she woke the next morning. Both of them looked tired. Erica smiled weakly. "It worked," she told them.

James leaned over her. "The poison is still in your wounds. It's still leaching into your blood. You need a healer to remove it and a cureman to treat you," he told her tensely. "We have to get to Pey as soon as possible."

Finally, the end of the ride, Erica thought.

'As if it's a good thing,' Zoe said. Erica's eyes widened in surprise.

"Are you all right?" Elsbeth asked. "That was the strangest look on your face."

Good lords. Erica shook her head. She sat up.

"Erica?" James asked fearfully. He took her shoulders in his hands and looked in her eyes. "Erica?"

She looked back at him. It sounded like he asked her name to see who she was. "'Tis fine," Erica responded and slowly stood with James' help. She noticed a funny sensation run down her arm, a trickle like sweat but she wasn't hot. *Now what?* She wondered. "Should we go? Can ride now."

James' brows twitched as he considered her. He eyed her then released her. "We have to eat first," he answered, "which won't be much. The pack horse fell on most of our food and it's about gone. We'll leave as soon as we're done." He gathered the few items he had for breakfast. Elsbeth saddled the horses.

Erica glanced down at her hand once they were busy and saw red on her wrist. "Son-of-a-bitch," she muttered and cringed.

"What's wrong?" Elsbeth demanded. She paused with the bridles and looked Erica's direction.

Erica looked up. She had spoken too loudly. She didn't want them to give her any more drugs, not even healer's paste. "Blood," she said softly and held out her hand. "No more healer's paste. Iridim can react with it. You be no cureman. Can't tell how much to use."

Elsbeth stared at her bloody hand. James joined them. "Is something-" he began to ask then saw Erica's outstretched hand. "You need to be healed again," he told her.

Elsbeth gripped his shoulder as he turned to get the healer's paste. "We can't," she informed him. "She's right. We don't know how much paste we can use. Healer's paste, even the stuff we have for her, can cause her problems. We are close enough to a cureman that we just have to ride."

"Let her bleed?" He glanced between the two women. "That's insane! You have lost too much blood already," he told Erica. "Did you see how much you left in the road?" He pointed back the way they had come.

"No." She tapped her chest with her good hand. "But my heart feels good today. Would keep it so. Should ride and find a cureman. Would be best." She pulled her bloody hand into her taped coat sleeve.

Elsbeth nodded. She agreed.

James frowned at them. "She'll weaken, lose too much blood."

Erica shook her head. " No more drugs. Feel good enough."

"I have to agree with her," Elsbeth stated once again with the authority of her rank.

"She could bleed to death," James hissed. He looked between

them frantically.

"No healing," Elsbeth told him with the tone of an order. He looked dismal and worried until Elsbeth relented. "Not at the rate she is bleeding now. She can tell us if it gets worse." She looked down at Erica harshly. "You tell us as soon as it does."

Erica nodded.

"You be sure to tell us," James demanded.

She stepped back from him. "So," she agreed softly. "Will."

He acted as if he wanted more, maybe to ignore both of them and heal her anyway.

"We cannot use the healer's paste, Captain," Elsbeth told him again. "Mount up."

"Can she at least have fresh bandages? Is it too much to bind the wound tighter?"

Elsbeth's eyes narrowed. They said nothing for several moments then she handed him the bridles.

"Finish," she ordered. "I'll put on fresh bandages but we're wasting time so be ready when I'm done." She went to her horse to get the first aid kit.

James sighed. "Thank you," he called after her. He shifted the bridles to one hand and pointed his finger at Erica's face. "You tell us if the bleeding gets worse. I don't want to hear about it later, after it's hurt you for hours or days. If you have any new pains you tell us," he warned then stalked away to bridle the horses.

Erica nodded after him with eyes twice their normal size.

"Stupid fool," Elsbeth muttered as she returned. She helped Erica off with her coat and shirt. "New bandages will bleed through before we ride an hour. Don't you dare tell him. Promise me that or we'll be stopping way too soon. You need a cureman not me. He doesn't need to know every detail of your health. Just tell us if you feel another heart attack but let this bleed unless it gets worse or you feel feint."

Erica nodded. "Promise," she agreed but she glanced at James to make sure he didn't hear. He was fitting the bridle on Elsbeth's horse far enough away. Elsbeth understood her concerns better than James. She didn't want to stop all the time either. Erica knew she needed a cureman.

"Good," Elsbeth growled. She opened the first aid kit and bandaged her arm again.

They ate their breakfast of bread and cheese and brandy. Erica drank a lot of brandy. They mounted and rode in silence.

It didn't take long before blood dribbled down Erica's fingers in a steady trickle. She held her hand on her leg so it disappeared into the black fabric of her pants. It felt sticky and warm and the constant drainage along her arm annoyed her. The wound on her leg opened as well. That bandage squeezed out more blood into her pants with every step that Turnbull took. She couldn't do anything to get comfortable.

"Are you all right?" James asked when she tried to wrap her coat sleeve around her arm differently. "Is it bleeding again? Are you strong enough? Can you make it? I can ride with you on my horse." He kept the horses walking. He rode beside her to shoot his aggressive questions.

Erica winced at his tone. "'Tis fine. It bleeds but not so bad." And she knew if he took her on his horse he would feel her soaking wet leg in a moment and be irate.

"Has it soaked the bandages?" he demanded.

She hesitated.

"Undoubtedly it has," Elsbeth told him. She twisted to look back at them. "Now leave her alone."

He reined his horse around Turnbull instead and came up next to Erica's bad arm. He pulled up the cuff of her coat sleeve. "Elsbeth," he called upon finding the bandage soaked and Erica's fingers dripping red.

"I know," Elsbeth said. "Move along James."

"We need to stop and change the bandage!"

"Can make a little longer," Erica argued. "Would finish this ride."

James glared at her for several moments. "You will not arrive a bloody mess."

"There is no avoiding it," Elsbeth told him. "It won't help to put a new bandage on her. The wound has opened. I could see that when I put this bandage on. For some reason the healer's paste disintegrated. She needs a healer and a cureman not me. It will bleed through again in no time."

James blinked at Elsbeth. He looked back at Erica and then brushed his hand over the spot where he knew they had bound the wound on her leg. When he raised his hand he found it covered in blood. He stiffened in his saddle. "They have both opened." His eyes narrowed on Erica. "You knew? You could feel this?"

"Can make it," Erica told him. "Quick be good. Would not stop to make me clean. Will last only a moment." Oh if only he had a lick of sense to think this through. She understood his concern, but she couldn't afford it right now.

The Marrilian

He wiped her blood on his blanket. "We are walking the horses as fast as we can with Turnbull hurt. If you can't stay on or if he falters you let me know and I'll hold you."

"Will," she agreed.

"Sure you will," he snapped under his breath. He made his horse jump into a faster walk.

Within the hour they skirted the edge of a town. Erica watched as they went by it in amazement. Wouldn't that be the place to find a healer and cureman? James and Elsbeth didn't seem to think so. They hurried on. A short distance after the town they turned off the road and made their way across a sparsely treed field. Erica hung on to the saddle up and down the small hills. She sighed in relief when a house came into view, one lone house nestled in native Quirni trees.

The house was two floors tall but it fit under the trees easily. It had long windows and several gables. Erica couldn't see the whole structure due to nearer shorter trees blocking her view. She could see it was big and white. Did they even know about other colors here? The grounds weren't what she would expect for such an enormous house but they served well for the ranch of which it was part. Nothing was ornamental. The drive between the house and barn was gravel. The fencing was wood, unpainted, and kept in grazing horses. There were no decorative flowers or bushes. There was a garden for vegetables down the slope to the side of the house. A windmill pumped water into a trough by the covered porch running along the back and the overflow watered the vegetable garden.

James trotted his horse ahead to the porch. An agent sat there with his back to their side of the field. James called out to him well before he reached the house and the man jumped to his feet. He came into the yard. They spoke hurriedly then the man went into the house.

Turnbull dragged himself to the hitching post and drank from the water trough. James had been prodding him to go faster all afternoon.

"We made it," Elsbeth breathed in relief as she dismounted.

James tied his horse. He helped Erica down. She continued to hold the saddle after he set her on her feet. She rested her head against the cool leather and tried to clear her mind. She felt dizzy and tired, probably from a loss of blood. She knew she must look like hell. Whether this was a Delegate house or a claimant's house or even Matilda's, she didn't know but in any case it was too bad she had to arrive looking and feeling like this.

Edwards

Blood dripped from her fingertips. She held her hand to her chest. She tucked her fist in her coat sleeve.

"What happened to you, Major? Why didn't you check in?" a woman demanded.

Elsbeth stopped brushing at her uniform and snapped to attention. James left Erica to stand at Elsbeth's side. "General Burk!" They both saluted with stiff hands to their temples then they both snapped their hands to their sides. "My telephone was broken five days ago. We were attacked outside of Nigh. Miss Kinsley was injured. She needs a cureman and a healer ASAP."

Erica came around Turnbull's back end to see the general. The woman was tall but slight of build with brackish blond hair and a pretty angular face.

Burk saw Erica and pasted on a big smile. "You are Lynn, obviously," she stated and left Elsbeth and James behind. She held out her hand as she approached. "I'm General Burk. I am pleased to meet you."

Erica didn't take her hand. "Pleasure," she returned in a tone that would have been more severe if she hadn't been so tired. This was one of the people who intended to use her for some unknown purpose. She wasn't going to be kind. But then she noticed Elsbeth stiffen and thought better of getting her in trouble. She didn't take the general's hand, however. She nodded instead.

"'Tis a kindness you see me," she said simply and lowered her eyes and head in an attempt to make up for her rudeness. She lifted her eyes again when the general didn't make the appropriate response.

The woman stared at her.

Erica stared back.

"Well, you were expected tomorrow," she said and seemed happy to change the subject. "We have several people who are looking forward to meeting you. They are here now by happy coincidence."

In other words, Erica knew, they had tracked her and knew exactly when to be at the house but she said, "How nice."

"Come with me and I'll introduce you." She reached for Erica's injured arm to lead the way but Erica backed off. "Is something wrong?"

"My arm be hurt," Erica explained, and, good lords, the heat! She took off her hat and fanned her face.

The general blinked at her. She stared again. "Oh, of course, the Major mentioned that." She glanced at Elsbeth with a smile

The Marrilian

and raised an eyebrow. Elsbeth wore a strained expression. Burk smiled at Erica. "Well, we have an excellent cureman inside. If we can induce her to take a look at you, she can fix you right up."

The general reached for her uninjured arm this time. Erica replaced her hat and went along but she didn't keep the general's step because her leg felt like it would buckle and then she stopped completely when she saw three people walk down the porch steps. The first was a man with dark wavy hair who was as sophisticated and as handsome as any man she had ever seen. He was young, tall, fit, smiling, and dazzling. He walked with a posture of complete confidence. He belonged on a pedestal.

The second person was a woman, somewhat plain with short blond hair but classy, just as young as the man and smiling. She had the same kind of confidence and the same walk. She expected to be looked at and admired as well.

The third person could only be Matilda Kinsley. Erica stared at her and Matilda paused in her step when their eyes met. It was almost like looking in a mirror. Matilda's hair was darker but other than that they were nearly twins. Matilda continued across the yard. She beamed a smile at Elsbeth.

"Major, how nice to see you again," she said with an open, friendly manner as the three people approached.

"At your leisure," the general instructed James and Elsbeth.

Elsbeth and Matilda exchanged a quick embrace. "I see you got my cousin here in one piece," Matilda remarked with a gay lilt in her tone then turned to James. "James, always a pleasure." She gave him a quick embrace and kissed his cheek. She then turned to Erica whom she looked up and down without expression. She gestured to the people who had accompanied her from the house. Their wide eyes suggested some surprise. "Miss Kinsley, this is Claimant Marcus Mois and Claimant Ella Mois." They both nodded to Erica politely.

Claimants! Oh lords! Erica's stomach twisted. She had never expected to meet claimants here! She never thought she'd meet one as a tenant. Her heart raced as she tried to return a greeting, just a simple one, the correct one! A motion, a nod, but her head swam and her leg felt weaker from the surprise.

"Lo," she managed to croak as her breathing came harder and her vision began to close in. No! Of all the blasted things! To feint when she met a claimant, a real honest to god claimant that wasn't hiding who they were. Damned if she would!

She stepped forward to meet them properly and her leg collapsed. She went down on a knee. If she could have dug a

Edwards

hole, she would have hidden in it. What was worse, she had to put her hands down to stop from pitching onto her face.

"That's certainly uncalled for," Marcus chuckled. "We aren't royalty."

"Marcus, she isn't kneeling she's hurt," Ella admonished in amazement at his stupidity. "Look at the blood on her."

"Oh," he replied and fell silent.

James and Elsbeth were at Erica's side before she could fall the rest of the way. "Come on, Doll," James whispered in her ear. He started to pick her up.

Erica pushed him back as much as she could. "Just help me walk," she asked as he helped her kneel. "Get me on my feet," she added but Ella Mois had already knelt in front of her. Erica's head hung. She had her eyes closed and didn't know the claimant was so close.

"Don't be ridiculous," the claimant said. "James, bring her up to the porch."

Erica opened her eyes. Good lords, she knew she stank with dirt and blood. Why would the claimant come so close? "Just need a clinic, my lady, please. Just need to see a healer."

Ella lifted Erica's chin with a cool clean hand and smiled at her. "I'm a cureman, Lynn, and a bit of a healer as well. Will I do?"

Lynn?

"Yes, my lady," Erica whispered. "My pardons, didn't know."

"Matilda, you could learn a lesson or two in respect from this one," Ella noted with a satisfied grin and then put her hand on Erica's forehead.

Her touch felt so cool. It was wonderful.

"She has a fever, James. Remove her coat."

Erica tried to help him.

"Keep still," Ella commanded and gave Erica a severe look by lifting her chin again and glaring in her eyes. "You will do as I say. Enough struggling understand?"

Erica had no idea she had been struggling and felt more than happy to relax especially given such a command from a claimant. Elsbeth and James slipped her coat from her shoulders.

"She has lost a lot of blood," Ella noted dryly upon seeing the soaked bandage and sleeve.

"That is the second bandage today," Elsbeth told her.

"Didn't want more paste," said Erica softly.

Elsbeth grunted in displeasure as she tossed Erica's coat to the side. It fell with a thud for all of the things in the pockets.

The Marrilian

"Her leg has an injury as well. Both have reopened. We tried to heal them."

"She carries a pistol?" Matilda half asked and half stated in surprise.

"Yes, Mati, and she saved our butts with it," Elsbeth told her. "Two archers attacked us outside of Nigh. She shot their bows right out of their hands before they could kill us. She defended us while she was pinned to the ground with arrows through her arm and leg."

Everyone stared at her.

"Their arrowheads were poisoned with red clay," Elsbeth added. "It's made her sick."

"Red clay," Ella repeated with alarm. "James, remove her shirt and belts. I need to see the wounds."

James unbuckled her gun and passed it to Matilda and then reached around Erica and untied the belt that held up her pants.

Ella unbuttoned Erica's shirt and slipped it off to reveal the bloodied and battered vest. She pulled the vest off and put it in a pile with her shirt and coat leaving Erica in a thin tank top. She removed the bandages.

"You tried to heal this?" Ella asked as she inspected the wound on Erica's arm.

"Yes. It was healed enough to stop the bleeding five days ago," Elsbeth explained.

James tossed Erica's belt on her clothes and waited for more instructions.

"Didn't you say she is an iridim patient?" the Claimant asked the general. She didn't wait for an answer. "Lynn, how does your heart feel?"

"Fine," Erica replied. She sat on her heals. It hurt her leg and bandage squished but she didn't have the strength to kneel anymore. "They gave me the antidote to clay."

"What?" The claimant's eyes shot between Elsbeth and James. "That was risky. That was very risky. Too much and she would be dead."

"Told them to, my lady. Was having an attack."

"I see," the Claimant said. "You waited. Good, but red clay antidote thins the blood and destroys blood clots and that's why the wounds opened. She needed to have the red clay cleaned out of the wounds and be completely healed first. But I guess, under the circumstances, you performed admirably," she said to Elsbeth and James. "I commend you."

"Thank you, Claimant," they both replied.

Edwards

General Burk stepped forward. "I'll call a transport for her, Claimant. She appears to need a lot of care. We can do that."

"Sophie, I'm quite willing and able," Lady Mois replied curtly. She stood. "She can be easily healed." She turned back to James and Elsbeth. "Stand her up. Lower her pants."

He pulled her to her feet. Her pants slipped down without the belt. Elsbeth took off the bandages. Erica hung on to James' arm.

Ella took one glance at the leg wound and shook her head. "Pick her up and take her upstairs," she told James. She stood back. "Mati, I need a bed. I suggest you cover it with a lot of old blankets or towels. It won't take much to heal her but she's bleeding rather freely." Matilda nodded and left as Elsbeth pulled Erica's pants up and James scooped her into his arms. He carried her to the house. He seemed to know exactly where he was going.

Several people finished preparing the bed as James laid Erica on it and stood back. Lady Mois retrieved her medical bag and removed items from it in a flurry of activity. She pointed to Elsbeth and a young female servant and told them to strip Erica of all her clothes. She put a temperature gauge around Erica's uninjured forearm along with a blood pressure band. She turned on a scanner and set it on the bed along with bottles, bags of fluid, needles and syringes. Then she drew blood, tested it several different ways, and started an IV, which James got to hold.

Erica wasn't as concerned about being stripped in front of all these people as being poked with needles and filled with things she didn't understand. She watched the Claimant who worked over her. Could she trust her any more than the SDD?

"We have work to do and I don't think you want to be around for it," Ella said kindly, winked, and then injected something in the IV line.

Warmth flowed into Erica's arm. She managed to fight sleep only for a moment.

When Erica woke she first noticed the warm bed and then how well she felt. She felt amazingly well. An oil lamp lit the room.

"Good afternoon," Elsbeth greeted and leaned forward in her chair. "We've been waiting for you. Did you have a nice nap?" She smiled like she had won a bet.

Erica flexed her arm and leg. They hardly hurt at all and her

The Marrilian

heart felt fine too. "'Tis really good," she exclaimed. "She's either an excellent cureman or have been here lots of days."

"She is excellent," Elsbeth assured her. "You have been here about five hours. She said you could get up when you woke. It sounds like she is right."

Erica slowly sat. Her arm was healed. The paste had closed the wound nicely. There would barely be a scar. She lifted the blanket and looked at her leg. It was healed too. Amazing. She was also clean. When she put her hand in her hair, it was still damp. Who had done that?

"You were a bloody mess. James and I washed you in the shower," Elsbeth explained and tossed her blue canvas pants, a blue shirt and undergarments. All were used but nothing she had seen before. She assumed they belonged to Matilda. "Get dressed then come on downstairs. We're on the back porch."

"James and you washed me. You held me in the shower?"

Elsbeth laughed lightly. "As if you mind after all the times we helped each other with baths. We know what you look like."

Erica thought about that. "So," she said softly but James had never been close when she bathed. She had a lot of scars. Not all her wounds had been healed as well as these.

"Get dressed," Elsbeth told her again and left.

The sun hadn't quite set when Erica joined her hosts on the back porch. The porch faced west. A pink sky lingered over the barns and pastures. Softly glowing oil lamps hung on the support beams around the porch and from a beam over the table. They cast a warm yellow glow. The remains of a meal lay upon the table. Erica paused in the door to take stock of the situation but no sooner had she appeared than Ella got up and came to her.

"Now *that* is better," she remarked and led Erica over to an empty chair at the end of the table. The spot placed Erica with General Burk to her right and Ella to her left. It wasn't the place Erica would have picked. She considered how she might take another chair but Ella's hand pushed on her arm. Erica sat down across from James.

Marcus and Burk were at either head of the table with Matilda, Elsbeth, and James to Marcus' left. The agent who had been sitting on the porch when they arrived sat to Marcus' right along with a stranger, then Ella, and Erica.

"Are you feeling better?" General Burk asked.

"Tons better," Erica replied. Since she was in the company of claimants, she tried to speak as they would. She tried to hide her Tenpole and, even more, she tried to hide Chaucer. "Thank you, Claimant." She didn't look at them but only turned towards them. She kept her eyes down as she had been taught to do when speaking to her superiors. She would do everything she could to let these people know how much she respected them.

Claimant Mois shook her shoulder, which would have hurt like hell a mere five hours ago. Now it barely felt sore. "It was a pleasure. I don't have much cause to use my arts since I've become a claimant." She gestured at the table. "You have to eat now. You look thin."

Erica glanced around at all the dishes which consisted of three roast chickens, green salad, a mixture of berries, a dish that looked like mashed potatoes, gravy. She hardly knew where to start. Ella handed her the potatoes and carrots so she started with them. She followed up with the berries and salad as the conversation around the table turned from weather then to ranch work and then to a topic she didn't understand.

"We'll need a transfer on Amonday," Matilda told General Burk as Erica leaned over her plate and enjoyed every mouthful. Amonday was the last day of their workweek. Quirni years and days were longer than the standard so they had added one hour, thirteen hour, to each day and one day to each week, Amonday. She realized she didn't know how far away Amonday was. She had no idea what day it was, or for that matter, even what month. She sat back to listen and declined Ella's offer of meat. "The shipment will have five-hundred units," Matilda added. She glanced at Erica then looked away, as if she disturbed her.

"Five-hundred? Why so few?" asked General Burk harshly.

"We had some supply problems," replied Matilda.

"Again? I thought you had taken care of that."

"I thought so too. Apparently not."

"This will put everything off once more."

"It couldn't be helped."

"Our demand for parts is outstripping the supplies," explained the man Erica hadn't met. She was surprised to hear his Marrilian accent. He was lighter skinned than typical Parcles, but it was an upper class accent from Parcles although diluted by Quirni tones. He must have lived on Quirni for a while. The Quirni spoke with precise, clipped-off words. Erica glanced down the table at the man to make sure she had never seen him before. That would be a hell of a thing if she had, but she didn't

The Marrilian

know him. Ella noticed her glance.

"Lynn, you haven't met Matilda's husband. Roger Serval, this is Lynn Kinsley."

Roger leaned forward and nodded to Erica. He had an average build with wavy almost curly, dark brown hair that badly needed a cut and eyes that made her think he had seen a lot of suffering in his days, an almost pained look from the way they pulled down at the sides. He wasn't handsome in the classic sense but a pleasant sight.

"Pleasure, I'm sure," he greeted. He spoke in the distinguished Marrilian lilt. "We have all been looking forward to meeting you."

His accent unnerved her. Tenpole didn't talk to Parcles except to be ordered about by them. "My pleasure as well, Mr. Serval," she replied and tried hard to mask her Tenpole accent. She had to think quick to say 'are' instead of 'be'. "You are recently from Marril, sir?" He smiled rather than scowl to hear her. Did he look amused? Did he know he was the type of person she targeted in her work? She would have left him alone for that smile.

"Yes, I am from Parcles, Miss Kinsley, but not recently. You are from Tenpole," he added but not contemptuously. His smile remained and it didn't turn mean or suggestive. Maybe he didn't hear Chaucer. Maybe she spoke well enough. "Ella tells me you have thayanite poisoning. You should be doing something about that." He produced a pack of smokes, bumped it, and then held them out to her behind Ella's back.

"Thank you" Erica took one. His type had never given her a damn thing in her life. She checked the cigarette to be sure it was real, that it was really a thayanite antidote smoke, and it was. The last thing she needed was a tobacco cigarette. She lit it with the matches he gave her then backed away from the table.

Ella touched her arm. "There is no need to be embarrassed, Lynn. Come, scoot back up here. More than one of us has had to get rid of thayanite."

Erica did as told and at the same time tried to ignore 'Lynn' if she could. Every time someone said it, she felt a drill of hate and anger.

"Perhaps we could continue?" snapped General Burk. No one disagreed but Matilda fixed Burk with a glare that clearly suggested she didn't care for the general's attitude. "We will pick up your work on Amonday," Burk agreed. "But if you can't get the supply problems resolved, Mati, then I suggest you work more closely with us. I am certain we could produce more favorable responses."

"I told you I would handle it. If the plans are pushed back, then so be it."

Erica wasn't surprised to learn a Delegate general and Matilda were at odds. Apparently Erica did have some things in common with her cousin other than murder. But why was the Delegate working with a mass murderer? Why would Claimants Mois work with her?

"Miss Kinsley." Erica had been thinking and focused on the mist rising from her smoke rather than stare at Matilda. She barely noticed Burk addressing her. "You must be wondering why we brought you here?"

So the time had come. Erica had expected to feel excited right now but instead she felt fear. "Yes, General," she replied calmly but thought she ought to get up and run. She tapped her smoke in an ashtray Ella pushed close.

Before Burk could continue the servants arrived to clear the table. They set delicate plates before each of them with a fork. The silverware seemed to actually be silver. It was the first metal eating utensils Erica had seen on the planet. General Burk waited until pies were served and everyone had taken a bite, exclaimed on the taste for the benefit of the cook, and quieted.

"Yes, well," Burk said, annoyed that her conversation was interrupted once more. Her face was now cast in the shadows of the lamps. The day had passed into night.

Elsbeth sat across from Erica but hadn't caught her eye once until now and to Erica's surprise she seemed amused with Burk's difficulty to keep a conversation in progress.

"You came to our attention some time ago," Burk began in the typical uninformative way of the Delegate. "When you were in the care of our Marrilian counterparts a general who knows Matilda saw you. He thought you were Matilda at first until he examined your records. He realized the exceptional opportunity you represented to facilitate plans here.

"We then learned you tried to buy passage to Sirrus. For reasons you undoubtedly know, they were not granted." Burk paused. A knowing smile played across her lips. From the corner of her eye Erica saw Elsbeth sit back with her arms across her chest. Burk wasn't facing her and didn't see her annoyed curl of the lip. "I don't doubt you know exactly what I am talking about?" Burk asked.

'Pissant,' Zoe said.

The Marrilian

Erica smiled at it. What a childish word, but it fit her feelings about the general. "I believe you refer to the twenty year exile from Sirrus," Erica asked with the smile still on her face. She didn't want to play the general's game. She had already shared this secret with Elsbeth. She would share it with everyone to disarm the general's attempt to use it against her.

"Yes," General Burk replied casually, but her forehead almost knit into a frown. "It seems you are a few years away from going back to Sirrus. With that in mind, we allowed a ticket here. I regret we couldn't send anyone to explain our reasons but that is what I am about to do now."

Regrets? They couldn't send someone? Who was White but someone they sent? And when hadn't there been time to explain themselves? She had been in the Padt City for months! She felt the tickle of a cough.

'Calm down,' Zoe warned.

"First, I want to tell you we are all very happy to have you here, Lynn."

All right, she had heard 'Lynn' enough. She put her hand over her mouth to hide a sneer, and cleared her throat.

'Erica,' Zoe warned even harsher.

"Here, take these," Roger said and tossed an entire pack of cigarettes to her. They landed next to her desert plate. She nodded her thanks.

"You bear a striking resemblance to Matilda," Burk continued as Erica struck a match and held it to the cigarette." You are also an iridim patient, as is she, so you are even like her in stature and you had to leave Marril so why not come here?"

Erica pulled the cigarette from her mouth and brought her eyes up. "Truly?" she asked and completely forgot to use Quirni vernacular. "Would you an answer?"

Burk smiled with an air of superiority. "Sure."

Erica's eyes narrowed. "Because this be a barbaric, pisshole planet without a shred of privacy, luxury or five nice people in one town."

The entire table fell deathly still.

Anger flashed across the general's face but was quickly hidden. General Burk stared at her and Erica stared back. She would not avert her eyes. Lynn was too close. Erica worked hard to control her.

"Succinct," Roger observed and sounded amused.

Matilda huffed in displeasure.

General Burk ignored his comment.

Edwards

Erica managed to gain some control and dropped her eyes.

"I understand you have been hurt on a few occasions, Lynn, but I feel we have acquitted ourselves well. You are here and whole."

Sure, Erica thought, *and why don't you meet Zoe?* She drew off her cigarette and kept her eyes on it.

"As for your privacy it seems preferable that you be with our agents and stay alive rather than on your own. The unfortunate attitude of the populace towards an individual that looks like you is deadly, as you are now aware." She paused to let that sink in and it did.

It brought Erica's eyes up again. She looked into Burk's face and wondered how in the hell she could say such a thing. *As you are now aware?* That meant the long trip on horseback, the attacks, not telling her about a murdering cousin was to be a lesson to her? That was how Erica understood this comment, *as you are now aware.* It had all been designed to teach her she needed the Delegate, which apparently Matilda had learned judging by their presence.

It explained the uniform on one of the attackers in Nigh as well but he had come close to killing her. Did Burk feel she would be better off dead than not on their side? It begged the question; how far would they go to get her on their side? And what did they want her to do? She remained silent but glared at Burk as her blood pressure rose.

Burk sat back confidently with her hands laced together and her legs neatly crossed. "You are aware of the reason you have been attacked. People think you are Matilda. I must admit we didn't expect the attacks to be so violent. We underestimated the feelings of the population but as I already said, you are here and whole so no harm done. In fact, it supports our decision to bring you into our care. Matilda is a very important person to the future of this planet. Her safety is paramount. She holds the key to bring this world those luxuries you clearly miss. Her needs are often interfered with due to the unfortunate circumstances of her reputation. You can help fulfill those needs."

Erica pulled her eyes from Burk. She looked at Matilda and found her gaze solid and curious. Good lords but Erica could hardly stand to look at her. How could they be so much alike? Could it be Matilda didn't care for the Delegate any more than Erica did? Matilda didn't appear to be sympathetic with whatever the General tried to say.

"Lynn," Burk said in a stern voice to get her attention once

The Marrilian

more.

She dragged her eyes from her cousin and back to Burk. "Continue to call me that and I leave. You know I don't like it or your counterpart in the Southern Padt City be a bigger ass than I gave him credit for."

All around the table people shifted uncomfortably. James and Elsbeth stiffened in their seats and glanced at each other.

Burk pressed back in her chair. "You will do well to consider to whom you speak," she warned unpleasantly.

"I speak to a scheming, eavesdropping, Delegate general." Erica let that sink in. "Or will you tell me 'tis your superiors that make all decisions and you just do as told?" Erica pushed away from the table and intended to get up but Ella held her.

"Stay." She squeezed Erica's arm gently until she looked at her.

Erica felt nothing but respect for a claimant, a person who could accomplish so much and lead so many people, and suddenly she felt ashamed. How could she let herself act this way in front of them? She shot Marcus a glance to see how he reacted. He appeared interested, not angry or annoyed at her outburst. Erica slowly relaxed and settled back into the chair.

"My pardons, Claimant."

"Pardons to the *Claimant*?" Burk mocked. "I think more is in order than that! We have treated you well. We have watched over you. We got you here!"

Erica suppressed the colorful retort she wanted to make then asked the question she thought Burk could not answer truthfully. She did her best to ask in a calm manner and tone. "Do you control the agents on this claim?"

Burk's brow knit in confusion. "Of course, I do. I am the general in charge of Northern Quirni Security."

"You alone?" demanded Erica.

Burk squinted in suspicion. "Why?"

"If so, you be responsible for the last attack. That be why. Was *agents* who attacked me near Nigh."

Burk sat upright in her chair. "I am responsible for no such thing!"

"Then explain why agents put two arrows in me," said Erica with as calm a manner as she could manage and she thought she sounded amazingly calm compared to the way she felt. "Why did your agent poison me, almost kill me, with that blasted red clay?"

Silence. Not one person moved or spoke but watched the two of them. Even Elsbeth, it seemed, couldn't believe what she was hearing but James sat with wide eyes and he nodded almost imperceptivity. He gripped Elsbeth's arm and gave her a look that widened her eyes.

"Good God!" General Burk finally exclaimed with her eyes riveted on Erica. "I was warned about this. This is ridiculous."

"What were you warned about?" Marcus asked. He sat forward and studied Erica intently.

"Claimant, I am sorry." Burk readjusted her chair back from the table which put her further from Erica. "They checked Miss Kinsley out in the Padt City and declared her fit for our purposes. Obviously the trip has been too much for her. She is insane. She is unstable and hallucinating and it is not for the first time."

A rustle of shifting bodies sounded around the table. Erica kept her eyes on Burk.

"Is this true?" Ella asked.

Erica looked from Burk to Ella. "Had problems in the past," she admitted. She turned back to the General. "Was why the Delegate took me wasn't it? My father accused me of being mentally unfit, but that be in the past. Was no hallucination on the road. Hallucinations do not make real wounds. Were cufflinks of an SDD captain on the man who attacked me. Saw them when he lifted his arm to shoot. Looked like those James wears. So how long has the Delegate planned to bring me here? When was my murder planned?"

Burk didn't answer. She stared.

Erica shot a glare at Matilda. "What would you with me, General? Die in her place? Would you kill me so she would no longer be hunted?"

General Burk shook her head. She honestly looked horrified by the idea. "You're sick," she accused softly. "That's sick."

"You scheming bastards. Call me sick? My problems begin after you got me. As for exile, that be twenty years for my father too but he went back! You fixed that didn't you? He went back and I can't. Now you ask for my help?" It wasn't easy but Erica stayed seated and stopped the coming rant. She had said enough.

Burk shook her head slowly as if in disbelief. "I see." She looked to the Claimants. "This girl had severe mental problems that we thought were cured. I can see now we were wrong." Eyes passed from her to Erica. "She can't tolerate being called Lynn because she believes there is another part to her, the part that she blames for all her past mistakes. She doesn't want to hear the name 'Lynn' because she thinks Lynn will be activated, don't

The Marrilian

you?" she asked Erica.

"You should know. SDD *treated* me."

"You brought her here knowing this?" Matilda asked.

"And we'll take her away as well," Burk told her in a consoling tone. "We thought she was well. I see we were wrong. If she believes agents were attacking her we were dreadfully wrong. I think another stint in the insane asylum is what she needs."

"What?" Erica's breath caught. Her mouth dropped open. She had expected they would take her back to the city or send her back to Marril. Burk's words hit Erica like a blow to the stomach. Burk smiled. "No," Erica gasped almost inaudibly. "No. You have no right."

Burk sneered and grinned together. "Yes, Miss Kinsley, I do. You are a menace and you need more treatment. An institution is just the thing you need and I'm sorry we ever tried to give you a life." She pulled her phone from her uniform then got up and walked off the porch to speak in private.

Erica stared after her until she was out of sight. Everyone watched Burk leave then turned back to stare at Erica.

What had she done? It never occurred to her they would put her back in an institution here. This was Quirni. How did they have such a place?

Then she thought of the clinic where Betty and Levitus worked. She had awakened and not known if she was on Quirni or Marril there was so much metal in the room. They could lock her up and start filling her with drugs all over again. How would she get away with the thing in her ear?

She put her elbows on the table and buried her face in her hands. She'd made a mess of things.

Edwards

Chapter 10 – The Servals

Delegate agents had brought Lynn out with drugs. All Erica remembered was disappearing into Lynn's hysteria. She didn't even know what happened during the time she lost. They never told her. Each time she returned days had passed.

They had done this at the medical institution on the MSDD base and they had been given free reign by her father. He had institutionalized her because she had attacked him. It didn't matter that he had tried to beat her and rape her again. She had had enough. She had attacked him and tried to kill him. His friends had saved him and had acted as witnesses against her. They had stopped her attack and then they had turned her over to the MSDD, called her a 'menace to society', and labeled her insane.

She was in the institution about three months when they decided she was safe. By then she was sick from the drugs, confused and feeling fuzzy, and weak. She had lost her job at the mines. A social worker got her cleaning work at the MSDD offices where she could be watched but it didn't matter if they watched her at all. She had lost contact with many of her associates. She was no longer wanted by Ilene since she looked so thin and ill. That meant she had to pay rent at the brothel. Her means to any income was all but gone and she had become so sick with thayanite poisoning all she could do was leave the planet.

Her father had gone back to Sirrus while she was in the institution. She had petitioned to return there as well and even though the Sirrian authorities granted the petition she never got a ticket. All the births on all of the ships were always full, private and SDD alike. She finally got the message that even though her petition was granted she couldn't really go back. They *had* to grant her petition because they had granted her father's but they didn't have to sell her a ticket.

Now she learned it wasn't Sirrus that didn't want her but Quirni that did. She looked like her cousin. She gripped her head in her hands and cursed her foolishness for angering the general. She might have worked something out with her cousin. She hadn't been thinking.

Edwards

After Burk walked away Erica heard a chair scrape against the wood of the porch. "You are not insane," Elsbeth told her as she put her hands on her shoulders. "You are fine."

Erica fought tears behind her hands. She couldn't, wouldn't face these people. She felt like so much less than a person. She shouldn't be in their company, people who did good things, who made claims. She should have dug out the aid in her ear and fled north.

"If she's insane then so am I," James admitted. "When I was fighting with one of those men I thought I saw Delegate insignia on his collar but I couldn't believe it. I didn't believe it so I kept it to myself." He paused. "Now I wish I had said something."

Silence followed his revelation. Erica stifled her sobs.

Ella Mois touched her arm. "Lynn, General Burk described what sounds like dissociation disorder? Is that what you have?"

Erica swallowed hard to push down Lynn's anger so she could speak. "Yes, Claimant." She held her forehead. She kept her eyes closed tight. "The trip was too hard. My symptoms be back." It had been fine to meet a claimant though. She could always say she had met the Claimants Mois as a tenant of this planet, not a whore. She gasped around a sob then quickly sucked it in. She covered her eyes with the heels of her hands.

"Have you been hallucinating?" Ella Mois asked kindly.

As hard as it was to admit, Erica nodded. "Vocal hallucinations," she answered with a choked voice.

Claimant Mois took Erica's arm and pulled on it gently. "Look at me."

Erica did but not in her eyes.

"I have never in my life heard more true things said to an Delegate general than what you just said. Scheming is an understatement of their organi-"

Erica looked up abruptly. "You must be careful what you say, my lady. They can hear you."

Ella blinked. She glanced at Elsbeth "Is she paranoid? Paranoia is not a symptom of a dissociative."

"She is not," Elsbeth replied. "I guarantee that. Although she ought to be."

"The SDD put a hearing aid in me. It tracks me and hears me," Erica told the claimant.

Ella sat back, as if she feared Erica and Erica's heart sank.

"How did you know that?" Elsbeth spat.

"Elsbeth!" James barked and shot to his feet.

"This is true?" demanded Marcus while Ella gaped at them.

The Marrilian

James looked horrified but when Marcus glared at him he nodded. Elsbeth did too.

Erica feared they would lose their positions or worse. She stood and took Elsbeth's arm. She looked between them in a panic. Her mouth wobbled open then closed then opened again. What could she say without making things worse? She didn't want them in trouble. "'Tis no need for this. This trouble be mine. Don't make it yours."

Elsbeth tried to look serene but she failed. She pointed to the end of the porch. "Go," she ordered faintly and touched Erica's ear.

Go? Erica hesitated but Elsbeth pushed her away. Erica stumbled into her first step then walked out of hearing range to the end of the porch. Elsbeth bent close to Ella. Marcus joined them. When Erica still picked up parts of their hurried conversation she walked down the steps and into the dark yard. There she stopped and dropped her head. *Say it, Zoe, call me a fool.* She scrunched her face up hard against tears.

"They've put you through hell."

Erica turned in surprise. Matilda stood behind her. Perfect Matilda with her perfect speech, beautiful easy manner, the confidence of a claimant even though she wasn't one, and maybe a bigger killer than Erica would ever be.

"You were a mess when you arrived here today and Burk is acting like they did you a favor."

Erica stared at her with nothing to say. This girl had cost her a ticket to Sirrus. She had cost her the family that she had longed for every day she lay broken in the hospitals.

Matilda sighed then smiled for the first time. "How nuts are you? I mean, did the Delegate make you nuts or did you manage on your own?"

Erica couldn't believe it but Matilda looked like she was perfectly serious. "You *are* a brat aren't you?"

Even at the insult Matilda retained a still, quiet air about her. She tipped her head to consider something. "Who told you that I am a brat?"

"Arlo."

"Ah, Arlo." She smiled gently. "How is he?"

"Broke."

Matilda nodded. "If he had done as I asked, he wouldn't be."

Erica ignored this. "He says to tell you, you owe him 23 million square." With that said Erica had discharged her one promise. She owed Arlo so much but it had come to nothing.

Edwards

Matilda nodded. "I like Arlo. I needed him to restart the business he ran for me but he wouldn't. He wanted his money. I guess he had invested his personal property in the factory and lost it when they seized all of my assets. He would be twice as wealthy now if he had only listened to me."

"Tell him," Erica urged. Matilda looked her in the eyes, which had the effect of looking in a mirror that skewed everything. Her expressions were so wrong, her hair was too dark, her emotions were wrong. Erica found it disorienting, almost like one of her other sides had hopped loose of her skin and stood before her, but it would be a new side, not Zoe, Sal or Lynn. Matilda looked too classy and serene to be any part of Erica's makeup.

"I did tell him." Matilda tipped her head to one side again. "I have a hearing aid as well. I wonder if they listen to me?"

Erica struggled to keep from calling her names. She didn't care about Matilda's damn hearing aid. She only wanted to stay out of a Delegate institution. She wanted to stay away from their drugs. She wanted to stay away from Matilda.

Matilda made a pinched face, as if she could see Erica's turmoil and didn't like it. "So, answer my question." She sounded serious now. "I want to know. Did the Delegate make you nuts or did you manage it on your own?"

"Why?" Erica demanded and she couldn't help thinking Matilda was rude as well as a brat. But hadn't Arlo said that?

"Just answer me."

"Managed on my own. They made it worse."

"Good," Matilda said and walked away.

Erica stared after her, standing alone in the dark. She spun when she heard the crunch of feet on gravel. General Burk spoke on her phone as she came around the corner of the house. Erica wanted to run. She wanted to dive into the woods like she had in the Padt City and hide but the GPS device was still in her. She had never been so well tracked and held by the damned Delegate.

Burk finished her conversation and returned the phone to her uniform. She paused then made up her mind and crossed the drive to Erica. She stopped before her.

"I just gave authorization for a direct medical transport to our northern base. I would like you to guess where that is." The malice radiating off the woman was nearly palpable.

Erica ground her teeth tight to keep from saying anything.

Burk grabbed her arm and pulled her close. "It's on Kinsley

The Marrilian

Claim and they'll know you're there." She hissed into Erica's unaided ear. "If you think the rest of the world is bad you should see how the Kinsley's feel about your cousin. You won't be leaving."

Erica yanked herself away.

"You are in my custody now," Burk informed her and grabbed her arm again.

"You will be on the ground if you don't release me," Erica replied through barred teeth and spun her arm to brake her hold. She backed away to kicking distance.

Zoe laughed.

Burk recognized the threat in Erica's movement and stepped back. "We drove here in a car, an SDD authorized business vehicle. You'll be on Kinsley Claim soon. Elsbeth! James! Mark!" She called towards the porch. "Come here and take her into custody!"

They all started down but Elsbeth stopped Mark before he stepped off the porch. Mark did a double take at what Elsbeth said.

James sauntered down the steps and into the dark alone. The porch light framed him. The red moon shone in his face. "Are you going to come peacefully or are you going to fight us?" he snarled.

If Erica hadn't known it was him, she wouldn't have recognized his voice.

"You keep bragging you know how to fight so is it true?" he demanded with amusement. "Or do you just brag for nothing?"

His attitude caught Erica off guard. He didn't sound like the kind man she had ridden with for the past three months. She braced herself to hurt him because it sure sounded like he intended to hurt her.

Marcus and Roger followed Elsbeth and Mark off the porch.

"Miss Kinsley, do you want to go with the SDD?" Marcus asked as they all approached together.

"No," Erica answered. Mark and Elsbeth flanked her. James stood in front of her. She was nearly surrounded. Mark pulled a leather strap off of his belt. A clip made the strap into a loop that allowed the leather to slide. Once he had the loop around her hand he could pull and draw it tight. The clip would keep it tight. Erica had thought the metal on their belts was only decoration. It was ties. "Put your hands behind your back," he ordered.

"Do as he says – *Lynn*," James sneered then jutted his chin at the other two agents. "Or if you think you can take all three of us, give it a whirl."

"Just get it over with. Tie her!" Burk commanded.

More than anything else, Burk's command made Erica fight. As Mark grabbed her arm she spun. He grunted as her foot sank into his gut. He fell. James grabbed her from behind. He pinned her arms at her sides. That gave Erica the height and leverage to use both feet and kick Elsbeth who fell but immediately started to get back up.

"You do fight pretty good," James told her and held on tight. He was too strong for her to break his hold.

So she bit his arm. It wasn't nice but effective. It was either that or dig out his eyes and his eyes were just too pretty. He yelped and dropped her.

She heard Elsbeth and stepped aside as Elsbeth kicked at her head. James received the kick in the chest instead and stumbled back. Elsbeth knew how to fight.

Erica ducked away as Elsbeth came at her again. Erica blocked Elsbeth's hit and used the force of it to spin, jump, and connect with a heel against Elsbeth's cheek. Elsbeth flipped onto her stomach and stayed down.

James tried to grab Erica again. She used the speed of his lunge to flip him to the ground. He landed on his back with a grunt and stayed still, winded. Mark got up. He tried to grab her and ended up on his back as well.

Claimant Mois stepped in. "Hold it!" he ordered as Erica turned towards him. "Come with me."

Erica blinked at him several times. Stopping serious fighting wasn't that easy. She straightened. James started to get up.

"Now!" Marcus demanded.

"Claimant!" General Burk protested. "She is going with me!"

"Move!" Marcus ordered Erica.

She hurried towards him.

Marcus took her arm and led her to Roger.

"Claimant!" Burk persisted.

"Take her," Marcus ordered Roger who grabbed Erica's arm and hurried her straight into the house, past the kitchen, the stairs, through a large ballroom and into a den at the front of the building.

Roger put her in the room. "Stay here." He closed the door and left her alone.

Erica stopped just inside. What the hell were they doing? She wiped the sweat off her forehead and began to cough. Oil

The Marrilian

lamps lit the den at intervals along the walls. They filled the large room with a soft glow. Another lamp sat on a large, carved desk. Its light fell over a fine leather sofa with deep cushions. Erica went to that, sat and breathed carefully until the coughing subsided. She was startled to her feet when the door opened. Ella entered with Matilda.

"You have stirred up a nest of vipers," Matilda grinned. "I have never seen Burk this mad." She motioned with her hand that Erica should sit, which she did, coughing once again. Lady Mois crossed to the desk. She wrote on a pad of paper. "Making people mad seems to come natural to you," Matilda added. "It is a gift I suppose?"

Erica opened her mouth but Matilda put a finger to her lips.

"So now you are mad at me and won't talk to me?" asked Matilda and kept her fingers close to her lips.

Ella handed Erica the pad of paper. It said, *'We can stop the SDD from taking you under one condition; you have to become our tenant. Will you?'*

Erica had to read it twice. She looked up at her, surprised and unable to answer.

"If I hadn't seen it for myself, I would have thought it was made up," Matilda chattered. "Three agents at once. I enjoyed your little display. Haven't you got anything to say for yourself? Are you that out of breath or are you just indignant?"

"What?" Erica asked. "You be for real?"

Matilda shushed her again with a finger to her lips and an angry frown. She pointed to the Claimant's note.

Ella grasped Erica's chin and turned her to face her. "She is very much real. I would have you behave. If you can't say something nice then be quiet." She pointed at the paper.

Why would they do this for her? What did they want from her?

'Please,' Ella mouthed then wrote the word as well. *'Let us help you.'*

Erica sat back in surprise. Please? What was going on that she didn't understand? *Zoe*, she thought. *You would understand. Come on, Zoe.*

Matilda stepped closer. "I meant no disrespect. I know you are from a lower class area. It doesn't matter. You are family. You are a Kinsley." She grunted in about as lady-like a way Erica had ever heard a grunt possibly made. "I never thought someone of our stature could fight three agents at once no matter their origin. It was really something. I didn't mean to sound insulting." She pointed at Ella. "Don't be put off by me."

Ella put the paper in front of Erica again.

Erica read it once more. They could keep the SDD from taking her? When it came right down to it she had a simple choice, go with these people or go to an institution. That wasn't much of a choice. Erica nodded.

"Ella, I think there is a great deal more to my cousin than we realize," Matilda said. "I have never seen anyone stand up to a general like she did let alone take down three agents. She is remarkable. And to think she came from Tenpole. Roger has explained to me what that means."

"It is remarkable," Ella agreed. "It is a shame to see anyone given such a poor start let alone someone from a family such as yours."

"Can you help her?" asked Matilda.

Ella smiled. She winked at Matilda and nodded. "I think I would be remiss if I didn't try. I would like to see her potential realized, Mati."

"So would I."

Erica frowned and looked between them. Ella nodded and wrote another note as she spoke. "Lynn Jillian Kinsley, I am formally asking, will you become a tenant of Mois claim? This would include customary pay and you will receive land and medical care as well as income in your old age. In return you will assist us in our daily tasks and be under our control." She showed her the note. It read: *Say you would be honored.*

"Would be an honor, Claimant, but I can't be much- "

Ella frowned fiercely. "Forget the 'buts', young lady. You will be valuable to us. You will earn your worth." Ella stood back. "Generally, this offer is something an individual should research. Do you realize it has a lot of consequences?" The Claimant flipped the page and showed her yet another note. *'You have to answer 'yes' to this question or the Delegate can claim coercion and terminate proceedings. They could impede our offer long enough to take you.'*

"Yes," Erica said after reading it quickly but had no idea what it meant. She only had a Tenpole vocabulary. That was enough to understand she had to say 'yes' or the Delegate could take her.

"Good," Claimant Mois told her. She and Matilda left.

Erica stared at the closed door. Could this be good?

'Could it be worse than being in the asylum?' asked Zoe.

Erica raised an eyebrow. Zoe approved? She dropped her

eyes to the pad of paper. She flipped a few pages but there was nothing else written on them. She tore off the top pages, crumpled them, and threw them in the fireplace where they fell behind the cold logs. She dropped the pad of paper on the table and sat again.

A tenancy was something few people accepted. All people living on a claim were called tenants but only a few held a tenancy. Even Erica knew it was something you researched and bargained for. You basically agreed to a working relationship with a claimant through which a person could become rich or ruined depending on the claimant's expertise in government and business. Erica would have never agreed to be tied down by such a thing but what choice did she have now?

The door opened again. Burk led the Claimants. She no longer seemed angry. "Miss Kinsley, I am told you have accepted a tenancy." Marcus stood behind the General. "Is this true?"

Erica rose from the sofa. "'Tis true," she replied cautiously.

"That isn't necessary. I admit, I think you need care but we can manage it without institutionalizing you. I do not wish to push you into a rash decision. I will not take you to the base since you feel so strongly."

Marcus put one finger over his lips just long enough Erica saw he wanted her to say nothing. She remained quiet.

General Burk cleared her throat. She twisted to glance at Ella then Marcus before turning back to Erica. "So, is that agreed? We'll treat you here?"

Marcus shook his head slowly.

"It 'tis not agreed," Erica answered and as hard as she tried to say 'it is not' like an educated person she could not. Her eyes almost dropped from her embarrassment but she wanted to keep an eye on Marcus. He had placed himself in such a way she could see him when she looked at the general.

"You should not take a tenancy under these circumstances," warned Burk. "You are mentally unfit to make that decision."

Erica took a step forward. How dare they bring her here, stop her from going to Sirrus, and then call her mentally unfit and try to dispose of her. She started to tell the general what she thought but Marcus stepped between them.

"We will assess her mental state before the papers are signed, Sophie. I wouldn't want to ask anyone who isn't able to understand the ramifications of such a choice to make it. That, however, is now in our purview and not yours. She has verbally agreed to become our tenant and the legalities fall to us."

"This isn't wise," Burk warned and glanced at Erica.

Erica didn't respond. She didn't think she could say anything without being rude. Not only that but what she said would obviously have a bearing on whether the Delegate could stop her from getting a tenancy and the Mois' protection.

Burk crossed the room to face Erica. She noticed the pad of paper on the table and picked it up.

Ella started towards them but Burk dropped the pad again. "Are you not surprised to be offered a tenancy? Can you imagine the reason for it? Could it be they only offered this to keep you from SDD Care because they know you fear it? That would hardly be in your best interests."

Erica set her jaw. She didn't look at either of the claimants but defiantly at Burk.

"Can I take your lack of response as an affirmative answer?"

Erica's eyes narrowed in puzzlement. "Pardons?"

General Burk glared at her, as if she thought Erica purposefully misunderstood. "Can I take your silence to mean you believe they offered the tenancy to keep you from Delegate care?"

"No," Erica replied. She chose her words carefully. "I fight good. Mayhaps they have a use for that."

"I see." Burk's mouth tightened. "Very well." She nodded to the Claimants. "I'll be in touch." She strode from the room. At the door she stopped and looked back but thought better of what she wanted to say and left. General Burk not only left the room but she left the estate taking the three agents with her.

Roger and Matilda came in after a few minutes. "They are gone," Roger told them with his gentle smile. He winked at Erica who blinked back at him in surprise.

Ella Mois picked up the pad of paper from the table. "What did-" she began to ask.

"El," Marcus warned, cutting her off. He pointed at his ear as he tipped his head toward Erica. "We have no idea how far the transmissions might carry."

"Over there," Erica told Ella and gestured toward the fireplace. She knew what Ella wanted.

Marcus crossed to it and peered in amongst the logs. He pulled out one of the wadded up papers and held it so Ella could see. She sagged and sighed with relief. Marcus smiled at Erica then took the matches from the mantel and started a fire.

He stoked it carefully, being sure to burn the papers soon after it started. Only the sound of the crackling flames filled the room as everyone watched him.

Erica sat on the sofa. They had saved her from the Delegate. She didn't understand why but she was grateful. Matilda broke the silence.

"Lynn, or, not Lynn. I admit I am confused. I was told your name but now it seems you don't use it."

All for this girl. Erica looked up at her. "Changed my name on Marril." Erica explained with a subdued tone, drained of energy. She cleared her throat and swallowed to stop a cough. "Delegate told me should change it here too but didn't. Legally, have to use that name on Quirni."

"I see." Matilda crossed over to the sofa. "So you are Erica Kinsley on Marril?"

"No," Erica answered and shook her head. "Changed it to Erica Ennis."

"Erica *Ennis*? You gave up the Kinsley name? Why?"

Erica found it hard to look at Matilda. She turned towards the fire but Marcus stood in front of it. He fixed her with a worried, searching expression that she didn't like much more than Matilda's. Erica looked away from him as well. Her eyes settled on the blank pad of paper.

"Don't want to sound insulting, but had enough of being a Kinsley."

Matilda nodded slowly. "Fair enough. So why haven't you changed your name here? You were in the Padt City. The Delegate offices are there. You should have been able to change it easily."

"Pardons, would rather not say," Erica told them and dropped her eyes to the floor. She touched her ear and hoped they accepted this excuse.

"I think we'll want to hear more about this later," Ella told them. "Now isn't the time. It has been a difficult day for our guest."

Matilda considered something then turned to Ella. "Claimant, she can stay here if you wish."

Erica rose from the sofa. Did she want that?

"It would be best," Ella agreed. "She would be safest here. I would stay as well but I need to research something on my computer. There are a few people I need to contact on Marril about this." She touched her ear.

"Very well." Marcus spoke slowly as he thought. "We have a lot to prepare." He crossed the room and extended his hand. "Welcome to Mois Claim, Miss Kinsley, which the Delegate is correct in calling you. I think a nickname of Erica would suit you fine, however." He flashed his handsome smile. "You will be safe and comfortable here." He extended his hand more.

Reluctantly, Erica shook it.

Ella extended her hand after Marcus stepped aside. She didn't take Erica's hand in the conventional way but patted it between both of her own. "If you are insane then I've yet to see it." She turned to Matilda and Roger. "Since you're doing the babysitting, tuck her into bed early. She needs a lot of sleep after the healing." With that they both left.

Which meant Erica stood in the room with Matilda and her husband. Matilda's stony face had returned. Roger, as calm as ever, turned to Erica. "Do you need a smoke? I heard you coughing after I left you in here."

"Yes," Erica answered. Her breath wheezed in her chest. They returned to the porch.

Roger sat at the end of the table with Matilda to one side and Erica on the other. He lit Erica's cigarette and his own then leaned back in his chair. "So, Erica is it?" he asked with a light conversational tone.

"Yes sir," she replied and kept her eyes cast somewhat down.

"Why don't you tell us about your trip here?"

He was relaxed and poised and smiled. She didn't want to scowl at the prat. Didn't he realize she didn't want to share stories of her trip? She only knew her future was blasted apart. Nothing else mattered.

But he was so damn typical of the upper class. They always talked about the weather and the scenery. Erica pulled her eyes off of him. She gazed at the table and took a long draw of steam and held it before beginning. She exhaled. "Quirni be a beautiful planet," she answered without much enthusiasm. "The most spectacular lakes and mountains."

"I think Roger meant to ask about the people you met," corrected Matilda. "How did they react to you?"

"Oh," Erica replied. She glanced at Roger who smiled serenely. She gave him a mental apology then thought about the question for a second. "Can't say they be good company. Arlo was the only one who spoke to me kindly other than James and Elsbeth." Now that she had seen Matilda, she expected that was because of Arlo's crush on her. He treated Erica well because she reminded him of her. "As for the rest," she shrugged.

"What happened exactly?" Roger asked. "How were you hurt? How many people attacked you? We'd like to know how dangerous it is for Mati." Maybe he wasn't being such a prat. Erica considered that watching his calm face.

"Quite," she responded and tapped her ashes into the tray. He wanted to know how safe it was for his wife. That wasn't small talk. She recounted the attacks since she first landed, the attitude of the citizens in the Padt City and then the attacks in Cluny, on Jennings Claim and outside of Nigh.

Matilda sighed after Erica finished. "I guess nothing has changed yet."

"Apparently," Roger agreed with a heavy sigh of his own. "You know, Erica, General Burk never did tell you why you were brought here did she?"

"No sir. Can assume it won't be good. 'Tis a Delegate scheme."

Matilda grunted.

"They intended to use you as a double for Mati. There are different projects that she needs to oversee but traveling is out of the question. They thought they might use you to confuse people as to her whereabouts so an attack couldn't be planned. They also hoped by advertising your presence they could convince people they may be attacking an innocent person and in so doing stop attacks altogether."

"Hadn't quite considered that play but expected it would be a thing like that."

"After that conversation with General Burk I assume you aren't interested."

What if this was the truth and she didn't do it? Why was Matilda so damn important? "General Burk didn't ask."

Roger chuckled. "No, she didn't. Still, you obviously don't care for the Delegate or their plans, whatever they might be."

Erica bumped the ashes from her smoke and studied the glass ashtray. The Delegate couldn't take her now and that meant so much. She drew a breath as she phrased her sentence to sound as proper as she could. "Would be willing if my claimants wanted me to."

Matilda and Roger were both shocked. "It would be dangerous," Roger warned and stated Matilda's sentiment given how she nodded.

"'Tis not the danger that worries me, Mr. Serval."

"Roger," he corrected.

Erica blinked at him, taken aback. A Tenpole whore talking to a Parcles prat on a first name basis? That was unreal. Parcles weren't above baiting Tenpole to think they were friendly then complaining about their 'forward' attitude. If she were on Marril still, she would ignore his suggestion to use his first name. Quirni was so different it took her a moment to consider the intent behind his offer and conclude there was none but friendliness. So strange, but she did know the correct response. "Thank you." She totally forgot what she was about to say. The silence dragged on.

"You would be a fool not to worry about being attacked," Matilda prodded impatiently.

And Matilda was the daughter of a claimant. Erica couldn't imagine the trouble this could cause her. These people always caused trouble for people like her.

"Think it be the bigger fool to not do a claimant's will."

Matilda's brow knit in confusion. "Aren't you afraid? Is that part of your disorder? You don't feel fear?"

"I feel fear," Erica replied gravely. "Other things be worse."

"What?" Roger asked. "The Delegate?"

Erica shook her head. "Yes sir but not just them." She had thought about this ever since she read the message Ella Mois had written on the pad of paper. They wanted to help her. Perhaps they had designs to use her as well but could it be any worse than the Delegate? Whatever the reason, they were going to help her. They would keep her away from more drugs. "'Tis stupid to such as you."

"What?" Matilda asked and sounded like she would think nothing was stupid.

Erica didn't want to say it even so. It sounded childish but compared to these people, she realized, she was childish so why not admit her fear? No doubt they had already noticed she didn't have their social skills. "Don't want to be alone. Has been nice to have good company. Even agents."

Matilda and Roger glanced at each other.

"Elsbeth and James?" asked Matilda.

Erica nodded. "Have been alone a lot since coming to Quirni and well..." She let her voice trail off but then she couldn't just leave them wondering what she meant. That was rude wasn't it? "Never realized how bad lonely feels. Never had such before."

"That isn't stupid," Roger assured her. "James and Elsbeth are the best of people. I am sorry they are gone. You deserve such company."

"A kindness," Erica told him with hardly a breath due to her feelings for James. Now he was gone. Burk had taken him away.

Matilda sighed. "So, you feel trapped and since you have to

take up with someone then you prefer us over the Delegate? Do I understand that correctly?"

"No," Erica replied, all too aware of the hearing aid. "I like James and Elsbeth but 'tis a shock, really. 'Tis a shock seeing you, being here."

"What is a shock? That you prefer the company of a mass murderer to the Delegate?" Matilda asked disdainfully.

Erica grunted to realize she no longer believed Matilda was guilty. After seeing the way Burk and the Moises treated her, as well as how unguarded Matilda was, Erica couldn't imagine her being the killer she was said to be. "Have known murderers. You don't strike me as the type."

"You know murderers?" asked Roger doubtfully.

Erica frowned at herself for giving away that bit of information. "Mayhaps Matilda's reputation be a bust wall."

"A 'bust wall'?" Matilda repeated. "What would that be?"

"There is nothing behind it," Roger answered. "In thayanite mines it is a wall of stone that can be easily busted through. They are used to control the atmosphere, hold up the ceiling, and slow water currents when the mines flood." He studied Erica as if searching for something deeper in her.

"A bust wall," Matilda repeated. "Why do you come to this conclusion?"

"People like you."

Matilda laughed outright. "Oh, that's charming. There are thirty million people on this planet that would kill me and you say people *like* me? When you came here this afternoon you were pretty bad off. Maybe you haven't recovered."

Erica saw her cousin's bitterness and didn't argue the point. The Moises had treated her well. They offered her a tenancy, protection, help. She could like it here despite the attitude towards Matilda. And what about Matilda? What had happened so that the Claimant's and the QSDD so fully supported her? "Do you like the SDD's plan?"

"I did," Matilda replied shortly. "I'm not so sure now."

"Why?" Erica asked and pulled her eyes up to see her expression.

"Because of your mental state and you are so young. I expected someone older and stable."

Erica almost laughed but only smiled. "How old do you think I be?"

Matilda's eyes narrowed. "They said you were twenty-six."

"'Tis not old enough for you?"

Edwards

"Are you twenty-six in Marrilian years or Quirni years?" Roger asked, uneasily.

"Marrilian."

"I see…" He didn't sound pleased. "What month were you born?"

Erica hesitated. "The sixth. Why?"

He looked at Matilda who shifted uncomfortably in her seat. "Nineteen in Quirni years," she answered quietly. "You aren't of legal age here," she told Erica. "You won't be for another year and a half."

"Thought the age I obtained on Marril moved with me?" Erica asked suspiciously.

"No, not exactly. It does for your Marrilian business, but that's all. Anything pertaining to strictly Quirni business will depend upon your Quirni age. You are not as old as we thought." Roger glanced at Matilda before continuing. "You need a guardian."

Erica laughed at this but Roger didn't smile. "'Tis ridiculous." She looked at Matilda's face closely. "And your age?"

"Twenty-eight. To give you an idea in Marrilian years I would be…" Matilda thought a moment then raised her eyebrows. "Wow, thirty-eight." Roger chuckled. Matilda smiled at him. "I told you I was a cradle robber."

Erica could hardly understand, thirty-eight? Matilda didn't look any older than herself. Then it came to her, the Quirni air, the long life Quirni gave its settlers had kept Matilda looking like a twenty six year old Marrilian when she was nearing the age Tenpole would be retiring. This made it clearer than ever why people actually chose to live on this planet.

"Now that you are on Quirni you are legally nineteen," Roger told Erica. "Mati is twenty-eight and we aren't even considering the number of *hours* you have lived, only days. You know Marril has shorter days. You may be younger than that if those hours add up to more than half a year. What the SDD has in mind is an alarming thing."

"None such. Life on Marril be fast. Everyone grows fast or dies or escapes. 'Tis twenty-six years I lived. 'Tis twenty-six that I be."

Roger shrugged. "You are on Quirni now. The Delegate, your claimants, the Council, no one will allow you any age but nineteen or less. You will have a guardian." He tipped his head at Matilda. "Your nearest relative."

Erica sagged.

The Marrilian

"And I don't want to put her in danger," Matilda declared.

"You may have no choice," Roger reminded her. "We have to consider the opinion of the Moises and the SDD."

"Seems the SDD made the decision already," Erica told them. "'Tis done. They put me in more danger than mayhaps the future. They let me go to Cluny alone."

Matilda's face darkened. "They told us about that. I find it unbelievable they allowed it. You are so young."

"Only in Quirni years." Erica forced herself to meet Matilda's eyes. "The SDD set their trap nicely. Fell into it. 'Tis all."

"You wouldn't be the first one." Matilda looked straight into Erica's eyes and then laughed. "Roger, I know what Ella meant when she said we were babysitting. She already realized Erica is underage."

"Of course," Roger smiled and glanced out at the sky. Amon had crossed more than halfway up it. Khepri had risen. Thoth's light was peaking above the horizon. "We had better think up a lie because it's past bedtime." He got up and gestured to Erica. "Come on. We'll show you your room. Don't forget to brush your teeth," he added and laughed at his joke.

Edwards

The Marrilian

Chapter 11 – Contracts

Matilda and Roger were eating breakfast on the porch with the Claimants Mois when Erica came down the next morning. "Lo," she greeted her hosts. She nodded politely to Ella and Marcus then wasn't sure how to greet the rest of the new people. The table was filled up with them. A tall man offered his chair. He had been sitting next to the Claimants.

"I'm finished, Miss." He dipped his head in an overly polite nod. He spoke with an amused lilt that didn't match his severe features. He was seven feet tall with a broad build and looked like he could kill and would enjoy doing it. He hadn't shaved that morning so a day's worth of dark beard shadowed his cheeks and underscored the testiness in his near black eyes. With his tan and his dark hair he could have passed for upper crust Parcles.

His amused attitude and burly appearance didn't intimidate Erica because his sort of person was the norm where she had lived. Big men were always amused at those smaller than them because they didn't know any better. "Thank you, sir," she replied and sat in his seat. He pushed her chair under her which was unexpected but fine. She smiled back at him in thanks.

"Erica, this is Bruce Sheline." Roger introduced the big man. "He is one of our ranch hands and doubles as security when necessary. He used to be an agent. He is retired now."

Bruce offered his hand.

"Pleasure," Erica told him and nodded.

He grinned and lowered his hand when she didn't take it. "It's a pleasure to meet you as well, Miss Kinsley. I saw your tussle with Elsbeth, Mark, and James yesterday. Maybe we will be able to spar?"

"Later, Bruce," Ella cautioned. "She still has the thayanite to contend with. When it's gone we'll let her throw you around all she wants." She smirked at Erica.

Bruce's grin grew broader. "Well, I won't say it won't happen because I know I couldn't take on Elsbeth, but a little thing like Miss Kinsley will be hard put to toss me about. There is a lot more to me than any of them, especially James." His grin went cockeyed, knowing, and he turned it on Erica. "He couldn't have been much of a challenge."

"The man be as he ought, Mr. Sheline. Not all be giants getting sore in their pants." Bruce's snide comment about James couldn't go without a comment and the way he straightened and tucked his thumbs in his belt told her she had made her point. As for his flirting, she ignored it.

Bruce's face dimmed. "You haven't been on Quirni long enough to know what a Quirni man ought to be, Miss Kinsley. Allow yourself the opportunity, and you will find we giants wear pants in ways runts can't hope to master. And my pants cover up the best Quirni has to offer." His grin broadened again. "I'll be happy to show you when you are ready." He picked up her hand from the arm of the chair and held it so his thumb kept it in place. "I insist. I can't allow the Kennedy boy to leave the wrong impression on such a pretty and storied lady as you."

Storied? She had no idea what he meant but she was amused. He spoke like the men on Marril who had wanted her but didn't have the money to pay.

"Bruce, let her be," Roger advised.

Bruce released her hand and stood back. "Of course. Pardon me for being forward, Miss Kinsley. Your exhibition last night charmed me. Nothing more." He winked then bowed to her, nodded to Marcus and Ella, and then strolled off the porch and onto the grounds.

Erica watched him leave, wondering at his insinuations, until Roger introduced Artur the cook, his wife Carol, and their two grown children, Heather and Destiny. Artur's brothers also worked at the ranch, Justin and Ted with their wives Judy and Adel. All of them looked Marrilian with their darker features.

Walter Rousseau was another hand but he was Quirni born like Bruce. He was tall and wide like Bruce too but with light brown hair and not a hint of amusement. He barely nodded to her. Roger explained how Walter ran the ranch, hired Artur from Marril along with his entire family, and made any breeding decisions for the horses. He had trained Artur's brothers to help him do the ranch work.

Due to the need to keep Matilda's whereabouts secret, trips into Pey were limited and as far as the town was concerned, Walter owned the ranch and Artur and his family were Walter's relatives. Bruce was Walter's hired hand. That story worked well because Walter naturally put off people so no one ever wanted to visit him.

Ella indicated Erica should eat while she listened to the

introductions so Erica started with the delicious looking bread. It smelled better than it looked.

Adel put some white spread on her bread so Erica decided to try it. It was fresh, fluffy butter. The bread had to be handmade. It was soft, heavy, and still warm. The butter melted. Erica slowly pulled the bread apart, inspecting every part of it, the tiny holes in the fluffy warm middle, the flaky crust. She bit out of the middle, savoring it. The conversation returned to Marcus who sat at the end of the table.

"Erica, I believe Roger and Matilda discussed the SDD plans with you. What do you think?"

He waited a moment but she inspected the bread and didn't hear him.

"Do you like homemade bread?" asked Artur with a pleased smile. He was an average sized Marrilian with an average build. He had wavy dark brown hair that was full and neatly cut in the long topped Quirni fashion that tended to fall over his forehead. It looked like a miner's haircut to Erica. They would wear it long on top to pad their helmets while keeping it short on the sides to stay cool. Artur's wide set eyes were as dark as his hair and deeply set. His pale skin offset his dark features so he almost looked unnatural.

"'Tis the most wonderful something," she declared and took another bite. That pleased Artur greatly. His wife rolled her eyes as his chest puffed with satisfaction.

"Perhaps they don't have homemade bread on Marril?" wondered Marcus.

"Probably not where she is from," Roger replied and Erica's eyes shot to him. He was right. They served the better food to the miners. They got fresh bread. So that comment meant he knew she wasn't one of them. She paled, swallowed, and set the bread down. She pulled out her cigarettes and lit one.

"Matilda and Roger discussed the SDD plans with you did they not?" Marcus asked again.

"Yes, my lord," Erica answered. She kept her eyes from the food and gave her attention to Marcus and smoked to stop her appetite.

"What do you think of it? Are you willing to help us?"

The claimant asked her what she thought? Since when would people of his importance care what she thought? She stared at Lord Mois' chin with wide surprised eyes. Smoke escaped her open mouth. She noticed and exhaled quickly. She closed her lips.

He cocked a brow at her.

"Don't know what to think," she admitted with great care to speak clearly, and not use a word of Tenpole idiom. If she was fortunate she could confuse Roger as to her origins but she had to speak slowly. Maybe that made her sound more confident. "I don't know General Burk's will but I am willing to help."

"I'll tell you what I think!" Matilda suddenly spat. She sat next to Marcus. She crossed her arms over her chest and glared at him. "I think she is too young and it's wrong. It's unconscionable to let a nineteen year old risk her life and I want to see this stopped. She will be valuable to our plans without this."

"I have to agree that she is too young but only by Quirni standards," Ella replied. "On Marril I would think nothing of it."

"You aren't on Marril," Matilda returned severely.

"No, I'm not, and I've been on Quirni long enough that I think Quirni," Ella told her and didn't appear the least bit taken aback by Matilda's tone. "On the other hand, Mati, what you have to do is important."

"Not that important," Matilda scowled. "It risks her life."

Marcus picked up his fork and waved it around above his plate. "Something as simple as this says it is that important so unless you want the SDD to distribute the information, which would be the worst possible plan so we won't let you, I suggest we work with Sophie. I think it her plan will work and it won't be the first time Erica has put herself in a dangerous situation either. I was on my computer last night doing some research. She didn't get that accent by working in Tenpole. She lived there and attended school there since she was about eleven."

Erica wondered how he had learned that. That sort of information required releases. Marcus noticed the puzzled look on her face.

"I learned a lot more than that. I will need to discuss it with you but after we take care of other things." He tapped his ear. "You have been a busy girl."

Ella nodded as much to herself as anyone. "I'm sorry to tell you, I can't remove the aid. No one but a Delegate healer can do that on Quirni."

"What?" Erica asked, alarmed.

"The equipment is too specialized. I would destroy your auditory nerve if I tried so I won't. The SDD will have to remove it and since they aren't allowed to have such devices on signed tenants without our approval, they will. Once you sign the papers they will have to remove it by law. I'll witness the procedure to make sure they do. They have already been informed."

"They be allowed to have the thing in me without me knowing?" Erica asked angrily.

"Not exactly," Marcus answered. "You have a case against them but I doubt you would want to pursue it." He lowered his chin and looked at her sternly. "They might prove they had the right to do this. To prove their case, they can secure all of your records. Do you want them to do that?"

That didn't require any thought at all. "No, my lord." The way Lord Mois asked the question, the warning in his tone, suggested he thought the Quirni Delegate shouldn't be allowed access to her records either.

"I thought not," Marcus replied.

Matilda leaned forward. "What has she done that they might have a case?"

"Later," Marcus cautioned, which left Matilda studying Erica like someone would a new breed of animal.

"Today Marcus and I are going to ride out to the canister project with you and Roger," Ella announced which surprised Matilda. Her eyebrows shot up but she smiled. "I think Miss Kinsley needs to see the reason she is important to us."

"Is that wise?" Roger asked. "We agreed as few people as possible should know where Mati works."

"Erica isn't going anywhere," Marcus told him frankly. "She cannot tell anyone what we show her."

Roger turned to Erica. "We have kept the place where Matilda works secret so she is safe there. In case you should leave, I would like you to keep it that way."

Erica dipped her chin in agreement then nodded that she understood as Quirni would.

His eye rested on her a second but he agreed with the claimants to take her along.

They instructed Justin and Ted to saddle the horses and soon they rode down the drive west from the barn. The woods closed in after they passed the last of the pastures and became rougher and narrower. No one said anything for a mile or so.

They hadn't saddled Turnbull for Erica and she had trouble making her horse mind. "Not much of a rider," she admitted self-consciously as they waited for her horse to get out of the roadside brush. "Turnbull be kinder to me than I realized." She tried to get her horse's attention by squeezing her legs around him and he jumped forward. Matilda caught his rein. He spun around so Erica ended up clutching mane and saddle with only one leg over the horse and the other hanging.

Matilda held the animal as Erica pulled herself back up.

"My pardons. 'Tis such a thing."

"It's all right," Matilda assured her. She released the reins after Erica took them. "I'll have Justin give you some lessons. With your athletic abilities you will learn quickly enough."

"Turnbull?" Ella asked. "Is he the animal you rode here?"

"Yes, my lady. James said he be from Turning's ranch." Erica smiled to think of James. "Guess 'tis good. He got me here and don't think he felt too well for the last." Erica noticed Roger and Matilda exchange strained looks. "My pardons, could walk," she offered as she tried to find the stirrups with her toes. She leaned over and grabbed them to place them over her shoes.

"You don't need to walk," Roger replied, troubled. "It's just I am sorry to say that your horse didn't make it."

"Make what?" Erica asked and straightened up from putting her feet back in the stirrups.

"He had to be put down," Matilda explained.

Erica gathered her reins and pulled on them. "What?" she asked. Her horse started backing up. "Oh blasted," she whined.

"Slacken you reins," Ella coached. "You are pulling too hard."

Erica let the reins droop. The horse stopped which surprised her and made her smile at Ella but she remembered what Matilda had said so her smile was brief. No doubt they would move on and forget they had said anything if she let them. The rich were always like that. Conversation with workers, especially whores, was about work. Any pleasantries were so fast and quick Erica and the girls used to tell each other how fast a man would get to business while at the same time trying act social. It was pathetic. "Put down where? He left the ranch?"

Matilda sagged and gave Roger a pained wince.

The expression spoke more than the words. "A thing?" Erica asked.

Matilda's horse obediently turned on one hoof to face Erica. "One of those arrows that had the red clay in them cut Turnbull's flank. By the time he got here there was nothing we could do."

Erica squinted as she began to understand. "Put down be…?" She paused in disbelief. "You mean he be buried?" Matilda nodded. Erica's hands relaxed. Her reins dropped and her horse put his nose down to munch on the roadside grass. "But he brought me all the way here. Was yesterday."

The Marrilian

"He was on his last legs to do that much," Roger explained gently.

She shot Roger an unbelieving stare and her horse walked sideways. She had had enough. She jumped off of him and stood in the road both shocked and dismayed and no longer willing to fight the animal. "My lords," she finally murmured. She bit her lip and closed her eyes. "Poor Turnbull."

Roger caught her horse as it began to walk away. He brought it back to her and offered the reins. "Here, get back on."

"Will walk," Erica squeaked around her grief.

"It's a long ways," Roger disagreed. "You can't keep up with us on foot."

Erica's tears fell.

"Come here," he told her softly.

She crossed to him but didn't go near her horse.

He put his hand down to her. "You'll ride with me. Take my hand." He took his foot out of his stirrup. Riding any horse felt like a betrayal to Turnbull. In her heart, that felt like a betrayal to James. He had given her Turnbull. Bed and a good, solid cry into a pillow would help, not getting on Roger's horse, but she couldn't get angry with these people or she would end up with Delegate drugs forced upon her again. She took his hand and Roger pulled her up behind him.

"I'm sorry," he offered when she settled. He gave her the reins to her horse. "Hold on to him would you? You can lead him."

Erica held on to the animal but hid her face in Roger's back. She tried to stop crying for losing the only connection she had left with James but the tears ran despite her efforts. Turnbull had been so patient with her, had such a soft nose, and he had been James' gift. Then it occurred to her what they had said, an arrow had cut Turnbull and she remembered how a horse had cried in pain when Noel let the arrow fly from the second archer. He had wanted to show Erica how nervous the man was, expected him to miss, and he had. He had hit Turnbull.

She shuddered and wept harder. Noel's bravado had killed Turnbull. Why had she trusted him when she knew he was like that?

The best she could do was keep Roger's back dry because she couldn't stop crying. She wiped her face with her sleeve and didn't look up until he told her they had arrived. They were nowhere special, as was the norm on Quirni. A grey brick building sat in the middle of a small clearing.

Edwards

It sat by a scummy pond. Thick algae covered the surface of the water. It smelled alive. That was the only way she could think of it, alive. If green, crawling things had an odor the smell coming off the pond would be it. It was the same odor that she had first noticed when she breathed Quirni air. It wasn't unpleasant except for being so strong. By the pond, it was thick and cloying.

They rode around the scummy water to a fenced pasture where they unsaddled the horses and turned them loose. Matilda took everyone to a back door of the building. To Erica's amazement the door had a metal lock. Matilda pulled a key from her pocket and let them all in. She flicked on a light switch. The ceiling lit up as a generator began to run somewhere outside. Next, she turned on several pieces of noisy equipment then stepped aside so everyone could come in after her. It was a lab.

"Are you surprised?" Roger asked Erica.

She blinked at the room with her red rimmed eyes and she was surprised, enough so the pain she felt was overshadowed by it. The lab had a row of huge metal vats full of various shades of water that smelled like the pond. Hundreds of canisters on shelves stood at the back wall filled with a golden fluid. Dozens more stood empty and uncapped.

"This is part of what Matilda is doing that is so important to Quirni," Marcus explained. "It's complicated but this lab was put here so Quirni can become a metal rich planet."

Metal? Erica gave him a doubtful look. She couldn't imagine how this lab could make metal. It used metal. It probably had more metal in it than most Quirni born saw in a lifetime. "Do I miss something, my lord?"

He laughed. "No." He took her arm and led her to a long black slate table in the center of the room. He pulled a stool out and gestured for her to sit. Once she had settled he folded his hands together and gave her the kind of look a teacher would when he gazed out at his class for an answer to his question. "Erica, do you know why thayanite is so important? Do you know how it is used?"

Volunteering any answer wasn't in her nature but she was the only student today. "Makes power. 'Tis used in space travel." She tried to give him her undivided attention but the lab had a lot of interesting and noisy things in it. Her eyes flicked about as she noticed them.

Marcus didn't seem to care. "Yes, but that isn't all. It's used throughout the settled planets to purify water, power motors,

The Marrilian

and make clean energy and any number of other things. What would happen if Marrilians didn't stay on Marril? What if they decided the money and lifestyle they led weren't worth the thayanite poisoning and not enough people stayed there to mine the mineral?"

That was a stupid idea but, of course, she didn't say that and she made certain her tone didn't reflect it. "Tenpole mine, my lord. 'Tis how they get money to get off the planet."

"I realize that. But what if that wasn't the case. What if they came to a healthy planet like Quirni?"

She shook her head. "Miners go to Sirrus. Tickets to Sirrus be expensive. Living on Sirrus be expensive but still, 'tis where miners would go after Marril. They must mine for it. No one gives them other jobs. Some die from mining and some from thayanite before they get enough money but they die rather than come to Quirni. 'Tis so. Pardons, but 'tis so."

"I know it is so," agreed Marcus and even though she was disagreeing with him, he remained calm. "Do you know how many people die on Marril? Did you know a disproportionate number of them are from Tenpole? The mining kills them. Thayanite poisons them. They can't make enough money to go to Sirrus soon enough so they just die there."

"So," Erica agreed with a dip of her chin. It was the way of it. She knew that. Not everyone could be born a claimant's daughter.

"So," Marcus repeated but he said it sadly. "You almost died didn't you? We were told you were only a few months away from being buried on Marril."

"That be the way it, my lord. Wanted to go to Sirrus so didn't buy a ticket to Quirni. Waited until time to leave and Quirni was the only option."

"You know what it feels like to have a bad case of thayanite poisoning," Ella reminded her. "You worked at Tenpole mine for about three years and you have thayanite damage worse than I've ever seen."

"'Tis the iridim, my lady," Erica explained, bewildered where this might be going. "It reacts with the iridim. Lots does. Only went in the mines part of the time because of it."

"I understand. Still, only three years almost killed you. Being an iridim patient or not is irrelevant to this discussion. It almost killed you and you chose to wait and get sicker rather than come here. But what if Quirni wasn't such a bad choice? What if this planet gave you a healthy long life in the lap of luxury? Would you have stayed so long? Would miners stay to mine thayanite?"

Erica didn't understand what Ella could mean because it was a bad choice. It was mean and had nothing of consequence; no computer network, no radio, no broadcasts of any kind. News traveled so slow she could walk across the continent and stay ahead of it. So what was Lady Mois after, a fairy tale? Erica answered her the way she expected she wanted to be answered because she was a claimant and maybe not in touch with reality. "Suppose not, my lady."

"Especially in your case since you are an iridim patient?" Marcus asked.

Why did they have to keep digging at this? "My lord, my lady, Quirni be a pretty planet, can say that, and has long life and health, but no luxuries. 'Tis barbaric here. Please pardon me saying, but Matilda's house be the first with metal forks. Takes her kind of wealth to get what you suggest a miner would want and that be a fork, 'tis it. Better off on Sirrus. Life be hard still but can call a friend on a phone and see what happens in the world. None such here. Don't even have computers."

"There is a reason I have metal eating utensils," Matilda said. "It isn't my wealth. I didn't import them." She took a seat on the stool before Erica. Their knees nearly touched. Marcus stepped back to allow Matilda a chance to speak. When she had Erica's attention she said, "I know where the metal is on Quirni."

It was the damn Quirni air again; it made the locals mad. Erica didn't roll her eyes as much as she felt Matilda deserved.

"Matilda, there be no metal. Even I know that. First days in school on Sirrus or Marril they tell us Sirrus has technology, education, and produces all perfect thinkers. Marril has money to make thinkers rich and clinics to keeping them alive to make it. Quirni," she shrugged. "You live a bit longer but have nothing to do."

"That story is going to change. The silver in my silverware is proof of that. It is from Quirni. The metal was mined on Mois Claim."

Erica studied Matilda and saw nothing to suggest she was mad or lying. What the blasted was she trying to say? "Was mined on Quirni?"

"It was," Marcus told her. "There is a lot of metal on Quirni. Matilda knows where it is."

Erica pushed herself up straighter on the stool. This could hardly be right, Quirni with metal?

"What would happen if Quirni was more like Marril?"

The Marrilian

Marcus asked Erica again.

"People might move here," she answered. She figured that was what they wanted to hear.

"Do you know how long people live on Quirni?" asked Roger. "It isn't something the Delegate allows to be published but what would you guess?"

Erica tried to think back to her early schooling. "One hundred years or so?" she replied but not at all sure.

Matilda leaned back to give Roger her 'I told you so' look. She turned back to Erica. She leaned forward and fixed Erica with her bright green eyes. "The first Quirni settlers were convicts. I've met some of them." She paused as if that was important.

Erica frowned. Matilda met them? No. "The first Quirni settlers came here two-hundred years ago."

Matilda nodded. "Two-hundred twenty-four, and I have met some of them recently."

Erica rocked back and squinted at her. "'Tis not possible. You be twenty-eight. Either way…" Her eyes narrowed as she considered just how long that had to be. "No one lives that long. 'Tis not possible."

"I looked up their names and crimes on rosters kept in the Padt City. They are old but I met them. They travelled to come and see me," Matilda said again and still fixed Erica with her intense gaze.

Erica squinted harder. According to Matilda people lived over two hundred years on Quirni. *Two hundred?!*

"The oldest man is 326 Marrilian years old," Matilda said. Erica's eyes riveted on hers. "And he came here from Sirrus when he was forty-three. What would a Marrilian, anyone, give to live on a planet with that sort of longevity?"

Erica was too stunned to answer.

"Especially if this planet had luxury?" Marcus asked. "Even if it was just metal forks and radio."

That made Erica's eyes grow. Three hundred years, she could build a blasted computer network!

Matilda gestured at Erica's face. "Does that answer your question, Marcus? She's speechless." She turned back to her. "My father stumbled onto the cause of this longevity when the Delegate asked him to produce air purifying canisters for their space stations. They built him a lab much like this one and told him how to produce the enzymes from algae. The alga on Quirni, when used for these canisters, not only purifies the air but lengthens life."

Matilda had blown up a lab, Erica remembered. "This lab belongs to the Delegate?"

"The Quirni Delegate. They built it."

"Same as they did for your father? The one you blew up?"

A flash of anger passed over Matilda's face but she smiled quickly afterwards. "Same as for him. Did Elsbeth tell you what happened?"

"So. Said you blew it up."

"Yes, that's when I got my hearing aid and the QSDD stuck in my life."

"'Tis true. You don't deny it?"

Matilda glanced at Marcus who nodded. He kept an eye on Erica. "My father found out about my relationship with the Trellians," Matilda explained. "I met them when I was only a little older than you are now. I traded with them and received documents that tell where all the metal is on the planet." She paused and leaned forward so her elbows rested on her knees. Erica stayed riveted on her. "My father learned I had those documents and tried to take them from me so he could play political games with them. It didn't allow that. I want them used to help all of Quirni. That made him angry and it led to the destruction of the lab."

Matilda took a breath and looked at her tightly clasped hands. "I was foolish. I knew everyone would want the papers. I knew they were supremely valuable and I knew people would do anything to get them, but I never expected my own father to be so greedy or vicious. Everything that has happened, thousands dead, has been because of those papers." She spoke quietly, paused to take a breath, then sat back and struck Erica with her intense stare once more. "Those same documents are causing your pain. I can't imagine how the Delegate found you. They probably scoured our entire family looking for someone. They must have been ecstatic to learn about your mental problems. They want to use you as a double to control how I disperse the documents."

The Delegate would only make safe areas that they chose. It would be easy enough to force Matilda's business with certain people or towns.

Erica realized if she were used that way she could also control the situation because she would be the means to make an area safe. The problem was she wasn't always herself so she wouldn't always be able to make a choice.

"Do you have some paper?" she asked quietly and touched her ear.

"We believe the noise and machinery in here will stop them from hearing us," Roger said.

Erica fixed him with a surprised stare; they had privacy here!

"Just speak quietly," he suggested. "Just in case the equipment in your ear is stronger than our research tells us it ought to be."

"Research?"

'Elsbeth,' he mouthed without a sound.

Erica's mouth formed an 'oh!' She helped them!

"What did you want to write?" Matilda asked.

"Why did they bring me here? To protect you? I think not. They could take your papers from you couldn't they? Those are what they want. Why do they want me?"

Matilda shook her head and her eyes dropped to her hands again. "That is perhaps my biggest mistake. I am able to remember things I see in detail, the gift of iridim therapy. I assume you have it too?" Erica shook her head and Matilda frowned, surprised. "After my father tried to take the papers from me I committed them to memory then destroyed them." She took a breath. "I am the only source for the coordinates of the metal deposits on Quirni."

"So, the SDD protects you to keep the documents safe?"

Matilda nodded. "I did it to stay alive but it has caused a world of hurt."

A world of hate as well, Erica thought. "Your father tried to ruin you so you couldn't use this information against him." She understood. "That be how the deaths on Cobal Claim happened? He blamed you to get rid of you or control you?"

Matilda looked surprised.

"She's a quick one," Ella declared. "I wondered when she would start putting her brains to use."

A frown flicked across Erica's face as she glanced at Ella but she quickly returned her gaze to her cousin. "Matilda, you be family and you have taken me into your home. Won't ever do anything to hurt you but you must know, you have to understand, am not the only one with a say in that."

Matilda sat back. She didn't understand.

"My presence here be a thing," Erica added.

"*A thing*, which is bad," explained Roger. "As opposed to *something*."

Erica nodded.

Matilda sighed and dropped her eyes. "I'm aware of that already."

To confess this took all of Erica's trust. She had to hope they continued to help her.

What she had to admit could be enough to make them walk away. If they wanted nothing to do with her after she admitted what she must then she would ask to have the hearing aid removed and leave. She could go north after all. "My presence here be a thing because there be parts to me that might not care about your secrets. Only rely on me if you know 'tis me."

They all looked concerned. Roger spoke. "Pardon me?"

"As long as I be 'Erica', will help you. 'Tis a promise. But am not always me."

Doubt and the touch of fear for her sanity covered all of their faces. They looked like so many people did when they realized she had more going on in her than normal.

Erica took a deep breath to fight back her fear that it was all going wrong. They might call the SDD but she knew she shouldn't conceal this. She had to tell them. These people were important and they needed to know.

"The Delegate took me when I had no problems. Was working with a doctor and then the Delegate came along. They tried to submerge me." Their questioning expressions told Erica she wasn't making her point. "Am not always like I am now," she added, becoming worried she couldn't explain. "Will change. The MSDD tried to make me change." She swallowed hard because their expressions were that same old mix of disbelief and fear. Her voice cracked. "Don't know what they did but my problem be back. What the doctor did be ruined. Had been fixed but got ruined."

Ella winced.

"I have an alternate personality that be-" Good lords she shouldn't say it. She looked down and bit her lip. "Well, she answers to my given name."

Matilda leaned forward to hear her over the stirrers in the big vats.

Erica pulled her eyes back up and found Matilda staring right at her. "They brought her out with drugs. Don't know what they did with her. Worries me especially now they put me here with you."

Matilda watched Erica as if wondering how insane she was. Her heart broke seeing that expression again. Her eyes burned.

The Marrilian

Because of this she never got close to anyone. When they saw a change occur it destroyed any relationship they had. Again and again it happened that way. As much as she longed for close friends she knew she would never have them. They always left. She had learned that lesson long ago.

Marcus stepped forward. "You can't say your name can you?" he asked and seemed at a loss.

Tears brimmed in Erica's eyes. "No," she answered.

He looked at her like she was some sort of pitiable freak. He saw her tears but didn't relent. Erica wiped her eyes angrily.

"Do you know claimants have the right to pull all records of a potential signed tenant?" asked Marcus.

Oh no, oh no, she shook her head. She looked away from him and wiped at her cheeks.

"Was it you, Erica, or some other part of you that tried to kill your father?" Ella asked.

"What!" Matilda exclaimed and gaped in surprise.

"Was me," Erica admitted. She slid off the stool and walked a few steps away so she could turn her back and wipe at her face. She blinked her eyes several times to clear them.

"Why?" Marcus asked.

Good lords they didn't waste any time getting to the worst of her deeds. She faced him. "Couldn't stand it anymore," she answered miserably. "He hurt me. Finally had to stop him. Was enough."

Matilda slid off her stool and stood by Roger. "Did you attack him with that fighting technique?" she asked. She had put more distance between herself and Erica.

That's right, fear me, Matilda. That's the smart thing. "Yes. Learned it for protection." She breathed hard.

"And it worked," she added callously. "It worked. Protected me." She stared at them, defiantly. As she calmed down, she began to cough.

"So it seems we have something in common," said Matilda. "At one time I would have loved to see my father dead too."

Erica caught her eye then shook her head. "Wasn't worth it. He got to leave Marril and he still lives. Didn't turn out."

"On top of that," Marcus added, "you can't change your name here. Our SDD will learn about your offences if you attempt to change your name so you have to call yourself a name you can't even say. If you did, they would have reason to deport you and you have nowhere to go but back to Marril."

Straight to the heart of the matter, Erica thought. She set her jaw against rising anger. "So."

Ella's face filled with pity, an expression Erica could not stand. It made her stomach lurch and her tears threaten to start again. Ella started to approach with her arms rising for a hug but Erica couldn't accept that sort of closeness, hugged today and snubbed tomorrow. Not again. She hurried around the table and left the lab.

Outside Erica faced the beautiful countryside alone, the fresh air and the potential for happiness if only she could be normal. She wiped her eyes again and took deep breaths to calm down but then started coughing. It brought her to her knees. She gave up her control and cried freely. Mercifully no one came out to witness it.

Erica didn't know when Roger did step out of the building. She knelt on the cement porch, sitting on her heels. Her tears had stopped but the coughing continued in short fits. She hadn't remembered to bring any antidote.

"I suppose you need one of these," Roger said and held out a smoke that was already lit.

He startled her. She jumped to her feet and stepped back. He held the smoke out, serene as could be despite her sudden reaction, except maybe a smile. She edged back towards him and took the cigarette. Should she even bother with it? When she inhaled the antidote started her coughing again. And all the coughing made her feel weak. Roger waited. He offered another of the cigarettes, which she lit off the first.

"I hope you don't hold it against us if we don't really understand your problem. You seem so normal."

"Usually," Erica agreed. She knew that was the case. There would come a time when her differences were obvious but no one had ever accepted them other than a handful of whores who thought she was acting.

He didn't say anything for a bit.

Colorful birds played in the trees around the pond. *A cesspool, the secret to long life.* Good lords but she felt for Matilda having to work with that slop. She gazed out at the thick water. Something jumped and a ripple of heavy algae lapped around the edge. She would have to make millions of those canisters to give all Marrilians longer life.

Her head hung from exhaustion. She wiped her eyes again. *Zoe*, she called, *can Lynn be used by the Delegate? Can they use her to hurt the Moises and Matilda?* She waited but there was no answer or any feelings. Erica sighed and smoked. She finished the second cigarette and ground it out on the cement. Her lungs felt clearer.

"We have a lot of work to do. Perhaps you could help us," Roger suggested. "We aren't here for a social visit."

She looked up at him.

He held out his hand and smiled the gentle smile that made her like him. She didn't take his hand like the child he seemed to think she was but she didn't turn away either. He smirked at her refusal, an *I know you* smirk. He dropped his hand and tipped his head towards the door. "Good?" he asked.

"So," she agreed and followed him back inside.

For the next several days Erica took riding lessons from Justin in the evenings. He worked her hard until she felt so sore she begged to stop, ate, and then went to bed. In the mornings she helped in the lab. The Delegate, she learned, had no intention of allowing Matilda to disperse her knowledge of the metal deposits on Quirni until Marrilians had longer, healthier lives. They had stopped her from revealing the contents of the SDD scans for years already. Somehow, they expected Erica's presence would help Matilda produce enough canisters. It was more Quirni insanity.

"We have people on Marril testing these," Matilda stated as they worked in the lab on the third day.

Erica had noticed Matilda glance up at her many times nearly every hour they spent together but she said nothing until now. Erica didn't respond. She actually hoped Matilda continued to work in silence.

"The initial tests indicate the canisters work well. A lot of people want to join the Delegate's 'Longevity and Health Initiative' and I can't keep up."

So that was for real. Erica grunted to herself as she glued another canister lid in place and twisted it down tight. She supposed she had to respond with more than a grunt to be sociable and she really did need to be sociable. Not only had Matilda taken her in but she hadn't said a thing mean about Erica's problem and she was family after all. She was the first family to ever do that, to ever help.

"The LHI," she stated. "Heard about it on Marril. No surprise you can't keep up. Thousands were joining." *Except Tenpole*, she nearly added but decided to keep that to herself. Matilda didn't need to know Tenpole wouldn't be lured by claims of long life and health. If such was to be had, it would be too expensive or simply not theirs to get.

"I can tell," Matilda returned. "Burk is getting more and more anxious about my slow production. I can't keep up with demand. I could at first but things are changing fast. Any help I get at this point I appreciate but considering who I am there isn't much to be had. Maybe I'll be able to travel soon if their plans work. If I can do that, I can set up more factories."

"What about Roger? He travels. Can't he handle your business?"

"He doesn't have a strong aptitude for business. He's more of an assistant than a CEO. Until I can take care of my end of things Marrilians will just have to wait.

"Burk keeps pushing though. She wants every Marrilian to have access to the canisters. She's insane to think I can do it alone. There are billions of people on Marril. Burk claims a lot of them live together in big buildings that would only need a few filters each month but still I can't make nearly enough."

She pulled another of the tubes close and began to put it together. It was already filled with the golden liquid from the vat. She added a powder whose description had sounded quasi spiritual to Erica when Matilda had explained its function, and then proceeded to wipe the lip of the tube, add seals, apply glue, and twist on the cap. Erica pulled her next tube over on her side of the table. Hundreds stood between them. They could see each other through a lane they had left between the canisters, those that waited for caps and those that were finished. It had taken a few hours to fill them with the liquid and ready them for the caps.

"I had factories that I could have used for production of these canisters before the SDD seized my assets. All of them ground to a halt and were eventually closed. Father and claimant Mois hired my tenants, except Arlo. He returned to his old banking job. He ran a glass factory and was, far and away, my most important employee. He is an excellent administrator. No one would work for me after I was found innocent without having it proven, not even Arlo, so I work at this alone now."

Erica shoved her finished container aside. "Of all the trials I ever saw, never saw a person found innocent but not believed. Not like this. Seen trials fixed but not like this. 'Tis a first."

Matilda paused with her hands holding either side of her canister. Her eyes narrowed. "You seem to be familiar with an awful lot of strange things. You study trials. You know murderers. You fight like you could kill. You don't shake hands.

The Marrilian

It's as if you distrust everyone. What's up with you?"

Erica shoved her finished canisters closer together to make more room.

'Your big mouth is what's up,' Zoe commented.

Erica frowned. "Well," she began. She looked back at Matilda and took another canister. "My first honest job was at Tenpole mine. Before that they weren't so honest."

Matilda stared at her, as if she wondered what else she might want to know. "What about now. How honest are you now?"

Erica dumped in the powder. She wiped the lip and picked up the glue. She suppressed her smile. It only deepened the corners of her mouth. Matilda's frown also deepened. "Don't like being locked up. Can tell you that. Like going outside when I want. But was nice to have lots of clean clothes and meals."

"Locked up?" Matilda's voice rose. "As in jail?"

Erica paused with the glue ready, nodded and glanced at Matilda. She wondered if she had shared too much. Was that possible? If Matilda decided she didn't want a convict in her house Erica might get the aid removed and then be asked to move along. That was the best possible outcome Erica could hope for. "Yes. Prison actually. For a year."

Matilda's eyebrows shot up. "Were you innocent?"

Erica laughed.

"Well, I guess that answers that," Matilda muttered. She eyed Erica sideways, as if she didn't want to look at a demon head on.

"You be the innocent one." Erica chuckled. "But never heard of anyone being declared innocent and not proven so. Nice trick 'tis all." She finished putting together the canister. It was none of her business what had happened at Matilda's trial beyond what the papers had said so she didn't ask.

"It was no trick of mine," Matilda told her hotly. "The people who would have been able to testify on my behalf disappeared. I had little defense left. On the afternoon that the verdict would have been given, and it would have been undoubtedly 'guilty', generals took me into the High Lords chamber and asked me if I would submit to Reagent 10 questioning. I said I would. Either that or I would have been hung."

Erica stopped to listen. "Really. Reagent 10? 'Tis supposed to be painful."

Matilda's face darkened. "It is, but more so if you tell a lie. I told no lies."

"It reacts with a lie when you tell a lie? 'Tis what I heard."

"It's more basic than that. It reacts with chemicals produced if you try to think which you do when you lie but not so much if you tell the truth." Her mouth tightened. "They asked me about my involvement with the Cobal Claim and I told them I had none. Then they asked me about the documents I had gotten from the Trellians. That was when they confirmed I had destroyed them. They stopped questioning me. They didn't want to take the chance of hurting me and ruining my recall. The judges learned I was innocent. Only four of the six judges actually witnessed the questioning so at that point four people other than the SDD knew of the documents. They didn't know what the documents were exactly but I expect someone realized what they were talking about."

"No one knows what you have except SDD?"

"Probably," Matilda replied. "Maybe. Those four judges know I have documents that are old and important to the Delegate and Quirni. And they know I am innocent because I was able to claim innocence without any pain while under Reagent 10."

"Why only four?"

"The generals didn't want any more people than necessary knowing about the documents, assuming I had them, and they didn't release the tapes of the questioning because I do have them and they didn't want that to be known."

"But they didn't say what the documents were? Didn't ask you directly?"

Matilda shook her head.

"So those four judges declared you innocent," Erica said in understanding. "And learned you have something valuable."

"'The vote was four to two." Matilda looked annoyed when she stated the fact.

"Nobody but four judges and QSDD saw the questioning," said Erica aloud, thinking through how things must have looked. "When four judges return from a closed room full of SDD, would appear the SDD convinced them to vote different even though you be guilty."

"Correct. It started riots in the Padt City. The SDD got me out and eventually brought me here."

"Was lucky you have the Claimants Mois as friends," Erica told her and could imagine how terrified she must have been to be dragged out of an angry court into the crowded Padt City. She had seen the photos of the riots and witnessed the mood of the town years after the event.

"Marcus was my defense council. He wasn't exactly my friend," Matilda replied.

"Oh," Erica understood that sort of relationship. Again she suppressed a smile. "Elsbeth said you had helped him so I thought he be a friend."

"I did help him but he knew I gave him information about the silver on his claim to strengthen him against my father. Mois claim had been under attack for years and I knew my father was planning something else. I wasn't sure what. I hoped to make an ally." Matilda picked up a few of her finished canisters as a grin flashed across her face. "It worked." She took the canisters to the shelves at the back of the room.

"So you be safe on Mois Claim but under the Delegate," said Erica when Matilda returned to the table.

"Under them, controlled, trapped, yes," Matilda replied offhandedly like she had come to accept that. "And under their protection as well. Your experiences show how important that still is."

"Mayhaps, but if not for Arlo that first day, would be dead while the Delegate stood back and watched." Or had they? Who had stopped the attack in Cluny and called Betty and Levitus? Where had they been? Had they come upon the scene or waited until she was hurt to interfere? Had someone been waiting to help her in the Padt City? If the people there had caught her would an agent have intervened? Who was it who saved her?

"Mati, they seem so clever at times, like finding me and bringing me here, but then they let Cluny happen. They attacked me in Nigh. They attacked me not you. 'Tis certain they knew it was me. But in Cluny, was an agent that stopped the beating. Saved my life." Her head tilted. "Barely. Were so late. The town nearly killed me. The Delegate plays a game. Don't understand."

Matilda set down the canister she held. "Do you want to know the two possibilities I've considered to explain these things?" she asked cautiously. "You won't like either."

Erica hesitated but then nodded. Matilda pulled open a drawer under the table and took a small metal music box out. She came around to Erica's side and pointed at Erica's right ear. "This is the one with the aid isn't it?"

"Yes," Erica replied.

Matilda put her hand over Erica's ear. The box played a tune Erica didn't recognize. It sounded like a waltz. Matilda put her finger to her lips. She held Erica's gaze. "I don't want you to speak of this until the aid is gone."

Erica's gut rolled. They were supposed to have privacy here. It appeared Matilda wasn't so sure about that. Erica was on a planet with little to no technology and yet here, on Quirni, she was heard and watched more than on Marril where surveillance, security, and technology of every sort watched everyone.

It had to be the minute amount of information collected here that allowed it. If they wanted to listen to everything she did, they could. She was one of very few people that interested them. Two people could handle the job while taking naps and long lunches. On Marril she had been among billions of people, computers, cameras, and such a large amount of data her crimes were lost. The irony of it was suffocating.

"There are two possibilities as far as I can figure." Matilda fixed Erica with her stare and Erica found herself too worried to think of looking away. "One is the SDD has split into factions so the orders are conflicting depending on whom they go through. That could be what delayed the help in Cluny or stopped it from coming in the Padt City. Or," she paused as if this would be difficult to say. "Or, they are trying to weaken you, make your condition worse, so they can control some part of you and use it. They let those attacks happen to make you suffer, to split you."

Erica had already thought of the second possibility and she knew they could do it. It worried her, but her mouth dropped open at the first. Factions in the Delegate? It seemed impossible at first thought but likely when she considered the way James had acted. He hadn't believed another agent had attacked them. Hadn't believed it so much that he didn't mention it until Erica verified his own sight.

Matilda rewound the box and put it back over Erica's ear. "Either possibility is bad," she said as she searched Erica's face, as if she desperately wanted to see what Erica thought. "Worse, both may be true. Actually, that is what the Moises and I believe is happening. If it is, then it is imperative you not be taken by the SDD. We fear Quirni would give a corrupt faction in the Delegate enough power to control all three planets in Ipet. They could–" she took a breath. "They could let me finish my plans then use you to replace me and control this planet through an alternate part of you and no one would be the wiser. Not even you."

The box wound down. The music stopped. Matilda pulled it away and wound it up again.

Erica stared at her mutely. Use her to *replace* Matilda? The SDD ruling? What had Betty told her? '*We have to follow the rules of the planetary councils. We get our supplies from the planets. Without them we can't exist.'* That wouldn't be true if the Delegate ruled a planet. They would have to kill Mati and probably Roger too. They would have to kill the Moises, anyone who could tell the difference between Matilda and Erica, if they wanted to do as Matilda feared.

Matilda bit her lip. It was the first time Erica had seen her unsure. She put the box back over her ear. She leaned close and whispered in her good ear. "When I first heard about you I understood this danger. When I saw you I understood the threat was far greater than I previously surmised. I hoped I was wrong but then Elsbeth warned us too. She told us they were getting conflicting orders about you and for Elsbeth to say anything it is serious.

"I discussed my fears with the Moises. They feel certain you are part of someone's plan and not just Burk's plan to protect me. That is why they are offering you a tenancy. You will be under Ella and Marcus' control as their tenant. The SDD can't touch you if you sign. Whatever your misgivings about becoming their tenant, whatever your past and your inclination, I am asking you to sign the tenancy papers. You said you want to help and that, more than anything, will help."

She leaned back and wound again. She watched Erica's face as she did so. She still looked strained. "The Moises are kind and generous people. They will treat you well. You need to sign no matter what you might think of the situation. The papers will be ready today." She lowered her hand and squinted into Erica's eyes while the box played then wound to a stop once more.

Erica turned away from Matilda. The table dug into her stomach when she leaned forward. Dealing with the SDD themselves was bad enough, but dealing with infighting? She had no idea what to do with that. Only Zoe might figure out how to pick it apart and work it. It horrified Erica. Better to sign the tenancy and let the Moises deal with any Delegate shit storms.

'Of course, you idiot, or they will kill you,' Zoe warned but then added, 'Matilda is family and they will kill her if you don't help her.'

Erica shuddered. Matilda gripped her arm and gave her a questioning look. "Are you all right?"

"Fine," Erica responded through a choked throat. Erica picked up a tube and began building another canister. She gripped it tight to keep her hands from shaking. Matilda hadn't moved from her side. "I'm fine." She spoke stronger this time.

Matilda didn't seem convinced. She stood by as Erica began working and only after Erica glanced at her and forced a smile did Matilda return to her side of the table.

"We need to get the rest of these completed today and then begin reducing the next vat of algae. Then we can go home." Matilda tried to sound conversational, as if nothing had been discussed.

"So," Erica agreed just as Tenpole would to any superior. They finished in silence.

When they returned to the house later they found the Moises and Roger on the porch once again. The Moises weren't wasting any time getting her under their thumb. She handed her horse off to Bruce who had jogged up to great them.

"Did you have a nice ride?" Bruce asked casually.

Erica smiled at him. "Thanks." She handed over the reins then followed Matilda.

Bruce started to say something else then stopped. His mouth quirked in a smile. He led the horses away.

Ella and Marcus greeted them with nods. Artur brought out platters of shaved meats and breads and cheese for lunch. Erica didn't feel hungry. Everyone else took a serving from the platters and transferred them to their plates. Erica took a slice of bread but she didn't eat.

"We have your tenancy papers ready," Marcus told her brightly once he had tasted his sandwich. He reached in a briefcase beside his chair and brought out an inch thick set of documents. "I'll explain these to you and then you can decide if you want to sign." With that he launched into a long explanation of the contract. He told her that they would have control over everything she did; where she lived, where she worked, what she said, where she went, and how they would punish her in the event she did anything wrong. *No one would be able to step in. No one could make her do anything without the Mois' permission.* He made certain she heard that and paused to be certain she understood the power they would have over her. She would be an extension of the claimancy.

In return she reaped a share of the claim's profits, became involved in its politics and business and set herself on the road to becoming a very rich and powerful person. She would be working closely with other tenants and meeting important people, making important friends. She would also fall directly and foremost under the jurisdiction of Mois Claim law rather than the laws of the Quirni Council or any other claim or legal agency. He paused and caught her eye when he told her this. "Do you understand?" he asked her seriously and for the fourth time.

Erica understood. The tenancy sounded like slavery for the chance to get into politics, which she didn't like, and to become wealthy, which she already was. That was with more than four million quid if she could ever get back to her businesses on Marril, which seemed less and less likely. Great.

Marcus slid the document over and pointed to a line halfway down the back page. "What you have to do is enter the number of years you are willing to be our tenant here and then sign. You must sign your full, legal *Quirni* name."

Erica picked up the document. It was filled with legal language. Under the line where she would sign her name was another line for the signature of an assenting family member of legal age. "Really." She looked up from the contract and tried to hide her disgust. "Not old enough to sign a contract?"

"Matilda can act as your closest relative and approve it," Ella told her. "You are old enough to work for us with her consent."

Erica shook her head in amazement. *Move from Tenpole mines to become a minor.* She could have smiled if the idea of becoming indebted and contracted to the Moises wasn't so horrifying. Once she signed she wouldn't be leaving for Sirrus. Once she signed she would be angering the Delegate.

Metal on Quirni, how did she end up in this mess? She didn't understand everything in the paper but what Matilda said in the lab had scared her so she knew she had to sign, especially after Zoe's input. Her return to Sirrus was fast becoming a dream. Well, at least this way she might survive to get back there some day.

The choice was how long did she want to be a tenant. If the SDD wanted to use her by dissociating her further, they could wait until she was free of the tenancy and then the Moises would be powerless to stop them once again. Marcus had pen and paper next to him. Erica took them and considered

What would Lord Mois do when he learned more about her? She studied him. Did she see any disgust in his face? What had he learned so far? She couldn't imagine him being too thrilled when he knew about all her past. He returned her stare with a gentle smile.

'Forget it. If you caused yourself trouble so be it.'

Sure, Zoe, you won't be around. You leave when it gets rough.

Her eyes dropped to the paper. The basic question was how long did Mati need protection? She wrote a question on the pad

Edwards

of paper, all too aware that the SDD could be listening. 'How long before you finish your plans?' She slid the pad of paper over to Matilda.

She read it then looked up. "It depends on a lot. Worst case," she wrote a number then something below it and slid the pad back across the table.

She had written '25 years'. Good lords, Erica sank in her seat. Did they think long term or what? Below the number Matilda had written, 'Linking the term of tenancy to one of the Mois' life spans could put them in danger'.

Erica cringed.

Matilda took the paper back and wrote another number, '50'. She gazed at Erica hopefully. Erica gaped at her. Fifty years on Quirni, guaranteed. The Moises looked hopeful as she considered Matilda's suggestion. They stared at her intently. Erica had been thinking two years. That was the time it would take for her exile from Sirrus to be over. But then again who was she kidding? She could only get a ticket if she convinced the Sirrian authorities she was a good risk and the QSDD could see that didn't happen. Her only hope would be an endorsement from a claimant.

'Fifty years out of two hundred,' Zoe noted. 'If you survive this. Are you sure you want to do this at all?'

Erica pressed her fingers into her eyes. *Quit changing your damn mind, Zoe. I've decided to throw in with Mati. She's the only family that has anything to do with me and she seems a decent person.*

'Exactly, this won't last long.'

Erica dropped her hands to the table and they landed on the tenancy papers. Zoe was right. She had no reason to be concerned. They wouldn't keep her around once they met all of her. They would remove the aid and soon after she would be asked to leave.

Matilda looked worried. Erica reached in her pants pocket for her smokes and a match. She lit a smoke and then used the match to burn the paper with her question on it. She placed the burning paper on an ashtray as she filled in '25 Q', the 'Q' for Quirni years, and signed the tenancy papers in triplicate, *Lynn Jillian Kinsley*. Matilda signed as well, *Matilda Lynn Kinsley*, when Erica finished.

Everyone seemed to breathe a sigh of relief as the last paper was signed. Marcus stood and held out his hand. "I'm sure we will have a long and productive relationship," he said with his all too handsome smile. Erica stood and after a fleeting moment of hesitation she shook his hand. He gave her a hug. Ella did the same.

Artur came out of the kitchen with a platter full of glasses and a bottle of wine. "I believe there is reason to celebrate." He held up the bottle with a flourish then poured.

They sat back and everyone but Erica began chatting, as if signing the tenancy papers fixed everything. "Well," Marcus sighed. "Now that we have your help," he gave her a cheerful smile, "the first order of business is Arlo."

"Arlo?" Erica repeated. "Arlo in the Padt City?"

"Yes, Arlo in the Padt City," said Marcus. He crossed his legs and placed his hand on his knee. He held his glass in his other hand which rested on the arm of his chair. "You know him and we need him. Ella and I think you are the perfect liaison to get him back."

"Me?" Erica asked skeptically.

"He ran a glass factory," Marcus explained. "We need that factory to make more glass cylinders. We keep running out of them."

"How would he start it? He be broke."

"We can loan him the funds but he will have to be given strict accounting rules so he doesn't make any more mistakes. We will explain that to you and then you can explain it to him."

They didn't know about her entire past, Erica realized now. Or if they did, they didn't care which struck her as ominous.

"After Arlo, you can work on the other five," Marcus added. "He had five friends working for him. We would like them back."

Erica raised her eyebrow. "Guess you were serious when you said you would use me."

Ella patted Erica's leg. "You'll earn your keep." She sipped her wine then smiled a little broader. "We can begin to improve your speech now too. You can start by using pronouns."

"Oh thank God," muttered Matilda.

Roger chuckled. "She might just tear up the papers," he said upon seeing Erica's horror.

Justin ran up to the porch and launched himself up the stairs. "The SDD are here, General Burk with three of her agents."

Roger set his glass down and sat up in his chair. "Justin, get Bruce, Walter, and Ted and stay close."

"Yes sir." He tipped his hat to the claimants and hurried to the barn.

Matilda set her face and leaned back in her chair. "This should be interesting," she muttered as Burk walked around the house with three captains, none that Erica knew. Where were

Edwards

James and Elsbeth? Erica remembered with a pang of guilt that she had kicked Elsbeth in the face and had not had a second thought about it. She hoped she was all right

"Good afternoon," General Burk greeted cheerfully as she mounted the steps. Everyone stood and the Claimants shook Burk's hand. The captains remained behind her until Matilda invited them to sit as warmly as could be, as if nothing was wrong, as if no one was worried. Artur even brought out more plates and wine so they could share in the lunch and celebration.

One of the agents walked behind Erica to go to his chair. He raised his hand to rub her arm and said, "You must be Lynn Kinsley."

She grabbed his wrist. She thought she saw something in his hand as he closed it. She forced herself to speak calmly as she twisted away from him. "Pardons, *Captain,* strangers don't touch me."

"Excuse me," he replied stiffly. He exchanged a glance with General Burk who nodded towards a chair.

Erica turned back around and noticed Marcus frowning at her.

"Be polite," he warned.

"Yes, my lord," she replied. Apparently she was supposed to be friendly with conniving SDD captains who might have come from Nigh? Erica looked away from Marcus and noticed Roger's little nod and smile.

"Lord Mois, command has informed me you filed intent to offer Miss Kinsley tenancy papers today," General Burk began.

"That I did, Sophie." He took one of the packs that Erica had signed and placed it on the table between them. "Would you mind taking your copy off my hands?"

Burk looked at it. She didn't appear to be displeased but she sounded like she was when she spoke. "I suppose this means you have researched her past?"

Marcus smiled serenely. "What I found was enlightening."

Erica's stomach twisted when Marcus shot her a glare.

"I hope you put a cancellation clause in this contract."

"Any good lawyer would," Marcus told her. "And I am a good lawyer."

General Burk nodded again. "That you are, Claimant. I'm curious if her trail was difficult for you to follow. It seems to lead everywhere. For example, did you know she spent a year in jail for a telephone scam?"

"Yes," Marcus replied.

The Marrilian

"Did you know she left Marril just in time to avoid being arrested for embezzling from the Consortium?"

Erica suddenly began coughing. She didn't even know that!

Marcus gave her a level look. "I think we have learned what we need to know about Erica, Sophie. And I think she will be honest and forthcoming with us. So go ahead and tell us the worst."

Chapter 12 – Lynn

"All right. Did you also know, Marcus, that this girl you wish to have as a signed tenant was a prostitute?" asked Burk as she continued to reveal Erica's past. "She serviced men on Chaucer Street in Tenpole. She probably serviced some of our own Quirni agents when they visited the place."

"I knew that the first time I heard her speak," Marcus answered and his face remained carefree. "No one needed to tell me."

Erica saw the barest hint of a wince around Burk's eyes when Marcus said 'No one needed to tell me'. She felt the color drain from her own face as well but that was because of Matilda whose eyes had grown and her mouth hung open. She didn't look disgusted or angry but, Erica couldn't explain it, impressed.

Matilda suddenly turned on Roger. "Can you hear that too?"

"Certainly," he replied and gave Matilda a raised brow and slight smirk.

"Then why didn't you tell me!"

He shrugged. "She can't do that here. It's illegal on Quirni."

"She's a prostitute!" Matilda exclaimed. "It doesn't matter where she did it! She's a prostitute!"

Erica lit a smoke and regretted where she had chosen to sit. She liked to see everyone so she sat towards the middle of the table in full view of Marcus. Matilda liked to sit near him and so did everyone else. That let Erica see all of their faces with a glance but today she would have been happy to be anywhere rather than see Matilda's stunned, gaping mouth.

"And a very good one," Roger explained, still smirking. "All of the Chaucer whores are in demand so if a Kinsley must become a prostitute then she could be in no better company."

Matilda fell back in her chair. She shut her dropped jaw. Her head tipped. "A good one?"

"A *very* good one," Roger corrected. "The ancient art is legal on Marril. You should remember that."

"Ancient art," scoffed Ella who only managed to pull her gaze off of Erica when Matilda started to yap. "Listen to you. I would think they create frescos the way you talk, Roger. What art could possibly exist for such an occupation." It wasn't a question.

"Chaucer's reputation *is* as art," Marcus told Ella and his tone left no argument either.

Ella's shoulders bunched up and her back stiffened. She gave Marcus a long, searching eye. "You don't know that personally *do you*," she demanded with a tone that told him only one answer was correct. "That can't possibly be where you were when you disappeared on so many afternoons."

"Of course not," he agreed with such a placid expression Erica wondered if he hadn't studied with the SDD on how to control facial features.

"But he is correct regardless of firsthand knowledge," said Roger. "Chaucer street residents are entertaining in ways most men would never suspect, or women. Theirs is an art form."

Matilda slapped Roger's arm. "How dare you! You went there! *You* know firsthand!"

Roger shrugged.

Erica sucked on her smoke and fought off her coughs. She did not want anyone looking her way.

"Please," Burk begged and shot a quick frown at Roger. "Chaucer is not the topic I came to discuss. She used the brothel as a base to work her schemes not to bed men. The point is, a good part of her four million quid was made from some sort of nefarious business."

"I am aware of this," Marcus returned and earned more open mouthed stares. "She, in fact, *did* sleep with clients so she might have a home on Chaucer Street but you are a right, Sophie, she also invented numerous scams. Among those were telephone scams but since there aren't many telephones on Quirni I think we can guard against her scamming us in that way and as for the other matter we will just have to be strong men."

"Telephones and prostitution are not the only concern," Burk warned. "She is also adept with computers. You have one."

"Which she won't get near. She will have no means to embezzle from anyone."

Embezzle? Erica was surprised to hear that too. "Never did such," she declared because she didn't need the SDD or Marcus adding that to her list of crimes. Her reference company had helped people get jobs so *they* could embezzle, assuming they cared to, but *she* had never embezzled anything. "Too risky. Too much data could be checked to prove a crime."

Everyone looked at her, Burk in surprise and Marcus in warning while Matilda and Ella blinked as if to clear away a fog.

Roger's typical expression of serenity with the sad eyes remained unchanged.

It was Marcus' near glare that convinced Erica she should not defend her case but shut up. She dropped her gaze to Marcus' tie and bit back her apology for speaking.

Burk kept an eye on her as she spoke. "So that wasn't you? Then do you admit to the numbers running or the illegal gambling?"

Erica didn't answer. She didn't look at her.

Burk turned back to Marcus. "Or will she admit to knowledge of the computers that track vehicle violations at the MSDD offices? Or did you become aware of a large charitable contribution that Silas Kinsley does not recall making? We expect Lynn is behind it."

At that Erica had to hold back a smile and wished she had studied with the SDD to control her facial features. That particular piece of creative banking *was* a work of art. Chaucer might be art to Roger and Marcus but the hack into the bank was Erica's idea of art. Dogs and cats on Sirrus got a hell of a hunk of money.

"Do you think that is funny?" Burk demanded.

"No, truly General none such." She cleared her throat, winced, and rubbed her neck, as if all the coughing had hurt. She kept her eyes averted. "'Tis a pain."

Burk slowly drew her eyes away from Erica and turned to Marcus. She poked the Tenancy Agreement several times with a stiff index finger. It lay on the table before her where Marcus had put it. "So you see, Claimant, why I asked about a cancellation clause. I think you should consider canceling it now and then we can take Lynn off your hands. She shouldn't be here."

"I disagree, Sophie, but I appreciate your concern. I, in fact, think this is the best place for her. We'll keep an eye on her, believe me, and your list isn't quite complete. I also learned about various other scams she was suspected of using. You forgot to mention she is also a thief and yet I still want her. She is obviously very clever and she has skills beyond anything I hired before."

Everyone stared at him, as if wondering what he might mean. What skills was he hiring her for? Ella crossed her arms over her chest. Matilda shot a glance Erica's way. Roger smirked. Burk sagged and dropped her eyes to the stack of papers before her, apparently defeated or trying to think of another argument.

Erica studied the glass of wine and her ashtray until General

The Marrilian

Burk leaned close to Marcus.

"She can endanger Matilda and her plans, your plans. Do you understand that?"

"Maybe all too well," he replied and held her eye. "She remains with us."

Burk sat back. She relaxed and nodded. "Fine. I can't say I trust this judgment but, I guess, I appreciate what you are trying to do. She is Matilda's family and maybe she should be with her."

That surprised Erica. She thought she might build on Burk's change of heart. She crushed out the smoke. "Would say something?" she asked Marcus, hesitant given how he has shushed her with that glare earlier. He nodded. "General, did such to survive. Would you know that. Chaucer got me a home and food. Was the best place. Had to do something. Wasn't always pretty. Was a means. Was the same for all the things you talk about. Was necessary but 'tis no more. Will do none such anymore." Not that she became entirely legal but if they didn't know about her other affairs she certainly wasn't going to tell them and it seemed, given what Burk had just revealed, they didn't know.

Burk thought about something for several moments. "We'll see," she eventually replied. She added, "Lynn" but said it as if she called her.

Erica carefully, concentrating, fought the emotions of Lynn but she knew her expression had changed. Lynn scared her. Then again, it was different. Lynn wasn't just angry…

Burk nodded ever so slightly. "Well, Claimants, it seems we have a medical procedure to perform on your newest tenant. We can't be leaving the hearing aid in her any longer. We've brought our iridim experts up to Pey along with the supplies they expect to use. You gave us enough warning so the procedure can be done tomorrow."

What had just happened? Erica wondered. What had she felt when Burk said her name like that? It had been so strong. She sipped her wine, considered it, and realized she had felt longing. Lynn wanted something. There was something Lynn wanted that went beyond her anger.

The conversation continued as Erica tried to adjust to the new feeling. Burk was speaking when she paid attention again.

"It isn't necessary you be there during the procedure," she told Ella.

"I will be anyway," Ella assured her.

"Very well." Burk nodded in terse agreement. She looked at

the three agents she had brought with her, all of them seated at the other end of the table. "Gentleman, please go wait by the car." All left without a word. Once they had turned the corner of the house Burk reached in her uniform and pulled out a six inch knife in a scabbard. She set it on the table and pushed it towards Erica. "I believe this is yours."

It was the knife Erica had imported from Marril. "That was lost that in Cluny," she stated with surprise. What a relief to have it back! She reached but Burk wasn't quite ready to let her have it. She had only offered it to prove it was Erica's. Now that Erica had identified it she covered it with her hand and drew it back to herself. Erica sat back again, wary.

The general picked it up and pulled it from its leather scabbard then turned the long slender blade so the Claimants could see it. A cutting edge was along one side until the tip. There it was sharpened into a thin stabbing point. The word 'ENZUS' was inscribed on the metal. "Would you tell us what this word means?" Burk asked.

Erica froze. Her breath stopped.

Marcus shifted uncomfortably in his chair. "What does it mean?" he asked her when she took too long to answer.

"Claimant, that be personal."

"Explain," Marcus demanded.

Erica's dropped her eyes to her lap. She had to answer. "Now," Marcus added.

She winced. "'Tis the first letter of…words, my lord."

"Words?" asked Burk. "What kind of words?"

"Names," Erica corrected.

"That's better. What names?" pressed Burk and sounded pleased, as if she already knew the answer and couldn't wait to hear.

"Erica, Noel, Zoe, unsaid, and Sal," Erica replied tremulously.

Burk pushed the knife back into the case with a snap then set it on the table. "And who are these people?"

Erica glared at the General.

Matilda picked up the knife. She pulled it from its sheath. "I can assume since Erica is one of the names you mentioned these letters stand for parts of yourself. It has something to do with that condition Ella told us about, the dissociation?" She turned the knife over in her hands and the tip cut her. "It's incredibly sharp!" she cried out and dropped the knife on the table. She sucked on her finger. The knife sunk into the wood, stuck upright before falling over.

"It's the type of steel that makes it so sharp," Burk explained. Matilda pulled her finger from her mouth and saw it bleeding. She glared at the knife which Burk picked up and slid back in the sheath. "It will keep that edge for years." She passed Matilda a napkin to put pressure on the cut. "And you are right, the letters do stand for different parts of her. What I want to know is what those parts represent and why they exist."

Erica clenched her jaw tight to stop a reply but she still breathed hard and fast. She couldn't let Burk anger her. She lit a smoke.

Roger sat beside Matilda and looked none too pleased. He took her hand to inspect the cut.

"I want you to explain," Marcus insisted so harshly that Erica drew in a sharp breath and looked him right in the eye without thinking. "Now," he added.

Erica dropped her gaze. "My lord," she answered. She wanted to explain nothing but how could she avoid it? He sat right here demanding she tell him and she had to tell him because she was his damn tenant now!

"Be one of five," Erica began. "Be the one who makes decisions and be out most of the time. Used to be, didn't know what happened when the others were out."

"You blacked out?" Ella asked. She reached across the chair between them to put her hand on Erica's knee.

"Yes, my lady." She hesitated to add more.

"Ella please, I want her to continue. I need to understand this." Ella pulled her hand back. "What happens when you black out?"

Erica forgot the burning cigarette. "'Tis not like that anymore, usually, don't usually black out. Usually know who be out and feel them, their emotions, even if can't always control them. Can't always tell when time be lost. Don't have a watch anymore."

Marcus' studied her through the corner of his eye.

That skeptical look, more than anything, worried Erica. She wasn't lying. Her problem wasn't a lie. It wasn't a ruse to get out of trouble and it wasn't fun. When she saw the look on his face, she stopped short.

"Who or what is Noel?" he asked.

Erica couldn't look at him. He wasn't going to understand. She spoke in a flat tone and gazed at her plate.

"Noel be for pain. He makes it less or takes over when it be too much. 'Tis the reason we could shoot when pinned to the road in Nigh." She paused to put out the cigarette that she wasn't smoking. "Zoe doesn't like me. Calls me an idiot because she figures things out before me. Hear her speaking." She took a breath. Her voice becoming quieter and duller, she continued. "The 'u' be for 'unsaid', my given name, and can't say it without losing time." At this she looked at Burk, at last feeling justified in expressing some anger. "Could be said until that so-called care from the SDD. Your people ruined me, made me black out."

Burk straightened. Brief surprise crossed her face but she said nothing.

"And 's'? You said Sal?" Marcus prodded.

"So," Erica agreed as she dropped her eyes back to the table, "She be a sexual thing and can stand the abuse from my father." Silence surrounded her. It seemed to go on forever. She didn't look up to see who believed her or who looked at her like she was a liar.

"I want her to go with me," Burk told Marcus once more but this time she didn't sound like she tried to convince him. It was only a statement with no force.

Marcus didn't answer.

"If she unravels she puts everything in danger. Don't you understand?"

"I understand she hasn't changed since I have known her. I also understand she has some problems. I still think she is valuable to us and she is better off here than with you."

"Before you make the mistake of believing that consider this. This becomes your problem if you give her a tenancy." She pulled an envelope from her uniform and held it out to him. He took it and opened it then spent several minutes flipping through a half dozen pages. At last, he pulled his eyes from the document. He met Erica's and she saw rage.

"Come here," he said far too calmly for the look in his eyes or the red in his face.

Everyone stared at Marcus with concern. They glanced at Erica who rose from her seat. Her legs felt week. He scared her. She had chosen to trust him. She wanted to trust him. She had chosen to do his bidding and now, seeing his rage, she dearly regretted it. Once again, the SDD made her life hell. She slowly stepped around Ella and stood before Marcus who glowered at her as he thrust the documents into her chest. He shoved so hard he pushed her back a step.

"Read that," he hissed.

The Marrilian

She unfolded the wrinkled papers and saw they were bank records. Her security at the Bank of Quirni had been tripped. The SDD had tried to take her money.

Marcus rose to his feet. He stood in front of her, inches away, towering. "I am beyond words," he sneered. "You tell us your illicit activities are in the past and at the same time you do this!" He slapped the papers from underneath so they flapped into her face.

She backed up a step and dropped her head to show her shame.

He grabbed the papers out of her hands. She backed up again in surprise. "I can accept a life of crime and deceit on Marril but you have had no reason for this sort of behavior here!" He flapped the papers under her chin. "You have been helped at every turn! You have had QSDD escorts! You have had QSDD cureman and healers!"

"The SDD took-"

"The SDD did not do this!" Marcus screamed. He tossed the papers on the table and then grabbed her hair and jerked her head back. He shoved his other hand under her chin. "You will look at me!" he snarled. "I will see your eyes and your deceit and your lies! Answer for this! Why did you do it?"

He bent her back and made her press close. She met his eye, could hardly help but do so. Her own eyes were wide with fear. He could choke her or break her neck the way he held her. Any defense she could use would be slight. He was too close, too big and his grip too tight. She struggled to not sob or close her eyes or let her legs weaken. Those things would bring more violence.

"Why!"

"They threatened me," she answered and was horrified to hear the tremor in her voice. "Threated to take my money." She answered then remained absolutely still. She felt his trembling just as he must feel hers.

His jaw worked as he fought to say something. "You God damned street imp!" was all me managed to growl. He pushed her aside hard.

She stumbled into the porch railing. The slats dug into her side. She didn't make a sound. She watched Marcus with wide eyes. He stomped off the porch and into the yard. He paced back and forth some twenty feet beyond the steps.

Burk hurried down to him. They began to hiss an argument back and forth.

"My God, what has she done?" Matilda asked at the table.

Edwards

"I've never seen him like that."

Ella already read the papers. "Good God," she muttered and turned the pages faster.

'Dummy,' Zoe remarked. 'I told you doing that would cause trouble.'

Erica lowered into a crouch by the railing. She wrapped her arms around her knees. She could curl further and protect her head easily like that. It exposed her back but that was better than the head.

If this had only happened after the surgery, after the aid was removed she could have run. Her lousy luck never ceased to amaze her.

"She has sabotaged our main banking system," Ella told them.

Erica closed her eyes and hid her face behind her legs.

"What!" exclaimed Matilda.

Erica ducked her head under her arms.

The papers rustled. "Can this be fixed?" Matilda demanded in a horrified voice. She jumped out of her chair and crossed to Erica. She shook the papers over her head. "Can you fix this?" When Erica didn't look up Matilda rolled the papers and swatted the back of her head hard. She only hit Erica's arms but the strength of the blow worried Erica. "Answer me!"

Erica pressed against the railing and lifted her head so she could see the next strike but Matilda's arm wasn't raised. "So," she whimpered. "Never expected to have help. They threatened me. They did. Never get help. Had to do the thing. Had to." Lords, she knew this would happen. Good things never lasted. Never.

'I told you,' said Zoe.

Matilda backed away several steps. "You had all the help anyone could give," she replied with disgust. "You refused to take it. Instead you did this!" She shook the papers.

Erica pushed backwards into the corner out of Matilda's reach.

"What made you think doing this would help you? Who would want to help you? You don't deserve it!" Matilda spat.

Claimant Mois returned and cut Matilda's tirade short. He mounted the steps as if each one took an effort. When he stood on the porch he looked down at Erica for so long she had time to slide her back up the wall of the house and stand to face him. She said nothing. From what she saw before he took the papers, the top fifty depositors had millions disappear. That included the

The Marrilian

Moises and the Servals. The money could only to be returned by her password or by her computer backing up the system. Every one of her scripts had been tripped. The QSDD had persisted despite the warnings.

"I want *all* of your secrets out in the open *now*," Marcus warned ominously.

'Erica!' Zoe yelled. Erica winced. Fear caused Zoe to react so, Erica's own heart pounding fear, and Erica could hear her heart it beat so hard. She swallowed back sickness. She wanted to run but the damn GPS wouldn't let her escape. It would tell them exactly where she went.

Matilda held the papers before Marcus. "She said she can fix it."

His upper lip curled in a sneer. His brow remained bent into dozens of lines and his nose wrinkled. His chin shivered with his anger.

"I don't doubt she can and she will before any other claimant learns about it," he said with a meaningful look at Erica. "But there will be no other surprises." He pushed Matilda aside with the back of his forearm. "Go back to the table and stay there." He took two large steps towards Erica.

Roger pulled Matilda into his arms.

Erica pressed her back against the house.

Marcus stopped inches from her. He glowered down at her. "Have you broken the law in any other way since you have been on Quirni?"

At this point she would answer anything to try and stop his anger. She kept her eyes lowered respectfully. She had forgotten his demand she look at him. "Yes, my lord," she said quietly. She spoke to his chest. "I stole from stores in the Padt City and Cluny, my lord." Her voice broke. She swallowed hard.

His eyes narrowed dangerously. "What did you take?"

"Food, a-a case of drinks, *thayanite* cigarettes, two candy bars, and a-a newspaper, my lord," she replied quickly.

He took a deep breath. His chest nearly touched her forehead. His jaw ground in anger. "Where did you get four million quid?"

Erica lowered her eyes further to show her shame but he grabbed her jaw and forced her head up banging her into the wall.

"Look at me," he growled. "And answer."

"Investments," she answered in surprise. He squeezed so hard her cheeks hurt. She whimpered without meaning to. She forced herself to keep her hands at her sides by digging her nails into a lip of wood on the siding. She could hurt him. He stood wrong this time. She could reach his face but she shouldn't. She couldn't attack a claimant. That would end so badly. "My pay from Tenpole."

"Quit lying," he growled and forced her head back again. He knocked her head into the wood siding. She felt it cut into her scalp. "No more bull! The truth!"

It had been the truth. She had spent her blackmail money. That had been in a different account. She thought of a lie. He needed a lie. "Running numbers, scamming, stealing, selling stolen goods." General Burk made a sickened noise in her throat.

"You will do nothing like that while you are here or so help me, Lynn Kinsley. If you do I will sell your tenancy to your Uncle and be done with you," Marcus hissed through his teeth. He banged Erica's head roughly against the house between each word.

"Yes, my lord," she gasped. Blood trickled down the back of her neck. He ground her head into the wall a little more. When she closed her eyes he slammed her into it yet again. Stars flashed.

"Look at me!"

"Yes, my lord," she sobbed, dazed and more than anything dismayed that her only hope had come to this already.

"I want to talk to Lynn." He spoke quietly now. "Do you hear me? I want to see Lynn." He almost whispered it at her.

Erica tried in vain to shake her head. He pressed her so tight against the house she couldn't move. She couldn't let Lynn out. *I have to run. I have to run! I have to fight!*

'NO!' Zoe yelled.

"No," Erica whimpered. She clenched her fists at her sides. She stopped herself from striking him. She could seriously hurt him where he stood.

'You fool!' Zoe warned harder still.

"Lynn! I will see Lynn!" Marcus yelled. He shook with rage. His face was red. He released Erica but she stayed stiffly in place. "God damned if there is such a thing as this Lynn character then, by God as my witness, I will see her!"

The longing, the fear, and the hysteria that was Lynn rose dangerously. Marcus seemed to recede as she fought to keep control. Every time he said the name she lost a little more. He didn't know Lynn would strike him. She wouldn't hesitate. Marcus stood too close. She would attack him if she came out. It

The Marrilian

wouldn't be the sort of hit Erica could deliver, Lynn didn't know how to fight like Tenpole, but her rage sometimes took multiple people to control.

"Say the name!" Marcus yelled and grabbed Erica's arms. He shook her. He lifted her. Her shoulders pushed up painfully against the siding. "Isn't that how she supposedly shows up? Isn't that the sort of crap you want me to believe? Say it!"

She was horrified by his demand but she still squeaked, "No."

He dropped her and then backhanded her so hard she flipped around. She folded over the railing, fell back and slipped to her knees with stars in her vision. "You can deny me nothing! I am your claimant! You will say it! Say it! Prove this isn't another lie you stupid, low life whore!"

What? Tears welled in her eyes. She gazed up at this man who she thought would be her savior. He towered over her in a rage. General Burk held Marcus' arm but only a moment. Her hands dropped and his raised again.

Matilda had lied. Claimant Mois wasn't kind. He was like her father! He was going to beat her! She covered her head with her arms and yelled "Lynn!" before he could strike.

She lay on her back in the grass. Burk held her right arm. It hurt like it was broken. Roger held her left arm. Matilda stood behind him looking stunned. Bruce pinned her left leg. Ella stood by Matilda, staring transfixed. Justin pinned Erica's right leg. Marcus knelt over Erica with his hand pressed hard on her chest. His head hung and he cried.

"I'm so sorry. Please, Lynn, forgive me."

Erica couldn't imagine how she came to be on her back in the grass held down by five people and her claimant crying over her. "She's not here," she told him fearfully, unsure of her surroundings. She sounded hoarse.

Everyone froze. Marcus met her eye. He blinked then gradually released the pressure on her chest. He wiped the tears from his face with his hands.

She took a deep breath. She felt like she had run a great distance and was weak as if she had used every muscle to its utmost.

"She's stopped fighting," Justin noticed.

"Erica?" Roger asked.

She saw pity in his face. "Can be fixed," she told him. "Knew they would try to take it. Tried to save it. Didn't know you then.

Didn't know it would hurt you."

Roger squinted in confusion. He shot Marcus a look like he had no idea what she meant.

They all looked at each other and then Marcus laughed hollowly. "Of course. The bank accounts." He gestured for everyone to let her go and stand back. They all did and Erica sat up. Marcus offered his hand to help her to her feet but she held her arm close to her side and stood without his assistance, managing to put distance between them as she rose, using an awkward and apparently off balance stumble backwards. She didn't want him touching her. It could be a trick. She knew those sorts of tricks. People would coax her to be still and then grab her.

But that was her father and his friends. Would other people do that? Would Marcus?

She backed away. She couldn't help it. She didn't trust his mood. Even if he wasn't the sort to tease her and lure her close she didn't trust his mood.

"Can fix it," she told him again, less sure now if it mattered since they didn't seem to care about the offer. She glanced at each of them.

Matilda put her hand over her mouth and looked as if her best friend had died. Tears glistened in her eyes.

"We know," Burk replied. "We'll have you do that."

She sounded different. They had seen something. They had seen too much. They would send her away without giving her the surgery first. "What happened?" she asked. Her voice quavered. They would fear her now. This had all happened too fast. If only it could have been after the surgery.

She stiffened her back and set her jaw. "'Tis only a part of me. She won't come out if not called. Ignore her. Would know what she did though. Would help to know."

Marcus shook his head. "You don't have to know." He wiped his hand down his face again. "Forget about this if you can."

Erica couldn't stifle the half laugh, half grunt. "Be a master at that in case you haven't noticed! 'Tis what I hope to stop!"

'Great, now lose your temper, you idiot!'

She gripped her sore arm closer and dropped her eyes. "Pardons, my lord." She backed up another step. The more distance the better if he got angry again but he didn't see it that way. He approached her. She took another step back until Zoe told her to stop. She flinched as he gripped her shoulders and bent to look her in her face.

The Marrilian

"You are right and I'm sorry." He drew her close and hugged her. "I'm so sorry. I didn't understand but I understand now."

Erica stood stiff in his grasp.

"We will talk about this later if you still want to." He put his hand over her ear with the hearing aid. She froze, expecting him to grab her hair again. "I can't begin to imagine what could do this to a person." He choked on his words. He blinked back tears. "I am never going to be able to forgive myself for what I did to you this afternoon." With that he stepped back.

Erica stifled the rising cough. Emotion always did this. She was an iridim patient and just about every damn thing would react with the stupid drug so when iridim was released into her blood so would be whatever was attached to it. Betty had warned her she would have to smoke more than normal people to get rid of all the thayanite but right now it felt like she was back to the first day on Quirni. She held her arm so she couldn't use a hand to cover her mouth. She bent and coughed towards the ground instead until Burk moved. Erica jerked upright and faced her. "Don't want to go with you," she warned and heaved to try for breath. Burk stopped.

"I'm not going to hurt you," the general cooed gently. She held her hands up, palms towards the sky, as if she offered friendship, and stayed still. "You can stay here. I won't take you away."

What? Erica tried to see if she lied then her throat filled with choking phlegm. When she tried to clear it, it built and worsened. She backed up several more steps and turned to spit. She managed to get her throat clear only to cough harder. Ella tried to approach her but Erica saw her from the corner of her eye. She backed away.

'You are making a mistake, dummy. Stop.'

She hesitated and stood her ground but Ella didn't move again.

Roger slowly pulled his pack of smokes from his pocket. "I think you need these," he said. He held it up for her to see then tossed them to her. She caught them but couldn't open them with one hand. The coughing worsened till she couldn't stand upright.

"Good lords," Matilda complained and strode past Marcus and up to Erica who only had enough time to straighten. "Why are we all standing around like she's broken?" She plucked the pack out of Erica's hand and tapped it to pop out a cigarette. "She's obviously had this happen before, for pity's sake," Matilda complained. She put the pack back in Erica's hand, put the cigarette in her own mouth and lit it. Her hand shook when she held it out to Erica who stared at Matilda as she took it. "It's over. You're unspoken part is obnoxious by the way. She doesn't even have a Marrilian accent. What's up with that?"

Erica managed to straighten. She inhaled and felt the steam break up the mucous in her throat. They stood face to face, almost twins, the same height, one slighter, narrower than the other for having fought so hard just to survive.

"Don't know," Erica replied. She dropped her head to blow the steam away from the rest of them. "No one tells me anything after lost time but would like to know."

Matilda crossed her arms over her chest. She forced a smile though it was weak. "Alright, would you rather accept Lynn is not an issue or would you rather we embarrass you with the details. I think all you need to accept about Lynn is she's not -"

"Not what?" Erica asked when Matilda suddenly cut herself off.

Matilda held her eyes. She didn't look away. She didn't seem to feel the same as the rest, pitying and shocked. She drew a breath and answered. "She's not sane, Erica."

Erica's eyes widened in surprise. She couldn't imagine what would happen to make her say that but her heart sank. Part of her was insane?

"I think you shouldn't say that name again," Matilda added.

Erica wanted to ask what Matilda meant, how she could know, but feared the answer.

"Would you come here," Ella asked and raised her arm to beckon Erica.

Matilda grabbed Erica's collar and pulled her over to Ella so she didn't have a chance to refuse or hesitate. Erica stumbled after her.

"I have to heal your arm," Ella explained. She detached Matilda from her collar and wrapped her arm around Erica's shoulders.

"Claimant, I would rather you waited," said Burk. "I want her to fix the banking computers. I brought a computer and our best operator in case we managed to talk some sense into her. I don't want her sedated by healer's paste and we have the changes to discuss as well. We expected that could be done tomorrow and it looks as if we will be going ahead with it."

Ella was annoyed but nodded. "Then make it fast but I am giving her pain medication." Burk frowned. "You want Erica, I assume, not Noel?"

"Of course," Burk said with a quick, intense glance at Erica and then headed off to the front of the house where her truck was parked.

Ella asked Bruce to get her bag from her carriage then she put her arm around Erica's back and pushed her towards the porch. "I'm sorry I didn't believe your problem really existed until now," she explained as they walked. "Marcus was heavy handed but we didn't understand. I am willing to believe you behaved badly as a means to survive even here on Quirni but only if you rectify your errors and never do anything like that again. General Burk admitted the SDD tried to confiscate your money. She says you protected it in a most imaginative way but you hurt a lot of people who have done nothing to you. You will fix it. That is the only way we will believe you really do intend to accept our tenancy and not run off the first chance you get. Will you do as we say?"

"Yes, my lady," Erica replied. There was no other reply possible since she had signed the papers.

Ella stopped and held Erica's shoulders. "Have you told us everything? There won't be any more surprises?"

"No more surprises, Claimant, unless they be surprises to me too."

'As if,' said Zoe. 'You should tell them everything.' Erica ignored her. 'Erica!'

A frown twitched across Erica's brow for the yelling in her head but Ella had already smiled and turned to walk towards the porch so she didn't see the expression.

"I would have thought that was a smart assed remark two hours ago," Ella said. "I'm sorry for how it came about but I am glad Marcus forced it out of you." She gave Erica a small hug around the shoulders.

As Erica sat she glanced out at the sun. Had it been two hours since she had said her name? She shook the pack of smokes and dumped one on the table. Ella took it and lit it then handed it to her. Erica wondered what could have happened for two hours.

She imagined Lynn would have been terrorized to wake in such an unfamiliar place with long grass, green everywhere, enormous trees, and people she didn't know. They would have spoken to her. She might have listened but how could they make sense of what she might tell them? They didn't know Lynn or the horror of her life.

If they had tried to touch her, and they would have, she

would have fought like a demon, screamed, bit, kicked and, of course, once held she would have expected to be raped. That was when Erica or Sal would come back. That probably explained the last two hours. But *two hours*? They had talked to Lynn for two hours? That had to be some sort of record.

It wasn't the longest time Lynn had ever been out, not by far, but it was the longest time she had been out and not done serious damage. She glanced around. No one had a black eye or torn clothing. What the hell had happened?

Should she forget about it like Marcus had suggested?

'Exactly,' Zoe declared.

Do you know what went on, Zoe? No answer.

Bruce arrived with the cureman's bag as General Burk returned with a portable computer and the agents.

Erica took the pill Ella gave her and then started to get up. "Need to get a notebook," she told Ella when she put a hand on her arm to stop her.

"Where is it?" Matilda asked. "You're hurt. Stay still and I'll get it."

Erica sat under the weight of Ella's grasp.

"Tell me," Matilda insisted.

Ella squeezed her arm, the good one. "You need to stay still. I don't want you moving your arm. Tell Mati where to find your notebook."

Erica suppressed a frown. Fine. "'Tis a red notebook, taped to the back of the dresser drawer, top drawer."

Matilda returned with it by the time the computer was connected. They had set it up in front of one of the agents.

"Ray will be inputting the information," Burk explained.

Ray looked at her expectantly. Erica opened her notebook. "Log into my bank account with the password fuuSDDaholes. Capital letters on the SDD only."

Matilda laughed.

Burk didn't. "Continue," she ordered icily and took a seat across from them.

Within the hour Erica's Bank of Quirni accounts were emptied and all the other accounts were back to normal. All of Erica's money was transferred to local Mois Claim banks and the Bank of Quirni had new security. "After we figure out what amount you earned legally, we'll return it to you," Ella informed her.

Erica thought that ought to be about five quid since they already accused her of not earning any of it legally.

The Marrilian

The Delegate agent closed down the computer.

"Ray, check it again in an hour and through the night," Burk ordered. "And stay available for the next few weeks to explain the new security to all of the employees. You can get a couple of your computer literate sergeants to help. There will be a lot of calls from all the branches."

"Yes, General."

"Good. Put the computer away and bring out the package."

He saluted her and left with the computer.

Now Erica didn't have a quid to spend. So be it. She glanced over at Marcus who sat at the end of the table. He had been watching her without a word. "Expected to be on my own and the Delegate meant to hurt me," she explained. "Wouldn't do things to banks except thought my survival depended upon it. Or," she added with a wince, "except where Sirrian dogs and cats need help."

He glanced at Burk.

"Excuse me, I missed that," Burk told him.

He blinked and looked relieved then sat forward so he could touch Erica's hand. "Tomorrow you can speak freely."

"Yes, my lord," Erica replied and forced herself to let him touch her, to keep her hand still.

"So am I to understand she is staying here as your tenant even with everything that has happened?" Burk asked Marcus. "Even with these things I have shown you today and what you have seen? I don't want you to change your mind about this if we go ahead with the plan."

"Yes," answered Marcus. "It's the least I can do at this point. She deserves to stay here with some protection and her family."

Erica shuddered and she didn't know why. Protection and family hit a nerve. Why? It brought up such feelings of longing.

General Burk nodded. "Erica, I know this might seem like ill timing but I have to press ahead. I have to tell you since you are staying here we would like to use you as planned. You agreed to help I'm told."

Erica dipped her chin.

"She agrees," interpreted Roger.

Burk leaned on the table towards her. "You were brought here to help keep Matilda safe. Her safety is our priority."

The pain pill began made Erica tired and fuzzy but she knew if Matilda's safety was a priority then that made her expendable.

"We want to use you as a decoy. You will have SDD bodyguards but the general population will think you are

Matilda and we will not try to convince them they are wrong. They will try to hurt you instead of her. They might succeed. Can you accept that?"

Erica dipped her chin again.

"Do you know why this is so important?" Burk pressed.

"So," Erica replied.

"And you will help?"

"Yes."

Burk smiled. "You can say 'no'. No one can make you do this."

Really, and where would she go? When it came right down to it there was no reason not to do it. "So," Erica replied. If things went dreadfully wrong, her problems would be over. That was one way to look at it.

Burk took a deep breath. "I want you to know I am not completely comfortable with the plan. I agree with Matilda, you are young and I don't know if your mental state can tolerate the onslaught of hate you are bound to encounter. Until today, I didn't understand what was wrong with you except that you had been treated for something. Now that I do understand, it seems cruel to ask this of you. I would feel no ill will towards you if you refused to help. That would be perfectly understandable."

Not completely comfortable? Why, because she didn't want someone insane helping her? Did she expect her to run off in a panic? What exactly was Erica supposed to take from Burk's sudden compassion or the expression on her face? The woman looked ready to run from a beating while presenting her back and asking to be whipped at the same time.

Whatever Burk felt or believed, didn't matter and the Delegate's opinion didn't matter. Marcus had made his feelings clear when he waved a fork around and told Matilda how important her work would be to Quirni. That was what mattered but Erica supposed she had to get the damn Delegate general on board with the plan or the plans would run into her constant waffling.

"My mental state be designed for hardship." She spoke softly in part because she would have to face more angry crowds and that was daunting. This whole thing scared her. "Won't do anything stupid but will help."

Burk glanced around the table. No one else had anything to say. She turned back to Erica. "In order for you to help there is something you have to do first." She paused as if to steady her nerves or decide if she were going to continue.

The Marrilian

Marcus eyed her.

Burk sighed. "Erica, if anyone saw you or Matilda together they could see the differences. Your nose is slightly different. Your hair is quite a bit lighter and your eyes are blue instead of green."

Erica didn't like where this was going but then again, she was calling her 'Erica'. What the hell had Lynn done?

"Tomorrow you will see Betty and Levitus. They are our iridim specialists and they will remove your hearing aid but we also want you to see another surgeon, a genetic surgeon. He can make you look exactly like Matilda. You two look so much alike this won't be difficult for him at all. It may take a week to recover from the surgery at most. We'll take care of you so you don't feel any pain." She took a breath.

"The most sensitive part of this change is your eyes. We want to inject them with a color that matches Matilda's, in essence tattoo them. It is semi-permanent and will give us a perfect match for several years. This next phase of our plan is the most dangerous part and now that you are here and have agreed to help us we can move ahead but we need these changes."

Matilda had sat down next to Erica to watch her fix the bank accounts. She leaned forward to speak. "We're ready?"

General Burk raised her palm. "I'll answer your questions later. My conversations with Erica seem to be cut short more often than not. If you don't mind I would finish with her." Matilda sat back and crossed her legs.

"Erica," Burk continued, "We want to change your appearance so you two could be side by side and be indistinguishable. The only thing we intend to leave as an identifying mark is that tattoo on your arm." She pointed at Erica's broken arm as she spoke. "We will then bring you into areas where Matilda needs to be. We will convince people you are Matilda. In that way we can identify who will attack, subdue them, and make sure the area is safe for her. We can't do that if they have a way of telling you two apart." She paused as the agent came back around the corner of the house. He placed a black plastic wrapped package on the table in front of Burk. "I understand the physical changes have not been discussed with you but I am hoping you will agree." Burk fell silent to let Erica think.

Erica didn't know what to think or even how to think about it. Matilda sat beside her, her arms folded across her chest. She wore a steely expression. She didn't say anything.

Edwards

Erica looked at Roger sitting across from them. He watched her intently. He would want her to help protect his wife but what would protect Matilda best, working with the SDD or not?

Ella also looked at Erica intently. Marcus didn't. He dropped his eyes to his lap. He sat back from the table with his ankle crossed over his knee as if to keep himself out of the conversation. He might have hurt Erica and cursed her and caused Lynn to come out but he was the only one who could speak up and protect her. He was the claimant. Ella was only a co-claimant. Erica knew he had good reason to be angry too, much, much more reason than her father had ever had. She needed him and she wanted his advice.

He happened to glance up and noticed Erica looked at him. "Respect your opinion, my lord. Please give it."

He frowned and shook his head. "This is your choice. These changes are permanent. I won't ask you to make them."

She looked at Ella who now lowered her eyes.

She looked at Matilda again. "Does this bother you?"

Matilda didn't seem to have an answer. She kept her eyes on Roger. When Erica glanced at him again he looked away.

"If we look any more alike, would it concern you?" Erica asked Matilda once more. Why where they acting like this? She needed to know if Matilda, or if any of them, still thought the SDD intended to replace Matilda with herself. A lot had happened since their discussion in the lab. Chances were they feared it more than ever now that they had seen Lynn. They should understand how Erica couldn't control her. "Would you have me do this?"

"I can't answer that," Matilda said. "As for you looking more like me, I'm not much concerned about that now." She looked back at Erica with a pained expression. "I think the only one it would cause problems is you."

Really. What had Lynn done? Why was Matilda no longer concerned about the SDD replacing Matilda with her?

"You said you understand how important Matilda is," Burk reminded her.

"Yes, General," Erica replied.

"We will protect you as best we can."

"I don't want her doing it," Matilda suddenly said and sat forward. "She has too much anguish from her past. We can't add this. I want to put off the plans until the anger towards me dies down."

"What if it doesn't?" Ella asked. "It has been years already."

The Marrilian

Matilda glared at her. "Then so be it."

Burk placed her forearms on the package and leaned on them to speak to her. "Mati, if something happens to you we will have lost the documents once and for all. It will take decades to find the ore without them let alone the way north. Unless you write them out and give them to us we have to protect you in any way we can find."

Matilda looked like she seriously considered handing over the information. Erica found herself horrified at the idea. If Matilda's suspicion about factions in the SDD was true then handing over the documents could doom them all.

"Good lords you stupid idiot," Erica said but it was Zoe who spoke, and she didn't speak with the thick, Tenpole accent. Erica vaguely wondered if she should try to shut her up but all she could do was listen. "Don't you even consider it." Matilda sat back and stared at her in confusion. "What makes you think you even have the *right* to consider it? All of us have a stake in what you do!"

Matilda blinked. "The right? It's my choice what I do with those documents."

"Is it?"

Matilda 's eyes widened. Her mouth opened but she didn't know what to say.

"It was bad enough getting the beating in Cluny only to find out you're innocent. But to be dragged to Quirni for nothing, well, that would top even that! I think your choices have reached an end."

Matilda stared at her.

Erica was as stunned as Matilda. Zoe was back in full force. She felt weak.

General Burk smiled and unwrapped the package, never noticing the change that had taken place. She pulled two vests from it. One was dark brown and the other was white.

"After we change your appearance tomorrow you and Matilda should be impossible to tell apart except by your tattoo which no one is to see unless they are one of the people sitting at this table or they are an agent you know. Those of us who work with you daily have to be able to tell you two apart, however, so we want you two to dress in different colors."

She slid the white vest across the table to Matilda. "You will be in light colors. I had this vest made so it won't be seen under your clothing." She pushed the brown vest towards Erica. "You will be in dark colors. We chose these because your own clothes seem to be that way." She pointed at the vests. "I want you both to start wearing those all of the time. We have already begun to arrange the first meeting between Matilda and the claimants and once people know where the meeting is someone could deduce where she is hidden. These will help protect you in the event that happens."

Matilda pulled the vest close. She prodded the hard plates in the cushioned fabric. "I hate these things."

"Wear it anyway," Erica told her. "One saved me more than once."

"That's why you are getting a new one," Burk said. "Your old one is a mess." Erica held her broken arm close and let the vest lay. "You will notice your vest is a little large," Burk added. "You're about twenty pounds under weight. You have to fix that within the next six months. You also have to learn to talk like Mati and Mati, you have to learn to talk like Erica."

They both raised their eyebrows incredulously.

General Burk laughed. "You already have the expressions down. Next, Erica, I want you to train. Your fighting is our ace in the hole. No one knows about that because you didn't use it but very little since you have been here. I assume that is because of the thayanite?"

"Yes, General."

"Fine, well, Betty insisted on bringing a thayanite therapy chamber with her. She says she'll have that out of your system in about two months. She wants to see you too," Burk told Roger. "She is certain you haven't cleared it since the last time she saw you. It doesn't go away easily on its own. Records indicate you never once used a chamber since the last time you saw her. She insists you do so now."

"I wouldn't miss it," he replied as he flicked his cigarette ash in the tray. He wore a gentle smile despite his dry tone then drew off his smoke again.

"Of course not," Burk agreed and turned back to Erica. "Bruce can fight, so can Elsbeth. Spar with them. However, you are not to fight unless you are explicitly told to do so or Matilda is in imminent danger. Can you do that?"

Erica dipped her chin.

Burk nodded as well. She leaned back with her hands outstretched on the table to either side of the tenancy agreement. "Well, that about covers it. Erica, you have an appointment in Pey tomorrow at dawn. Get there in the dark. Your claimants said they would take you. They want to be there when we work on you. They'll pick you up in a closed carriage." She looked at Matilda. "Now, you have a question?"

"Yes. Does this mean the canisters have tested out? We are actually beginning?"

"It does. They have worked beautifully and we'll be pressing into full production. That is another subject for another day. I think Miss Kinsley is about done."

Erica blinked and raised her eyes to look at Burk. *Kinsley still huh?*

"It's the pain pill," Ella said. "It's time I healed her arm."

"We could take her to Betty and Levitus in my car right now. No one would see her in it. They could heal her at your new clinic," Burk suggested. "There is room for you to stay there if you wish. It's quite an improvement over your old place."

Ella liked the idea. "I haven't seen the inside of it since they started," she said to Marcus. "It's been months. Ever since they began preparing for this."

He smiled. "By all means go."

She helped Erica stand. Burk stood and collected Erica's vest. "We'll take this with us. I want her wearing this starting tomorrow."

Ella and Burk started to lead Erica away but she stopped and looked down at Marcus. "I would speak to you in private, my lord."

He tapped his ear. "Maybe after tomorrow."

She shook her head. "Doesn't matter, my lord, please."

He frowned.

She shrunk back from him and opened her mouth to excuse herself for asking but then he slowly rose from his chair. She kept a few paces away from him as he led the way to the middle of the drive. He turned to face her.

Faced with him giving her his complete attention, Erica didn't know how to say what she wanted to say. She had to think.

He waited.

She decided to ask outright and chance insulting him and if he hit her again she deserved it.

"Do I remain your tenant or do you stop the agreement after this plan of the SDD's be done? When you no longer need me? Would know in order to make plans." She looked at his chin.

The question didn't seem to upset him. "You can't want to stay. You are terrified of me now. I can tell that just by looking at you and you have every right to be."

Edwards

She drew a long breath to try and steady her nerve. "Mayhaps, my lord," she said and fought a grimace but that only made her twitch around the eyes and mouth. "But please, my lord, please I need a home and Mati be my cousin. Would that I stay at least as long as she lets me." She asked Marcus because of Lynn. That part of her wanted a family more than Erica did and if not family then maybe a home. "Will you let me stay?"

He relaxed. "You will remain my tenant for as long as you want but you are putting yourself in harm's way not with me but with the SDD plans."

"Yes sir." She dropped her eyes. She couldn't keep looking at him. "Can accept that if-" She took a breath and forced herself to look at him again. "If when I change you don't make me leave. Can accept what happens. A home would be something." She searched his face. Could she plan on it? Would he keep his promise?

"You know you will be depending upon the SDD to keep you safe and it seems they do nothing kind for you."

It was so true but she wasn't going to discuss it while they listened. She put her fingers over her ear.

He squinted and took a deep breath. "Thank you for doing this." He touched under her chin then lifted. She flinched until she felt his gentle insistence that she raise her gaze to meet his. "You have beautiful blue eyes and I'll hate to see them changed but you will do a lot of good by protecting Mati. She is hard headed, smart as can be, and has incredible resolve but I think you are her match." He smiled. "You're Enzus to me. You're all the parts, not just the first. I will remember that."

"Yes, my lord," she replied as he brushed his fingertip over her cheek where he had hit her. She felt the bruise he had made and it worried her that a man who had hurt her that afternoon could touch her so gently before the day ended. Perhaps he tried to make a point by stroking that spot. He tried to convince her he wouldn't hurt her again. He would remember his error. She knew better.

She hoped he would let her stay no matter what happened. That was all she wanted, not his concern, not his promise to never hurt her. She had to believe he wouldn't send her away. That was all she hoped to get. That hope was enough to make her do and live as he expected, that and she had nowhere else to go, no other family, no money for a home, nothing.

She had no one but this look-alike girl that would transform Quirni into something strange and new. All three planets would change their relationships to each other if Matilda was successful and Erica was to help. If she did well, maybe in the end there could be a permanent place for her here with good people, maybe a family.

Edwards

Chapter 13 – Peace for Healing

Someone touched Erica's shoulder.

"Wake up dear."

She recognized the voice. When she tried to open her eyes she couldn't. She raised her hand to her face but someone held her wrist.

"You have patches over your eyes. They'll be there for three days. Don't rub."

"Betty?"

"Yes. Claimant Mois is here too. She slept in the chair. That is quite an honor to have a claimant sleep in a chair for you." She sounded pleased.

Was it an honor or a mark of how little they trusted her? "She stayed all night?"

"She's never left your side even during the surgery. So how are you feeling?"

"Hungry."

"We can fix that. I'll be back soon." She heard Betty cross the room and the door bumped closed.

Erica gently touched the pads over her eyes. Again, someone took her hands away. "As soon as her back is turned you do exactly what you shouldn't," Ella remarked with a sigh. "Your appearance is not the only thing you share with Mati. You both do exactly what you want."

Erica laid her arms down on the bed. "Pardons, my lady."

"We'll take you home soon. It will be dark in a few hours."

"Dark? Been sleeping all day?"

"Yes. It took a while to make the changes. The eye color is perfect though. You look so much like Mati now I won't be able to tell you two apart once the bruises are gone."

"Truly?"

"Truly," repeated Ella.

"Hope it 'tis the right thing."

Ella squeezed her shoulder. "It is. The tenancy contract you signed assures that."

Erica turned her head. The sounds of the beeps around the bed changed. "Can't hear out of my right ear. The aid be gone?"

"You may speak the pronoun 'I' now, Erica. Roger told us

how the young people working on Chaucer Street are not allowed to use the pronoun. Well, you are no longer working there and frankly it is expected here. As for the aid, yes it's gone. You can have a regular one when your ear heals. It should take about a month."

Erica tried to sit up and found it made her dizzy. She lay back down.

Ella chuckled. "That is the pain medication."

"She tried to get up already didn't she?" Betty commented.

"She did. Somehow we both knew she would."

"That is certain. I have seen enough of her to know this child is usually petulant, often guarded, and always obstinate."

Erica had no idea what the hell that meant but it didn't sound good and had Betty called her a child?

"She means that in the best way," said Ella. "Don't you."

"It was entirely a compliment," said Betty as she raised the bed. She took Erica's hand and put two pills in it. "Take those and then you can have your sandwich." Erica swallowed them then received the sandwich in her outstretched hand. "I hope you like ham and cheese."

Erica didn't but she was too hungry to care. She forgot about Betty's comment and ate quickly both to get past the taste of the ham and to fill her stomach. Shortly after she finished eating, the pills took effect. She fell to sleep again. They had meant it when they told her she wouldn't feel any pain. She couldn't stay awake.

When it got dark Ella and Betty roused her enough to help her into a carriage. It took them back to Matilda and Roger's. Erica slept for the short trip. She woke when someone slipped their arms under her.

"Time to get up, Doll," a man said near her left ear.

She recognized the voice. "James?" she murmured with a smile and a tone that didn't hide the thrill she felt. He helped her stand from her seat.

"None other." He lifted her down from the carriage. He didn't allow her feet to touch the ground but a moment before he picked her up again.

She didn't object. She leaned against him and inhaled. He smelled good.

"How are you feeling?" he asked.

"Sleepy," she replied. "'Tis nice to have you back. My pardons about flipping you."

She felt his chuckle rumble in his chest. Even without her hearing aid his voice enveloped her. Everything about him

The Marrilian

comforted her.

"Elsbeth has shown Mark and me how to avoid that maneuver next time," he said. "Not that you will try but someone else might."

"Elsbeth? She be all right?"

"She has a bruised ego." She could hear his smile.

"I'm fine," said Elsbeth. "Including my ego."

Erica lifted her head from James and smiled towards her voice. "Oh, you both come back! My pardons for any hurts!" She started to touch her eye-patches.

"Don't touch those," Ella warned. She pushed Erica's hand down. James stopped.

"Would see Elsbeth, my lady. Would say my pardons properly. Hurt her when we fought."

"No pardons are required," Elsbeth told her and held Erica's other wrist.

"None at all," agreed James. "We were doing our job. It was a bad day for it."

"You can apologize properly when we say the patches can come off. These two are staying here so they will be available for whatever pardons you feel like heaping upon them," added Ella. "Elsbeth has a nursing degree and she will be putting it to use again. She will take care of you until you are healed. They will also provide you with extra security now that the plans have begun."

"That means we are back and half of us are wiser," announced James. He began to walk again. "Elsbeth has been pushed off her high horse."

"High horse?" Erica asked.

"I have never been knocked like that before," Elsbeth explained.

"Knocked?" asked Erica again.

"Knocked down, taken down by a kick from someone six inches shorter than her and nearly a hundred pounds lighter," James explained and he sounded delighted. "She hasn't been knocked down since she passed her fight tests or whatever they call it."

"*Belts*," Elsbeth corrected him dryly. "They call the levels *belts*. After your demonstration, Erica, it occurred to me your tattoo is your belt so I looked up the Tenpole schools." Elsbeth chuckled slightly. "You earned a full ring of circles and thorns. You were being nice when you left my jaw intact. I mean it when I say that no pardons are necessary."

Edwards

"And you finally believe she can fight," James declared. His feet crunched over the gravel drive and then his shoes echoed on the wooden stairs of the porch. "I believed her a long time ago just because of the way she moves. All of you kicking fighters move the same way."

"Kicking fighters?" Elsbeth asked. "As opposed to you bludgeoning boxers?"

"Who have more finesse," James told her. "Just listen to your captain next time. He knows what he is talking about once in a while." A chair scraped across the porch decking. James bent and set her down.

"How did it go?" Matilda asked.

"Fine," Ella answered.

Erica heard the scrapping of more chairs. She leaned back into the soft glow of painkiller.

"Her hair is already darker," Roger noticed in a hushed voice, as if he would disturb a sleeping person.

"What did they do to my hair?" asked Erica.

"It's a genetic dye on top of a regular dye," Ella explained as a few more chairs scraped across the wooden slats of the porch. "As her hair grows now it will be the same color."

Erica felt someone close to her. They put a hand on her shoulder. "I can't really tell in this light but it looks exact." It was Matilda beside her.

"They matched it to that sample we took from you, Mati," Ella explained. "It was quite incredible to watch and her eyes are perfect."

"Good gracious but the things they can do," Matilda declared and sat in the chair next to Erica. She touched her hair again. "I like the haircut."

Erica felt it. Her hair was not as long, just at the nape of her neck. It curled. She could feel the ends flipping up just like Matilda's. Somehow they had added curl along with the color because thayanite had straightened and lightened her hair.

"How are you feeling?" asked Matilda. She placed her hand on Erica's arm.

"Buzzed," Erica replied. "And hungry."

Matilda squeezed her arm then got up. She came back with a plate that Erica heard set on the table. She picked up Erica's hand and placed it on a pile of hard and soft things. "Crackers, cheese, fruit, stuff you can eat without a fork and knife. Is that good?"

"'Tis, thank you," Erica replied. She closed her fingers on a something soft and bumpy, a strawberry she hoped.

The Marrilian

Matilda patted her arm. "I want to thank you instead. This is a big deal. Because of your choice to do this for us, the SDD is going to let me begin the plans. I will be giving out the locations of metal deposits soon. It is incredibly exciting to think of all the things we can do with metal."

Erica stuffed the soft something in her mouth and it was a strawberry. Her hand settled on a cracker next. She ate that too. Eating blind was sort of interesting. She explored the plate and didn't reply. Metal didn't impress her that much so it didn't require any reply. Quirni did all right without it. She found a strawberry.

Everyone fell quiet for a while. Erica noticed and stopped eating. She sat back. "What happens?"

James cleared his throat. "Nothing."

"James," Erica warned. "You and Elsbeth chatter like a bush full of birds. Your quite be no good."

"I uh," James started and then stopped. "Do we?"

Everyone around the table laughed and it was the type of laugh that came after tension, diffusing it upon realizing the worst was past.

Matilda replied in a Marrilian accent. "James, our good captain, simply told us a thing or two about you *Doll*."

"Doll?" Erica repeated.

"Yes, *Doll*."

No one said anything for several moments then Erica finally sighed. "So…you make me live with that." She put a grape in her mouth. "All because Quirni be brutes."

"Absolutely," James told her and she could hear how he grinned. "And 'tis the first time to be called a brute," he added sounding like a Chaucer Street puff. "Usually be called a runt!"

Erica sighed in resignation.

"The Runt and I have been sharing stories of our trip with you," Elsbeth confessed.

"Like the look on your face when I asked you get the boar," James laughed. "That was precious. I could have sworn you were going to punch me in the nose."

"Or finding you up the tree," Elsbeth added. "I thought I was going to die laughing when your gear fell on James' head and then to see you hanging from that branch and James ready to race up after you. I had to keep a straight face and it nearly cracked off. God. Then we were supposed to get you to talk about your past only to learn you knew about the aid all along so you wouldn't. In the meantime, General White was trying to get your records with no luck. He has no tact so no one would willingly give him a damn thing." She laughed again. "And you were angry about the aid so you told us nothing either. That was lovely."

"They found out enough without my help," Erica said dryly.

"General Burk did. She looked in Delegate records, not just police records. It never occurred to White you would have been picked up by the Delegates for something other than medical treatments or that incident on Sirrus. Desante didn't mention it. Like I said, nobody likes to give White a thing. Desante and White both, actually." She paused a moment and several around the table chuckled for no reason Erica could hear.

"Burk still had a lot to guess at," said James. "That ENZUS thing had her going for weeks."

"Don't you take a chance talking like this?" Erica asked. "They might hear you."

"No," James told her. "We have devices in our uniforms that we can activate with a phone call. No one listens to us otherwise. They only locate us."

"So they listened through me?"

"They could if they wanted but that sort of listening is expensive. They just waited for us to send interesting information," explained Elsbeth. "We could upload an hour of conversation if something interesting happened. Terry was the one waiting for reports. He was begging us for something, anything. When you told me about your sisters he went nuts only to find out White already knew about them."

"Her sisters?" Matilda asked in a Marrilian accent. "Might we another story?"

Neither Elsbeth nor James replied.

"'Tis a sad story," Erica told her. "Some other time."

"Were you being bad again, Erica?" Matilda asked with pleasure. "Because I have learned enough to know you are quite capable at being bad."

Erica swallowed her cracker and set the other half back on the plate. "So," she replied with the tone that conveyed the sadness she felt. She changed the subject. "Where be Lord Mois? Don't hear him."

"Home," Ella answered. "He wanted to be here when you got back but they needed him in Nigh. We have a project down there. He's been on the computer and phone all day."

"Nigh?" she said thoughtfully. "Has anyone found the agents that attacked us there?"

The Marrilian

"General Burk is looking into it," Elsbeth answered and had lost her delighted tone. "She has to be careful how she handles the situation. She doesn't know what the agents were doing or who sent them but at least she believes agents did attack you."

"That is part of the reason we are back," explained James. "She isn't sure who she can trust but she knows she can trust us."

"And we can vouch for Mark, Sati, and Rami," Elsbeth added. "They are being brought in as well."

"Interesting," Matilda said, using her Quirni accent again. "Handpicked guards and more than I ever needed before."

"Very interesting," Ella added. "To think Sophie is unsure of her own staff is disheartening at the very least."

"I told you there have been conflicting orders," said Elsbeth. "General Burk won't take any chances with Matilda's safety until she knows why."

Erica crossed her arms over her chest. "So how come you and James could come so quick? Why didn't you go south already? You two be part of White's group. Thought you would go back."

"You two *are* part of White's group," Ella corrected. "Use the proper verb, Erica."

"Yes, my lady," Erica agreed contritely.

"General Burk requested our transfers," James answered. "She had us stay to debrief us repeatedly about the attack in Nigh. I think she used that as a delaying tactic until our transfer came through."

"She did," agreed Elsbeth. "White didn't want to approve it but Burk wouldn't accept any of his crap. James and I knew Mati already and now you as well, Erica, so she had good reason to want us. She went over his head."

"I'm happy with the change," James told them. "But I have to admit at first I was concerned. I wondered if I might end up working with one of the attackers. I thought I'd gone nuts that afternoon. Those agents weren't trying to scare you, Doll. They tried to kill you."

"How did they know we were there?" Erica asked and she did her best to talk like the Quirni and avoid Ella's displeasure. "They had no time to bring that boat, set up the rope or walk all those men there after we arrived in town. They had advance notice."

Elsbeth agreed. "Undoubtedly. All agents were told when we approached their area. They helped keep us safe supposedly."

"Did you keep General White informed of your position?"

asked Matilda.

Elsbeth and James didn't answer out loud.

"I see," Matilda murmured.

"See what?" asked Erica.

"She's right," Ella said quietly. "I hadn't thought of it that way. Could it be him?"

"I don't know," James replied. "He told us after we entered Lund Claim that Erica was safe. I guess the attackers expected she would take off the vest but she never complained about it so we had her leave it on."

"Since she did we continued to wear ours as well. That way she wouldn't get any idea to leave hers off," Elsbeth told them. "If I hadn't done that, I would have been shot in the chest."

Silence again. Erica couldn't imagine how Elsbeth felt knowing another agent had shot the arrow.

"Burk believes there may be more going on than we thought," Elsbeth added. "She would have you know, Claimant, that up 'til now we believed it was only a few people who didn't want Mati getting help. Now it looks bigger than that or we're getting paranoid."

"We've thought it was bigger for some time. What we don't know is who is behind it. You have helped to change the direction we'll look."

"Not White," James said.

"More so than Sophie Burk," Ella answered.

"General Burk would have gladly gotten rid of Erica. That first day she was ready to commit her," argued Roger. "I thought it was her who attacked them in Nigh. I felt sure of it."

"No, I never thought so and I told you that," Ella argued. "I have known Sophie too long. She is loyal to us. I trust her more than I trust White."

"No, it's not Burk," Matilda agreed. "She didn't want Erica here. That is for certain. She saw Erica as a danger and tried to stop her from being with us for our sake. After she met Lynn that changed. It changed us all. No one could use her. If they brought her out everyone would know it wasn't me and there is no way Erica would work for them either. Or Zoe," she added as an afterthought.

Erica felt the longing from Lynn as her name was said. She shifted uncomfortably in her chair.

Matilda laid her hand on her arm.

"What happened? What are you talking about?" asked Elsbeth.

The Marrilian

"Well," Matilda began carefully. "Erica has another side to herself. She's a bit wild and she shows up when Erica says her given name, Lynn."

Erica bit her bottom lip against the rise in emotion. Matilda patted her leg but continued. "Marcus forced this other side of Erica to come out. After Burk saw it, she realized she wasn't a threat. She was grinning about it. She was actually happy Erica had become a signed tenant. She said no one could touch her now and *everything* was safe."

That surprised Erica. "Never was told that."

She heard Ella get up beside her.

"You weren't around for anyone to tell you," Matilda explained. "You were sedated. But her reaction made me believe there is much more to this problem than a general or two. She said '*Everything is safe*'. I don't think that means a few local generals are causing local problems. It's bigger than that."

"As in Quirni?" asked James.

Silence followed.

"It was prudent that she has become a tenant," said Roger thickly. "That was quick thinking on your part Ella."

"Marcus' part," Ella corrected.

"A wise man," Elsbeth noted.

"He is," Ella agreed.

"Erica," Roger said, "thank you for changing your appearance. I've been worried about Mati for a long time but for once, I feel better. Something is being done about all of this."

Erica didn't know what to say.

Ella saved her the effort by picking up her hand and putting a few pills in it. "It is time for more medication." She put a glass in Erica's other hand. Not long after swallowing Erica could hardly stay upright.

James startled her when he picked her up. "Say goodnight, Doll."

She muttered something approximate to what he said and fell to sleep. She woke when he bent over to lower her into a bed. He pulled her shoes and pants off and covered her.

"Good night," he said softly near her ear and that woke her one last time. She fell back to sleep with the feeling of a kiss on her cheek or perhaps she had dreamed it.

The patches came off Erica's eyes three days later but for a lack of mirrors on Quirni, Erica had to accept she looked like Matilda. Further proof was only Roger seemed to tell Erica and

Matilda apart at a glance. Even before they changed into light and dark clothes each day he could still tell them apart.

Erica thought he might be able to do so because she still coughed. She made sure to use Betty's thayanite antidote chamber every day. It had been moved to the lab where there was electricity to plug it in so she wouldn't have to go into town repeatedly and risk being seen. Elsbeth rode out with Matilda and Erica each morning to maintain it and also to give Erica eye drops and pills throughout the day. Erica was convinced Elsbeth liked this part of her work.

"You should be a healer or a cureman," Erica told her when Elsbeth brought her more pain medication than Erica thought she needed. Drugs could make her dissociate, especially narcotics, so now that she felt better she was back to her old habits of avoiding them if she could. With the antidote chamber mask inches from her face, she frowned up at Elsbeth. "You like harassing people."

"I can't tell you how much fun it is," Elsbeth replied and held out the pill.

Erica refused and placed the mask over her face.

Elsbeth's fingers folded around the pill as she grew an evil smile. "In about an hour your eyes will begin to feel like sandpaper and then I will enjoy scolding you before I let you have this. By the time I finish your eyes will tear up from the pain and the tears will make the pain worse, salt in wounds hurts. Taking the pill will avoid that. It is my duty to tell you so but feel free to deny it and give me the pleasure of saying 'I told you so'. It is one of the easier ways for me to get my thrills." She held the pill out again. "You have about three seconds."

Erica didn't know it was for that. She slapped Elsbeth's hand as she took it.

Matilda laughed at them and received two glares. "Pardons," she begged and sounded so much like Erica they both stared. "I've been doing a bit of practicing," Matilda added and began to measure out some chemicals.

"Which you should be doing too," Elsbeth told Erica.

Erica put the mask back on without a word. That afternoon she began practicing her Quirni accent with James' help. He said she didn't sound at all Quirni and he could say that sounding like a Marrilian puff. Each day she took walks with him in order to practice and half the time he rolled with laughter. He wouldn't stop laughing long enough for her to talk to him seriously. It was almost as if he avoided any serious conversation. After a few weeks, in spite of his sense of humor, he said she had improved and returned to the ranch happy with herself.

"Hel-lo!" she called to Matilda as they rounded the barn and waved. She had a table at the side of the drive near the barn.

Matilda grinned as she approached them. "Care for a bit of a competition?" she asked and sounded very Marrilian although on the upper class side. Erica suspected that was Roger's influence.

"Like what?" Erica asked suspiciously and with short, curt Quirni sounds.

"Saw your pistol on the bedpost. I have one too. I'm pretty good with it."

Erica's eyebrows rose. "Really," she said with disbelief. She grinned. "I'd love it."

Matilda's eyes narrowed. "I never say 'really' like that, Erica." She got a mischievous grin. "Shall we make our competition more interesting? I say we trade pistols."

They both grinned. Elsbeth and James went to the porch to watch. A thick wall of straw bales with paper bullseyes stood out in the field. Matilda already had Erica's pistol sitting on a table.

"Nothing like expecting me to agree," Erica commented in her best Quirni.

"You could at least try to talk like me," Matilda told her and picked up Erica's gun and immediately achieved a cluster of shots about three inches around. She retrieved the target and showed it to Erica. "Now, dear, tell me, 'tis impressive, so?"

"I have never called anyone 'dear' in my life," Erica growled and picked up the revolver. She aimed and missed the rings on the target altogether although a poof of straw flew out from beside it. She corrected and missed again. Her own gun's sites were dead on. She emptied the pistol and only managed to creep into the center ring.

Neither of them saw Marcus arrive since their backs were to the house. He stood by James and Elsbeth to wait and watch as Matilda shot another six rounds then collected her target again. "Now tell me if it 'tis not perfect," she said in her Marrilian accent and waved the target about. She was obviously delighted in speaking like Erica as well as flaunting her expertise with the pistol.

"Give that here," Erica muttered stiffly and took the target. She poked her finger through it so it had an extra hole to the side and handed it back to Matilda. "Better luck next time." She loaded Matilda's revolver and, still not seeing Marcus behind her, said, "I will make one hole when I figure out your lousy pistol, Mati."

"Enzus?" Marcus said in surprise. Erica lowered the gun and looked over her shoulder.

"My lord!" She started to unload the revolver but he motioned for her to turn back.

"Let's see how good you are." She hesitated but he insisted.

Less confident now, she aimed and shot six times. When she returned with the paper Matilda looked at it and smiled.

"Boo-hoo" she pouted for Erica, pleased. The spread of holes was a lot bigger than Matilda's.

Marcus nodded. "I suppose you're better with your own weapon. Not that you have to be with the way you cheat."

"Yes, my lord," Erica replied fearfully until he grinned. She managed a weak smile. "'Tis nice to see you, my lord."

He stared at them both, first Erica then Matilda then back. "Amazing," he said then walked forward and put his arm around Erica's shoulders. "I have a job for you, *Doll*."

Erica grimaced. "James did tell the whole planet to call me that."

"Just don't get confused and call me that," Matilda told them. She started picking up the spent cartridges of the automatic pistol. Marcus led Erica away.

"Would you care to chat with Arlo?" he asked and tried to sound Marrilian too, which Erica chose to ignore.

"Arlo? He's here?"

Marcus shook his head. "He's still in the Padt City but I have set up a phone call. I want you to talk to him about coming back."

They sat down on at the porch table. Elsbeth and James left as Marcus began to explain the deal she could offer to Arlo, the amount of money available, the terms, and the expectations. "Can you explain that to him?"

She shrugged. She couldn't figure out why she would need to.

Marcus frowned.

"Yes, my lord," she agreed quickly.

He pulled out his phone and dialed but with an unsure eye on her. "We'll be calling through an agent at the bank," he explained as he waited for the call to go through. "He might be listening. Keep that in mind. He spoke to the agent briefly then handed the phone to Erica.

"Hello?" Arlo greeted on the other end when she put it up to her ear.

The Marrilian

"Arlo!" She grinned to hear him. "Lo! 'Tis Erica."

Claimant Mois leaned in close. She gave him a puzzled frown until he pointed to his ear and then the phone. She leaned towards him so they could both hear.

"Erica," he remarked dully. "You didn't get away from them."

"No, but 'tis fine. What you feared doesn't seem to be the case. Do you remember?"

He sighed. "Yes, I remember. So how are you?"

"Fine, fell in with a good group."

"Really? Like who? The Dirty Knoll Gang?" he asked with a disdainful laugh.

"No." She frowned. Who were the Dirty Knoll Gang? "The Claimants Mois."

"No way! You found good people?"

"Yes."

Arlo laughed a little easier. "I used to live there. They're nice."

Erica smiled as Marcus sat back looking pleased then leaned in close again. "They are, Arlo. Lord Mois does a lot for me. Guess he took pity. Actually, Arlo, I use his phone to call you. Matilda knows him. She introduced me."

"She would. He was her attorney."

"Gave Matilda your message."

"You remembered? It's been so long I figured even if you saw her you would have forgotten. What did she say?"

"That she likes you and 'tis a shame you didn't take her offer to work again."

He grunted. "Some offer. Go right back and start all over so I can lose everything again? What about my 23 million?"

"What about an opportunity to make more than that?" Erica asked. "And have it protected so you can't lose your own money. Guess there be some fancy way of doing business so no one can take it again. The Moises will front the money to start."

Marcus sat back and frowned at her.

Erica shrugged.

Arlo didn't answer right away.

"Arlo, don't know what happened before but know what happens now. There be glass canisters you can make in your factory. They be in demand, so much so my cousin, Lord Mois, *and* the QSDD be involved. Don't know if you can get the old factory going but, if you can, you will be on the ground floor of something big."

"Are you suggesting I come back to Mois Claim?"

"So. But you do as you will. You be successful there, 'tis for sure, but felt I owed you."

"Erica."

"Yes?"

"I got your message."

"What-"

"The message you left for me on the computer," he interrupted.

She stilled, expecting him to yell at her.

"I understood it but before I could do what the note instructed it was fixed."

"Fixed it from here," she explained cautiously with a glance at Marcus. "Was a rough day."

"Did the Delegate take your money?"

"No, the Moises have it."

"All of it?"

"Yes."

"Sorry."

"Have something better," Erica told him with pleasure although much of that pleasure was an act. "Have a home and friends. Also have a signed tenancy."

"What? No way! A tenancy with the Moises?"

"Yes. Twenty-five years to give an idea how much I trust them." She gazed up at Marcus when he sat back and frowned at her once more. "'Tis how I know coming back be something. Won't be for naught. Would something for you. Will you come?" she asked as she smiled sweetly at Marcus and tried to disarm his anger a little. It worked. He shook his head, perturbed, but listened in again.

"With you as a tenant, absolutely," Arlo agreed. "That gives me extra leverage doesn't it?"

"Anything for you, Arlo."

"Just me or are Pete and the others invited back as well? They used to work with Mati too and lost a lot for their effort."

Marcus' eyes grew wide as he nodded vigorously.

"Sure. They can come. You can all be rich," Erica told him. "Think you and your friends could stand that?"

Arlo laughed. "I'll have to give notice at the bank then pack. It'll take me about three months to get there, maybe more."

Marcus frowned and shook his head.

"Three months? Why so long?"

"You've traveled this world. We don't use mass transit you

know. I'll have to buy a cart, pack it, get horses. I'll probably go in with the guys. We'll come up together. It takes time to plan something like that and then the travel time to Mois Claim from here is at least a couple of months when the roads are in perfect condition which they rarely are."

"I suppose," Erica agreed. She saw no way around this.

Marcus put his hand out. "Let me talk to him," he said softly.

"Arlo, would you talk to Lord Mois?"

"He's there?"

"Yes. He listens. 'Tis his phone."

"I thought you sort of took it. Knowing you."

"No." Her eyes narrowed as the implications. "Knowing me? Who tells you such?"

"QSDD, Erica. They told me about you. They said you were such a slick scam artist, thief, and computer hacker that they didn't blame me for getting mixed up with that computer mess."

She shook her head. "Mayhaps once but not now. Never had a chance like this. Claimant Mois be here just as I said. Did not steal his phone and he wishes to talk, like I said. The need for the canisters be big. 'Tis a great opportunity. I know how to make money and this be a good one."

"You know how to make money illegally, according to the agents, but I guess it's all the same to you."

"You guess?" Erica looked up at the porch roof in exasperation.

She didn't like the hostility in his tone. She wasn't sure he would come. She suspected he told her what she wanted to hear. What reason did he have to leave his job except for what she said? That didn't seem like enough given what he had learned about her.

"Arlo, how many people live on Marril?"

"What?"

"Can you answer?"

He signed. "About 2 billion."

"If you sold a filter to each of them and only made a quid profit, how much would that be?"

He laughed. "So that's it. You want the glass for those filters Mati started making. She told me about them. Apparently, the trial period is over and they are going into production?"

"So."

"How well do they work?"

"How healthy does Quirni make you?"

Arlo grunted. "Damn. We could make a whole lot more than

one quid off of each filter."

"You will not lie about coming, will you?"

He chuckled. "Lie? You accuse me of lying? Of all the people, *you* accuse *me* of lying?"

"Do not accuse. I know you do," she said. "'Tis such for sure."

Marcus tensed at the following silence then Arlo sighed again, this time with a long exhale. "Fine, you're right, although I can't imagine how you know. I used to be good at this sort of game. No one ever called me on a lie. What did I say that you don't believe?"

She shrugged. "There be no reason to believe what I tell you but you did."

"Ah," Arlo replied. "I guess that makes sense."

"You can be rich again," Erica told him. "You be respected here and your work be needed more for this than counting."

He made a scoffing sound. "I didn't expect Matilda could ever make any headway with those things. Quirni has so few exports. Our High Lord has to negotiate the trade with Marril and frankly, he isn't one to put much effort into it."

"Know nothing about that," Erica admitted. "General Burk, Lord Mois, and Matilda know such. They begin exports. That I know. They need you too. Will you believe me? Will you come? Bring your friends and come?"

"For factories with full production, yeah, I suppose I will. I'll come. That is worth more than I can imagine. For Matilda to let me in on the ground floor, well." He grunted. "That's repayment as long as what you say is true and the Moises front the startup costs. I'll need a lot to attract the workers I'll need. I don't have that kind of money. He will confirm that part, won't he?"

"Ask him," dared Erica.

"Oh, I will. Put him on and I will. And thanks for doing this. It couldn't have been easy for you to make this call after what you did to my bank."

"So," she agreed and added a dejected note since it seemed to be what he wanted. She hadn't thought of it as 'his bank'. She thought of it as 'the bank he worked at' and how he would be in trouble for giving her access but she had fixed that. She had protected him by leaving her computer.

"Maybe they can clean up your act," said Arlo. "I hope so. You're too damn smart to be part of a thieving, cut-throat, bunch of pick-pockets and scam artists. You're better than that, Erica. You can change. Put your mind to it and you can."

"There already be big changes in me. You will see when you

The Marrilian

get here. That includes no more messages. Promise."

"Good lords, I hope so. I nearly shit my pants that afternoon."

"Pardons, Arlo. My deepest pardons."

He took a breath, exhaled. "Accepted," he said. "God, how could I not with you? I was ready to give my resignation when I saw how you had used me. Then I realized that was why you gave me your keys. You would have backed me up in everything wouldn't you? Just like you said."

"Yes. Only all of mine would have been yours. I would the Delegate not have it. Was the only change."

"I thought so. It looked like that could be the case. It was a nice gesture. I'm just glad it wasn't necessary. This is better. I'll bring your stuff, all right?"

"That would be great. Now here's Lord Mois. He waits. Would he wait no longer."

Arlo chuckled. "Only you would keep a claimant waiting at all. Good God."

"Mayhaps, Arlo, thanks. See you soon."

Marcus took the phone with a beaming smile. "Hello." He winked at Erica. He told Arlo helicopters could bring him and any of the others north. The need was such that the laws governing the use of the vehicles would sanction it. General Burk would send agents and trucks that day to help Arlo and his friends pack. Arlo could arrive within a week. Then they talked business while Erica waited. None of it mattered to her so she didn't listen.

When they had made their plans, Marcus hung up the phone and turned to her with an approving smile. "We've been trying to lure him back for years. Good job."

"My pleasure, my lord."

He grinned. "You have an odd way of making a business deal. You didn't give any of the financial details. You just promised riches and told him to trust you and here he comes even with the misgivings he had."

"'Tis a thing, my lord?" she asked doubtfully.

He shook his head. "That is charisma, Erica. It's only bad depending upon how you use it. Which reminds me, what was this about keys and backing everything up?"

"Was instructions on how to return the bank accounts to normal."

"You left instructions with Arlo? The head of the bank?"

"Yes, my lord."

Edwards

"Why?"

Erica thought that would be obvious. She tipped her head in confusion that he should question it. "He helped me, sir. Couldn't let him lose his job because of it and do nothing. If he fixed it he would have inherited all my money. He deserved it."

Claimant Mois looked perplexed but accepted her explanation.

Arlo arrived without mishap the following week with four others. He thought Erica was Matilda until she spoke and explained what she had meant by changes. He didn't like it and didn't like her helping the Delegate to protect Matilda but Claimant Mois had him working on a factory so fast he hardly had time to object.

After two months the production in the lab died down as the production in Arlo's factory, and soon two factories, ramped up. Erica's mornings became free because she no longer needed to assemble canisters or use the thayanite chamber. She began training to improve her fighting. Bruce sparred with her.

By the sixth month Erica battled with him barring only moves that could seriously hurt or kill. That left them dirty and sweating. When they sparred they would often end up on the ground. When done they clawed their way to sitting positions while they caught their breath and then they helped each other to their feet.

One afternoon Matilda sat on the porch steps to watch them. "You two act as if that is fun," she observed as they stumbled up the steps past her and fell into chairs. She stood and watched them shed the sparring equipment onto the table all around a pitcher of water and glasses.

Bruce laughed and took a long drink of water. "She actually took me down! The little pipsqueak Marrilian can actually take me down!"

"Three times," Erica reminded him. "Again!"

"God!" he declared as he poured some more water and drank that glass too.

Elsbeth came out of the house and glanced at Erica then Matilda. "Don't bother to dress in light colors any more Mati. Erica is always covered in dirt." She continued down the steps. "Anyone can tell you two apart."

Bruce and Erica looked at each other then laughed harder than before. "You're an absolute mess," he told her.

"Me?" She gulped down some water. "Take a look at

yourself, Mr. Sheline."

He looked down to find dirt and grass stains all over his shirt. His pants were just as bad. He laughed again.

Matilda came up the steps. "That is no way for a lady to act," she scoffed and went in the house.

Erica's eyes followed her until she was gone then she looked back at Bruce. "They don't care for our fun."

"Ah hell." He waved his hand at the house. "Their problem."

"Yes, well, I was told we would leave tonight. Guess I'll clean up."

Bruce grabbed her hand as she got up. He stood. "Be careful." He was suddenly sober.

Erica squeezed his hand. By standing on her toes she could just reach the bottom of his cheek. She intended to kiss him there but he turned and kissed her on the mouth. He tried to pull her closer but she pulled back. The kiss made her think of James, which upset her.

She was trying to not care about James. After six months of her attempts to all but throw herself at him he wasn't interested. Still, she loved him. She didn't love Bruce. Nothing about him gave her the feeling of safety and wholeness like James did.

She shook her head. "Sparring be done," she warned and went in the house to shower, leaving Bruce staring after her.

The days were cooler now and the breeze traveled down the porch. That made it uncomfortable to sit there after the sun went down so they ate dinner in the house. The dining room had a highly polished table that could seat fourteen people. Candles lit the room and glinted off the white china dishes. All of the seats were full because General Burk went over final plans. Matilda would be giving out information about metal deposits in two days and they had worked out the safest way to get her to the meeting.

"The meeting is in Pey," Burk told them. "That isn't far from here at all. We don't want to attract people to this area thinking they can find Mati so we're going to move Erica over to Meadows. From there we will take her down to Pey and let people see her on the way. We expect everyone to be so intent on Erica so they won't see us bring in Matilda.

"On the day of the meeting we'll bring Mati in the building as Erica leaves the hotel. If all goes well, Erica will get inside and Matilda can walk right out to speak. At that point no one will know Matilda has a look alike."

"What if everything doesn't go well?" Roger asked what was

on everyone's mind.

General Burk didn't like the question but she addressed it. "If Erica is hurt then they will think Matilda is hurt. We will still bring Erica into the building and Matilda will still be able to talk. That is the beauty of this plan but it will change part of the agenda. There are two last minute changes. One of the changes will depend on Erica getting in safely."

"What last minute changes?" Matilda asked suspiciously.

Burk smiled like she had gotten the best present. "I have managed to convince my superiors to let us show the tapes of your questioning."

Matilda sat forward. "The Reagent 10 questioning?"

"Exactly."

Matilda looked at Roger. "My god! Do you know what this means?"

"It will help prove your innocence," he said as his eyes widened, equally excited.

"We will bring in equipment to show them both video and audio. You may not like to see it, Mati. It's distressing to watch but I think it will go a long way to prove your innocence. You'll be brought in on the truck with the equipment disguised as one of our techs."

"And the other thing?" Marcus asked.

"I want to have Erica introduced," Burk replied. "Assuming she gets through the crowd unhurt I want her introduced. She'll come out on the stage with Mati. I want people to see you side by side so from now on no one will know if they are attacking an innocent person or Matilda, assuming they don't accept the tapes."

"They have to accept them," Matilda said desperately. She leaned on the table. "If people don't stop hating me there is no way we can continue the plans past the southern claims."

Burk didn't reply. She looked back at the notebook in front of her then up at Erica. "I want to remind you again, no fighting unless we specifically tell you to do so. Don't take any orders from any agent you don't know. Don't forget to wear your vest."

She turned to Matilda. "You, I have the same instructions. Keep your vest on and keep it tight. Both of you keep them tight. I don't care how uncomfortable you are." Erica nodded while Matilda frowned. "You will both be wearing your side arms but they are only there as status symbols. Don't use them. If we have to we will take them and use them ourselves. The last thing we need is Matilda to have more killings added to her name."

The Marrilian

Erica and Matilda both nodded.

Burk smiled weakly. "That's all. Ready?" she asked Erica.

She refused to show her anxiety so she forced a smile instead and willed her shoulders to relax. "Yes General."

"Good. We'll be going to Meadows in our staff car. We have a house out by the lake. It belongs to one of our generals. We'll be there overnight then go down to Pey in a nice slow coach."

They said their goodbyes and wished each other the best of luck then Burk led Erica out of the house. James came with them. Elsbeth stayed with Matilda.

The staff car turned out to be a truck with blackened back windows. Erica could barely see through them as it picked its way down roads, usually used by wagons, for two hours before arriving in at Meadows.

It was dark when they got out of the vehicle. Trees whispered in the breeze. Erica paused to listen and look up at the moons and sky. The stars winked at her. She took a deep breath and exhaled slowly to calm herself. Levitus had given her a new hearing aid the week before and it picked up all the night sounds, insects, and frogs.

"It might not be safe to stand there," Burk told her and gently pushed on her back. The house sat on a hillside overlooking an enormous lake. Something cawed and splashed into the water. A dog barked far away in the woods north of them.

They entered the building and lit oil lanterns. Four agents were with them, Mark, Sati, Rami and James. They fanned out to check the rooms. General Burk and Erica waited in the marble foyer until all of them had returned and declared the house safe. They settled in for the night but Erica couldn't fall to sleep until late. Burk wouldn't let her take off her vest and she struggled to get comfortable as well as clear her head of the next day's possibilities. She understood the necessity however, and wouldn't argue about the vest.

"We have allowed information to leak that Matilda is traveling from here," Burk had told Erica. "There will be people who expect this house to be used. Anything could happen from this point on." And in her dreams everything happened.

Before the sun rose Sati woke Erica for breakfast. She had her dress in one of Matilda's black suits with a dark gray shirt. They ate then the horses were saddled and a coach was hitched. Erica rode in the coach with Burk. The SDD guarded the coach from horseback front and back, much like Elsbeth and James had done when the three of them rode together. Rami drove the carriage. Traffic passed them on the road and sometimes slowed to take a look. They left the draperies open on purpose so they might see Erica.

"Nervous?" Burk asked her, as they got closer to the city.

"Yes, General," Erica answered. She stared out the window at the passing trees and occasional traveler.

"You realize this is a very important thing you are doing don't you?" Erica looked at the General. "You had a choice to do this. You have done everything I asked but you didn't have to. You could have been difficult. You could have said no."

Erica dropped her eyes. She didn't want to talk right now but it was practice. Using pronouns and saying words like the Quirni did, came hard. The same for looking everyone in the eye and so many other things, from how she stood to how she ate. She needed practice so she talked and focused on using her pronouns.

"I was brought here to help and it 'tis what I will do and I would help Mati and Roger. I like them, plus, this be easy."

"I can see you like them but I don't know about this being easy. Still, we all appreciate it. I want you to know that. We will accomplish a lot."

Erica shrugged. "Do you expect this to be bad? How many people will come to hurt her?"

Burk gazed out the window. "Hundreds if not thousands. People have come from long distances. It's Matilda's first public appearance since the trial."

Erica looked back out the window then drew a long breath and released it.

"We have every agent here that could be spared."

That did not calm Erica in the least. Agents they didn't know could be agents who had attacked her in Nigh. They had discussed that possibility but Burk felt certain she knew those loyal to the QSDD and picked them out of the rest.

They rode in silence.

"We're here," Burk said and shook Erica's shoulder.

Erica was surprised to find she had fallen to sleep. The carriage lurched to a stop in front of a four story, red brick building.

"We'll be staying here. Tomorrow we have to get over there," Burk said and pointed across the street to a theater. "While you are being moved from one side of the street to the other Matilda will be brought in the back."

"They actually have theater on this planet. Who would have

thought that possible," Erica remarked dryly.

"Use a Quirni accent now," Burk warned but she smiled at her comment.

"Yes General," Erica responded in a clipped, hard voice.

"And say 'is' not 'tis' or avoid the word."

"So," Erica agreed, then realized her error. "I mean – *alright*."

Burk patted her leg. "You'll be fine. I won't let them hurt you. So relax."

"Yes General."

Outside James and Sati dismounted amongst a dozen people who had stopped to see who was in the carriage. James put his hand in to help Erica down. Immediately the crowd began to chatter. Erica glanced around and saw horrified expressions on their faces. A few children ran off, calling to their playmates. "It's the murderer!"

Burk held her right arm and James her left as Sati fell in behind. Ten steps up to the front doors and they were past the people and into the hotel without any problems. More people sat in the lobby around the fire. They lounged in red velvet chairs reading papers and conversing in pairs. When they looked up they stared in stunned disbelief. A man in a fine gray business suit jumped from his chair. His paper fell to the floor as he left. He hurried up the stairs at the back of the lobby.

The SDD led Erica to the stairs and went directly to the rooms they had reserved. There another agent met them. General Burk introduced him. "Matilda, this is Agent Philip Wahls. He's been sent up from the south to help us with security."

Erica nodded to him. She glanced around the room. They were on the second floor. Long windows looked out onto the street. The room had two beds. A sofa and two chairs sat by the fireplace.

"Mark and Rami will be in the room through there." Burk pointed at a door on the left. "Philip and James will be through there." She pointed to another door on the right. "Sati and I will be in here with you." They sat down to wait.

The city grew louder as the night approached. Burk went out several times and left Erica alone with Sati. Erica tried to sleep in a chair but yells in the street woke her around eleven. She sat up and saw Sati standing to the side of the window. The lamps burned low. Sati turned when Erica came close to see. A crowd milled in the street. Agents stood throughout it.

"It's just a bunch of drunks," Sati told her.

James knocked on the door and entered. "Get ready to

move." Philip stepped into the room after him. Mark and Rami knocked twice then stepped in from their room. Erica felt her heartrate double. They hadn't covered where they would move to if they needed to leave the hotel. The one thing she could rely on was her trust in James. If she was with him, everything would be okay.

"Why?" Sati asked James. "They're just being loud."

"General's orders."

Sati glanced back out the window. "They seem harmless enough."

"She's had six people arrested from that harmless group." He put his hand out to Erica. "Come on." She went to him and he took her into his room with the others where she perched on the edge of a chair, stiff, waiting for a thing to happen, listening for the walls to crash down. Every sound against the hotel walls was a bomb ready to explode. Any loud shout from the crowd below made her jump enough that she caused the agents to jerk.

She caught James' eyes and he smiled a little at her. She had to relax, or this night was never going to end.

No matter what happened right now, she could do nothing about it. Even if the riot broke into the hotel and ran up the stairs, she could do nothing. Her job was to attract this angry mob so they were distracted from Matilda. She had to be Matilda and if Matilda were in her place, she would relax. At the very least she would act unconcerned so Erica focused on that rather than the angry mass of people.

She slid back in the chair and tried to sit like Matilda then realized Matilda wouldn't sit on such a hard, straight back chair so she moved to the stuffed chair by the fireplace.

The fire had burned down to embers when Burk returned. Erica heard the door and sat up to see who entered. "General?" she asked and forgot to speak with a Quirni accent.

Burk looked at her severely. "Yes, Mati?" she said with a glance at the back of Philip's head. He turned and gave Erica a considering stare.

"What's happening?" she asked with the Quirni accent and didn't even attempt to say 'is'.

"We tried to tell the crowd they should be around for the end of today's meeting. There would be information regarding you. It took a while to convince them. We caught a few people trying to set fire to the hotel before that." She looked spent. "I'm going to get a few hours of sleep." She handed James a pocket watch. "Wake me at seven."

The Marrilian

Erica relaxed in the chair again as Burk went into the next room and lay down.

"Get some sleep," James told her. He nodded towards the bed. She didn't question him. She took off her suit coat, shirt, and pants and lay down. As stressful as the night was, it seemed to be over.

The sun had risen when they woke her.

Sati got out a new suit, black with and gray shirt. "Dress," she said simply.

Rami and Mark went out and got them breakfast then they had to wait until nine. That was the hardest waiting Erica had ever done. She paced. She could hear the crowd in the street. She didn't say a word, not trusting herself to get it right in front of Philip. At nine o'clock General Burk came back and nodded to her.

"Matilda, it's time for us to go." She didn't sound encouraging. She fixed Erica with a long stare like she expected her to refuse.

At this point Erica would do anything to stop the waiting. As she stepped forward, Burk smiled. She rubbed her shoulder gently and led her to the door. They made their way down the stairs. When they got to the lobby Erica saw numerous brown uniforms outside at the front door to the hotel. The lobby was empty when they crossed it. Philip and Rami preceded them. They opened the doors to the street.

Yells and calls from the crowd tangled into a mass of hysterical hisses and screams. The volume rose when the nearest of the crowd caught sight of Erica. The mass pushed forward. Agents held them back. They kept the crowd behind the designated line as Erica and her escort moved outside onto the steps.

"You deserve to die!" a man yelled at her.

"Kill her!" a woman jeered.

More shouts were drowned out as others saw Erica and started to scream their threats.

Erica paused, stunned at the number of people that had gathered. The agents pulled her down the steps. They kept the crowd at bay but their line bent and had to fight. A man put his leg through the agent's legs. Erica and Philip tripped. James and Rami dragged them back up but their stumble darkened the mob, fueling their anger like dogs getting a whiff of blood.

"Hurry," Burk yelled at them. She walked in front of them. "Let us through!" she yelled both to the agents with their backs to her and the crowd around them. The mass of people pressed in. Hands grabbed at Erica's hair. James shoved her head down so she ducked and stumbled forward. She hoped none of the agents hated Matilda as much as the crowd seemed to hate her. Any one of them could be the man who had shot her. That thought fueled her legs and lungs. She held to James as hard as she could and did her best to keep step with him while crouched down over her.

"Die, die, die, die," someone began to chant and quickly the rest of the crowd took it up.

They only had to cross the street but SDD were being overwhelmed. Burk drew her pistol and fired into the air. The report of the gun stopped the chanting. "Get back!" she yelled.

James tucked Erica under his arm with his fingers around her belt to keep a tight hold. He pushed Burk along with his left hand and held Erica with his right. Rami and Philip quickened his step by taking his arms. The wall of agents around them opened and let them push through. James, Philip, and Rami walked three abreast with Erica no more than a package between them. The rest of the agents pushed men and women to the side not caring if they pushed them off their feet or hurt them.

Erica's toe hit a step. She glanced down to find the red carpet of a theater. James set her down. He pushed her up the steps with Burk. The crowd wasn't moving beyond the banisters of stone that stood to either side of the carpet. Burk and Philip stepped aside at the door. James and Rami pulled Erica headlong into the building. The doors shut behind them and dulled the noise of the crowd.

"Hurry," James urged and didn't pause but quickly led Erica through the lobby and into a back hall. Rami stopped to guard the last door to the backstage area. James pulled Erica down enough halls that Erica got lost and finally he took her into a room where they met Elsbeth and Matilda.

Matilda smiled in relief. She looked unhurt and fresh. It appeared no one had noticed her entry into the building. Matilda paused to take in the mess of Erica's hair and the derangement of her clothes then hugged her soundly.

Chapter 14 – The Vest

The theater was full with the planet's claimants and co-claimants, thirty-two tables with at least four people at each. Every claimant not only brought their co-claimant but their trusted signed tenants as well. Tables fanned out before the stage on ascending levels.

At the back of the theater the box seats raised three stories. No one had been allowed in them or on the upper floor. Only the main floor was seated. Everyone visited each other's tables and whispered in agitation. No one had any idea why the Delegate had brought them there but rumors circulated wildly. The only certain thing was the Moises were part of it. Usually any gathering of claimants met in the Padt City at the Council Halls not in the capital city of a claim.

A drum sounded three times for them to sit. Once the last claimant was settled General Burk strode onto the stage. Everyone politely clapped for her as she walked out, including other SDD generals who stood up from their chairs behind the podium. Most of them wore more stars than Burk, more rank, but they allowed Burk the introductions.

Erica could see part of the audience through a gap in the curtains. She stood with Matilda and James in the right wing where it was dark enough no one could see them except Burk and the generals sitting at the back of the stage. The Claimants Mois sat directly in front of the stage with some of the claimants Matilda believed remained friends despite her trials.

"Good afternoon ladies and lords," Burk began. A cordless microphone carried her voice over the crowd that had quieted to perfect stillness. "The press and our invited guests," Burk continued and nodded to the back rows of tables. "Today I have the pleasure of bringing you together so we can set Quirni on a new road and I am delighted to be part of this auspicious event.

"Your present day lives on Quirni are due for a change. This is a difficult planet to live on and difficult times have set many of you at odds. Quirni's metal poorness has strained your relationships with the other planets. It is time these difficulties came to an end." She moved a paper over on the podium, scanned the new sheet, and took a breath.

A whispering buzz of surprise rose from the claimants who looked perplexed or annoyed. No one had guessed metal would be the topic of this meeting. It seemed implausible to them a meager one star general would have anything to say about such an important topic if any real change was due to take place.

Burk waited for them to quiet. The men and women of the press listened intently. The whispers dimmed then finally stopped. After all, they were there and might as well hear the rest.

"Before the first settler ever came to Quirni in search of land and longer, healthier life, the Defense Delegate scanned the planet to locate metal and mineral deposits. That is dangerous on a planet as mountainous as this one and an accident occurred. The Quirni scanning team lost their lives and the documents were never recovered. The Defense Delegate chose not to rescan since superficial scans from space indicated metal was scarce.

"Quirni, according to those scans, was such a metal poor planet it was a perfect place to quarantine criminals. It was understood they would never have enough metal to fight their guards or leave.

"In the Quirni year 80 the first claimants decided to come here to enjoy the same health and longevity the convicts seemed to be enjoying. When the Solar Defense Delegate realized the planet would be claimed they initiated a second scan but this one they did on the ground.

"The methods used to scan from the ground are arduous but less dangerous. Unfortunately, that team also met with disaster. The SDD searched for them and found only parts of their equipment spread over a wide area. Orchedon's were the assumed culprit since the area was home to several of the animals.

"If their documents could have been recovered we would have had most of the data for Quirni. The team had all but finished their work except for a few soundings in the North but the scanning documents were never recovered. To this day it is accepted that Quirni is a metal poor planet."

The audience listened with bored interest. Many of them wore expressions of disdain for her long introduction.

"This is all well known history," Burk continued. She didn't respond to the attitudes of disrespect. "We have heard it in classes throughout the three worlds. Few of us give it a second thought," she paused, looked out at the dimly lit crowd, then added, *"but for one."*

The Marrilian

She paused again and much of the audience straightened in their chairs to listen more intently.

"A student of that history made a supposition and began inquiries. This student believed a group as well equipped as the SDD scanning crew wouldn't fall prey to Quirni's native animals and the student didn't believe those animals could drag away an entire vehicle, or the heavy scanners, or boxes of munitions. The student believed such behavior was due to a more cunning animal, fellow man. This was considered by the SDD as well but searches among the first settlers of Quirni turned up nothing and what we knew of orchedon's did allow for such behavior.

"This student disagreed and so, did a different sort of search. The student collected notes of all search missions. The student painstakingly read thousands of details and unlike any agent who had done the same, the student remembered every detail.

"The student realized parts of the scanning equipment and parts of the transport vehicle were actually found. Less and less was at the sight every time a crew returned to search the area. Where the Delegate blamed animals, the student did not. The student thought the equipment was being disassembled not attacked.

"Nothing the student read suggested the scanning documents had been torn apart either. They were stored in blue, metal cylinders. An orchedon would probably rip them but no blue cylinder or parts of the same were found. The SDD had concluded animals carried them off. The student concluded no such thing. The student looked to Trellis, to a settlement that held a grudge against the Delegate and new claimants. It had been over a hundred years and the student hoped feelings had changed. The student carefully approached them."

The claimants began to erupt again. This time General Burk raised her hands to ask for quiet. They calmed down but the theater rustled with agitation. The few that remained seated were at the front.

Burk raised her voice and the microphone carried her words over the noise. "The Delegate scans are found!" Claimants froze and stared in disbelief.

"Please sit," Burk asked them in the silence. They were too stunned to do anything different. She waited for them to settle. "The student traded with the Trellians for the documents. The student has the information from those Delegate scans in their possession."

The theater remained transfixed with what had to be the

next question. Who?

Matilda stood with Erica behind the curtains. There, in the right wing, Erica could feel the excitement of the audience. She glanced at Matilda to see how she reacted. She stood still, collected and waiting.

The buzz in the room rose. Chairs shifted. General Burk raised her hands to silence them once more. She waited patiently but her patience only served to increase the tension. "This individual," Burk said in a more serious tone, "has suffered for finding the documents. She was young and didn't protect her discovery. She did not know how to use it. She has had to struggle to keep it safe from unscrupulous hands."

The room quieted as everyone, no doubt, wondered if Burk could be talking about Matilda and her father. Still, Erica noticed, Matilda seemed ready to walk out there and speak. She even looked eager. Erica knew if she had to go out there she wouldn't be able to move a step.

"She has endured attacks on her character, her possessions, and her person and was loath to give up the very reason she had endured those attacks. The QSDD helped her to survive. We did not force her to hand over the papers. Under the laws of lost treasure the Delegate abandoned the documents. We did not continue the search so when the student found what amounts to a treasure she has the right to keep it and use it as she sees fit.

"She sees fit to share the information but has not been able to do so until now. Today she comes here to share the SDD scans with you and the information is staggering in its content and depth. She asks you to join her in bringing this planet to a metal age."

The auditorium stilled.

"Please welcome and accept our guest who has come to you at great personal risk." General Burk stretched out her arm towards Matilda. "Matilda Lynn Kinsley." She stepped back from the podium.

Erica bit back upon hearing her name and at the same time heard Matilda take a long breath. That was the only sign Matilda was nervous.

"Good luck," she told Matilda quietly. Matilda didn't acknowledge her. She crossed the stage to Burk.

Not a soul clapped. The only sound was Matilda's three inch heels hitting the wood floor. Burk stood beside the podium until Matilda reached her, shook her hand, and then Burk sat down in the line at the back of the stage with the five other generals.

The Marrilian

Erica feared Matilda wouldn't know how to proceed. Burk had told her how she would introduce her and what she needed to say but now that she stepped out into the silent theater with the low lights and the room full of frowning faces she couldn't imagine her being able to remember anything.

Cameras flashed as she stood behind the podium and bowed her head. There she stood for many seconds, head bowed, silent, before looking up. "Thank you for that moment of silence. I have yet to honor the victims of the Cobal Claim Disaster with my friends. I appreciate the opportunity."

"Here, here," muttered several people in the front row.

She nodded to the people there. "Claimant Vaughn, a pleasure to see you again. Thank you for coming from so far away."

"Glad to make it, Mati," he called up to her.

"Claimants Paulson," she nodded.

"Claimants Mois," she nodded to them too, then several other tables. She averted her eyes quickly when she looked at the table behind the Paulson's. Erica peeked out the curtain to see who Matilda wouldn't look at. A fold in the curtain obscured the area.

Matilda took a breath and began. "General Burk explained why we have invited you here today. It has been a long time since I have wanted to share what I found. The Delegate, however, has held me back." She paused to let that them understand she hadn't kept it secret voluntarily.

"The metal on Quirni will enrich our planet. With the long life we currently enjoy and the luxuries metal will soon be able to provide, the balance of power between the worlds will shift. Quirni will become a planet of power with enough tenants to use that power. All of us will benefit from it. Those who support my efforts will benefit most of all." She didn't read from a prepared speech like Burk but she still looked down at the podium to pause. Every time she did the claimants began to shift in their chairs. They seemed to be thinking with the sudden deepening of frowns, who would want to support her efforts?

"The Southern claims have metal deposits," Matilda continued and didn't seem to notice the scowls that faced her. "Centuries ago the Defense Delegate understood deposits in the North were more plentiful compared to the south. The early scans showed this. What they didn't show is southern metal is deeper so it appeared scant when it is not. That is the reason they do a second scan, to evaluate depth of deposits, purity, and tonnage.

"Wrong assumptions based on the early data led the Delegate to believe metal on the southern half of our continent was scant. They didn't understand the relative nature of the information, namely the metal in the South isn't scant but deeper *compared* to the North."

The generals appeared as surprised by this information as the claimants. They shifted forward in their chairs and gazed at her in what had to be shock no matter how hard they tried to hide it.

"Due to this misunderstanding, no one has ever looked for metal," Matilda explained. "It is here. It is often in places that are not settled. We have so few tenants much of our planet is not settled and for that reason as well, metal has seldom been found. The few deposits we stumbled across thrilled us. Well, you will all be thrilled but for your own sakes. Every claim has metal to be mined."

Claimants glanced at co-claimants. Whispers began again. Scowls dropped from faces to be replaced by looks of amazement and hope. Matilda didn't smile or frown but waited for the claimants to turn back to her. They did so quickly unlike for Burk.

Erica loved this. It was good to see Matilda spend time in the spotlight. She deserved it. It was fantastic to hear her sounding so steady, unconcerned and content.

"The balance of power between the worlds is due to shift," Matilda continued. "Likewise is the balance of power between our claims. My difficulties have arisen due to this expectation but I have survived them thanks to the help of the SDD and the information of the SDD documents remains intact."

Not a sound. Erica wondered if anyone understood what she meant. How could they not? She looked out over the audience. They stared back at Mati like she was some sort of specter.

"If you would all take up your place markers you will see they are letters. Please open them and I will explain their significance."

Throughout the theater the claimants picked up the folded papers they had thought only told them where to sit. They looked at the envelopes front and back and then tore them open. The ripping continued for some time. Cards were withdrawn and comments were made as to their meaning.

Matilda didn't wait for them to quiet. She began talking over the low rumble and made them quiet for her. "There are limited mining companies on the planet. If I gave all of you the information about the metal deposits, the bidding for these companies would be fierce. The mining companies would love it, I dare say, but only the richest claims would benefit. I have taken this into consideration as well as a suggestion by my cousin.

"My cousin, Lynn Kinsley, came from Marril to help bring my plans to action. She convinced me that those of you who have supported me and will support me should be among those to receive their information first and therefore be able to bid for mining companies first. Likewise, those who have ores of particular use for building Quirni's infrastructure should receive their information first."

A murmur began to rise. "If you hold a card with today's date, split it open. Inside you will find a set of co-ordinates and a description of the ore to be found at that location."

The theater rustled with the flipping of cards, more tearing, and claimants leaning over to show their co-claimants.

"Those of you who have other dates on their cards will receive the information on those dates," Matilda continued. "By those dates we will-"

"How dare you keep this from us!" a man yelled.

Erica saw Matilda look at the same table she had looked past before. Her face went steely blank.

"This information should be freely available to every claimant at the time they claim! It is the duty of the SDD to supply this *when* we claim! You have no right to ration it. Least of all you!"

General Burk began to get up but stopped when Matilda turned and faced the man squarely. Erica left the gap in the drapes where she couldn't see this person. She wanted to circle around to the other side of the stage. There was probably a gap over there too.

"Erica!" James whispered after her sternly. He lunged and grabbed her arm. He stopped her in her tracks. "What are you doing?"

"I want to see who it 'tis," she whispered and tried to twist her arm free. She pushed on his bicep. His arm felt like an iron bar. It bulged more as she tried to get away. She blinked at him. He had never held her with such strength. She realized there was no way she had broken his grip by biting him. Her eyes lifted to his. He had dropped her on purpose the day they had fought in front of Mati and Roger's. He had let her go.

"It's your uncle. Stay here."

Edwards

"'Tis?" she asked quietly with her eyes wide. "Haven't yet seen him. Want to see him. Let me go." She pushed on his chest but that felt as hard as his arm. She wouldn't get free unless he allowed it. She stopped struggling and looked up at him with a mixture of awe and amazement. She had never felt such a hard muscle.

He smiled, as if well aware of what she was thinking. He pulled her back with one arm and set her at his side. He held her around the waist. "You will see him soon enough," he whispered.

Was she so light he could pick her up with one arm like that? She felt her ribs. Had she lost more weight? James leaned with her in his arms so she could see through a crack in the drapery. She frowned as she peaked with him.

Matilda addressed her father. "Least of all me you say? Then perhaps you think you would have been the better person for the job?"

"Get off that high horse you insolent girl," Claimant Kinsley sneered. "I have nothing to do with this information."

Matilda smiled serenely. "No, because I stopped you but you tried." She almost spoke too quietly for the audience to hear.

"You still accuse me? I would not trust her if I was you," he called out to the theater. "She plays these games as all of you know. Do not condone the use of this information to her benefit!"

Marcus Mois stood and faced Cyril. "Where is her benefit, Claimant Kinsley?"

"Obviously there are strings attached to this. She speaks of the North. She would enrich herself by claiming the North and she would use our metal to get there!"

"Someday someone will claim the north," Matilda told him. "I once hoped it would be me but in the present atmosphere of Quirni politics this seems unlikely. Indeed, if I were to go to the North I do not doubt I would have to go alone and a lone *girl* with a pick ax would not become very rich now would she, Claimant?" About half the people in the theater laughed. "If you would sit, I will finish explaining the plan which, by the way, is sanctioned by the Delegate and intended to meet everyone's needs."

"Only to hear what other hype you toss at us, yes I will sit," he replied angrily.

Matilda seemed perfectly calm. Erica's own heart beat like a hammer. She would have yelled in Cyril Kinsley's face, bloodied his nose if she got close enough. She hadn't even seen the man yet but she disliked him. What an ass! James squeezed tighter around her waist. She looked up at him and smiled sheepishly then relaxed.

His steely eyes melted and he smiled at her warmly.

She could have kissed him right then and there. Hell, she could have done more than that. She turned back around to watch.

"As I said, there will not be enough mining companies to mine all of the sites. They will be in high demand. To help you assess what you should bid for a company I have included the estimated tonnage and the purity levels of your ores. I have also listed the depth at which these ores will have to be mined and the geology of the area from which it must be mined. I have included all information that will help you decide what the mining company will be worth to you. Or, indeed, you may wish to assemble a company yourself but I warn you it is not easy getting miners from other planets to come to Quirni."

A burst of excited chuckles and conversation started then died as Matilda continued speaking.

"I wish all of you luck in your bids. Some of you, however, deserve more than my best wishes. You have supported me despite my troubles. Lynn has helped me decide how to compensate those who remained steadfast as my friends." Matilda glanced at Erica who wondered what she talked about. "This is the way I thank you."

Matilda walked to the edge of the stage. Roger waited there for her on the floor. She handed him a second set of cards and he passed them out to the eight foremost tables in the room.

Each of those claimants looked at their second cards and smiled, including Marcus Mois whose mouth dropped open. He passed the card to Ella who gaped then wiped her eyes.

Matilda continued speaking as the eight sets of claimants looked over the new cards. "It is due to Lynn's help that I arrived here safely today. It is due to her help that we have met the Delegate's criteria to pass this information on to you. She has a gift for business as well as convincing people to do what we needed and what we needed involved the Marrilians."

"Many of you come from Marril. Marril has but one thing to offer, riches. Quirni will someday be on a par with Marril. The SDD had become aware of this when they questioned me with Reagent 10 years ago. They learned I had these documents then. They did not force me to hand them over, nor could they for reasons I won't reveal." She paused. The claimants waited, intent upon her.

Edwards

"The SDD fear Marril will become a ghost planet if Quirni becomes metal rich. No one will want to live on a planet that kills them by the age of 45 or 50 if they can live hundreds of years in luxury here. Enough thayanite would no longer be mined in that case and this cannot happen."

Now the claimants began to listen politely. The scowls were gone and they leaned back in their chairs in relaxed manners. Matilda had won them over. At least Erica wanted to believe that was why they sat back and listened. It seemed possible.

Matilda continued. "To our benefit, the SDD has a means to help Marrilians live longer and healthier lives. They learned air purifiers made on Quirni included extra health and life lengthening benefits. They insisted I make these purifiers and test them, create a market for them on Marril, before I shared the SDD scans. In effect, convince the Marrilian's they could stay on their planet and live a long and worthwhile life.

"Through Lynn's help I have finally been able to get factories running to this end. Marrilians will no longer suffer as badly the damaging effects of thayanite. I have tried for years to accomplish this but Lynn has managed to bring it to fruition. She is the reason we are here today rather than many years from now. She has benefited me and every one of you as well." She glanced at Erica again. "If I may, I would like to introduce you to my cousin, Lynn Jillian Kinsley." Matilda stood back from the podium, stared straight at Erica and clapped. The claimants politely clapped with her.

Erica was fine watching from the wings but now she froze. She wasn't going to go out there! General Burk and the five generals sitting with her stood. They faced Erica and clapped.

"Is someone in there capable of walking?" James said in her ear. "Move it, Doll!"

Erica flashed him a frown just as he shoved her past the edge of the curtain. A quiet chuckle rose from the audience due to her stumbling, frowning entrance but it died quickly. Once moving she found she could continue. She walked out to Matilda in a theater that became steadily quieter.

Matilda grinned. "My cousin, ladies and lords, the press, and our invited guests, Lynn Kinsley." She took a few steps from behind the podium to stand side by side with Erica. Except for the height of their shoes and their clothes, they looked identical.

The flashes of cameras exploded. The claimants sat stunned at first then began to talk louder and louder. Photographers ran up the isles to get closer photos. Burk returned to the podium.

The Marrilian

She raised her hands to try and regain silence but the noise of the room built until Erica couldn't hear what Lord Mois said to her from the front row although she saw he smiled broadly. She smiled back then glanced down the tables until she saw a man and women who stared at them in open shock.

Cyril Kinsley, it had to be. He looked like Mati. He had the same fine features, pretty, with long brown hair that he had tied back. His shock turned to a frown but not in anger or fear but thoughtful, as if a fog cleared and he understood.

"Ass," Erica told him and hoped he might be able to read lips. She gave him her sweet smile when his face dropped into disapproval.

He got up, infuriated, and left the room with a woman.

Erica leaned close to Matilda. "Was that your mum and da?" she asked.

Matilda glanced at the receding backs of the two claimants. "Yes," Matilda replied and nodded as well in case Erica hadn't heard her over the noise.

"Called him an ass. Do you mind?"

Matilda looked at her in disbelief. "Father? To his face? Here?"

Erica nodded with a mischievous glint in her eye.

Matilda laughed. "Do you waste any time making enemies?"

Erica raised a brow and smirked.

"This is too much fun for you," Matilda said as Burk began to quiet the crowd. Matilda took Erica's arm and led her from the stage as Burk began to speak.

Burk thanked Matilda and Erica then started into an introduction of the 'Reagent 10 Tape' as she called Matilda's questioning. They could hear her from backstage but Matilda didn't want to stay and Elsbeth already ushered them into the dressing room.

"You two have to exchange clothes now," she told them. "We're going to take you out of here together on the carriage."

Matilda wore a light gray suit with a white shirt. They both stripped and exchanged clothes, guns, and shoes.

"The vests too," Elsbeth told them when she saw the dark vest Erica wore could be seen through the white shirt. She wrapped a tan band around the black tattoo on Erica's arm as they wordlessly removed the shirts again, then the vests, threw them to each other, then dressed once more. Elsbeth quickly brushed their hair and ushered them out into the guarded hall.

The carriage waited at the front door. Twelve agents on

horseback and as many on foot waited around it. The crowd started to chant 'Die Kinsley!' when Erica and Matilda came through the doors but seeing two of them threw them into confusion. The chant stopped and the crowd watched in surprise as the women they hoped to attack climbed into the carriage with James and Elsbeth. It started away without any problems. Soon they had left the town and headed east towards Meadows and not one tenant had attacked or touched the vehicle.

Matilda leaned back in her seat with a grin. "That went well," she nearly giggled she felt so relieved and happy.

Erica sat across from her. "Quite," she agreed. "Loved the looks on their faces."

"Did you notice when I walked onto the stage?"

"Not a sound in the place. Don't know how you managed it," Erica laughed. "Would have stuck to the spot."

"Which is exactly what you did. You stuck even with that big introduction I gave you. I'm certain you would not have moved if James hadn't pushed you."

"Yes, well," said Erica and glanced at him.

He kept his eyes trained on the window.

The introduction. She frowned. "So, Mati, uh, why did you decide to help your friends like you did?"

"Why?" Matilda asked with a grin. "Because of you. You protected Arlo when you gave him the directions to fix the banking computers and look what happened? He came back to work for you not me."

"You decided to give out extra sets of coordinates based on that? At least I assume that's what was in those second cards you gave out?"

Matilda sat up straighter. "Of course, we discussed it. That and a mining company I hired for the Moises."

"Oh," Erica responded and tried to hide her surprise. She had never had such a conversation with Matilda.

Matilda settled back in her seat. "Are you saying you don't remember talking about it?"

Erica forced a smile. She fell into her old way of dealing with this sort of thing, wait for a clue and be noncommittal. She shrugged.

"We were talking in the morning, over breakfast," Matilda added to try and prod her memory.

"Oh," Erica replied again. "Must have been half asleep still." She would let Matilda believe she remembered but Erica's chest tightened with worry. Was she losing time? Were her other parts coming all the way out? She hadn't thought that was happening. She thought she was just feeling them, dissociating but not all the way.

"I see," Matilda replied. She eyed Erica with a frown then looked out her window for several moments. "So, if it wasn't you, with whom did I discuss it?"

Her tone was lighter than Erica would expect. Whenever Erica had this sort of conversation people always ended up in hurt feelings. They didn't like being forgotten especially important people.

Erica shook her head. "Don't know," she muttered. "Like I said, probably was half sleeping."

Matilda made a scoffing grunt.

Elsbeth and James listened but didn't say anything. They continued to watch the road out the windows. Elsbeth sat next to Matilda and watched towards the front and James sat opposite her so he could watch the back.

They rode in silence for a while. The carriage rocked over the rutted road.

Erica kept her eyes on the floor. Other than the day Marcus had forced her to say her name she did not believe she had dissociated again. She knew she was feeling less than she ought to, a sort of filter on her emotions, but she had convinced herself that was the effect of being partly dissociated and it wasn't all the time.

Dissociation occurred by degrees and she didn't think she was at the far end of that scale. Now to learn she had spoken to Matilda about a complicated subject at length floored her. It meant she wasn't just partially broken but completely so. Any of her other parts could have been out. So who?

She wanted to know so she might do some damage control. Sal in particular could screw things up so fast and so completely that Erica would be kicked out of the house before she could ask why. Could it be Zoe? Zoe always liked to give her opinion so she supposed it could have been her. Lords, Erica hoped so.

"Well, it doesn't matter," Matilda finally determined.

Erica took a long breath, ready to ask about the conversation and learn who had been out, but exhaled and didn't ask. It could ruin Matilda's good mood and she didn't want to have Matilda in a bad mood. She was horrible in a bad mood so Erica examined a dry spot on her finger and kept quiet.

"It was good advice," Matilda told her. "Did you see the expressions on Marcus and Ella's faces?"

Edwards

Erica nodded. She tried to change the subject. "You certainly made them happy."

Matilda stared at her. "Me?"

Now what had she said? "Yes. You gave them the coordinates."

"All of them for their claim," Matilda replied, as if to jog Erica's memory. "Don't you remember suggesting all of them?"

Erica went back to looking at her hands. She had to be quiet.

Matilda made an annoyed huff. She leaned forwards and pulled Erica's hands apart so she'd quit picking. "I thought Lynn was the only one who could take you over?"

Erica averted her eyes towards James.

"Oh," Matilda said softly. "Well, in that case, I think you'll have to introduce yourself to me more often. Erica?" She smiled and reached across to place a finger under Erica's chin and raise her head. "Erica?"

"Yes," she said with a scowl at Matilda and pulled her head away. "Don't do that. Don't like that."

"Then look at me when you talk."

Erica kept her eyes on Matilda's and replied, "So," with such a harsh inflection she made Matilda raise a brow.

"You certainly get a lot of use out of that word." She laughed, her good mood still intact.

At least there was that because Erica's turned dark with the stupid finger under the chin thing. They all did it to her. Quirni looked in eyes when they spoke. Anything less and they thought you were hiding something from them. What a damn weird planet.

The carriage slowed. Elsbeth peered out the window but didn't seem alarmed.

"So who do you think it could have been?" Matilda asked conversationally. She clasped her hands in her lap. "I liked her."

Erica tried to shrug off her annoyance. Matilda's continued upbeat tone helped. "Don't know." The carriage slowed down further then rolled to a stop.

"*I* don't know," Matilda corrected.

Erica drew a breath. She glared at Matilda. Were they really going to do this now?

"*I* don't know," Matilda repeated and her eyebrow shot up again.

"Mati, the morning be enough work for me today. Let the speech thing go would you?"

Matilda smiled and shrugged. "Fine. It doesn't matter. Like I

The Marrilian

said, it was good advice." She clucked her tongue and rolled her eyes in a way Erica could never hope to copy. It was cute, ladylike, and pretty. "Hell, it was great advice," Matilda said and crossed her legs. She looked over at Elsbeth. "Why are we stopping?"

Elsbeth pulled back the drapery to see a little more of the road. "An agent is coming. I don't know him."

He knocked on the door. Elsbeth reached forward and opened it. The young agent saluted her and she saluted him back. "We have received word there is a large gathering of tenants on the road ahead, Major. We think you should get out and proceed on horseback with Matilda." He glanced between Matilda and Erica. "We can cut through the woods and go around them."

Erica glared at the man. She wasn't about to do as he said.

"Stay where you are, Mati," James said and touched Erica's leg.

A second agent opened the door on the opposite side of the coach.

"Her!" The first agent pointed at Erica and before she could react the second one reached in and grabbed her arm. He yanked her from her seat.

"Stop!" James yelled and grabbed for her. James' hands slipped off of Erica's leg as the unknown agent flung her free of the carriage. She tumbled onto the hard dirt road.

"Down!" Elsbeth yelled.

A gun fired three times. Erica had been instructed not to fight unless Matilda was in danger. This qualified. The agent who had dragged her out of the carriage still held her wrist. He jerked her to her feet in front of yet another agent who had his gun out.

Erica used the momentum of his jerk to twist and sank her knee into the agent's gut. He gasped and doubled over enough she was able to deliver a blow with her elbow to his skull. He gulped in surprise and collapsed to his knees then splayed out on his stomach. He would no longer be a problem.

She turned to face the other agent but hardly started towards him when he shot. Pain hit her gut and spread across her chest. The force of the shots threw her back and she fell with a jarring thud. James yelled. More shots rang out. Everyone ran past her or over her and then there was nothing but the sky. Gunshots erupted up and down the road. Warmth drained behind her and it pooled there.

Edwards

What could be warm and draining down her side? It was such an odd feeling.

Elsbeth sprang from the carriage firing what sounded like Erica's gun. Matilda had been wearing it. Elsbeth must have taken it. She launched over Erica and ran.

Multiple shots fired in quick succession. Horse's hooves pounded on the road. Erica felt them as they galloped away but not for long. When more horses galloped she didn't notice. She felt less in her body with each moment. Her guts and breathing hurt most. Breathing shallow helped but it was hard to breathe at all. This shot to her vest felt nothing like the last one, the arrow in the back. The pain was deep and the draining wasn't sweat. She realized it was blood and the vest hadn't worked.

Her damn vest hadn't worked. She reached up to feel for the bullet holes. He had hit her three times, twice as she fell. She touched her shirt and didn't feel any blood but then her hand was numb and cold. She could barely feel her fingers. The holes were there but her finger had to sink into them to recognize them.

She found one mid-chest and another one lower down. She thought she had felt more impacts than that. Three? Or had she felt a bullet passing through the vest behind her?

The holes were dry. The vest kept the blood underneath it?

She let her arm drop back to the road. It took too much effort to move it.

How the hell could the vest not work? The shooting stopped. She tried to roll to her side and sit. Had they killed everyone? Who won? She managed to get her leg up to push herself over but the effort of rolling hurt so much she faded and when she woke again she was on her back once more. She stared at the sky.

The horses pranced nervously so the coach jerked back and forth beside her. She heard Elsbeth talking on the phone to Levitus and Betty. "Come to the transponder signal stat! There is a field next to us! Land there!"

"Get this man out of here," she ordered then slid down next to Erica. She hovered over her so she could look into Erica's face. "Are you all right?"

Erica started to shake her head and answer but blood filled her throat. She choked. She coughed and the vile taste filled her mouth. Her gut cramped. She tried to curl to relieve the pain but that hurt more. Her vision dimmed, tunneled.

"Oh my God!" Elsbeth breathed in horror. She ripped open

Erica's suit coat, shirt, and the vest. "Bring me the first aid kit now!" she yelled back at the carriage.

Someone ran towards them and handed over a red box. Elsbeth smashed it to the ground next to Erica's head and flipped it open.

Erica felt so heavy that breathing, moving her chest, took more effort than she thought she could manage. She did breathe but it tired her to keep doing it. She needed some of those pills she used to have, the ones to help against Quirni's gravity.

She doubted James could pick her up now. She was too heavy.

Elsbeth pulled out handfuls of white fluff from the box. "The vest didn't work!" she yelled to those around her. "The God damned vest didn't work!" She pushed hard on the wound in Erica's stomach.

Erica gasped as knives and fire shot through her gut.

"Help me," Elsbeth ordered. Mark knelt down. He pulled Erica up to a sitting position as Elsbeth stripped off Erica's clothes and the vest all the while pressing hard. They laid her back again, using her shirt and coat to protect her from the dirt road.

Erica grunted in pain from the movement. More blood filled her throat. She choked. Elsbeth grabbed her jaw with a bloody hand. "Stay awake! Breathe!" she snarled and turned Erica's head to let the blood drain out of her mouth. She pulled her phone from her bloody uniform and tossed it at Sati. "Call medical and tell them to hurry! And call Burk!"

Matilda appeared. She crouched beside them. Her shirt was torn open but the vest she wore seemed intact. She hurriedly handed bandages to Elsbeth.

"I can already hear them. They're close," Matilda said breathlessly. She looked down at Erica. "Don't you die, damn it! You stay awake!"

Erica wanted to tell her she wouldn't die but coughed then vomited up blood. Her vision faded again.

Elsbeth rolled her to her side and held her head to clear her throat. "Just shut up and breathe!"

Erica tried. She concentrated on breathing until the *thump, thump, thump* of an engine distracted her, the helicopter bringing Levitus and Betty from Pey. Burk had them stationed there. They had a brand new clinic. Erica appreciated Burk more.

Elsbeth leaned close. She pressed hard with her arm in Erica's abdomen and chest. She laid on her to hold her tightly front and back. Mark continued to stuff bandages against the wounds, shoving them under Elsbeth's arms.

"Stay with us," Elsbeth urged in Erica's ear. "They're coming. Betty and Levitus will be here any minute. Come on and breathe. Breathe deep." Elsbeth squeezed.

It became harder to breathe at all. Erica's chest felt dead. At least that helped the pain but the blood was horrible. It drained from her mouth. It tasted foul. Air wouldn't go past it. It strangled her. She felt the warmth of more blood spilling out of her belly when Elsbeth changed her hold. It was so much blood. Was she going to die?

"God damn it!" Elsbeth yelled in her ear and pressed into her stomach even harder. "God damn it, you friggin nightmare! Stay awake!"

Erica gasped at the pain Elsbeth created. More blood filled her mouth. She tried to spit it out, managed a little, and drew a long rattling breath.

Someone drove the carriage away. The helicopter landed on the other side of where it had been. Erica watched the skids touch the ground and Betty then Levitus take red, yellow, and blue boxes handed down to them. They ran towards Erica as three other people ran up the road with their own set of boxes. Levitus dropped his cases next to her and quickly pulled out a scanner and healer's tools. Betty shoved the first aid box aside and dropped her boxes behind Erica. Elsbeth continued to hold her tight.

"She's bleeding bad," Elsbeth told them. She sounded strained. Her grip was weakening.

Levitus pulled several syringes with thick needles out of a bag and turned on the scanner. "Let her go," he told Elsbeth and started scanning immediately as she sat back. "Who is this?"

"Erica," Elsbeth answered quickly.

Betty started an IV without so much as a swab. She gave Mark a bag to hold then another. The healer and cureman worked in silence and fast.

Erica tried to keep her eyes open and stay awake even as Levitus plunged a long probe into her chest. The day darkened as she almost feinted from the sudden piercing of the wound but Betty's medication quickly took away the pain. He emptied another two probes into her back then a forth in her belly. The pain in her chest returned, a fiery cramp, but then the wash of painkiller dulled it.

When Levitus finished they turned her to her back and let

her lay still.

"Thank God it's Erica," he told Betty. He pulled the bloody cloth off of her tattoo as if to be certain. "That was a lot of foam." He ran his scanner over her chest and stomach. "The plugs have stopped the major bleeding for now."

He looked up at Matilda. "Are you okay?"

"My vest worked," she answered weakly. "They shot at me. It knocked me down but I'm fine."

He turned to Elsbeth who knelt at Erica's feet. "You are covered in blood. Is any of it yours?"

"No," she replied.

His sudden exhale showed how relieved he was to hear that. "Call another medical team. Then call General Burk. She needs to see what happened here."

"We have called Burk," Elsbeth told them as she got up and soon Erica heard her talking on the phone again as she called for more medical assistance.

Levitus pointed at Matilda. "Get out of sight. Get back in the carriage."

Matilda left.

"Erica?" he asked. "Are you Erica?"

Talk, Erica thought. She could hardly breathe. "So," she managed to choke out.

"Were you wearing your vest?"

"So," she answered again with more effort than the question seemed worth.

He frowned at Betty. She left them then came back with the bloodied white vest. Three holes pierced the front of it. She spread it to see the back and grimaced.

"There are more holes in the back than the front aren't there?" Levitus surmised.

Betty held his eye as she nodded. She turned it so he could see the back side.

His mouth tightened.

She set it on the road at Erica's feet.

"Call me if any of her vital signs change," Levitus instructed and hurried away.

Erica stared at the sky as the cramps receded. *Breathe*, she thought. *Breathe*. She felt tired, so damn heavy and tired.

Betty kept touching the monitors she had snapped around her arm.

Elsbeth returned. Blood covered her from her cheeks to her knees. She squatted beside Betty. "Is she stable?"

Edwards

"For a bit." Betty glanced nervously up the road to where Levitus had gone. She touched the monitors again. "Did you talk to Burk?"

"Just now. Again," said Elsbeth as she continuously scanned the road and woods about them. "I expect her within a few minutes. The claimants realized something had happened and wanted answers so she didn't get away directly. I guess Jesse took over so she could leave."

"I can't believe this." Betty sounded sick. "Are they agents?"

"I don't know. There are too many faces here I haven't seen before. Burk and Jesse called in a lot of help for the meeting."

Erica's gut cramped. She closed her eyes to concentrate on ignoring the pain. Betty laid her hand on her forehead. "God, I hope she gets whoever is responsible for this."

"We got one who might talk," Elsbeth told her. She pointed down the road. "She took him down without a weapon. He isn't going anywhere soon."

Betty glanced where she pointed then back at Elsbeth with her mouth open, as if she wanted to say something but her eyes dropped to Erica. She closed her mouth.

"He pulled her from the carriage and regrets it. He might know something about the plot against us or at least the leaders."

Betty touched the monitors again. "If he can talk."

"Yeah," Elsbeth agreed. "I recommend one of your surgical teams give him priority."

"I'll see to it."

Erica felt numb, like lying in ice. Her throat wasn't filled with blood anymore. "C-c-cold," she told Betty. She didn't even want to imagine how much it would hurt to start shivering.

"Lev!" Betty called.

He didn't return at once but when he did Betty was anxious. "We need to move her."

He nodded. He pointed at Elsbeth. "Come with me." They hurried off.

While they were gone Erica felt rumbling in the road then heard another engine. A car door slammed. Soon afterwards Burk stood next to Betty. "Who is this, Major?"

"Erica," Betty answered and wiped more blood off Erica's tattoo.

Burk sighed in relief then glanced around. "Where's Matilda?"

"In the coach."

Burk walked away. She returned with Matilda. "I want you

The Marrilian

to take them both back to Pey with you."

"Yes, General," Betty agreed.

Burk took out her phone. She dialed a number then waited a moment. "Yes. I want charts of where each agent was in the area surrounding me in a five mile radius for the last hour, then ahead for the next hour. Where are the agents now?" She listened. "How many?" She sounded skeptical. "Shouldn't be," she muttered as she looked over the scene then listened some more. "Just record it and chart it."

Levitus returned with two stretchers. He had Elsbeth take one up the road.

"Who can tell me what happened?" Burk asked Betty.

Betty shook her head and began packing up the equipment so Burk looked to Levitus.

He pointed. "I think James knows but I'll tell you this, the shots went right through the vest like she wasn't even wearing one."

"She was wearing it?" Burk asked in disbelief.

Betty tossed it to the general. Burk looked at it then cursed under her breath as she strode away.

"How are the others?" Betty asked Levitus as she closed her supply box.

"Unconscious, shot, dead, you name it." They laid the stretcher beside Erica then carefully lifted her onto it. "They'll bring them along. She's the worst off that I can still help."

They lifted her onto the stretcher then flew her to Pey without another word.

The news that Matilda and her cousin had been attacked had already reached the population of the city. As the helicopter landed people hurried to the clinic. Agents had secured the area but a lot of people had come to see the aftermath of the attack. They carried Erica through ranks of SDD closely followed by Matilda. No one yelled for a Kinsley to die this time.

They entered a clinic that General Burk had made into a state of the art facility because of the dangers this part of their plan entailed. Erica wondered if Burk might not be a better general than she had ever given her credit for. She had brought the genetic surgeon to change her appearance and it seemed Matilda had survived unhurt because of it. They had grabbed Erica instead. But then Erica realized with a start, if Matilda had been taken, she would be all right. They had shot Erica in the chest through the vest. Erica's vest, the brown one, had worked. Matilda's vest, the white vest, hadn't.

Edwards

They hadn't shot her in the leg or arm. They hadn't shot her in the head. They had taken the easiest shot like all Quirni would who were sure their target was unprotected, a shot to her chest. They knew the vest wouldn't work.

So who made the vest? Who could have told the agents it wouldn't work? Who but the person who made it or had it made? As Betty injected a sedative that was all Erica could think about, who had made that blasted damn vest so it wouldn't work?

The Marrilian

Chapter 15 – Aftermath

James crashed through the double doors into Pey's clinic and stopped short. The waiting room was full. He hadn't expected that. The investigatory work at the scene had been left to General Burk so, apparently, everyone else came here; two three star generals, his own mother General Jesse Kennedy, and General Desante, the planet's two four star generals, Clair Pearl and Darcy Lufkin, as well as Elsbeth, the Claimants Mois, Roger, and Matilda. He stopped in the door. They all squinted or blinked at him.

Elsbeth had cleaned up a little. She had shed her outer uniform coat and washed Erica's blood from her face and hands but she still wore bloody pants. Her shirt showed the hole where she had been shot. She gave him a disapproving frown, the one that told him to think, and James realized the mistake he had just made.

Now he had to explain his arrival without showing his concern for Erica which had been the only thing driving him for the last four hours.

He had come for her but he wasn't supposed to have personal feelings for her. Like an idiot he hadn't been thinking and entered the room so harshly everyone stared at him. He didn't know why they were all squinting. The light! He still held the doors open. They squinted at the light behind him. He stepped into the room and closed the doors.

"Excuse me," his mother begged and got up from the group of generals surrounding her.

Jesse Kennedy was half a foot shorter than her son. She had light brown hair and a motherly figure but she wasn't motherly. She and John aimed to raise agents not civilians and half of her children were agents because of that. She used a stern attitude and controlled every expression on her face all of the time.

She gripped James' arm and dragged him towards the double set of doors leading towards the offices. It was the farthest point away from all the other people in the room. The only person who might hear them talk would be Gina, the receptionist. Jesse glared at her.

Gina left her seat behind the reception window. She found

some filing deep in her office that would keep her busy.

"What are you doing here?" Jesse hissed at James.

He closed his eyes and dropped his head. He had been wrong to come. He had let his feelings for Erica override every reasonable thought.

"A show of personal emotion is the worst damn thing you can do for her. Are you too stupid to understand that?"

"Yes Ma'am," James answered and felt a surge of agony for having stirred her up. Her glare made him reconsider what he had just agreed to. "No Ma'am."

Her chin lowered and her eyes rolled up. If she were a bull he would have a horn in his gut. "Lufkin is here," she snapped and hissed. Angry as she was she still managed to speak in a whisper. "He wants his nephew on this case. Do you intend to give him the excuse to remove you and assign him? This is the sort of behavior that will do it! That is the last thing I need! A God damned Lufkin reporting to me! Exactly how much information do you think I'd get?"

"Yes ma'am," James replied." Except-"

"Stand straight! Look at me!"

James stiffened. He looked his mother in the eye. He had to tuck his chin in to do it.

"Now tell me what the hell happened out there. Make it convincing. As far as I am concerned that is why you came here. Get that fixed in your head. You are not here to see your precious *Doll*." The sneer Jesse made cut James. He loved Erica and his mother hated her. "You came here to report to me and to check on Elsbeth. Look at her right now and see that she is all right."

He set his jaw. How the hell had she heard about him calling her Doll?

He had to get through this. He looked over at Elsbeth. She smiled and nodded at him. He made a show of relaxing. He nodded to her then looked back to Jesse. "I thought General Lufkin's nephew wasn't going to be a problem," James said quietly. "He isn't a captain. You have to be a captain to be involved with Erica *and* he's on Sirrus. He isn't here is he?"

"He can take a test. If he passes, he is a captain," she snarled. "I have heard rumors that Sirrus has a ship that could get him here in two months."

"Two? It's a three month trip."

"Not anymore," Jesse told him.

"Damn," said James. "So is there anything you really need to know or should I stand here and make shit up?"

Edwards

"I don't know nearly enough. I'm told you saw everything including that child in there knocking an agent's skull in," she said and tipped her head towards the surgical suite.

James nodded. He made the motion he had seen Erica make with the downward strike of her elbow. "I think that is what did it. She got the guy doubled over then did that on the back of his head."

Elsbeth came over. "Is that how Erica injured her attacker?"

He nodded. "When he was doubled over." He touched the spot on the back of his own head.

"She must have known right where to hit," said Jesse. "Isn't that right?" she asked Elsbeth.

Elsbeth nodded. "Regardless, it would be hard to cause the injury she did unless the man had a previous injury."

"He deserves what he got." James growled.

"She put an agent in a coma," Jesse reminded him.

"He was trying to kill Matilda," James shot back. "We got lucky because he happened to grab Erica!" He made sure he spoke loud enough that Lufkin heard.

Jesse jerked his arm and made him face the wall, as if to quiet him so Lufkin wouldn't hear. "Better," she sneered at him.

Elsbeth slid in on his other side. "She'll be fine," she said softly.

"We got an update about ten minutes ago," Jesse added. "They have all the shrapnel out."

"Shrapnel?" asked James.

"The bullets broke up," Elsbeth explained. "They were a mix of some cheap metal."

"She's survived so far," Jesse continued. "Levitus will keep her alive. They are closing her wounds now."

"It's been hours," James complained fearfully. "How much damage was there? How many pieces of shrapnel were in her?"

"What do you want me to do take up a collection and count the bits?" Jesse demanded with a glowering curl of her mouth and forehead. "Be satisfied she has the best care and forget the shrapnel. It's none of your business."

James drew a deep, slow breath then released it. He kept his eyes firmly on Jesse.

"You know the miracles he can work," Elsbeth reminded him.

"If I have to send her up to the space station to finalize treatments I will," Jesse told him. "She has done enough to earn that."

The Marrilian

"Do you think?" James asked acidly. "Matilda would be dead if it wasn't for her."

"Is this a private conversation?"

All their heads spun. Darcy Lufkin and Clair Pearl approached behind Elsbeth. Darcy waited stiffly for his answer. He was the four star general that Quirni's Commander had selected from Sirrus. He was six inches taller than James with dark brown, wavy hair and brown eyes. He had broad shoulders and straight, strong stance. He appeared to view those who were less accomplished than him as lesser beings and that was most people.

Clair Pearl didn't like him much. Actually, no one did. She had to be careful of him every moment so she followed close behind when he crossed the room to learn what the Kennedys discussed.

"I would like to debrief him before I make my report," Jesse answered. "I hoped to hear a few answers now but, obviously, this is an emotional situation for James. Two of his charges and his partner were fired upon. He wants answers as much as I do.

"All of the vests should have worked but we have someone in surgery because one of them didn't. I suppose if I were in his shoes I might not be able to keep my voice down either. But we have civilians present," she added with a glare up at James. "They would be upset to hear you." She tipped her head towards the Moises, Matilda, and Roger.

"I understand James is the one who saw most of what happened," said Pearl.

"So I am told," replied Jesse. "He helped subdue the man who shot Elsbeth and Matilda and then he was able to return through the carriage in time to overtake the man who shot Erica. He witnessed more on that road than most people."

"It sounds as if you are already well briefed," Darcy noted.

"Not by James," Jesse told him. "He has been helping with the investigation until now. I still want to hear what happened from him but I don't want to do it here. I would rather do this where he can sit and recall everything in order, without disturbing others, and without distractions." She tipped her head toward the waiting room full of people. "The Moises, Matilda and Roger are all far too attached to Erica. They would not welcome his report." She turned to James. "You should be making notes not putting civilians in a situation like this."

He dropped is head and nodded. "Yes ma'am. I made a report with General Burk. I thought her interview would be the only paper copy. I just came here to check on Elsbeth."

"Is Burk the top ranking general in charge of Erica Kinsley?" Jesse demanded harshly.

Her tone was so severe James winced and stiffened to attention. "No ma'am."

"Then don't assume she can take your statement!"

"Yes ma'am," he said stiffly and stared straight over her head.

Darcy walked away.

"I have a room at the hotel around the corner, room twelve. Go there and wait for me." She glared at Elsbeth. "Go with him and make sure he follows protocol."

"Yes general," Elsbeth responded. She saluted Jesse and led James out of the Clinic.

They said nothing as they walked to the hotel. They went inside, found the room, and closed the door behind them.

"Why the hell were all of those people in the waiting room?" James asked immediately. He shed all of his Delegate behavior. "What interest do so damn many generals have in Erica?"

Elsbeth pushed away from the door. She stepped very close so she could speak low. "Because one of them is likely our traitor."

"What?" James quickly ran back through the scene in his mind. "Desante, Lufkin, or Pearl? Impossible."

"There is no other explanation," Elsbeth told him. "The traitor would want firsthand knowledge of whether Erica survives and what her condition is if she does. Their plans undoubtedly hinge upon her."

James' jaw dropped.

"Now a warning, Captain, do not let anyone else know that you love her. It was bad enough you informed your mother."

"I never told her!"

"Did your mother not just warn you to stop chasing after Erica?"

"She never-"

"She never said what?" demanded Elsbeth, cutting him off. "Did she or did she not realize you entered the clinic like a lovesick boy to check on your *Doll*?"

James stared.

"I know what she said because she said as much to me. And not an hour later you proved her point."

All of the stiffness in James' back wilted.

"From now on you must do everything you can to cover the

fact that you care for her. You have been obvious about it too many times." His shoulders fell. His eyes betrayed his worry. "If General Lufkin gets any idea you are involved with her, he will have you off this case. He never liked the Kennedy's being in charge of her to begin with. You know that. He thought Desante should have had the rights to use her."

"He can't remove us. Powell put us in charge."

Elsbeth eyed him until he felt nervous. She always understood more than him. "Maybe," she finally agreed. "Powell trusts your family implicitly. Your father and mother have helped him too many times and kept far too many of his secrets for him to wonder about their loyalty. He knows they will do everything they can to support him which is why they got control of Erica. She is a means to help find the disloyal agents. If you haven't been briefed, or don't understand, then at least do as you are told. Follow basic training." She stabbed him in the chest with a finger. "Stop being stupid so your parents can work without distractions. They have enough to manage without you mucking something up."

She was right.

"I suggest you pay attention to how you act around Matilda and act that way around Erica. You smile around Erica far too much and touch her every chance you can."

"I do?"

Elsbeth nodded. "You get it under control or I'll post you in the barn. You and I will be returning with her. We are at a critical point in this case. There is no doubt now that agents are trying to kill Mati and we don't know who leads them. You, I, Sati, Rami, and Mark are all going to be assigned to watch over her and Erica."

"Assuming Erica lives," said James stiffly.

"She'll live," Elsbeth told him. "She's a damn Kinsley. They don't die that easy."

He closed his eyes. God he hoped she was right.

She gripped his shoulder. "You can show your feelings around me. You can talk about her to me when we are alone and behind doors but other than that, don't. You will make it harder on your mother, your father, all of us. Lufkin is begging for a reason to remove you from the case. An attachment to your charge would be enough for him to do it and it wouldn't look good for your mother or father either. Do you understand? Don't give him what he wants."

James nodded.

Edwards

She squeezed his shoulder harder. "Good. I hope you know Erica feels the same way about you. Your feelings can wait. She will."

"Really?" His eyes brightened and he lifted his head. He hadn't realized it was sagging.

"Oh you moron," Elsbeth griped. She would have shaken him if he wasn't such a strong man and her chest didn't hurt from the shot in her vest. "Wake up. Yes she does. I told you she does. That first day she saw you she practically swooned."

"She was weak from lack of food. She wasn't carrying anything to eat. I told you that. Why can't you accept it?"

"Because she was eating the plants that she picked! Lords, James. Take off the blinders! She cares about you. *You* accept *that*! If you do maybe you will start to see the signs that I'm right. You will see you don't need to rush her. She loves you. She'll wait. Hell, she probably realizes more than you how foolish she would be to show her feelings for an agent. She's the smartest little thing to walk off a ship in ages."

His eyes narrowed as he thought.

"You'll see it," she told him. "When you do, just keep control. Don't get all giddy."

He continued to look at her doubtfully.

"You are such an idiot," she moaned. "Pay attention to me and I'll let you know if you're screwing up. In the meantime, did you hear that your father is back from Marril?"

He nodded. "Yes, for a few weeks."

"Then you have spoken with him?"

He shook his head. "My sister told me he got back safe. She worries about things like that and thinks all of us should. She was on the base when he got off the ship. She sent us all a message."

"Lynsey? She doesn't seem like the type to worry."

"No. Charlotte."

"Oh."

James didn't like the way she said that. "*Oh* what?"

Elsbeth shrugged. "I'm surprised she made it through basic. I'm surprised she joined."

"She shouldn't have," James grunted. "She isn't the type."

"Everyone is the type."

"You haven't met her. She's pink and lace."

Elsbeth hesitated to say anything. Her mouth twitched. She fought what wanted to come out. James waited. He knew she couldn't hold her tongue. He lifted his chin. Her upper lip twitched harder.

"What?" he asked.

She smirked then grinned. "Pink and lace? A Kennedy? And your father didn't shoot her before she finished crawling?"

"She grew on us."

"You mean she grew on your mom. I'll bet Jesse was so thrilled to have a girly girl she probably cried the day she joined."

James shrugged.

"She did?"

"She didn't cry."

"Damn, I never thought I would hear a Kennedy secret as big as that one," Elsbeth grinned. "There is a real woman in your family."

"Keep it to yourself," James told her.

"Oh of course," she agreed. "I suppose you intended to make up for it by bringing Erica home? Your father would love how we found her in a tree."

"Make up for it with a whore?" He shook his head. "Hardly. Mother almost bit me in two back there. Did you see that?"

"At the clinic? Over Erica?"

"She hates her."

"No way."

James nodded. "Sometimes I feel like I have to protect her from my mom's command decisions as much as I do the people attacking Matilda."

"No. That little Kinsley is fantastic." She thought. "Well maybe. Jesse has been harsh, hasn't she?" She shrugged. "At least your father knows what she's worth. I talked to him. He learned a lot on Marril. Maybe he can keep Jesse off your ass later when you two have a chance. Talk to him about her. Tell him everything. She is far more impressive than we gave her credit for."

"I give her a lot of credit," James warned. "I appreciate her."

"Not enough," Elsbeth told him and smiled her impish smile. "Not nearly enough."

"Why?" he asked. "What do you know?"

She glanced at the door. "I shouldn't tell you. If your mother came in, I would have to stop talking and you should hear this from your father."

James frowned. "You are wasting time. Tell me."

"I will if you want to chance hearing only part," she agreed. "Jesse is headed this way right now or I'm not in the SDD."

"Tell me."

She shrugged. "You know she was raised in a place called Tenpole right?"

He nodded.

"She ran away to there. Her father didn't move them there like we thought. She left her father and ran to Tenpole so she could escape his beatings and molestation."

"What?" James looked sick. "Molestation?"

"Yeah. Do you remember how she wouldn't tell us what her father did to her? She wouldn't tell us how she got all of those scars? It was her father. She has medical records all around the area where she lived with him and those are only the incidents that put her in clinic."

"Why didn't anyone help her?"

"Who can say? It's Marril. The planet can be barbaric. But that isn't my point," Elsbeth told him. "My point is what makes her extraordinary."

He squinted, unsure that this was something he wanted to hear.

"Most children who suddenly end up on their own drop out of school and take to the streets. She, unlike most children, enrolled herself in Tenpole's school and finished her grades. She didn't do great but according her the teachers she could have. They think she held back in order to fit in. She was a Kinsley in Tenpole. She wasn't welcome. Only her age and the obvious fact she was beaten and harassed at home kept the other children off her back. She often arrived at school bruised. She even had casts on at times which implies she had so many breaks a healer couldn't use enough healing paste."

"Because she's an iridim patient? Like when I wanted to heal her and you two wouldn't let me?"

Elsbeth nodded. "The bruises showed up every time her father took her. Sometimes she would disappear from her school for a week or two. John assumes her father tried to keep her at home and it took her time to escape back to Tenpole. Eventually she figured out a way to stop his abductions. She moved to Chaucer Street. That is where the lowest class Tenpole live. Chaucer houses the whores of Tenpole. Marrilians can hear Chaucer in a whore's speech. They can hear it when *she* speaks. It is why she doesn't use the pronoun 'I'. It is just like Roger said, she would have been punished there if she had."

James wondered how much of that could be true. It seemed unreal. Who could treat their child so horribly to cause such scars. Then he wondered how she could get the scars if she were

The Marrilian

being cared for properly.

"According you what your father learned, after she started to sound like a Chaucer whore Samuel Kinsley, her father, didn't want her living with him anymore. From there on she was free to finish school un-harassed. She learned to fight and she saved money. She came to Quirni with over four million quid."

His brow rose while Elsbeth gave James time to process the information. He tried but the more he considered it the more it amazed him. He knew she had money but the rest of it was a surprise.

"Where was her mother?" he asked, because that was what really struck him. How could her mother allow her to be so mistreated?

Elsbeth looked annoyed. "That's all you get from this?"

"Well, yeah. She has a mother, doesn't she? Why didn't she help her?"

She sighed and answered. "She lives on Sirrus with Erica's brothers and sisters. Erica never saw them. She told us that."

"Didn't anyone help her? Other than a Tenpole brothel?"

"Do you remember how surprised she was whenever we did things for her? Do you remember that first time we helped her bathe? She was more grateful than any other charge I ever tended but she didn't readily accept our help either."

"She was suspicious of our motives. Like we expected something in return."

"Exactly."

He held her eye. "Did you know she offered herself to me? She thought that was what I wanted."

"Exactly. I heard that offer and, as I recall, she offered to service both of us. It explains a lot about her temperament and expectations doesn't it? She doesn't expect help for nothing."

James couldn't answer. He stared at the floor.

"It might be hard to convince her that you care about her," Elsbeth told him. "Which is for the best right now. Keep it calm, alright? For her sake and yours."

He nodded. "I never realized I was obvious."

"You aren't the worst boy I've seen in love. And it didn't matter when we were at Matilda's but it does now. Lufkin could notice. Your mother indicated she would like to still use you as Erica's escort if she has to go to any functions but only if you can learn to act right. Otherwise, we'll have Rami escort her."

"Are you kidding me?" James demanded and scowled. "He will be worse than me! Quirni are like horses to hay for Chaucer!"

Edwards

"At least it would be lust and not love. He would be reprimanded but everyone would understand and move on. Erica probably wouldn't even care. That was her job."

"Which she left!"

"How do you know she didn't like it? She chose it."

James was speechless.

"You don't know," Elsbeth told him. "That is a point, isn't it? You don't know her that well. Maybe she isn't the person you think she is and you only feel infatuation for a provocative little woman you saw up a tree."

His jaw ground shut.

That only made Elsbeth grin. "Don't get angry at me. You are the one that can't behave."

He turned his shoulder to her to hide his face and to stop getting angrier at her smirk.

"Oh, come on," Elsbeth complained. "If you love her and she feels the same, I'll be the first to help you two get together, but do the right thing and be sure. Cool it off. Do your job. You have to for everyone's sake, especially hers. Lufkin wouldn't think twice to remove you and then who would protect her if Jesse really does dislike her as much as you claim?"

"I thought I was doing my job," he said then heard how strained he sounded. He swallowed and inhaled then turned back to her. "But thanks, I would rather hear this from you than mother."

"I'm certain you will hear it from her too. At least the part about acting like an agent instead of a kid with a new toy."

"No doubt endlessly," he mumbled. He sagged and took off his cap. His head felt hot. He ran his fingers through his hair then put his cap back on and looked at Elsbeth. "This case needs to end. We need to find out who made that damn vest. Someone needs to go back to Marril and track it down."

Elsbeth shook her head. "We already thought of that and can't. Marril is locked down. It appears to be time for their Council soon."

"Aw hell," he complained. "Seriously?"

"Yeah. Tickets, information, communication, everything is slow or shut down."

"Good lords, I hate it when Sirrus and Marril have Council. Ours doesn't affect them in the least but theirs shuts our economy down without warning."

"At least this time we have a ship on Marril," Elsbeth consoled.

"For repairs," James hissed. "They probably won't repair it during Council. They wouldn't want Quirni to get any information off the planet."

Elsbeth didn't respond to that.

"At least father got back before they stopped ships."

"They probably kicked him off," she said with a chuckle. "He can be as determined as your mom for digging up the truth."

James grimaced. "What now? How are we supposed to figure out who is working against us?"

"We go back to Mati's," Elsbeth told him. "And we wait for someone to think of a way. They'll let us know when they do."

That meant it could be a long time. His mouth hardened. "Do you think I could get in to see Erica while she's in clinic?" He searched Elsbeth's face for some hope in that.

She relented and smiled. "We'll all see her. I don't we'll be alone with her. She'll need to be guarded here as well as at Mati's."

That eased his mind. "Maybe I can give her some idea that I like her. If I don't say something, she could be taken by any number of men. You and I both know it. She's rich and Chaucer. She's a catch and she doesn't know it."

Elsbeth laughed. "You are an idiot." She pushed off him and went to the sofa. She sat.

He stared after her with his lips parted, confused.

"Sit down," she ordered and pointed at the other end of the sofa. "Your mom will be along shortly. I'm shocked she isn't here already. She will tell you Erica is still necessary to our plans. I hope now you are prepared to hear it."

His mouth twisted with dread. He sat on the edge of the sofa. They remained silent for a bit then he thought of something. "She won't get in trouble for hurting that agent, will she?"

"No. He's a traitor. He wasn't acting as an agent. She did the right thing." She gave him a face. "One of these days you might just start thinking rather than worry about nothing."

She was right about that. He had to think but she didn't give him time to.

"Marril knows when we have Council."

He wanted to ask 'and?' but he didn't. He had to start thinking. He looked over at her. "Every five years." It was this year.

"Isn't it odd they choose to have a Council about the same time as us?"

It was odd. He couldn't remember it ever happening before.

Edwards

"What are they up to?"

"You know who the High Claimant on Marril is don't you?"

"Of course, Silas Kinsley," answered James. "I might be just a captain but even a grammar school kid knows that."

"Well, Captain, why would a Kinsley on Marril be interested in shaking up his government at the same time that the Kinsley's here are bringing Quirni into metal? Could it be coincidence that he calls for Council now?"

"No," James replied.

She smiled. "So why?"

"He doesn't like something he sees and maybe he can change it?"

"What doesn't he like?"

James tried to come up with a reason. Nothing seemed obvious. "It's something to do with the government," he said for lack of anything else. "What else might he change during Council?"

"Or who might he meet?" suggested Elsbeth. "Who is drawn together in one place during Council and no one would be suspicious of them talking?"

He might have drawn a conclusion, which was rare for him since his parents did most of his thinking, but Jesse knocked twice then entered. James and Elsbeth stood. Jesse carried the bloody white vest Erica had been wearing. She closed the door and dropped it on the floor. It fell open. The inside of it was all dark, dried blood red.

James saw it and suddenly felt hot again.

"What is wrong with you?" Jesse demanded as she crossed the room to them.

He pulled his eyes from the vest. "Nothing."

She glanced where he had been looking. "She almost bled to death a few times," Jesse said without a trace of emotion. "She is out of surgery now."

James released a breath he hadn't realized he held.

Jesse eyed him.

He held her gaze.

"I'm sorry to tell you that she could still die," she told him. "Levitus said the wounds are bad enough. He said he had to do some quick surgery to save her. She had a heart attack while he was working. Her iridim levels got out of control from the blood loss and the lack of iridim in her system induced the attack. He believes they revived her in time but they won't know for sure until they get her iridim levels back to where they belong. Then she'll be back in surgery."

"God help her," Elsbeth muttered softly.

"Everyone is praying for her," Jesse agreed. "It's amazing you kept her alive in the field, Elsbeth. Levitus was shocked to see the damage. He said you kept her alive with the help of a miracle."

James couldn't take the conversation. His legs went weak. He sat down.

"Keller and Welsh died," Jesse informed him.

"Who?" James asked and looked up at her.

"The two men you shot."

"Oh." He didn't care.

"And the fellow who shot Erica has a concussion, broken jaw, broken arm, and five broken ribs. I have to wonder if you were upset when you tackled him."

"Heh," James grunted softly. He looked at the vest.

"He fought you didn't he," said Jesse.

He lifted his eyes to hers. "Yeah," he replied. "I was there to protect Matilda and Erica and he thought he shot Matilda. I would say that was fighting me."

"That isn't what I meant."

"Tough."

The narrowed eyed *'I'm going to slap you until you turn to mushed shit'* look hardened her expression. "I want to see an emotionless SDD face this instant!"

James drew a breath and managed to relax his frown. He stared at her with blank eyes.

"Stand up. Face me and maintain that while I speak to you and keep your mouth shut."

He stood then didn't twitch while she waited, eyeing him, doing her best to find some chink. She couldn't so she continued.

"If your whore survives, you will be with her again. I don't want to hear one report from Sophie or Elsbeth that you have misplaced feelings and I sure as hell don't want to hear anything from Lufkin or Pearl. *If* she gets out of that bed, then treat her like any other person you defend or have to sacrifice. In the meantime, we have to devise a means to lure out the person or persons who orchestrated these attacks. That will require we use your whore again. I don't want you to twitch one hair when we do."

Jesse paused to wait for a reaction but James remained impassive.

"My bet is Desante is involved," she added.

James blinked.

Edwards

Jesse glared at him. "He was on Marril. He had time to set up the treatments that ruined the brat's therapy. She was whole and cured from what John learned. Something happened while she was institutionalized by the MSDD."

James' shoulders tensed.

"Captain Kennedy, you are a disgrace to me," she hissed. "If you can't listen to this from someone who you know is trying to goad you then how are you going to act when you are surprised by real news?"

He breathed evenly and relaxed again.

"We'll practice his control," Elsbeth promised.

"Do it for a couple of hours each day," Jesse told her.

"Yes ma'am."

"That white vest was made on Marril," James said. "Desante isn't from Marril and neither is Lufkin."

"What is your point?" demanded Jesse.

"The person who had that vest made wrong has to be an agent on Marril. Lufkin hasn't been there so he doesn't know anyone. Desante was there but he is too much of a Quirni snob for a Marrilian to follow his orders and I can't imagine him following orders from Marril."

"Then who do you suggest?" asked Jesse.

"General Pearl. She is recently from Marril."

Elsbeth made a pained face. "Consider the problem with that. Why would she follow orders from Marril when she just received a forth star and has the chance to become a commander?"

"Ditto for Lufkin," Jesse added. "And he has been to Marril. Sirrus and Marril exchanged officers for a few years. He was one of them."

Every time James thought he had a good idea, they shot it down. He didn't try to defend it.

"We don't know who it is but we know who it isn't," Jesse told him. "I meant it when I said we will probably end up using Erica to lure them out. Be ready for that. I'm sorry but be ready."

He drew a breath and dropped his face into pure military non-emotion once more. "I want to be at her side. I'll be ready."

"It is Matilda that has to live," Jesse reminded him. "It is your job to save Matilda not Erica. Be ready for *that*. If you can't be then Mark or Rami will take your place. They will be ready when needed."

'*When* needed?' not *if* needed. Had that been a deliberate slip or an unintentional one? Either way, Jesse told him she had lost

The Marrilian

her confidence in his work. He had become less of an agent in her eyes. This was a blow he hadn't expected. He did his best to not respond but it cut to lose her respect. His first thought was how to restore her confidence. His second was of Erica and that validated his mother's concerns.

Why did he have to fall for this girl? Of all the times and all the people, this was the worst. Maybe Elsbeth was right and he was being a fool, an infatuated fool, but it didn't feel that way and he could list a dozen reasons that Erica was worth their effort, *his* effort, his love.

God help him if he had to jump in front of the next bullet but he knew he would if that was what it took to save her. He stared at his mother. She could be the death of him by putting Erica in harm's way. He didn't allow the shudder. He cleared his mind so his face remained passive. Jesse nodded her approval.

James controlled his breathing. He turned his thoughts upward. *God help me because no one is going to hurt Erica again if I can help it* and that wasn't the way a good agent should act.

27863225R00202

Made in the USA
Lexington, KY
07 January 2019